Frank P. Ryan is a multiple-bestselling author, in the UK and US. His other fiction includes the thrillers *Goodbye Baby Blue* and *Tiger Tiger.* His books have been translated into over ten different languages. The first two books in the Three Powers series, *The Snowmelt River* and *The Tower of Bones,* are also published by Jo Fletcher Books. Born in Ireland, he now lives in England.

Also By Frank P. Ryan

The Snowmelt River
The Tower of Bones

FRANK P. RYAN

The Sword of Feimhin

Jo Fletcher
New York • London

Jo Fletcher Books
An imprint of Quercus
New York • London

First published in the United States by Quercus in 2016

ISBN 978-1-62365-642-3

Library of Congress Control Number: 2015956913

Distributed in the United States and Canada by
Hachette Book Group
1290 Avenue of the Americas
New York, NY 10104

Manufactured in the United States

10 9 8 7 6 5 4 3 2 1

www.quercus.com

For Catherine and John

Strangest of all are the suggestions that Tír is linked to a sister world, variously known as Geb, Jörd, Gaia—or even Terra, a name akin to that of our world, Tír. Manifold are the references to this sister world in the legends of Tír, notably those of the warrior races such as the Fir Bolg and Shee. In both traditions the two worlds are spoken of as twins—as if worlds, like infants, might share a single cosmic birth. Communication and even passage between worlds is said to be possible through Dromenon or the power of the Fáil. This same passage is said to have allowed the seeds of war to be carried from one world to the other, though such history is uncertain and largely denied. Most intriguing is the suggestion that the fates of the two worlds might also be entwined, as is occasionally seen, even dramatically so, in living twins. The implications are unknown, perhaps even unknowable. Yet one is tempted to question if the answers to the afflictions of one world might be discovered in the struggles and tribulations of the other?

Ussha De Danaan: last High Architect of Ossierel

CONTENTS

London

"Smoke!" Nan exclaimed in surprise, as she performed a small pirouette while still holding on tight to Mark's left hand, lifting it to duck under his arm.

"Try not to draw attention to us."

"What is this smoke in the air?"

"We call it smog." Mark watched her from the corners of his eyes, aware of the nervousness that had consumed her since their arrival here on Earth from Tír. "There are power shortages. I think people must be opening up the old blocked fireplaces. They're burning coal and wood—and probably any old rubbish they can lay their hands on."

His old leather jacket, the jacket he had worn on leaving Earth perhaps two years earlier, had proved to be too small for him on his return. He had been no more than a youth on leaving Earth but he had grown and matured to a young man. Back in Clonmel, the southern Irish town where the Temple Ship had brought them on their return, he'd been obliged to buy new trainers, jeans, several T-shirts, a new black leather jacket—artfully scuffed so it didn't appear too new—and a navy beanie to hide the oraculum in his brow. As for Nan—she had had a field day becoming acquainted with popular fashions for teenage girls. And now, kitted out in black leather boots that rose to mid calf, a chunky-weave purple pullover and blue jeans under a thick navy woollen overcoat, she twirled around again, then gazed into the distance. "But I can see plumes. There are buildings on fire."

"Yeah—maybe."

Somewhere not too far away, judging from what he had gathered on the news, some buildings would still be smouldering from the recent riots. Anarchy appeared to be endemic in London these days.

It was mid-afternoon in a dank October; the light was poor, cloaked by dense cloud and smog. People just thirty or forty yards away looked like ghosts moving through a mist. Even Mark felt nervous about their situation. He sensed, as Nan did, that they were surrounded by danger. They were walking through a thickening smog that might have harked back to the pea-soupers of half a century ago, the ones they had learned about in school. And smog was not the only reminder of more primitive times when poverty was rampant and life was cheap.

It was important that they didn't draw attention to themselves. But that was proving to be a problem with Nan. On Tír she had been queen of her own dominion: the Vale of Tazan. A teenage queen, but a queen nevertheless. That royal heritage showed in her face, in her eyes, in her bearing and it made her stand out. He glanced at her, worried. *She must be feeling lost and confused here at every step,* he thought. Only yesterday, at the airport in Dublin, she had stood and stared at the queue working its way towards passport control. "These women," she'd exclaimed, "have painted their lips as red as cherries."

He had squeezed her lightly. "Try not to stare—it's just a fashion."

"On Tír, it was only the recusative priests who painted their faces—they painted them black, along with the palms of their hands."

Mark chuckled. "There—you see, it's just their fashion."

"Fashion? These women—they should ride six miles a day for exercise."

"They do. They ride six miles or more, on buses, and tubes, cars and trains."

"But this is just sitting on their bottoms with no exercise, other than their lazy imaginations. I suspect, upstairs—is that what you would say, upstairs?—they are as lazy and complacent as they sit on their—how do you say . . . ?"

"Bottoms?"

"Arses."

"That word is considered impolite."

"Hah! Yet is it not so? They sit on their arses in their buses and trains. And surely those arses would be a deal less padded if they could desist from eating this execrable fare you call fast food."

He grinned. "It would be difficult to ride horses here in the city."

"There are machines—iron horses. I have seen them."

"Motorbikes."

"Well then?"

"It is thought a little unladylike—though some do."

"I would like to try that—to ride an iron horse."

He laughed. "I'd love to see it."

"And as to the appalling drink you call tea . . ."

"Hey, don't let anyone hear you criticise tea!"

"And no servants—you are sure?"

He nodded. "I'm sure."

"It is no wonder they are consumed with despair."

How lovely she looked, with her olive skin and her cascade of blue-black hair. Mark hugged her to him. He kissed her eyelids, first one and then the other.

He loved her deep chestnut eyes, which contrasted so sharply with the faintly blue-tinged whites. He loved the umbrage in them right now.

"I'm sorry," she whispered.

"Don't be sorry."

"I grumble too much?"

"Grumbling suits you."

It was hardly surprising that Nan felt uncomfortable here. She came from an utterly different world, closer in its customs to Earth in medieval times. Her lips moved as she spoke, but they didn't pronounce the words in any Earth-based language. She was speaking one of the many languages of Tír and Mark, a native Londoner, heard her words as though spoken in English; not through his ears, but mind-to-mind, a gift of her power. Right now, walking the smoggy streets of the city, he wanted them both to appear as normal as possible. She said, "I shall desist from grumbling."

"I feel like doing some grumbling myself. This Church of the English Martyrs—we need to find it."

"Yes, we do."

Bridey, the housekeeper of Kate's family back in Clonmel, had given Mark instructions on where to find the church where Bridey's uncle—Father Touhey, a retired Roman Catholic priest—was expecting them. But the church was small and obscure and Bridey had never been to London in her life. Her instructions had been vague, to say the least, and thanks to the destruction brought about by months of rioting, travel had proved to be difficult in the inner city, now a maze of roadblocks and impassable side streets. Their only hope was to find some helpful local, a shopkeeper or a policeman, who might be able to give them directions. Mark shook his head, directing Nan into a side street away from any curious gazes.

He had difficulty in coming to terms with the shocking anarchy and violence that was now commonplace here in London. He had even more difficulty coming to terms with all that had happened to him in the last two years—a passage of time that had felt much slower on Tír. He had crossed, with his adoptive sister, Mo, and his American and Irish friends Alan and Kate, into an alien world ravaged by war and dominated by an extraordinary and very dangerous spiritual force known as the Fáil.

When he had kissed her closed eyes a moment ago, he had found himself gazing into Nan's jet-black oraculum, startled by the metamorphosing matrix deep within it, tiny arabesques that appeared and disappeared in time with her heartbeat.

Although he couldn't pretend to understand how, he believed that the power conferred on him and Nan through their oracula was linked to the same Fáil. On Tír the triple goddesses of the Holy Trídédana were incredibly powerful, especially Mórígán, the goddess of death. The black crystal triangles they bore in their brows were oracula empowered by Mórígán herself. He had wondered if that force would still prevail back on Earth. But now, walking these dystopic streets, the very fact that they were able to communicate through their oracula suggested that it did—at least to some degree.

And that was as surprising as it was disturbing—even frightening.

"It'd be nice if we could test the situation, Nan. We need to know how strongly Mórígán's power extends to Earth."

He felt a tremble in her as she kissed him softly.

At Dublin Airport, Mark had steered the inquisitive Nan further along the crocodile queue of prospective passengers, praying they would get through passports and boarding cards without drawing attention to themselves. The passports had been a bit of a problem, even with the help of a certain Mr. Maguire, a useful acquaintance of Bridey's. He had registered them with what looked like genuine green-covered Irish passports, with false names and dates of birth. It might have proved hilarious had he registered Nan's true date of birth, which, if he translated Tír to Earth years, would have placed her birthday somewhere back in the Bronze Age.

As they had passed under the bilingual signs, heading for the X-ray machines, her eyes, round with amazement, had been darting everywhere, from other people, to the "painted" women, to the overhead monitors and television screens.

Worried that air travel would terrify her, he had offered to take her across the Irish Sea by boat but she had insisted on flying. Then in the departure lounge she had pressed her face against the plate glass windows, twirling a strand of hair in her right hand, staring out in open astonishment at the aeroplanes landing and taking off into the cloudy grey skies.

"Flying for the first time can be a frightening experience."

"You promised me it would be exciting."

Mark had tickled her waist, his free hand fingering the battered old harmonica he had somehow managed to retain: the only physical possession that linked him to a man who he assumed was his biological father. A fleeting memory passed through his mind, of standing close to Nan, sharing the view of their reflections in the window, gazing out on the planes soaring into the sky.

When they got to London, she had told him what she'd thought of flying. "All through the flight I was close to fainting with terror."

"But you made it—you're here!"

"Yes, I'm here! And you told me London will be interesting. Instead I find myself fearing for my life."

"Oh, come on—let's not—"

"You tell me"—she tapped him on his leather-coated shoulder—"you will protect me from whatever danger we encounter. So what is the likelihood I shall end up saving *you*?"

He laughed, squeezed her mildly resisting body close to his own. "I'm sure you will do it with elegance and aplomb."

"You might forgive my thinking that anything that could possibly go wrong will go wrong—and I shall be picking up the pieces."

It had been that journey from Ireland that had created today's immediate problem. He had been unable to bring along the Fir Bolg battleaxe bestowed on him by the dwarf mage, Qwenqwo Cuatzel, back on Tír. A twin-bladed war battleaxe, almost three feet long, would hardly pass unnoticed through the obligatory X-ray machines. Vengeance, he had named it—and now he sorely missed his weapon. Even during his imprisonment in Dromenon he had imagined it, sensed it, always there strapped to his back. He had never otherwise been parted from it since it had been conferred on him—not until the day before yesterday when Bridey's contacts had arrived to smuggle it across by truck and ferry, concealed among a consignment of agricultural machinery. Since being parted from it he had felt himself incomplete. Even now, he was consumed by the paranoia that he would never get it back.

They headed past tall office buildings and apartment blocks with broken windows into Soho. People were sitting in doorways, smoking and staring. Mark asked a passing woman if she knew the way to the Church of the English Martyrs. She ignored him, hurrying on by with an averted gaze. Mark found it hard to believe that this was his native city. The London he had grown up in had the confident and attractive hustle and bustle of one of the greatest cities of the world. In more normal times he would have enjoyed strolling along here with Nan, like any other couple.

Nan linked her arm in his. “I have the sense that we are being followed.”

“I feel it too.”

“In an hour it’s going to be dark. We need to find the church.”

They ducked into Archer Street, passing the boarded-up shell of a theatre that still had the tattered shreds of its posters hanging from the walls. Mark decided he would try a dingy pub on the corner. He slid a ten pound note across the bar and asked again.

The barman glowered. But he took the note.

“Keep going the way you’re headed. You’ll come to Peter Street. It’s a small church off to your right—close to the end of the road.”

When they came to it, the shops and houses on either side of Peter Street were boarded up and the street itself was blocked by a ten-foot barrier. Across the barrier was a giant poster with a central logo. The logo was a triple infinity. The poster read:

DISCOVER THE PROTECTION OF THE
INFINITE TRINITY
DISCOVER STRENGTH, LOVE, SANCTUARY
BE WELCOME TO THE ISLINGTON CHURCH OF THE SAVED

The Islington Church of the Saved was the church founded by Mark’s adoptive father, the Reverend

Grimstone. There had never been much Christian love in Grimstone's theology, any more than in his treatment of his adoptive children. Now Mark stared, speechless, at the clever way the poster had warped the Tyrant's symbol of the triple infinity into the Christian concept of infinite trinity.

Now that Mark considered the poster, there was no mistaking its significance. That same sigil had decorated the hilt of the twisted cross Grimstone had used as the foundation emblem of his church here in London. And it had decorated the hilt of the great sword that Padraig, Alan's grandfather, had shown the four friends in the barrow grave in the woods behind his sawmill. That grave was the burial chamber of a Bronze Age prince, called Feimhin. But when Mark and Nan had revisited Clonmel, they had found the sawmill burnt to the ground, with Padraig missing, believed dead. The barrow grave had been desecrated, the Sword of Feimhin stolen. Mark and Nan did not believe that Padraig was dead. They believed that Grimstone's followers had kidnapped Padraig and stolen the Sword. The robbery had to be important. Padraig's family, over countless generations, had been keepers of the Sword. Padraig had explained a little of its history—and the danger it carried. When that ancient prince, Feimhin, had originally wielded it in the Bronze Age, it had led to bloodshed on a colossal scale. Padraig's term for it had been "endless war." He had also shown them that its dark magic was unchanged, even today. And so it was in search of Padraig and the sword that they had now arrived in London.

It was a cross that wasn't a Christian symbol at all, but the symbol of their arch enemy, the Tyrant of the Wastelands. If ever Mark had questioned whether Tír and Earth were linked, he was looking at its confirmation.

Nan was tugging at his arm. "What does it mean?"

"I don't know."

They were jostled to one side as some teenagers barged past, not caring if they knocked them over.

A moment later, a girl's scream came from the direction that the teenagers had been running in. Mark wondered if he should go and investigate, but his instincts told him to forget it. The girl screamed again—a long drawn out strident wail. Then it stopped. He had no idea if it was just kids playing around or if somebody had just been seriously hurt. But he had no intention of abandoning Nan here while he investigated.

Two well-dressed and clean-scrubbed young men appeared out of nowhere, asking if they were lost and offering to help them. Under the immaculate charcoal suits they looked fit and well toned—like trained military recruits. Mark wondered if it had been these two who had been following them. He said, "Maybe you can help us. We're looking for the Church of the English Martyrs." They ignored his question. Their expressions remained studiously bland. Each was hugging a small leather-bound prayer book.

"Grace be with you, brother and sister."

Nan squeezed his arm, affecting a smile. "Thank you. May I enquire? Are you members of the Grimstone church?"

"We are members of the Saved."

Our Place

"*Stop, look, listen!*" She had said. Now Gully Doughty heard Penny's words inside his head again. "It's okay," he muttered to himself. "There ain't no 'urry." He stopped for as long as it took him to shove his grimy spectacles up his nose.

Thinks she's smarter than us. An' maybe she is.

His mind reeled, just thinking about it. He didn't want to think about it. Only he didn't rightly know how to stop thinking about it. That was the trouble with thinking. You found yourself thinking about things you didn't want to be thinking about in the first place.

"Now you got to 'old yer breath an' listen," he muttered to himself again. He held his breath. He listened.

Maybe she's a whole heap smarter than me while I'm a whole year older than her. A whole year! Only she goes right ahead and says it.

Shit! The truth of it was that, when it came to it, he didn't really mind thinking about Penny. And he didn't mind thinking about Penny at all when he considered it that way about.

Gully made himself listen again. He heard nothing because there was nothing to hear. Then he shoved the cardboard box up through a crack in the wall and into a soot-stained shaft.

So wot—so Penny is smarter than me. But it's only smartipantsness. She ain't a deal smarter when it comes to finding the bleedin' food so's we can eat. I'm the one who has to go out and do things.

It was dark in the rubble-strewn basement. The temptation was to hurry, but Penny was right. There was no need to. His brown eyes swept the gloom, making sure there was nobody about. There was only this one way in, but it was kind of awkward because the box was so heavy and he didn't want to shine no torch into the gloom; that might let someone know he was there.

The basement was ankle deep in soot and ash from the fire that had burned above it. There wasn't any kind of a door into the shaft, only the crack in the wall where you could squeeze through a gap between jagged bricks and the edge of a wrecked car that stank of piss and cat shit. His bladder always seemed to respond to them smells, like now, so it felt like a balloon just about to pop. But he didn't want the bleeder to pop right here and make the stink worse. He just shoved his back up against the wall, so as to balance the box, and bent his knees up so that the soles of his trainers were pressed against the rusting metal of the other side of the shaft. That way he could shimmy up the first two floors in the dark, keeping the box safe in the curl of his belly, all the while feeling the muscles of his thighs bunching so hard they was just about splitting the seams of his pants. Foot by foot, he slid his back along the wall, all the way up past the boarded ground floor.

Sometimes there was dossers there. They pulled off the boards and kipped down in the mess and lit fires and scrapped among themselves.

"*Don't forget to wait and listen . . .*" she always reminded him.

He waited, just for a little, time enough so as to get his puff back, making sure there wasn't no dossers who could have heard his scratching.

"Fuckit—they's too pissed to hear anyway."

He'd come to the bit wot Penny called the air lock.

"*It's the airlock that keeps us safe, Gully. It stops anyone who tries to climb the shaft. It puts an ocean between them and us, leaving us Our Place like a secret island rising above the ocean.*"

He liked the idea of that. He liked it when Penny talked about Our Place like it was a secret hideout. It was a mystery to Gully how a lock could be made out of air. But it was a good thing as far as Our Place was concerned. It made it safer. For sure, Penny was smart. He had to grant it to Penny how she got her angles just right. Gully couldn't deny that about her. She had the brains for stuff like that.

He shoved the box out before sliding his body over the big muck hole—wot Penny called the cave of wrack and ruin—where, if you listened when the wind was blowing, you could hear the clatter of parts of the roof still falling in. When it rained, the water came through here like a river. The fire had burned out them floors in between the roof and the basement. He had watched it happen: flames roaring like a horde of demons through all five upper storeys. The crashing and cracking as the innards tumbled down amid the smoke and the heat had been so loud. When you looked up, you could see a massive crack in the roof. Penny said that this was because the internal walls had gone. He was sure them fire demons was still alive, creaking, up there in the concrete of the roof where it sloped and dangled all over the place.

Emerging out of the shaft, he slid the box along so he could sit astride the I-beam. It was a bitch, because his back was grating against the scratchy cinders. At least the glasses wouldn't come off—he had heated the ear pieces in a candle flame to bend them around his ear lugs. He stood to relieve his busting bladder, while simultaneously removing his glasses with one hand and washing the lenses with his spit between his finger and his thumb. He laughed now to think that he could have shown Penny how well he could multi-task—and all the while perfickly balanced on the one-foot-wide flat of the I-beam. He wiped his glasses dry again on his hooded denim jacket.

Lens-wiping and dick-shaking-off all done, he made a point of resting a calf against the box and holding still for another few moments of self-congratulation on his multi-tasking, while still waiting and listening.

He heard a slithering noise from the floor below. Could be he heard the whisper of dosser voices. Maybe somebody felt the rain of his piss coming down out of the dark. Gully giggled again. But might be it wasn't such a smart thing to do.

"Check if Our Place is secure." He heard Penny's warnings in his head again.

He felt so guilty that he stopped right there on the giant iron beam, holding himself rigidly still. He closed his eyes so he could listen better.

Once ain't enough, he thought

Gully made his way over the rusted I-beam that bridged the devastation of the collapsed upper stories; a thirty-foot crossing with the cardboard box balanced on his dark mop of curly hair, one hand steadying it. Stepping cautiously in the dark, he felt around with the edges of his trainers with the other hand, registering the hard sharp side of the beam, until he arrived at the junction where iron merged with the ledge of concrete. Manoeuvring himself, and then the box, he pushed himself through the trap door that opened into the shaft and dropped lightly onto the rusting roof of a big, unmoving lift. He hauled the box down off the ledge.

The box held the stuff he had bought from the sale of Penny's drawings. The honey—a tiny pot of the waxy sort Penny liked—wos a surprise he had for her. Maybe it would make her think about him like any normal gel should.

"Weird she is. Won't let me touch her or nuffink!" Gully wanted to kick something right there and then. His fists bunched. "Why won't she let me touch her—not even give her a little hug?"

Penny was smart enough, her ma and da coulda been professors. Yeah—professors or the like. Only she wouldn't talk about 'em. Never. Only thing she ever said, maybe like she was recalling a thing somebody must have said to her, was, "You are the strangest thing—the most disruptive child." The hoity-toity accent Penny put on it made it sound like a school teacher mighta said it. Or more like some bleedin' professor. Not that Gully had ever met a professor in his life.

"Won't let me touch her, she won't. Won't even let me pull up close to her in the cold. Don't feel the cold, she don't—not ever. Not even when her 'ands are blue with it and her skin is covered in goose bumps. Not let me come close, just to warm one another. Paranoiac—that's wot she is!"

Might be a good thing, being just a bit paranoiac. Might keep you alive. But you didn't want too much of it.

Gully stopped and listened again and only when he heard not so much as a rat squeak did he slide across the rusting roof, heading to the porthole in the wall, where he shoved the cardboard box into the dolly. "Dolly"—that was what Penny called it. She knew the words for things like "dolly." Gully would give her that. She was smart with the sums, and she was smart at remembering the pictures. But for all of her smartipantsness, there was that weirdness about her, in so much as she would think about things nobody in their right mind had any right to think about. There was scumbags who called her Cat and made meowing noises when they saw her coming. Like they knew that Penny had claws. All the same it frightened the life out of him at times, the way she took no notice. Like she didn't seem to know how to be afraid when anybody with 'arf a brick o' sense knew there was times when you needed to be afraid.

On his knees now on the gritty ledge, he slid the box further forward, finding the port hole in the dolly. He opened the porthole and slid the box into the empty chamber inside. He got it so it was sitting right in the middle and then he pulled on the cord—three sharp tugs. It didn't ring any bell at the top, but it made a soft noise, when the leather spring opened and shut. He waited for Penny to give the single tug back that would tell him she got the message three floors above. She would then haul it up and pass the knotted rope down the other shaft so he could follow.

While he was waiting, he thought back again to the night of the fire.

Razzers had started it in the small tube station next door. That too had been derelict—the entrance boarded up. Gully had watched them tear off the boards and go inside with their cans of petrol. He had watched it burn. The fire had quickly spread to the five storey red-brick office building next door. He had waited to see if the fire engines would turn up, but nobody bothered. The buildings was empty and there was more important fires elsewhere. So the fire had it all to itself, gobbling up the tube station, until the roof and the walls caved in. But the old red-brick office building had stood the worst of it. Penny said it was because of the I-beams and the reinforced concrete up there in the roof. That and the water storage tank that was perched right up there on the topmost corner, right over the surviving two rooms that were left to them. Our Place had been saved when the tank had split and the water had deluged onto the topmost floor and covered the corner of the lift shaft and a few other bits and pieces, like the dolly, two rooms and the I-beam wot came out into the dangling metal sleeve of the dolly. Otherwise, all that was left was a big empty space, a black hole of cinders and broken concrete and twisty bits of rusting iron.

In the two or three minutes he had been waiting, his knees had begun smarting from kneeling on sharp grit and there had been no answering tug on the cable. Sometimes it took a while, like when she was up on the gantry, drawing her pictures. But this time Penny was taking too long. The thought grew in him that she just wasn't there.

Penny shoulda been there. She shoulda waited for him. She had promised she would.

A mixture of fury and apprehension caused Gully to jerk upright onto his feet, cracking his head on a protruding ledge of concrete.

"Ow—ow! Bleedin' 'ell!" He no longer gave a ratarse shit if the dossers heard him. Wincing and holding his head, he was forced back over the I-beam and the rusty roof of the trolley car. Here he extricated a plastic torch from his pocket, directing its beam into the well of the lift shaft. Only then did he notice that the knotted rope was down.

Penny really had gone out.

But she had taken the precaution of pushing the loop of rope into the corner and fixing it out of sight under a brick. Gully shoved the glasses back up his nose.

"Wot's Gully to think, gel?"

He clambered up the knotted rope within the lift shaft and when he got to the top there was no sign of her. That did not come as a surprise. He didn't even bother to look for a note. He was the one who left notes.

He moved over to the dolly and hauled on the chain in the channel by its side, muttering and fretting all the while. He hauled out the box and carried it into the kitchen area.

I suppose it must 'a' been some kind of impulse, not some emergency situation?

He sat down, his arm lying over the box. He let a puff of air out between his pursed lips—a habit that Penny would have complained about if she was here. *Well, that's the price you pay, gel, for not being here!* He hoisted out two heavy bottles of drinking water, which he been allowed to fill up at Mrs. Patel's corner shop for free, and set to preparing two sandwiches—beef for Gully and salad for Penny. He placed his sandwich on a small, clean square of toilet paper, right there on the pink-tinged Formica table, carefully wiping away the crumbs so that it became shiny again. He had so wanted to tell Penny how he had bargained on the Hawksmoor picture with that Reverend woman. He could rip off her high-pitched la-di-dah voice just perfick. She was an old biddy that ruled the same church as in Penny's picture, the one who made him laugh with her purse dangling on a bleedin' chain.

"Squeezed twenty quid out of 'er, I did, wot bought the groceries, lots of fruit and vegetables and such like—an' the lice comb. She tells me the picture makes the church come alive. I just thought you'd a liked to hear them things."

He flopped down on the concrete floor by the side of the dolly and lit up a cigarette, gathered together from the dog ends he had collected. He took a drag on it—still damp from his spit on the paper glue—and thought about all them things as was going wrong, and was going wrong all the time, all over the place. That was what made him feel so worried. He wanted to talk about his worry with Penny. He needed to see her here. He needed her. What she did, what she cared about, what she told him, was right. Mrs. Burlington had hit the nail on its head. That was the thing about Penny—the magic about her. She made things beautiful. Her pictures made buildings come alive.

Just about all of the money from Mrs. Patel had gone into the box. He had so wanted to impress Penny with his haul. He picked out the little pot of waxy honey. He wanted to see the look in her eyes when he gave it to her.

But then, he asked himself, wot would Penny see if she looked him back in the eye? Goggle-eyed glasses, flecked with eye crud and finger marks. He had a sloppy bridge to his nose that caused the glasses to slip down, no matter how hard he tried to stop it happening, even to the extent it was putting wrinkles on his face.

He had chosen the denim jacket he wore because of its six pockets; the upper two zipped and the lower four flapped, so he could carry stuff when he was on the move. Now he emptied what change he'd kept from the ten pounds fifty pence Mrs. Burlington had given him when another station picture got sold at the post office on Clemshod Street. He placed the note and coins in a tin.

"One of us is doing it, Penny. One of us is keepin' body 'n' soul alive!"

But that wasn't really fair. Penny painted the pictures.

There was still light enough in the sky to see the sights—pigeon fashion. It was here Gully and Penny would have come to celebrate his success. Only she wasn't here like she promised. He grumbled some more about that, moving around in the gloom, spreading the blinds he had rigged up, pulling them all tight before he lit the candle in the wax-splatted saucer.

"Mrs. Patel," he heard himself tell Penny, " 'as these two evil cats: a black tom with 'alf his ear bitten off, called Spike, an' a tabby wots more cunning and sinister, called Moll. Soon as they get me all to themselves they come rubbing up against me calves. Moll does all the begging, with her smoky blue eyes. Spike's eyes is a kind of snake-like yellow, so he got no begging appeal at all. They think they can read my mind—honest—even before they makes a move. Cats is mad about food, especially food that's nice and bloody. That's how I get them in my control. I gives 'em the juicy giblet bits of me trapped birdies."

"Those pigeons will be the death of you, Gully."

"Nah!"

"*You go crawling out onto that broken concrete roof, you never know when it's going to give way.*"

"Listen to me. There's folks down below would pay good money for fresh pigeon. I could set up a market stall."

"*You're just dreaming, Gully.*"

A Psalm for the Dead

White-haired and unshaven, Father Noel Touhey paused in his shaky progress down the main aisle, to announce the words for the dead into the clammy emptiness of his abandoned church. The light coming in through the oriel windows above his head was so poor he had borrowed a brass candlestick from the altar, its uncertain flame casting dancing shadows into the echoing nave, with its silent rows of pews.

"*De profundis clamavi ad te, Domine.*"

His hands were blue with cold and stiffly arthritic, so he rested the candlestick on the lid of the coffin—the first time he could recall the need for candlelight since he had been a child in his grandmother's white-washed cottage on the foothills of the Comeraghs. Or had it been an oil lamp? At eighty eight years old, it was hard to recall. An age ago, certainly. Just thinking about it caused him to lose track of his progress. He picked up the candlestick again, reminding himself of where he was and what he was doing.

"We have to show respect for the dead."

"Yeeesss, Fadah Toowee."

"Touhey," he corrected her for what must have been the dozenth time.

"Toowee, Fadah," she acknowledged.

His Belizean housekeeper, Henriette Boleyn, was a tall, elegant woman who exuded presence. She dragged a brass bucket over the black and white tiled floor, causing the round-headed brass brush to clang against its sides, like a bell. She was wrapped to the ankles in a pea-green gingham dress and a matching band was tied around her brow, with a big knot holding together her bun of ink-black curls at the back.

"It's hard to remember at my age."

"Weh, de good Lord forgive you Fadah."

My good and faithful Henriette!

She had taken care of him for a long time. Or at least, she felt so familiar he thought she must have. Tsk! If only he was not beset by a failing memory. These days there was a part of him that wondered if his entire life was a dream; his memory playing tricks with him. A lot of recent events were missing. He found himself shaking his head with bewilderment. He even wondered if it was true that the Lord would forgive him. His thoughts lagged behind his legs these days, so that he stood still for a moment or two on the glazed tile floor and waited for his memory to catch up with him.

The words, in English, wandered sluggishly through his mind as the Latin of the Tridentine Mass for the Dead emerged from his lips.

Out of the depths have I cried unto Thee, O Lord,
Lord hear my voice,
And let thine ears be attentive to the voice of my supplication.

No wonder they had changed from the Latin to the vernacular. What did words like these mean to ordinary folk grieving over their departed loved ones? Yet still there was a place in his heart for the lovely Latin cadences and the poetry of it.

The young curate was surely gone—gone as every single one of the parishioners was. They had fled . . . or worse. Father Noel turned and looked around at the shadowed emptiness of both nave and chancel. The church had a presence all to itself. It was something he had always felt about it. It was as if it were watching, listening, feeling. A silent presence, sadly observant, as an old man being tended to—only its melancholia was deeper, more poignant.

Folk were afraid. Who could blame them?

I'm afraid too. But I have nowhere else to go.

There had been no electricity in weeks. Cabs and buses no longer frequented the area and half the tube stations, including the one nearby, were no longer functioning. All that was left was him and Henriette; faithful Henriette, who had cooked him a pot of her "Caribbean beenz soop" just before the service, ignoring his grumbling and complaints about it. Oh, and she had such a lovely alto voice in the hymns. But there were no hymns to sing any more. No altar servers. No parishioners. No relatives to mourn the dead.

Reaching down with a trembling hand, he removed the brush from the bucket, its black horsehair wetted in the holy water, and he continued his progress around the coffin, his course widening to avoid the wooden horses that supported it at the furthermost limit of the central aisle, just within the locked and bolted doors.

"Are you all right, Fadah?"

He was far from all right. His heartbeat felt irregular, as if an upended turtle were struggling to find its feet in the empty bowl of his ribs. Where in heaven's name was the curate? It was cruel, at his age, making him remember the details of the service. Latin had fallen out of favour for a while. But then it had been permitted again for special circumstances. And surely these amounted to special circumstances. And its poetry and majesty comforted him, reminding him of the old days, familiar in a way the vernacular had never really been.

The elderly priest stood amid the flickering light and attempted to clear his mind. He was expecting visitors. He thought it was today, but he could be mistaken. He did get the days confused. A young man and a young woman. No point in attempting to remember names, he found that almost impossible now. And he had no way of confirming the date or day since his mobile had died.

His thoughts alighted on the object he had to give them. "You put it somewhere safe?"

"I hide it good."

He didn't ask her what she meant by that. He'd rather not think about the "it," or know where she had hidden it. The thing frightened him. When it had arrived, brought into his flat by two hard-faced fellow countrymen, he had taken one look at it and refused to handle it.

Now he carried on, walking around the oblong shape of the coffin, splashing the holy water onto the waxed yellow wood. Oh, yes—if there was a place and a time for the ancient resonance of the *De Profundis* . . . His mouth moulded itself around the psalm again, as if the words were metamorphosing into something deeper, something solid as a shield, against the morbid hush of the empty church.

If Thou, O Lord, shall observe iniquity, Lord
who shall endure it?
For with the Lord there is mercy and with him
plentiful redemption
And He will redeem Israel from all its iniquities.

"Hurry up, Fadah!"

"I'm doing my best."

Father Noel had been thinking about the message from his niece, Bridey. Lost in his thoughts, he was startled by the arrival of a high pitched musical tone, as if the finest pipe in an organ were sounding directly into his ears. The hackles rose on the back of his neck.

"Hurry up! It startin' again."

He was struggling to think clearly, already sensing the change. There was a tingling over his skin, as if the air had become charged with static electricity. Then the eruption of shouts and cries from outside.

"What in the world?"

"De Razzamatazz, Fadah."

"The what?"

"De young people. Jigi-jigi!"

Her patois was so strong at times he had to stop and try to figure out what she was saying. Did jigi-jigi mean what he suspected?

"Are we secure?"

"I lock all de doors. But de light . . . !" He followed her gaze to the uncurtained windows. His trembling hands were unable to do it. It was Henriette, wetting finger and thumb in the pail of holy water, who snuffed out the flame, plunging the church, and Father Touhey, into deeper shadow.

The Feral Girl

Oggy's Café was on Lower John Street, the bottom floor of an ancient multi-storey block in which all of the upper floors looked forsaken. Inside Mark and Nan found a half dozen or so Formica-topped tables in an otherwise empty room. They chose one by the window, with stools that were screwed to the floor. Outside the window the air was so smoggy it felt as if dusk were falling.

The situation in London was far worse than Mark had anticipated. It had been such a miraculous stroke of luck when they found a way of returning to Earth from Tír. Being subsumed, body and spirit, by the Third Power had left him and Nan marooned in Dromenon. They had been devoid of physical substance. For all they knew they might have been dead. They had risked everything on a foolhardy plan. Recalling a legend told around the fireside by his friend, the dwarf mage Qwenqwo Cuatzel, in which the Temple Ship was referred to as the Ark of the Arinn, Mark had gambled on the possibility that the ship might carry them back to Earth. The gamble had paid off.

Just to have made it back, to have recovered his flesh and blood again, should have been more than enough to satisfy Mark. But now, with the discovery that Padraig was missing and the Sword of Feimhin stolen, their joy had been short-lived. And now they had arrived in London he and Nan found themselves lost in a dystopic nightmare, with raving mobs rioting in the streets and fires making a wasteland of large areas of the city.

And now, heading over to the galvanised-zinc counter in the greasy café, Mark was confronted by the male reincarnation of the Willendorf Venus. The eponymous Oggy was no more than five foot four, but looked equally wide, with pendulous man boobs and a belly wrapped in a curtain-sized apron that overflowed half way across the counter. A wicked-looking meat cleaver dangled from a hook by his shoulder.

"Yeah?"

Mark looked over the menu, which had been drawn in chalk on a blackboard amid numerous "For Sale" posters and ads for cheap accommodation. The safest item looked to be the English breakfast.

"English breakfast—for two, please."

Dark eyes in a face that merged, with a mere dimple of a chin, into a truck-sized chest, looked Mark up and down. The voice that wheezed out of the fag-decorated mouth said, "That'll be twenny pahnd."

The price was outrageous. But very few cafés had survived and Mark was obliged to shove the twenty-pound note across the greasy metal surface.

"I'm looking for the Church of the English Martyrs."

Oggy ignored the question, affording Mark a slanted perspective of his backside as he swivelled around to shout the order through a serving hatch in the poster-strewn wall behind him.

Making his way back to the window table, Mark thought that Nan looked increasingly restless. He saw it in the pallor of her bronze-hued face, her skin lit by the neon streetlights, which had been fooled by the murky light to come on early.

Moving so he was sitting adjacent rather than opposite to her, he reached across to take both her hands in his. "Come on—don't look so worried!"

"I sense danger. I sense it very strongly. But I cannot say what it is—or why it should so alarm me."

"The state of the city is alarming, even for me. I can't figure how it could have deteriorated so much in the short time I was away."

"I'm confused by so much that is unfamiliar. But you know what is the most challenging?"

"What?"

"So much despair in the hearts of the people here. I have gone for so long without experiencing such sentiments. Feelings can be overwhelming when you have become unused to them."

"It's the oraculum, Nan. Maybe you should switch it off?"

Her hands were cold, the skin waxy. He reached up to brush the outside of his fingers over her face. "Hey—I won't let anybody, or anything, hurt you."

She took his hand, kissing it, then clutching it tight between her own. Her eyes darted about the empty café. "This place—it is not a good place to spend any time!"

"It's just a greasy café."

Mark looked over at Oggy, who was pulling a stainless steel teapot down onto the working surface. He scoured it with steam, dumped a couple of tea bags into it, then slapped it under the stream of boiling water. Glancing across at Mark and Nan, those piggy eyes glowered before he carried the pot over to their table.

Nan had released Mark's hand in Oggy's presence. But as soon as he had gone, she caught hold of it, squeezed it tight. "I sense the same unease growing in your mind too. You're sensing danger."

Oggy was back, slamming a tray with the two breakfasts onto the table. Lifting the plates, cutlery, the tiny pot of milk and then the two mugs, he used his filthy apron to wipe sweat from his face before waddling away again, avoiding any direct eye contact.

Mark waited for him to go. "What is it?"

"He knows something. They all do."

"Such as?"

"He's refusing to help us. He knows where the church is—it is surely somewhere near to here."

Mark lowered his voice. "So why is he doing that?"

"He's afraid."

"Afraid of what?"

"I don't know."

"But you sense something?"

"I think everybody we meet is afraid. That's why they are all refusing to help us."

"But what are they afraid of?"

"Maybe they know something we do not know."

Mark thought about that. What could be so important about some tiny church that it scared someone like Oggy? He shook his head. It didn't make sense. He saw that Nan had pulled her overcoat tighter around her throat. She had refused the food, even the tea, leaving her mug untouched on the bare wood surface.

They know something that we don't.

Sipping despondently from his mug of tea, Mark had also lost his appetite. He peered at his own reflection in the window—at his beanie-covered head, the rim pulled down low over his brow. Looking further, through the steel mesh that protected the glass on the outside, he saw the occasional person hurrying through the spoiled streets. Were they really as scared as Nan suspected?

Mark shouldn't have been surprised by Nan's reaction to London. A modern city must appear completely alien to her. He wanted to comfort her shock at the size and complexity of the city, at the electric lights, the speed of mechanical things, the cars, and cabs and buses—even the bicycles—that rushed about through some of the streets.

"Do you want to go back to our hotel room, Nan? Call off the search for today?"

"No."

"All right. But you must try to relax."

"How can I relax when there is so much that dismays me? These people who press by you, never meeting your eyes!"

Mark kissed the palm of her hand, an awkward kiss, with her fingers close to scratching the skin of his cheek. It was so good just to be able to touch her, the living girl he loved. Not very long ago he had so longed to be able to do just this; they had been trapped in Dromenon as nothing more than soul spirits, unable to touch one another, even to communicate with each other except through thought alone, unable to express their feelings in any physical form at all.

"You know, maybe it's understandable that people are frightened. So much is going wrong here. They don't know where to turn."

"Mark—there is something wrong here. It isn't merely the people."

"What's wrong? Do you sense something specific?"

"I think I do. I think what I'm sensing is the proximity to great evil."

"What does that mean?"

"It's the same feeling I sensed before the calamity."

Mark glanced back out through the filthy window. Those streets out there were grimy and threatened with anarchy, ruin—but Nan was suggesting a more arcane danger. He presumed that by calamity she meant the war and invasion of her mountain fastness by the Tyrant's Death Legion, which had resulted in the fall of her civilisation two thousand years ago, in Tír.

"Proximity to great evil?"

Nan was a lot more experienced with her oraculum than he was with the same power embedded in his brow. It was possible that she was more sensitive. He felt a prickle of disquiet constrict his scalp.

A sound: a faint rapping on the steel mesh beyond the glass, so close it seemed only inches from his mind, startled him, and focused his attention on somebody who was standing on the other side of the steamed-up window.

Unkempt fingernails, like claws, withdrew from the mesh to be replaced by a spectre. A face was peering in at him, through the white lettering of the words HOT SANDWICHES painted on the window: a pale face, the skin semi-transparent. The eyes were a pale shade of grey that looked almost as clear as glass. The large black pupils were starkly highlighted. He saw tawny yellow hair, filthy and matted, tied into rat tails with rolled-up strips of silver foil. It was a girl, maybe fifteen or sixteen years old. She was pressing her cheek and brow so hard against the mesh that her face was distorted by it. When she moved back slightly, Mark could see she had a beaky face, a pink tip of nose, a sharp little chin, and heavy lids over those pallid eyes. The confrontation was so direct and unflinching he felt obliged to shake his head, motioning her away.

But she refused to be dismissed.

The feral girl withdrew from the screen but she still stared at him as if she somehow knew him. Her eyes darted from his face to Nan's. Mark saw that Nan's fringe had parted. The black triangle in her brow, with its pulsating arabesques, was visible. Mark felt at the rim of his beanie to make sure he was hiding his own. He guessed that the girl had spotted the oraculum in Nan's brow and now there was a heightened restlessness about her, an urgency that he felt unable to ignore. She was scribbling something into a grubby little spiral notebook. He sensed something very strange, something very needful, about her. And he sensed that it mattered to him, and to his purpose here.

"Nan?" he whispered.

"I see her too. Her mind! It is so difficult to enter, so different to read. It's as if she were erecting barriers to every effort of my probing. All I'm getting is . . . is pictures. Extraordinary pictures."

"Maybe she was following us through the streets."

"Yes—I think so."

The girl pressed a single page of her notebook against the glass. Mark thought it was whatever she had been sketching. He was gazing at the drawing of an entrance to what might be a church.

"She knows what we're looking for."

"But how?"

"I don't know. But she might be able to help us."

Mark had forgotten his chair was screwed to the floor. In his hurry, he almost tripped over his own feet. He stumbled out of the warm café, with its comforting food smells, and into the refuse-strewn coldness of the street. But the feral girl had melted away into the smog.

The Dragon Graveyard

Kate Shaunessy's teeth were chattering with cold as the dragon Driftwood descended from the obscuring banks of pure white cloud onto a vista that took her breath away. This couldn't possibly be their island: huge rocky buttresses rose sheer out of forested slopes and needle-like pillars soared into the air. Yet even these, as they descended and neared them, were capped by small plains dotted with mature pine trees. It was in a wheeling arc, directly towards one of the tallest of these pinnacles, that the dragon's descent took them. Major changes were in the air. But then, how could she have possibly imagined that there would be no changes when Driftwood himself had changed so very much?

Somehow, and she hadn't understood it then any more than she did now, the power bestowed on her by Granny

Dew—the Second Power of the Holy Trídédana—had resurrected him from a petrified death. He had perished long ago at the end of a terrible war fought between the dragons and titans, led by Fangorath, a being that was half divine. Driftwood—or Omdorrréilliuc, as the Gargs had called him—had been the King of the Dragons and himself half divine. To save the world from imminent destruction, the dragons had sacrificed themselves to Mórígán, the goddess of death. Mórígán had defied Fate to accept the sacrifice, thus bringing an end to the Age of Dragons. But this had ultimately led to her arrival here on Tír, along with her three friends: Alan Duval, the young man she loved, and the adoptive brother and sister, Mark and Mo Grimstone.

And now she was returning to the same land where she had been tormented and hunted by the Great Witch, Olc, to see if she could save the Momu and thus restore the hope of fertility and rebirth to the people known as the Cill.

They were alighting on a broad, flat ledge of stone hundreds of feet above a valley verdant with trees. The dragon had become so enormous that their landing involved Kate first climbing down from her comfortable nest in the brilliant green and yellow feathers of his ruff, then making her way through the valley of his wings and down the stairway of his spine, to the very tip of the hundred yards of tail. She walked around the scaly body until she could sit, cross-legged, by the grounded head, to one side of a huge nostril and beneath a reptilian orange eye as large as a tractor tyre. The membrane of the eye performed one of the dragon's sideways blinks.

His voice was so deep it rumbled like thunder through the ground beneath her. Kate knew that she could not possibly interpret his communication through the minuscule ossicles of her human ears. She was hearing his words and translating them from the language of beginnings, through the oraculum in her brow, which was one with her mind and her being—what the people here called her soul-spirit.

"I wanted you to see our island once again."

"Oh, Driftwood, I'm enchanted by it—what you have made of it."

"I did not create this wonder—you did."

"I don't understand."

"The bed of rock on which you slept—it was not a single grave. It was the graveyard of many."

Kate's heartbeat rose into her throat. Was Driftwood saying what she thought he was? Had she resurrected not just one dragon, but a race of such extraordinary and wonderful beings?

She had to take his word for the fact that this was the same island where she had discovered him. How it had changed! It was as if a magic inherent in the land itself had been awakened. The ecology, even the geology of the entire island landscape had evolved. It was as if aeons, rather than weeks, had passed, during which time it had become lusher than before. Even the trees had changed. Staring up into a dense canopy hundreds of feet overhead, Kate saw that these were no longer the oaks and birches that she herself had planted. These soaring titans resembled . . .

"Oh, my! They're the ancient trees you showed me—they really are. It's where the baby dragons nested in your dreams."

"Not my dreams. In the memories you saw as dreams. You and I, Kate, girl-thing—we need to talk."

"I love to talk with you."

His snort rumbled and echoed throughout the ground beneath her feet. "You must understand the value of patience—and the need for caution."

"Caution?"

"Blood 'n' bones! Guts 'n' gizzards!"

He had resurrected his childish exclamations. She didn't know if he was joking with her or genuinely mad with her.

"Don't be cross with me."

"Pah!"

"Please?"

"This has ever been a perilous world. And things have begun to change."

"What changes are you talking about?"

"The Tyrant feels threatened. The situation has become far more dangerous even than the struggle with the Great Witch. It is inevitable that he will take measures to rid himself of that threat."

"But you are hungry, and weak. You need to rest and prepare yourself for the ordeal that is to come."

Ordeal?

Oh, heavens! Driftwood was right, as always. She really was starving, and frightened too. The use of her oraculum, the Second Power, had drained what little remained of her reserves of strength and will. She was only slowly recovering from her torture in the Tower of Bones, where she had been Olc's prisoner. She needed to rest.

"Should I be worried, even when I'm here with you?"

"You should be worried anywhere and everywhere."

"What am I to do?"

"You must heed the fact that the Tyrant has access to the Fáil."

Kate shivered, recalling what she had witnessed of the third portal. It had been hidden within Dromenon, at the spot marked by the Great Witch's Tower of Bones. The colossal power of it frightened her—the danger it represented.

Driftwood pressed her, gently. "But there is a more immediate danger."

"There is?"

"You think of the Cill as pure."

"I wouldn't have put it that way."

"How would you have put it?"

"I think they live in innate harmony with nature: they have a sense of oneness with what is good in the world. This, surely, was why the Great Witch, Olc, tried to destroy them."

Driftwood took a great breath in through those scaly nostrils. When he exhaled his breath was hot, sulphurous, like throwing open the gate on a furnace capable of melting iron. “You are indeed naïve, Kate girl-thing. There were other reasons why the Witch sought to destroy them.”

“What do you mean?”

“A conflict of power.”

“I don’t understand.”

“Your kindness, when coupled with your oracular gift, is a temptation more dangerous than you might realise.”

“For goodness’ sake!”

“Have you already forgotten your time spent with the Momu?”

She had spent many hours in the company of the Momu, during which she had been introduced to mysteries of being that were deeper than mere images, or words, or even feelings. She had experienced a transcendent level of communication, something deeply intimate, enabled by the harmony of thought and being that was intrinsic to the Cill—even now the memory of it was so moving she didn’t want to lose it. Still, Kate recalled how Driftwood had warned her even then to beware the Momu.

“Beware her hunger . . .”

But what had he meant by hunger?

Kate wasn’t altogether sure. She felt so ordinary in herself. She wasn’t brave. All she had, she believed, was a deep, instinctive empathy with what was natural, what was living—and somehow, although she couldn't define it altogether logically—with what was decent. Yet the Momu had sensed something special about her. They had become very close, spiritually intimate—whatever that really entailed.

Kate had no memory of being brought back to her chamber in the Cill city of Ulla Quemar from the cave of the Momu, and yet, at the moment of first waking, it felt as if her mind had expanded with important knowledge. It was as if she had, during the short time they had spent together, absorbed a new level of . . . the word that came into her mind was wisdom.

"I don't have your understanding of what's going on, Driftwood. It all seems so complicated."

"Yet you know what I mean by understanding the need for patience. And you know what caution means."

"Yes, of course."

Her lips were pressed together to stop the tears of frustration that threatened to break free.

Wisdom! It was such a weighty word!

I'm frightened that too much might be expected of me. I'm terrified that I'll make a dreadful mess of things.

The one thing she did understand, something vital to the survival of the Cill and their lovely underwater city, was the fact the Momu was dying. It was clear that her time was very limited. And this presented Kate with a dilemma.

"A new Momu, young and fertile, must be born."

Driftwood snorted again, provoking another echoing rumble through the landscape. The membrane over those enormous orange eyes performed another sideways blink.

But before the Momu could give birth to her successor, or whatever was necessary—Kate felt a stab of panic in realising that she had no real idea what would be required—she would have to get over her feelings of inadequacy. And to do this she must have hope.

Driftwood's grumble cut across her thoughts. "I cannot accompany you into the city of the Cill. As for you, I very much doubt you are ready for such a trial. Yet I can see you are determined on this course."

She found her perch again within the sanctuary of his neck, ready to soar above the mists that were rising.

"Remember—there is no happenstance, only Fate."

"You're teasing me with riddles."

"Friendship is not a matter of reason or even of experience."

"No. It's a question of caring."

"Pah!"

"Thank you, Driftwood. You know that I care for you and I know you care for me, but we're never going to agree on this."

"For a trifling girl-thing, you require a considerable bulk of caring."

Kate smiled, despite her misgivings. "Is that a joke?"

"I might fail to make you laugh, but I do care for you and you have little understanding of the perils of what you are attempting to do."

"I will do my best to be scrupulously careful—I promise."

"Such a promise is doomed in its very inception. To do one's best implies the potential for failure."

"I can only try."

"No, you must do better."

"How?"

"You must determine to do, not to try."

Kate hesitated. In the distance a giant bird, possibly an eagle, hovered over a pinnacle on which she presumed there might be a nest. The bird was magnificent in its ordered movement, the perfect symmetry of its flight and its delicate landing on the topmost point.

Then she realised that it was no eagle.

"Oh, my goodness—it's another dragon!" There had to be . . . oh, wonder of wonders, a nest. Baby dragons.

Driftwood ignored her wonderment. "I fear for you."

"What exactly do you fear for me?"

"Of all the races on this world, the Cill are the least predictable."

"In what way?"

"They answer to a central being—a force, a mind—which can hardly be entirely unselfish."

"You're talking about the Momu?"

He made a sound that might have been the dragon equivalent of a *tsk*. She looked around herself again, with new eyes. How exhilarating was this landscape? It had been a dragon graveyard, but was now utterly transformed into a landscape of life.

"Please explain to me what you are really worrying about."

"I would urge you to think again—to consider the true nature of the people you call the Cill."

"Why? They are the most beautiful, the most perfect beings I have ever seen. Their city is a wonderful union of ocean and land. They take pains to protect the ecology and environment of their world. They venerate the cycle of life, in a perfect balance of people and nature."

"There are no perfect beings any more than there are perfect worlds."

"The Great Witch, Olc, weakened it, as she destroyed all the other Cill worlds."

"No."

"No?"

"You were invited into her realm. What did you learn from your time with the Momu?"

"I—I don't rightly remember all of it."

The dragon snorted. Maybe it was meant to convey irony.

"We met in her chamber—well more like a cave. There was a birthing pool I had to wade across. She was waiting for me in the roots of the One Tree."

The dragon reared, his wings extending to a monstrous proportion, before settling back onto their beautiful, if terrifying, prominence. Kate had to cling on to her perch at the root of his long neck.

"There you have it."

"What do I have?"

"The nature of what will most likely threaten you."

"And what is that?"

"Where is her power derived from?"

"The One Tree?"

"And the One Tree in turn?"

Kate recalled her experiences back in the roots of the Tree. The Momu had attempted to persuade her to stay in Ulla Quemar, when she was so desperately needed to help end the tyranny of the Great Witch, Olc, and the more dangerous Fangorath. She recalled the words of the Momu, desperate to save her world.

"Nidhoggr, the serpent-dragon—who gnawed at the roots of the world—fertilised a seed of the Tree of Life. That seed grew into the One Tree whose branches make up the roof this chamber: a chimera of serpent-dragon and Tree of Life. Sadly, the One Tree is dying, as is her beautiful city, Ulla Quemar. I, the first child of Ulla Quemar, I who am almost as old as the One Tree herself, am dying with her. There will be no more Shaamis."

"The One Tree is an offshoot of the Tree of Life."

"Indeed. And thus you would stumble headlong into a maelstrom of peril."

Kate sat back, deep in thought. "This peril? Are you referring to the Tree of Life—or the serpent-dragon, Nidhoggr?"

"Both."

"Then all I can do is to promise you that I will take the utmost care to conserve my own safety."

It took Kate a moment or two to recognise that the thunderous resonations that were booming and echoing through the landscape were the dragon's laughter. "Alas, Kate Shaunessy, foolish girl-thing, still more do I worry."

"Then tell me what to do."

Those huge eyes gazed back at her.

"Rest a while. Take time to consider what you will face in the challenge. Though you possess the Second Power of the Holy Trídédana, you are not ready for what you will face in the city of the Momu. You are naïve. Beware the trap of kindness."

Kate experienced a sense of déja vu: the Momu herself had said something very similar when they had first met.

A Murder of Tramps

Mark and Nan continued to explore Soho, straying into a narrow street lined with crumbling four-storey Georgian buildings. The lower storeys consisted of small shops, few of which retained intact windows. Those without broken windows were readily identified by their steel-mesh protective screens.

After a few twists and turns they emerged onto a famous street, the giveaway sign straddling the upper stories, supported by metal brackets but riddled with what looked like bullet holes. A third of the black lettering was missing so it read, WEL-C--E TO -A-NAB-S-RE-T. Carnaby Street. The fashion boutiques had been replaced by dusty caves selling second-hand clothes, bags of coal, candles and staple war foods such as corned beef and condensed milk. Mark found himself blinking at one surprise after another, hardly daring to think who might inhabit the upper stories. He turned to Nan.

"Can you still sense the girl?"

"I think so."

"But you're not sure?"

"My instincts tell me that she's leading us to the church."

"I hope you're right."

At the top of the street they turned right onto a broader lane overhung with concrete and glass offices. These sheltered small pavement cafés where jack-booted men in camouflage uniforms of light grey dappled with ochre and brown, were sitting around, drinking coffee and stubbing out cigarettes on the plastic table surfaces. Paramilitaries. Mark didn't bother to ask them for directions. Further on they passed tall office buildings and apartment blocks, many with peeling plaster and broken windows.

They arrived at another obstruction, which forced them to enter a narrow street to their left where an office block carried a dangling fragment of a blue-and-white circular sign: a historic marker that meant somebody famous had been born or worked there. Most of the street was boarded and grim, invaded by squatters lounging in doorways. They hurried on through, eyes averted, and emerged into an open market. "You think your adoptive father, Grimstone, is behind all this?"

"I don't know. I don't understand what's going on here. Last I saw him he was gathering a church of toadies about him."

"You could approach him—confront him."

Mark had a childhood memory of Grimstone standing with his back to him, staring out into the town of Clonmel. Evening faded through the wide round-topped window of one of his make-do churches. He was coming down from the high of a service; his black silk shirt stuck to him with sweat, sculpting his heavily-muscled body, reminding Mark of a panther ready to spring. Mark recalled the sense of danger, of impending hurt.

"Grimstone is not the sort you would want to confront—unless you were sure you were going to win."

They ambled, single file, between rows of vegetable stalls. There was a scattering of overripe fruit, cheap clothes, spices, shoes, the occasional offer of flowers and one surviving newsagent. On either side of the market were boarded-up cafés and restaurants.

Nan clasped Mark's arm and whispered, "We're being followed again."

"Not the girl?"

"No."

Glancing around, Mark caught sight of a tall leather-coated young man with short-cropped dyed blond hair. He sported a tattoo of a triple infinity on a shaved patch of scalp above his left ear. Placing a protective arm around Nan's shoulders, Mark ushered her into a narrow channel at the back of a dilapidated theatre. They hurried through to emerge into an alley that skirted a block of run-down buildings, and were confronted by a young woman standing in a doorway. Her carroty red hair was awry, her voice thick as treacle.

"Excuse me, sir—live shows!"

Mark could see the signs over the doorway. REVUE BAR. WORLD CENTRE OF EROTIC ENTERTAINMENT. In the reflection of a window he caught sight of their pursuer again, the blond with the tattoo.

They were standing before a sign that read MADAME JO-JO'S.

They turned away and squeezed through a hole in a breeze-block wall to enter a cul-de-sac. The tattoo-head squeezed in after them, abandoning all pretence of concealment. They were forced to risk running through a doorless entrance, and then to face the obstacle race of the derelict building beyond, emerging into a yard that must once have been the loading area for a small factory. It had evolved into a junk market. Edging through it, Mark saw the refuse of butchering: lumps of bone flecked with bloodied scraps of meat; entrails laid out over the rough planks like prime cuts. A voice was shouting out prices: "three a pahnd!" or "five a pahnd!"

Mark ushered Nan in front of him.

There was a glimpse of movement at the corner of his eye. Mark spun around and spotted the feral girl. She had stopped, as if pretending to look over the contents of a particular stall. She turned to look at him directly.

He sensed it again—the invitation to follow her. Then she took off. Feeling an overwhelming urge to catch her, Mark grabbed Nan's arm and they half-staggered on through the filth and the averted faces.

Within thirty yards his heart leaped as he caught sight of her again. The pale skin and ragged mop of hair were unmistakable. God alone knew what she had been through out there. She was peering back over her shoulder at him. How curiously intelligent she seemed, in contradiction to her apparent age. She was tall, maybe five foot nine or ten, slim and willowy, as if she might bend about corners, and her movements were lithe, the grace of a cat. But her face, her eyes, were startlingly young, shy and evasive.

She allowed them to catch up with her, as if she too were frightened by the surrounding tramps. She muttered, "I saw the thing in her head—and in yours too."

Mark caught her arm. "Who are you?"

She screamed. His contact with her really frightened the girl, causing her to tear her arm away from him.

"Hey, I'm sorry." Mark spread his arms. "I didn't mean to frighten you."

Nan did her best to calm the girl. "We don't mean you any harm. We sensed that you wanted us to follow you."

She looked from Mark to Nan with a stubborn intensity. "Why do I hear you talk to me inside my head?"

Nan smiled, attempting to reassure her. "What's your name?"

"Penny." She was so unusual Mark didn't know what to make of her. "Quickly—wannabe Skulls are hunting you. I heard you asking about the church—I'll show you."

Mark glanced at Nan: *wannabe Skulls?*

"You know where it is? The Church of the English Martyrs?"

"Come—quickly!"

She led them through a derelict workshop and into a square of abandoned buildings. Gaunt faces followed their progress. Discarded glue tubes, vials, syringes and needles littered the ground. The tramps here were younger than elsewhere, and were gathering about them. They bore little resemblance to the homeless of old who huddled under the bridges in their beds of newspaper. Those had maintained some kind of fellow human empathy. These looked vicious.

It was a mistake to hang about, but when Mark tried to push his way through the shuffling crowd he felt a sharp kick at his ankle. He caught a glimpse of a jean-clad leg with a steel-capped boot at the end of it and, wincing in pain, turned fully to find a short thick-set thug staring at him. He was wearing a leather overcoat and Doc Martens boots. He was joined by the blond with the tattoo, his face pockmarked with acne, a cigarette clamped in his teeth. The blond's leering blue eyes squinted at Nan through the trickle of smoke.

"Bleedin' rich tart! Give us a note or I'll kick yer nancy boyfriend's bollocks up into 'is throat!"

Mark muttered, "Shit!"

"What do we do?" Nan whispered.

"Leave it to me."

Mark looked around for some kind of advantage. He found none and the first thug was blocking their only escape. Mark saw a triple infinity badge sewn into one arm of his overcoat. Now he could see them closer to, the badge and the tattoo on the blond's scalp looked amateurish. He understood Penny's reference to wannabe Skulls: he was dealing with common thugs with professional aspirations. They shoved up hard against him, close enough for Mark to smell their body odour. Both wore stud earrings in their left ears and the smaller one had a ring through his right nostril, from which a scabby sore festered onto his lip.

Mark wondered if his oracular powers would help him here. He had no experience of using them on Tír and he wasn't filled with confidence he would know how to use them here, even if they did work.

When he turned to look for Penny, the girl had vanished.

"Damn!" he said, and turned suddenly, using his elbows to attempt to force a passage through the junkies, but it was hard work to make any real space and there was no escape from the two leather-clad thugs. The blond backed into him, distracting his attention, as the shorter thug grabbed Mark's beanie, draping it rakishly over his own tight-knit curls, horsing around with it. The blond was groping at his pockets. How likely were they to be carrying weapons? Mark didn't give a damn about a few coins of change. But his harmonica was in his right hip pocket and he had no intention of letting any of these thugs get their hands on it. Mark punched the blond in the centre of his face, giving him a bloody nose.

He fell back a little, giving Mark the opportunity to grab Nan's arm and run. His injured ankle slowed him down, but after thirty yards or so he saw a derelict shop and kicked his way through the rotting boarding to usher Nan into yet another alley.

They were startled by a rousing gallery of heads; filthy faces, missing teeth, mangy scalps with untended straggles of hair. Every crevice and doorway was taken up: a legion of homeless had taken over the alley. They had cannibalised most of the doors and frames for firewood and were sheltering from the weather in the holes in the walls. As they got to their feet, Mark hurried Nan onwards and they stumbled on, tripping over the jumble of legs, evoking an increasing chorus of curses.

They recoiled from the grotesque faces, the open hatred in every eye, the overwhelming stench.

They heard the two thugs before they turned and saw them, running down the alleyway toward them. The blond, with his bloody nose, was slapping a lump of metal against his palm. The shorter of the two was swinging a pickaxe handle, tossing it into the air and catching it again.

Mark heard Penny call out. "Come with me!" For some reason he couldn't fathom, the homeless were allowing her some leeway. She beckoned Mark and Nan after her.

Under the light of one working street lamp, he suddenly saw her face in great detail: her right eye was surrounded by a yellowing map of bruising and her skin was a rash of healing cuts and abrasions. Mark reached out as if to touch her cheek with the back of his hand, but she dodged him and made off at a run.

They had to hurry to keep up with her, leading them through a maze of ruined streets, then through a hole in a wire fence and into a side door of what had been a shopping centre. Unwashed faces peered out at them from more holes in the walls as they hurried past.

But then the two thugs appeared behind them. They separated to block their exit then they closed in on them from both sides. Mark concentrated on the shorter of the two, the one with the pickaxe handle, waiting until he came closer. Taking a couple of running steps forward, Mark kicked him hard on one knee. The thug dropped back, limping and cursing. Mark was on the point of turning when he felt a heavy blow to his temple from the lead pipe in the blond's fist. As Mark toppled sideways, the blond's elbow came back at his face and hammered against his teeth. Half conscious, he couldn't stop his shoulder and head hitting the wall next to him.

Still limping, the shorter of the thugs grabbed Penny by the hair and she screamed. From a pocket he took out a half bottle of vodka and, still holding onto Penny, took a swig then tossed the bottle to his partner, who was grinning at Nan, wiping a furred tongue over his cracked lips.

There was a blur of movement and the feral girl was standing over Mark in a protective crouch. The thug was down, blood spurting from a hole in his thigh immediately above the knee. It took a moment for Mark's brain to catch up: Penny had taken the shorter one out and was now crouching just in front of Mark like a wild animal, making cat-like snarling sounds and facing off the blond with something long and metallic clutched in each hand. As Nan helped Mark struggle back onto his feet, the blond moved in to attack Penny, swinging at her head with the lump of lead.

But every time he swung the weapon, she ducked and swerved out of the way, as sinuous as a ballet dancer.

Mark must have blinked, because he missed her strike with the long narrow blades; she was already back in that defensive crouch as the taller of the two thugs fell onto his knees, blood pumping from the side of his throat. Mark saw that the blades in Penny's hands were as slender as needles—sharpened meat skewers, perhaps. The narrow blades, now beaded with blood, moved about Penny's fingers as if they were extensions of her arms.

"Come—quickly!" she said, running ahead.

They emerged into a small street of three-storey brick buildings. The girl was pointing to twin oak doors in a gable end of a church. The sign next to the doors read CHURCH OF THE ENGLISH MARTYRS. For "Enquiries" they were directed away from the main entrance. Mark began to search around, but Penny shook her head and headed down a narrow cobbled mews, one wall of which connected with the church. Mark attempted to read what she was thinking, mind-to-mind.

"No!"

She really had sensed his attempt at mental contact. And she clearly hated it. She hated it just as she hated contact skin-to-skin.

"It's okay. I understand—I won't do it again."

Nan was already hammering on the door.

Mark took his cue from Nan and he pushed in the letter box and shouted through it. "Father Touhey! Father Noel Touhey! Bridey sent us here to find you."

First Light

Standing on a desert island, just one of the archipelago of a thousand islands that was the equivalent of the Garg royal city, Alan Duval watched the welcoming of the dawn by Shah-nur-Kian, mother of the Garg prince Iyezzz and queen of the Eyrie Gargs. He would never get used to the fact that Gargs had no use for roads or houses, or towns and cities for that matter. They revered all that was natural, inhabiting a metropolis of sand and rock and caves which, to a human without the ability to fly, was a labyrinth. In the sand, by his bare feet, Alan noticed the zigzag trails left by some sort of sidewinder snake. He wondered whether a Garg would avoid treading on that imprint, imagining its natural origin might be sacred to them in some way. He returned his attention to the silhouetted figure ahead, watching closely as she turned her back on the landscape to venerate the rising sun, which within a few minutes of the dawn, was already three quarters above the liquid-gold line of the oceanic horizon. He saw Shah-nur-Kian lift her head to the sky as if studying the wisps of cloud or the strength and direction of the coastal breezes. Mind-to-mind, he heard her dutiful homage as the sea took fire, the golden incandescence devouring the tall, erect outline of the Queen.

Over the naked prow of her breastbone, between the powerful pectoral muscles that tensed as she opened her eight-foot span of wings, she bore the radiant gold-and-turquoise regalia of her royal rank. Her scaly, grey, membranous wings were tattooed with emblematic scenes of the dawn on her left and the ocean and its inhabitants on her right. Glistening arcs of those same royal colours decorated her great bulbous eyes; gold above the left and turquoise above the right.

Her voice was deeply melodic, incanting a repetitive psalm. Alan caught snatches of meaning. It was a hymn to the deities of dawn, sun and moon, which were the daughter-sisters of the Creator-of-All.

Taking his cue from the nearby Iyezzz he bowed his head, honoured to be there, but also puzzled at the honour.

What is it? What's really going on here?

As if reading his mind, the Garg prince explained: "Mahhh-nur-Sakkk, Sacred Lady of Tide and Oceans, saved the ancestors from drowning in the great flood, which was sent to punish the first people, who built the City of the Ancients. She did so by conferring wings upon them, so they could ride the storm that was to come. And here, in Utna-Harruscum, the place of sanctuary, the ancestors of the Eyrie People made sacred these islands, which were birthed from the consummation of golden desert and the blue ocean."

Alan was careful to demonstrate his respect for the Garg way of thinking. He now regarded Iyezzz as a true friend. The prince had shown himself to be both brave and resourceful in leading them out of a perilous swamp, helping Alan to find Kate after she had escaped from the Tower of Bones. How he wished that Kate was there right now! The Gargs respected her a lot more than they did him, and he was only just beginning to understand how much they revered her, with her emerald-green Oraculum of the Second Power: the power of healing and birth itself. Kate had greened the wasted lands of the Gargs, restoring life to the sacred tree. But she had left him to go back to the city of Ulla Quemar, the only surviving city of the Cill, where their leader, the Momu—a strange being that Alan had met in the cave of the City of the Ancients—was dying. She felt she had to help the Cill by saving the Momu.

Kate! I need you here!

Later today, Alan and his company would be heading for a formal confrontation with Iyezzz's father,

Zelnesakkk, the Garg king. That meeting would decide whether or not the Gargs would help them invade the Wastelands to take the war to the gates of the Tyrant's capital city, Ghork Mega.

Alan should have been spending time preparing for the meeting, discussing tactics with the young Kyra, Ainé, her spiritual adviser, Bétaald, and his friends, Mo and Qwenqwo. Instead, Iyezzz had enticed him here to observe this ritual of veneration by his royal mother, Zelnesakkk's wife. Alan knew that Iyezzz understood how critical the help of the Gargs was likely to be—and that suggested that Iyezzz had a reason beyond the obvious for bringing him here.

Alan took a deep breath, reining in his frustration.

The estuary was vast and windswept, but still hauntingly beautiful in the morning light. It was icy cold, with dew twinkling like diamonds in the fronds of lichens, coating those spiky, rocky outgrowths that sprang upwards like miniature steeples.

Alan turned to Iyezzz, keeping his voice low: "Your father—surely he's not opposed to helping us?"

"Do not imagine that my father has forgotten the Vale of Tazan. And he values the advice of the high shaman, Mahteman."

"You think Mahteman will be difficult?"

"Yeshhh."

Alan knew that the Gargs still referred to him as Duval the Slayer following the bloody battle at the ruined sanctuary of Ossierel. Thousands of Garg warriors had died there fighting Alan and an army of Shee, including Iyezzz's brother and Zelnesakkk's eldest son. It was asking a lot of the Eyrie People to help their former enemies now in an endeavour that might prove even more hazardous than Ossierel.

Alan and the invading army of Shee were now intent on destroying the Tyrant once and for all. Zelnesakkk and the wily shaman Mahteman were well aware of how dangerous that undertaking would be, given that the Tyrant had access to the Fáil. He would always be one, maybe several, steps ahead of them. And that, in turn, made the help of the Gargs vitally important. They knew this landscape: they could scout ahead and fly above obstacles that might be dangerous, or impenetrable, to forces that had no option but to advance on land.

Tense, shivering with cold, Alan reflected on the quandary that faced him while observing how, over several minutes, the emblematic patterns on the Queen's wings underwent a series of changes in colour and pattern. He had been mistaken to think them tattoos. The colours were, instead, generated by the scales of her skin; like the colours of a butterfly's wings. The display was mesmerising. Shah-nur-Kian controlled the chameleon-like changes within her own being. What an amazing visual devotion to the Sacred Lady of Tide and Oceans!

"I'm glad you brought me here, Iyezzz."

Iyezzz flushed a plum purple over his entire skin. It was a statement of emotion, accompanied by a musky scent exuded from his scent glands. When he spoke, his voice hissed through the gill-like slits that vibrated in his elongated throat. "The Queen performs this ritual to honour you. She alone has the power and grace to do so without needing the permission of the King."

Shah-nur-Kian sprang from the cliff-top, her wings beating the air powerfully, slowly, to give her lift, then she soared out over the glittering gold waves. Alan glanced towards Iyezzz, thinking about what he had said, but the Garg prince revealed nothing more, his reptile-like eyes hooded and his features blank.

A hundred thousand Shee warriors would accompany Alan on the landward journey. They would be commanded by Ainé and Bétaald. The Shee would be assisted by half as many aides, the strange, largely silent women who played many important supportive roles to the Shee. All those lives would be placed at risk under Alan's command.

Alan stared at the distant cruciform figure of the queen under a sky that was a patchwork of cotton-wool clouds, which caused her silhouette to move between a mixture of azure and shadow.

Maybe she's looking for something. Perhaps a sign?

Iyezzz cried out. His wing talon pointed far away, into the distance, where the great ball of the sun was lifting free of the horizon.

Flying fish—a great school of them—had erupted from the ocean. The shimmering cloud of silver bodies merged flight trajectories with Shah-nur-Kian, chasing her graceful leadership. They rose and fell in a giant delta-shaped cloud. As they circled against the golden glow of the rising sun, coming closer and closer to where Alan and Iyezzz observed them, the rain from their wings ensheathed the queen in myriad rainbows of iridescence.

Iyezzz was trembling with emotion.

Alan sensed some profound communication, body to body, spirit to spirit, between the prince and the queen. Iyezzz drew his tall body erect, throwing his wings wide.

He was humming, as if in unspoken prayer, through the vibrating clefts of his gills.

"What is the gain from such a perilous enterprise for the Eyrie nation?" Zelnesakkk demanded of Alan.

"Honour—redemption." Iyezzz interrupted.

The King snorted. "Have we not already afforded you and your army of witch warriors every assistance? Your fleet is cluttering up the bay; we have not hindered your army disembarking; you go about your purpose unchecked—what more can you possibly expect of us?"

Alan gazed around at the extraordinary setting in which the Garg elders were gathered. There was a crescent of basalt columns low enough to provide seating for those who chose not to stand, and landwards, the backdrop was an encircling cliff of much taller columns, some of them hundreds of feet high. Amidst this, tiny blue rock flowers blossomed, like furtive eyes peering up out of the shadows. Whether the Gargs had done a little sculpting of the natural, Alan couldn't say, but he had no doubt that the choice of place was another example of the Garg passion for nature.

"Sire," he said, "you know that our enemy is your enemy. The Tyrant can hardly be unaware that you helped us defeat the Witch—his ally. What do you think he will do to you if he wins this war? Do you think he'll come here and offer trade?"

The King shook his bat-like head, causing the heavy, jowled cheeks to wobble. "You scorn us with your sarcasm, but it is not as simple as you paint it."

Seekers were flying in and out of the Garg-inhabited caverns in the surrounding cliffs. They were so abundant that Alan wondered if the place was the site of origin of these bird-like spies.

The King had insisted on keeping a certain distance between him and Alan, which allowed his shaman, Mahteman, and others among his advisers, to be close enough to whisper in his ear. Was he aware that Alan was capable of reading their minds—of eavesdropping on their whispered conversations? Was the King testing Alan and his respect for their privacy?

The King spoke again, loud enough for the entire assembly to hear. “We have suffered enslavement—and worse—for tens of thousands of years. Briefly have we tasted this freedom, yet you would press us to risk this in your cause. What you are really asking of me, of the entire Eyrie nation, is that we risk annihilation.”

“We risk the same fate.”

“But your need is not ours. The continent of Monisle, with its witch warriors, has been at war with the Tyrant for thousands of years. Your purpose has ever been as it remains today—to destroy him. What you demand of us would mark out a very new purpose, and danger, for our race.”

“Father,” Iyezzz spoke from his position between Alan and the king. “I would ask that you allow Shah-nur-Kian to speak.”

Alan stiffened. Was this the opportunity that Iyezzz and the queen were waiting for? Would she explain whatever sign she had drawn from her dawn communion with Mahhh-nur-Sakkk, the Sacred Lady of Tide and Oceans?

The king turned to bow to his wife who stood beside him with her head held high and her regalia gleaming, but he did not invite her to speak. Instead he turned his eyes in the direction of Mahteman, who lowered his head to stare down at the sand between his feet.

Alan sighed. Perhaps neither king nor shaman needed the queen to explain, because they knew already. They, or their spies, would have observed the queen in every minutiae of her dawn ritual.

The wily king climbed to his feet. “We shall pause for refreshment. While we do so, I shall take counsel with my advisers, as you, Duval the Slayer, might take the same opportunity to consult with yours.”

Returning to his own camp, Alan could hardly control his disappointment. He couldn’t really blame the Gargs for their reluctance to engage in this coming war. They had lost half their armies at the battle for Ossierel, when the Gargs had been allies of the Tyrant’s own legions and Alan and the Fir Bolg had been their mortal enemies. Now they were asking these same people to join forces in fighting the Tyrant in his capital city, Ghork Mega, some three-hundred leagues to the north of the Garg kingdom. It was true that the king had allowed them to move their advance party from its limited beachhead, surrounded by impassable marshes, and make a much easier landing in this sheltered bay. The main fleet now lay out to sea, a vast army of sails filling up the spaces between the islands. But as yet they dared not land. And all the while they were losing time.

Alan felt nauseous with doubt as he watched Mo, Turkeya and Iyezzz leave the camp to explore some nearby cave-dotted hills. He found himself joined by Qwenqwo and Ainé at the moving hinterland of the surf, where the brisk shore breezes fidgeted with the grasses growing out of the black volcanic soil about them.

The Kyra was uneasy in the proximity of so many Gargs. They were joined by Bétaald, who was the first to speak.

"You must understand the Gargs' fear. All of their lives, and for countless generations past, the greatest power—a god-like, if ultimately malignant power—has ruled their every thought and action. Now you, a stranger, demand that they go to war against that same power."

The breeze was building up. It dried the sweat on his brow even as it formed. Alan shrugged. "I have the feeling that they are waiting for something. But for the life of me I can't figure what it might be."

"Perhaps they await the return of Kate?"

"They're not alone."

"Have you no word from her?"

"Nothing."

Kate was lost to him again—as if they had never been united at the sacred pool, in the City of the Ancients. The thought infuriated Alan. Where was she when he really needed her to be by his side? And Mark too—Mark who had cleared off on a desperate errand, determined to persuade the Temple Ship to take him back to Earth. And for what? To discover whether or not he was still alive. For a moment, Alan was lost in thinking about his friends, both armed with their own oracula of power, wishing that they were here to help persuade the Garg king.

He felt the hand of the dwarf mage around his shoulders, and heard the belch that informed him Qwenqwo was seeking recourse in the bottle. But why should he not? When called on he fought without fear or self pity. There was no one Alan would have preferred by his side in times of danger.

Alan said, "We've lost another day."

"The king plays for time. He must be seen to be doing the right thing, by his son and the queen—by his people."

"Do you have any idea what Zelnesakkk is waiting for?"

Qwenqwo tamped a refill of tobacco into his pipe, but he paused before lighting it, deep in thought. "Knowing the Gargs, it will have to be a force of nature. A portent, perhaps?"

Alan rubbed so hard at his brow it felt bruised. He looked out at that same ocean the queen had skimmed, reflecting on her ritual, and on Iyezzz's insistence that he should attend. The Garg prince had expected something to happen. And, so far as Alan could see, something had happened: the flying fish had risen out of the sea to fly in communion with the queen. Iyezzz had been excited at the time, but it hadn't been enough to persuade the King.

Was there some additional reason why Iyezzz had been so insistent on Alan accompanying him to witness the queen?

The Garg prince's behaviour had been tense, as if he was hinting at something he had been forbidden to talk to Alan about. Some game the devious Mahteman was playing? Something so big in the minds of these superstitious beings that Zelnesakkk held back from any alliance of their peoples.

Magtokk the Mischievous

Mo and Turkeya were just as intrigued by Iyezzz's behaviour as Alan. Iyezzz had taken the two of them out of the Garg city, and now they peered out over the golden waves of desert that stretched northwards, as far as the distant slopes of the Gargs' Flamestruck Mountains. The Garg prince had been very secretive when he had taken them out of sight of his own people and then ferried them up here, one by one, to discover this nondescript plateau high in the hills that encircled the Thousand Islands. Then, with the promise that he would shortly return, he had left them alone in the rarefied air. His yellow eyes had been so liquidly bright they had practically glowed, and his skin had shone in a way Mo had come to recognise as excitement.

Turkeya turned his downy face to the sky, where the dark silhouette of the Prince was clearly visible, hovering several-hundred feet above them. In Turkeya's frown, as in his tall stature, Mo glimpsed his distant bear-like origins. He muttered, "I have a bad feeling about this, Mo. Look at him—he's up there watching us."

Mo wasn't too worried. She guessed there were thermals up there that would be pleasant to float on. The plateau was one of hundreds amid the conical peaks that were peppered with caves.

"I think he's more likely to be looking out for us."

"You're too trusting by half."

Mo had to admit that Iyezzz *was* playing some game. Turkeya had never trusted their Garg companion, in spite of the fact that he had very likely saved their lives on the perilous journey to the Tower of Bones. "How," he'd demanded on a number of occasions, "could anyone trust a creature with eyes like a snake's?"

"I don't know why he brought us here any more than you do—but I think that whatever it is, it must be purposeful."

"Huh!"

Turkeya performed a quick sweep of their surroundings with his eyes. There were thorny bushes bearing clusters of scarlet berries and the shaman plucked a handful, sniffed at them, then tested one of them between his teeth. "Mmmm—sweet."

Immediately he jerked and squealed.

"What is it?"

"Something bit me on the bum!"

Mo couldn't help but giggle.

"It's not funny."

"No," she grinned. "But the look on your face!"

"Huh!" He dropped the berries into the dry grey dust, his eyes darting here and there, searching for the teeth that had nipped at his bottom.

Mo narrowed her eyes, peering closely at the arched entrance to a nearby cave. Even though Mo trusted Iyezzz far more than her companion did, she still fingered the Torus that dangled on a leather thong around her neck, her nervous fingers also finding the bog oak figurine suspended on the same thong, a strange shape carved by nature that resembled a female figure with three faces. It was one of her most precious possessions, a gift back on Earth from Alan's druidic grandfather, Padraig.

"This place gives me the creeps," Turkeya grumbled. "What's the great secret? What could be so important we have to hide the fact we're coming here, not just from Alan, and the Kyra, but even from the other Gargs?"

Mo shrugged, having no idea.

But just as Turkeya was about to add to his grumbling, Iyezzz returned, descending through the air with a noisy fluttering of his wings.

"I think it is safe—you can now appear."

Who was Iyezzz addressing? Mo and Turkeya looked around the empty plateau. "I've had enough of these games," Turkeya exclaimed. "Either he tells us what's going on or I shall insist on returning to the shore."

"Certainly I will explain." Iyezzz's skin flickered through shades of cooling colours, greens and blues and golden, as if to placate the young Olhyiu. "The Mage Lord, Alan, has pressed me, again and again, as to why the Eyrie people should keep their own counsel on the impending war against the Tyrant."

Mo looked up at him, confirming the impression of high excitement in the red-veined yellow eyes. "Is this why you brought us here—to explain the reason for your father's cautiousness?"

"Yeshhh! For you—for the sake of our friendship and alliance—once more do I accept the risk of my father's ire. *Kwatekkk!* I break taboos."

Mo recognised the word, kwatekkk—it was the Garg word for forbidden. She murmured, "What is it, Iyezzz?"

"These are times of great change. The rules that once served us must be broken. I will introduce you to one whose presence here is our greatest treasure—a secret that must be protected at any costs."

Turkeya rolled his eyes. "What secret? What's so special about this place?" Turkeya was increasingly apprehensive, staring at the landscape of conical-shaped hillocks of rock, with their hundreds of caves. He gestured at the caves, "They might be teeming with watchful eyes."

Iyezzz sighed, in the sweeping way that only a Garg could. "Even the most unsophisticated shaman might know of a sage known as Magtokk."

Turkeya stared at the Garg. "Legends. Tales of magic and mischief to amuse children around the winter's hearth."

"Magic and mischief?" Mo grinned.

"A real being—as you are about to discover—but one so loathed by the Tyrant, your sworn enemy, that he has been persecuted and hunted through ages past."

"Oh—you're claiming he's here?"

"Ach—my pupil, and most protective ward, has no need to explain. It was I who asked for this meeting."

As one, Mo and Turkeya spun round to discover the source of the voice. There was the strangest impression, as if they were gazing at nothing more than a cloud of smoke. Mo continued to examine it as a presence solidified out of the empty air in front of them. All she could make out, at first, was an enormous bundle of shaggy brown-orange hair perched on a boulder within feet of them. But, gradually, Mo found herself gazing at the strangest creature: an animal that resembled an enormous male orang-utan. Mo had only ever seen an orang-utan up close in London zoo, but this creature was much larger, and far shaggier, than those she recalled. His eyes, which were chocolate-coloured, deep set and surrounded by wrinkles, were partially clouded with age and peered out of a huge face of matte black skin, massively widened at the cheeks with flaps that arched from his mouth to the top of his head and a drooping moustache that fed around the mouth to become one with a luxurious reddish beard. His thick tangles of hair fell in waves from his shoulders and arms to shower over the ground at his feet. He was the shaggiest, most wonderful, creature Mo had ever seen.

"Who—or what—in heaven's name are you?" Turkeya said.

"Ach," she heard a great bowling whisper of a voice, as if it issuing from the depths of an empty barrel, "a poor miserable excuse for a magician. Magtokk is my name, known to my friends as Magtokk the Mischievous, given my fondness of trivial and even wanton delights."

Mo pealed with laughter. There was such a mischievous twinkle in those chocolate-brown eyes she just wanted to throw her arms around his neck and hug the improbable monster.

"You . . . you're an orang-utan!"

"A seemly creature I lifted from your mind."

Mo simply blinked.

How had he arrived so close to them without either of them noticing? A hairy hand on the end of an enormously long arm beckoned Mo closer.

"Mo Grimstone—I think it was fated that we meet."

Turkeya placed a cautious arm on her shoulder, but she shrugged it off. Magtokk the Mischievous had an immense physical presence she just couldn't resist. Soft fingers enveloped her hand, as if their owner were intent on consuming her whole. His eyes widened as they fell on the Torus dangling on its thong. He lifted his eyes to meet her own. Mo enjoyed being the focus of his all-consuming curiosity.

Iyezzz bowed his entire upper body, his skin flickering through waves of colour like rainbows. "My friends, Mo and Turkeya, allow me to introduce my most revered and respected tutor who, despite his fondness for self-deprecation, is known to the Eyrie people as Magtokk the Wise."

Mo copied the Garg prince in bowing, not knowing how else she should greet the elderly mage.

"Magtokk the Wise—if that is how I should address you?"

"Magtokk the big head, according to some. But I am fonder of Magtokk the Mischievous."

Mo was recalling the creature that had nipped Turkeya's bottom. "It was you—you bit him?"

Even Turkeya couldn't hide the fact that the slow grin that was making its way over the huge face, with its sea of grey leathery wrinkles, was infectious. "I could not have the bear cub gobbling my supper."

"But you were invisible!"

"All knowledge is invisible until one's eyes are opened to it."

Mo paused to consider what he was saying, or perhaps hinting at. "Iyezzz said that you wanted to meet us?"

The prince spoke. "Magtokk's people, like our own, were persecuted—not by the Great Witch, but by the

Tyrant himself. He is rare indeed—a fugitive who has escaped the clutches of the great enemy for millennia. His presence here puts us all at risk. This is what my father, the King, has been at pains to conceal from you."

"What do you mean, Iyezzz?"

"So great is the Tyrant's loathing of Magtokk that, were his presence to be discovered, he would destroy us all."

"But why, then, have you risked this secret by bringing us here?"

"I will admit that I have talked about you at length with my tutor—talked about all of you, including Greeneyes. Magtokk was curious to meet you."

Turkeya was visibly tensing. Mo's hand reached out to touch his shoulder, to reassure him as Magtokk spoke.

"I am most obliged to my young ward. The prince has spoken eloquently of you. But now you are here, we have much to discuss."

"Magtokk, will you help us to destroy the Tyrant?"

"Come, Mo Grimstone—and you too, Turkeya, son of Siam! Come join me in my hall of splendour—what you imagine to be a cave."

Mo must have blinked, and in the act of closing her eyes, even for the briefest moment, Magtokk had disappeared from his perch on the rock and was nowhere to be seen.

* * *

"Since the bear-cub has taken such a liking to my berries, perhaps he would like to indulge himself, this time with my permission?"

Turkeya didn't look remotely interested in food. Mo saw how he was twirling on his heels, his eyes widening at the strangest, most magical, chamber he had ever witnessed. Its shape—if it had a shape at all—was like viewing the carapace of the strangest, most exotic insect from the inside. The light in the atrium fell to a modest glow that pervaded the walls and roof and there were shadowy niches that contained sculptural objects—though they could also have been natural oddities, chosen for their shapes.

"Observe," Magtokk declared.

Mo's eyes held the image of Magtokk for a brief moment, before he disappeared to be replaced by a shimmering blur of movement. And then he reappeared, or, rather, dozens of him reappeared. She heard the magician chuckle, a deep throaty laugh that filled the entire atrium.

"So you see how easily I hide. Such disguises do I affect while living always on the go. Yet I dream. Ach, how I have dreamed of liberty over the ages I have lived! I don't know if I am the only survivor of my people. I have prayed that there may be others living in secret like me, waiting and hoping for the day when a new force might come along, one capable of challenging the Tyrant's vainglorious rule. And now here you are, Mo Grimstone, one of four friends who have journeyed far—from another world, no less—accompanied by Turkeya, shaman of the stout-hearted Children of the Sea. Already you have destroyed the Tyrant's most dangerous ally, the Great Witch Olc, in her Tower of Bones."

Mo couldn't believe what she was hearing. "You've been waiting all this time—for us to come here?"

"Indeed."

Magtokk was himself again, a robust shaggy figure with a great rounded dome of a head atop burly sloping shoulders. He leapt into the air, landing atop a projection, where he hung upside down, holding on with his feet, his fur dangling at all sorts of improbable angles. He didn't seem to notice, or perhaps care, how ridiculous he looked.

"This war into which you are heading will be bitter and dangerous."

"I think that Alan understands the danger. We all do. That's why we need every bit of help we can find."

Turkeya was staring at Mo, as if he couldn't believe that she was trusting the creature. The orangutan leaped again, discovering another equally precarious perch, this time holding on with one hand.

"On that we are agreed."

"So, will you help us, Magtokk?"

He was more interested in traversing a section of wall, swinging from one precarious perch to another, all the while humming a tune. "Forgive my need for exercise. It really does help me to think. I worry, you see, that my help might prove more of a hindrance—even a potential danger to your brave purpose."

"Oh, Magtokk, please stop this capering. You're making me feel so dizzy I can't begin to think."

"Surely it is you, young lady, whose very presence is bedazzling me."

Turkeya was looking sideways at Mo, baffled by the behaviour of Magtokk the Mischievous.

Mo pressed him, "Why does the Tyrant hate you so much?"

"That is a very long story. Long . . ." Magtokk leaped clean across the atrium from one wall to another. "Long, long . . ." He leaped again, this time performing a somersault before he came to rest, patting his drapery of fur back into a comfortable blanket around his shoulders, and taking a seat on a stone immediately opposite Mo. He brought his huge face up close to hers, exposing two scary horseshoes of teeth in a yawn. "So long," he concluded, "that it will have to keep for another time—a time perhaps when we are not so hard-pressed."

"But we are not in the least hard-pressed."

"You think not?" A shaggy hand had curled around an ear as if anticipating the warning horn that sounded out from far below in the clearing before the beach. "Alas, it would appear that we must think of today and forgo worrying about what will happen tomorrow."

"What are you hinting at?"

"Ach, my two young friends—Iyezzz has brought you here so I can impart a secret. One that your friend Alan should know—a secret that you might use to your advantage with the reluctant King Zelnesakkk and the wily High Shaman Mahteman."

The Scalpie

Mark ushered Nan and Penny through the side door into the modest nave of the Church of the English Martyrs. A tall, colourfully-dressed black woman, who was carrying a candle in a tall brass candlestick, slammed the door shut behind them, confining them to a gloom as deep as twilight.

"Thank de good Lord! Fadah Toowee is expectin' you."

There was the flare of a match in the near distance—Mark saw a yellow flame appear a short distance away. In the feeble light of the newly-lit candle, he could make out a diminutive stooped figure which, closer-to, revealed itself to be a white-haired priest, clad in heavy gold-brocaded vestments over his black soutane. He was standing by a coffin, set on trestles in front of the vestibule before the arched main doors. The illuminating candle, in a candlestick identical to that held by what he took to be a West Indian woman, was perched atop the coffin lid. On the floor, by the priest's polished black shoes, was an ornate brass bucket containing a brass-handled brush. There were no funereal flowers bedecking the coffin, just a splatter of brightly reflective droplets of water glistening over the lightwood top.

"Father Touhey?"

"Indeed, that's me. But who are you?"

Mark could hardly contain his relief. "I'm Mark Grimstone. I believe that Bridey will have sent a message. You have something for me?"

"Hush," he said, with a finger to his lips.

"De Razzamatazzers is ganging up outside."

Mark turned his attention from the white-haired priest to the woman "The what?"

Penny answered, "Razzers!"

"Henriette, my housekeeper—she fears they're trying to break in."

"Razzers?"

"Dey all juiced up."

"Juiced—you mean they're drugged?"

"Juiced up on de spirit. Dey hammerin' off an' on, all day. Dey sense it like we hear de music—de wave."

"You're Henriette?"

"Yes."

Mark was about to ask her about what kind of wave the Razzamatazzers sensed when he sensed it for himself through his oraculum. Something was signalling, sending a message that wasn't audible through his normal hearing. When he attempted to probe it, it became a deafening scream so uncomfortable he instinctively clamped his hands over his ears.

He glanced at Nan. *You hear it too?*

Her wide eyes were answer enough.

Nan addressed him, urgently, mind-to-mind.

<This razzamatazz thing?>

<Yes?>

<You must ask Henriette what it is.>

But before he could speak to Henriette, there was a thunderous hammering against the main doors. It sounded as if somebody was using a sledgehammer against the Victorian box lock.

"O Lord—dey breakin' in!" Henriette immediately put out her candle flame between her moistened finger and thumb. She was reaching out towards the second candle on the coffin, but it was too late. There was a violent crack and the lock crashed inwards onto the tiled floor. The twin doors sundered, throwing splinters of oak into the darkened hallway of the church. The old priest had fallen against the coffin, causing it to slip on its trestles, so it teetered on the brink of plunging to the floor. Henriette moved quickly, dropping the candlestick and steadying the tottering construction with one hand, while supporting the ageing priest with the other.

The interior was flooded with light as the headlights of a vehicle shone directly in through the breach. Father

Touhey froze. His mouth dropped open and his eyes widened, staring past Mark towards the shattered door. When Mark spun round he saw a swarm of flying monsters pour in through the gaping entrance to invade the church.

"Grimlings!" the girl exclaimed.

Mark spoke quickly, urgently, "Father Touhey, Henriette, Penny—all three of you get behind me and Nan. Make yourself into the smallest possible target."

"But you'll be killed," said Penny.

"I'm not sure we're killable."

"I don't understand."

"Makes three of us."

Father Touhey muttered a prayer but Mark wasn't listening. He was studying the swarm more closely. The flying monsters looked like chimeras of mammals and insects. As big as tawny owls, they had transparent wings almost a foot in span. Their heads were obscenely human-like, with faces that reminded him of goblins. Their eyes were amber and glowing, glaringly fierce, and the jaws looked lethal, crowded with piranha-like teeth.

He heard Penny's warning. "Grimlings bite!"

As if with one mind, Mark and Nan grabbed a heavy brass candlestick apiece. The air within the entrance now buzzed and swarmed with Grimlings, their wings a whirring blur; but the repellent faces moved more slowly, more purposefully, assessing the situation within the church. Mark and Nan turned back to back, waving the heavy candlesticks to best ward off attack.

<Penny! Her mind!>

Mark followed Nan's alert. Through his oraculum he invaded the mind of the feral girl, to be startled by the strangeness of what he discovered there. He recognised that he was looking around himself at the nave of the church, in which the headlights threw everything into lurid contrasts of light and shadow. But there was an additional, astonishing perspective. It took him a moment or two before he could even begin to grasp what it might be.

<She's analysing every moment, constructing a kind of three-dimensional blueprint of what's going on from moment to moment.> It was too complex for Mark to follow in detail.

Penny screamed. "Watch out!"

Within her mind Mark saw that the seemingly random movements of the vicious little brutes was coordinated into a purposeful weave. She was predicting their impending attack. He had the disorientating sense that it was Penny who was directing his mind and not the other way round.

<Nan—do you see?>

<How very disturbing!>

<But I think I see what she's attempting to do.>

<She's helping us—predicting their movements?>

Mark found himself testing her predictions, moving the heavy candlestick towards an incoming Grimling head with its snarling maw of teeth. The crunch of contact was satisfying. In seconds he and Nan killed a dozen of them, but then the gaping main doors were flung wide open. An enormous man, built like a Sumo wrestler, strode into the church. His head was smooth-shaven, and embedded in the left side of his skull was the glowing silver sigil of the triple infinity. The Grimlings changed their pattern of attack to flow about him, like the shoal of pilot fish about a hunting shark.

"Grimlings bite—Scalpie kills," hissed Penny.

"Shit!" Mark felt the oraculum take fire in his brow. He shouted to Nan. "I'll deal with the Scalpie if you can deal with the Grimlings. Look after Penny!"

The Grimlings had altered their pattern, extending out into a dome enclosing all five of their prey. But they kept their distance, deferring to the giant warrior. The Scalpie was in no hurry to attack. His behaviour suggested ritual. He lowered himself to a kneeling position on the floor, placing a casket of polished ebony on the tiles in front of him and making a bow before opening it. He took out a single gauntlet, made out of articulated matte black metal, and drew it onto his left hand. With his mailed hand he lifted a dagger from the casket. It was heavy and ornate and the Scalpie handled it reverentially. The blade was a tapering spiral; it too was black—darker than the mere absence of reflection—and the handle gleamed with inlaid silver. There was a sigil of the triple infinity embossed on the hilt.

Mark stared at the dagger with disbelief.

Alan had described exactly such a dagger back on Tír. It was the weapon of a priestly caste known as preceptors, who fulfilled some darkly spiritual role within the armies of the Tyrant of the Wastelands. Mark guessed the Scalpie was the equivalent of a preceptor here on Earth. When the burly warrior spoke it was in a guttural alien language, he didn't recognise, though he heard the meaning of the words through the oraculum.

To the clay shall I sacrifice such
dung as irritate my Lord.
Thus, in a spirit of humility do I
consecrate my unworthy offering.
In blood shall I honour Thee, my life
and soul unworthy, at your call.
Spare me not!
Tear the still beating heart from my
breast, if it pleaseth thee,
Oh blessed and everlasting Master!

Mark felt a shiver pass through him at a reminder from Nan of where their own power came from. *My oraculum is the oraculum of the Third Power. And the Third Power is Mórígán, the Goddess of Death.*

But what did all of that mean here on Earth?

He thought back to when Alan came to terms with his oraculum, the ruby equivalent—something he called the First Power. Mark had discovered that it worked best through instinct, when he didn't have to think about it, but as Alan himself had discovered, that wasn't such an easy thing to do.

The Scalpie was climbing back to his feet, the dagger clasped within his mailed left fist. There was an eerie glow about the fist and the dagger, the sigil pulsating with silvery light in concert with the logo embedded in his skull. The Grimlings were moving again, the swarm's complex formations suggesting imminent attack. The air about Mark's head was filled with their buzzing and bumbling. He glimpsed a goblin face just inches from his own, the amber glow of the eyes, the flash of teeth. Within moments he had been bitten several times.

But he couldn't afford to focus on the swarm.

"Nan—you okay?"

"I've got them—deal with the warrior!"

Mark took a firm hold of the candlestick. It was likely to be useless but he didn't have the confidence to throw it to one side. He tried to engage the oraculum, but he was untested in using it in combat. All it seemed to achieve was a tingling at the ends of his fingers.

Out of the corners of his eyes, he saw that Nan's eyes were all-black. The oraculum was blazing in her brow. He was glad to see it; she was far more experienced in wielding the power of Mórígán. Blue-black lightning flared, followed by squeals from the Grimlings as their bodies burst into flame.

"Quick," Penny called, her voice high-pitched, curiously cat-like.

Mark found himself back within the strange landscape of her mind. The Grimlings were ignored, her entire focus on a centre of incandescent power. It had to be the Scalpie's dagger. In her mind Mark saw the lines of force radiating from it, its purposeful trajectory bending and distorting the space around them.

There was a sudden rush and the gauntleted hand, with its flaring blade, was coming for his throat.

He moved instinctively, striking out with the heavy candlestick at the naked forearm above the gauntlet. He encountered flesh and bone and prayed to hear it crack, but a dreadful force rebounded against his strike, turning the candlestick black and searing his hand. The spiral blade of the dagger caught his right shoulder, moving diagonally down across his chest as he fell away. At the same time a tremendous bolt of black lightning struck the Scalpie, ensheathing him and whiting out his eyes. He fell back, turning as he did so, yet still he came back around to face Mark, his purpose unchanged.

Mark found himself on his knees, leaning on his uninjured left hand. He was trembling from the wound. He had no time to think, he had to force himself back to his feet.

Nan prompted him: <The girl!>

Mark switched his focus back onto Penny, re-entering her mind. Within her vision the Scalpie was just completing the act of turning round. His whole figure was illuminated by moving wavelets of power. As if in slow motion, the gauntleted hand rose to threaten Mark full square. At the centre of the lines of force, Mark saw the dagger approaching his throat once more. Then he saw another, faint, familiar power.

"Vengeance!"

He roared the name through his throat and oraculum at the same time, thrusting his left hand into the air above his head. In that strange distorted world of Penny's vision, Mark saw the emergence of a new force within the battle arena. He sensed Penny's own astonishment as she saw the walls of the coffin exploding, a blue-black sun erupting from the mass of disintegrating wood. A wrack of lightning followed the twisting motion of the Fir Bolg battle axe, its sigmoid blades effulgent with Fir Bolg runes as it spun towards the raised hand of its master, striking home to be enclosed in Mark's fist, sheathing him in such a storm of power he felt his feet lift slightly off the floor.

There was no time to think. He heard Nan's whisper, mind-to-mind: <Let the power of Mórígán flow through you. Be one with it!>

Mark knew, suddenly, that his eyes were as terrifying as Nan's. He didn't know if he could actually die, or if he was in fact already dead, but he was certain that something fearful was about to happen to him. He recalled Alan, when similarly threatened, with his ruby oraculum blazing. Alan had held the Spear of Lug, reaching out into the thunderclouds in the sky overhead, bringing down the lightning onto the Temple Ship and shattering the frozen lake in which they were trapped. He had looked so all-powerful in that first call upon his power. At the time, Mark had felt utterly diminished by the spectacle, but now he had to do the same. He had to draw on his oraculum if he was to destroy the Scalpie—and the threat of the dagger with the twisted blade.

All of this passed in a moment, but during that moment, Mark felt as though the wound no longer existed: he felt stronger, more confident.

The loss of the Scalpie's vision after the axe had burst from the coffin in a lightning storm was to his advantage, but the blinded Scalpie was now sniffing at the air, trying to locate Mark through scent, instead. He was sweeping the spiral blade in great arcs before him, advancing towards where Mark now crouched with the battleaxe raised. Mark waited until the sweep of the blade passed by him, inches from his face, then he struck, stepping into what Penny saw as the next vicious arc. Mark brought down the wyre-glowing axe, severing the Scalpie's dagger arm just below the elbow. He ignored the tumble of limb, with its dagger. His eyes were on the white eyes of his enemy. His mind was focused on the anticipated next movement of the huge right hand, which was searching for his throat. Jabbing forward with the tip of the battleaxe he scored a line across his attacker's brow. The force of the strike, flared with lightning, caused the Scalpie to rear back, exposing a throat as thick as a normal man's thigh.

Mark brought his arm around through a horizontal arc, hardly registering the contact between the blade and the Scalpie's throat. No mortal flesh could have withstood the ferocity of the strike. He knew he had beheaded the Scalpie without needing to look. His own proximity to such terrible power frightened him. He felt his consciousness waver, felt his heartbeat so fast in his ears and throat it seemed impossible that he should survive, then he felt the release, which was so debilitating he fell to his knees.

He was unable for the moment to rise to his feet, blinking repeatedly, wondering what it all truly meant.

Nan spoke. "We cannot delay here."

"No, you're right." Mark forced himself back onto tottery legs. His voice was husky as he called out, "Henriette—are you still here?"

"Here—I been hidin'."

"Father Touhey—is there someone who could look after him?"

"His friend—de dean at Christ's Church."

"Then we'll help you get him there."

Nan called out, "Your wounds!"

Mark's wounds were self-healing. He looked at Nan and saw the whites of her eyes reappear and the irises contract, returning them to a more normal chocolate-brown. But her eyes had not just changed superficially, they had metamorphosed into something else. He felt the sense of fright again: the sense of wonderment at what they had become. *She can see the same thing happen in my eyes too.*

He sensed the same fright in her.

He stared at the rubble-strewn nave of the church with its wrecked coffin, a coffin in which there had never been a body, just his Fir Bolg battleaxe. Mark needed a few more moments to take it all in: the beheaded body of the Scalpie and the dead bodies of Grimlings that littered the small church aisle, and then Father Touhey, who was sitting, head bowed, in one of the pews, and the housekeeper, Henriette, who had her arm around the elderly priest but was staring at Mark and Nan open-mouthed. Only then did he notice that the feral girl was nowhere to be seen.

"Where's Penny?"

"Gone."

"The Scalpie's dagger?"

"Gone too. She took it an' ran."

Return to Ulla Quemar

How very differently Kate Shaunessy felt now, standing on the same stone ledge as on her last visit to Ulla Quemar, the sole surviving city of the Cill. The same waves broke against the cliff face below her feet, the same sea-breezes wailed like banshees through the rocks. But the foul air rising from the opening in the cleft was ample confirmation of Driftwood's warning. Things had changed for the worse since her last visit. Had she left it too late to help the Momu?

The dragon had been too large to drop her off as before and had been obliged to hover in mid-air while allowing her to descend the staircase of his tail. Now, as the down-draught of his take-off blew her auburn curls around her face, Kate's heart pattered with apprehension. She steeled herself in front of the cleft before letting herself go, tumbling down the chute she recalled from before. This time, there was no soft bed of moss at the bottom, only a stinking morass of rotting seaweed. There were no welcoming eyes waiting for her in the dark, no Shaami to greet her. She had to make her own way using the green glow of her crystal that permeated the smooth-walled cavern; in actuality, a carved entrance chamber leading to the hidden openings that led to the water locks, which in turn protected the city from unwanted visitors.

The complex doors of finely-carved stone, which had irised open at Shaami's musical incantation, now stood agape, and the guardian water-locks had been allowed to drain away, with just a residue of stinking brine at the bottom of every fall, making her headway difficult and smelly before she eventually emerged into a world abandoned to ruin. Even the light in the city had decayed, with only a misty glow permeating the open spaces. Pools of darkness made sinister the twists and turns of what had, so recently, been entrancing labyrinths of organically-shaped buildings. Previously, the buildings had been like nautilus shells, the curving beauty of oyster shells, or the lovely radial symmetries of sea urchins and starfish, all bedecked with a proliferation of colourful plants, butterflies and damsel flies.

All too soon she discovered the explanation for the failing light, as well as the sulphurous smell, as she made her way through the warren of streets and waterways to the great seal. It had once been a marvellous construction that united city and ocean, but now the coral reef was overwhelmed by red growth.

She came close enough to examine it, holding her nose against the stink of decay, and noticed that a toxic scum had spread everywhere. It had suffocated the brilliantly-coloured life of the reef, choking the underwater sunstealers, whose life-giving oxygen bubbles were no longer rising.

"Poor Ulla Quemar!"

Kate looked about at the buildings and streets, lustreless and untended. And even here Shaami was nowhere to be seen. All that she encountered were the fierce warriors, with their massive heads, protruding jaws and huge interlocking canine teeth, who wandered, disconsolate, here and there amid the despoiled streets, and who regarded her passing with indifference. How could it have deteriorated so quickly? Was there nobody sensible she could ask?

Kate made her way along the ruined shoreline, gazing around in consternation. She looked upwards, towards the point where a transparent curtain-wall fell in a graceful arc from the roof and filled three-quarters of the entrance, extending out in a wide semicircle into the ocean. A series of fractures had appeared over the quartz of the wall. It looked as if the seal might give way at any moment and the pressure of the ocean would swamp the city. The thought was so frightening that Kate reached up to touch the oraculum in her brow. She needed to be reassured that she still possessed the power of healing and restoring life. Now she closed her eyes and cast those powers about her, as if testing the pulsating green oraculum against the ravaged scenes that she was witnessing. But she soon realised that, even with the Second Power, she was helpless to cure the city. No power was capable of making it well again. The beautiful city would not return to healthy life.

The finality of it caused her to fall to her knees.

"Greeneyes—is it you?"

Kate's eyes lifted to be confronted by a distressed figure, standing several yards away in the reddish gloom. The voice addressed her in a way she would have expected of her friend, but the figure didn't look like Shaami at all. The voice was so hoarse it was little more than a croak.

"Oh, Shaami—is it truly you?"

He had looked so delicate and graceful when last she saw him, but now he more resembled the hurt and tormented figure she had first encountered in the Tower of Bones. His flesh was so wasted it had become as transparent as smoke and those gorgeous turquoise eyes were now shrunken and abject within wells of grief.

"Come closer to me."

Kate watched the lovely irises contract and open again with what she knew must be deep emotion. "I cannot."

"Why not?"

"I am not worthy."

"Then I shall come to you." She climbed back onto her feet, went to him and hugged him to her breast. How scarecrow thin he had become! He resembled a wraith. *This is the despair the Momu talked about when she begged me to help her and her city.* Kate hugged him more fiercely. "I have come back to help you."

"It is kind of you—as indeed you have ever been kind. But it is too late for Ulla Quemar. Too late for the Cill."

How it ground her heart into the dust to hear no music in his voice. The despair of loss had robbed him of that spiritual delight. Even the cruelty of Faltana, and the Great Witch herself, had not been capable of that. Kate felt tears moisten her eyes.

"Please don't say that. Oh, Shaami, I hardly dare to ask you. But please tell me the Momu is not yet dead."

"I don't know." He began to tremble in her arms.

Kate comforted him, but even as she did so she was struggling to come to terms with all she was witnessing. She tried to think beyond the contagious despair. She must find a way to help the Cill.

Lifting her own tearful face, she was startled to be confronted by a kneeling creature, whose shrouded arms were crossed over its breast and whose face was coldly indifferent. Its eyes were reflecting grey mirrors, its octopus-like head shrouded in a heavy veil that trailed to the ground.

She kept a protective arm about Shaami's shoulders. "What is this creature?"

"It is a keeper."

“What does that mean?”

“I do not know.”

Kate felt a shiver of dread. *I should have listened to Driftwood.* How often had Bridey warned her about jumping into things with both feet. *Oh, Bridey—how I miss you and Darkie, and Uncle Fergal. How you must all be worrying about me, after I’ve been missing for so long. What must you be thinking? I couldn’t blame you if you were assuming the worst?*

Kate gritted her teeth. She took a breath or two to make herself calm down. The truth was that there were dark forces at work here that she didn’t understand one bit. She had sailed on towards calamity like . . . like what Bridey would have called the very worst feckin’ eeejit. The Kate Shaunessy who had returned from Africa, alive but wrecked, wanted to run. The Kate who lost her mammy and daddy and her brother Billy—that Kate was screaming in panic, deep inside her. She felt so weak she couldn’t have taken a single step. Her hope withered.

“You must go now,” Shaami whispered.

No! She was done with being afraid. She was done with running. She refused to be cowed by her rising panic. She stubbornly shook her head. “Shaami, take me to the Momu.”

“Please listen to me. Ulla Quemar is doomed. You must abandon it while there is yet time to save yourself.”

“Shaami—from what I can see, we don’t have time to argue about it. You must take me to the Momu right now—to the chamber of the One Tree.”

He reluctantly led her deep into Ulla Quemar, to the chamber that opened into the solid rock in the oldest quarter. But even though Kate kept her oraculum searchingly open, there was no choir of harmonious voices to flood her mind, none of the hauntingly beautiful atmosphere she had sensed before. Their way was blocked by more of the aggressive warriors who seemed drunk on grief or, worse still, on the verge of losing their reason.

Shaami tried to hold Kate back when she arrived at the entrance to the chamber. "Oh, please—I beg you for a final time. Don't enter there."

"Why not?"

"I fear what you will find."

Kate remembered with a cruel clarity her previous welcome arrival into the chamber of the Momu. But now the warriors' eyes were flatly hostile, half-shaded under bulging brows. Their armoured limbs, with powerful lobster-like claws, were tensed against her entry. They knew who she was, but still they obstructed her.

"I must go in. I have to speak to the Momu."

"The Momu cannot speak."

Kate saw a hint of madness in their eyes—a madness born out of the loss of the hive control, which depended on the central focus of the Momu.

"Be careful." Shaami raised his hands, with their podgy nail-less fingers. "The warriors are apt to strike without warning."

Into Kate's mind came cautionary words spoken with a gentle voice: <Beware, Greeneyes. You should listen to Shaami's advice.>

"Oh—Momu! Is it you speaking?"

There was a long pause, and then she heard it again, though terribly faint, the soft, deeply musical voice: <There is little reason left. All is failing. All hope is lost in the growing equivocation.>

Kate didn't understand the meaning of the strange words, but she was sure that she was speaking mind-to-mind with the Momu.

"Please address the guardians. Make them let me through to you."

The door was probably the last to be under any formal control in the city, but now it irised open. With a jarring crash of their distorted right arms against the shell-like carapaces of their chests, the warriors made space enough for Kate to squeeze between them, but then they crossed arms again to ensure that Shaami could not follow her into the chamber. The great door irised shut behind her, casting Kate into a terrifying gloom.

She searched the large cavern through the eye of her oraculum; the chamber had been transformed with dark energy. Flickering arcs of lightning flared over the natural rock walls. Where the Momu had hailed her arrival across the birthing pool, Kate now faced a freezing shower of sea water falling from the roof. Wading through, she discovered the Momu lying on her back between the massive roots of the One Tree, which had proliferated around her body, entangling her limbs. There was no sign of the hand maidens who had cared for her on the last occasion Kate had come here.

The Momu's lips flickered, to allow the softest whisper. "My dearest Greeneyes. I regret that you should witness my final humiliation."

"Oh, Momu—I have come back to save you." She came close to whisper into her elongated ears, the lobes perforated and widened to take spools of ivory a full six inches in diameter.

"There are creatures out there. Shaami called one a keeper, but he couldn't tell me what that meant."

"When a civilisation is about to end they come. They observe."

When a civilisation is about to end?

"On whose behalf do they come and observe?"

"The Keepers of Night and Day have their duty to observe."

"Oh, Momu, you're talking in riddles."

Kate had no idea who, or what, the Keepers of Night and Day might be, but they sounded ominous. She desperately wanted to help. She had learned so much from the Momu's friendship, their mental and spiritual communion. She recalled waking from a restful sleep in the sea-urchin-shaped chamber where she had slept, whose walls had glowed. She had hugged the eiderdown bedcovers to her nose and mouth, with no idea just how long she had been immersed in this dream-like state, her mind still floating in a kind of ecstasy of revelation with the Momu. The level of communion had been altogether deeper than what would have been possible with words alone. Through the love and kindness of the Momu, she had acquired an understanding more complex than any other she had ever encountered before, a sense of wisdom.

This understanding had changed her, made her aware, physically and spiritually, of her own role, of the power and use of the emerald triangle in her brow. But in absorbing such a level of understanding, in being immersed, mentally and spiritually with the Momu, Kate had also come to understand that the Momu was dying, that her time was limited, and that she, Kate, was being asked to accept the responsibility that such knowledge brought with it.

A new female—young, vigorous—must be born. But before the Momu could give birth to her successor, she had to rise from her despair. And to do this she must have hope—hope for the future for her people, so that her successor could bring a new joy of life, and communion, into the world.

But how, in the circumstances Kate found herself, could she promise hope for the future of the Cill?

Kate sat down among the roots, willing herself to be one with the strange and wonderful being who had befriended her when her need had been equally great.

The falling brine had caused the Momu's hair to adhere to her elongated skull. Those beautiful mother-of-pearl eyes were drifting closed, and now that Kate was close enough to hold the great webbed hand, she saw that the tree's roots were not merely growing around the Momu, the rootlets were invading the flesh of her legs, and rising to cocoon the rest of her.

"Oh, no—they're devouring you."

"There is no unkindness intended. The roots of the One Tree merely respond to their own growing hunger."

Kate gazed down at the heavy crystal of greenish-blue hung on a gold filigree chain around the Momu's neck. The crystal of power retained but the faintest glow.

"Please advise me. Tell me what to do."

The Momu's golden eyes performed that slow blink, and she placed her hand on Kate's arm. "The One Tree is a mere twig of the Tree of Life. Like me, it is dying. Long ago it called upon Nidhoggr, the serpent who gnaws at the roots of the world, to give it life. Now Nidhoggr demands its return. He would also take me back." She sighed, a long, mournful sound. "You must not stay here. It is too dangerous. My reason is ebbing fast. I cannot save you, any more than my people, for my mind has been invaded by the phantoms of despair."

"I'll stop it. I'll stop Nidhoggr. I won't allow it."

"You cannot stop it—not even with your blessed power. Go—go now! Leave this chamber while there is yet time."

"I will not go. I came to save you and your people. I won't abandon the Momu or the Cill. Where you go, I go."

Drawn by the Sword

Under a whitewashed gothic archway in Christ's Church Hall in Spitalfields—a space twice the size of the entire nave of the Church of the English Martyrs—Mark sipped at a mug of tea while watching a queue of hungry people move across the galley. At the head of the queue there were four women doling out food, all wearing baseball caps. The homeless, numbering well over a hundred, each picked up a tray and then collected their bread, chicken, vegetables and finally milky tea poured from huge aluminium teapots into plastic cartons. Once the food had been collected, the figures shuffled away to an assortment of tables. There was little talking and even fewer smiles, and there were so many hungry that they crowded the space, overfilling the tables so that a small oblong meant to accommodate four was made to fit seven or eight.

They called it The Refuge, but as far as Mark could see that was just a euphemism for a soup kitchen. Soup kitchens were hardly a novelty in London, where there had always been homeless people, penniless and desperate, eking out a troubled survival on the streets with little or no privacy and even less protection. But the expression on these faces reflected more than hunger. Mark had seen the streets where they lived. He understood the desperation, the sullen fear in their eyes. At least Father Touhey would be well looked after here.

They had accompanied the elderly priest across the mews and into a small terraced house. Henriette had helped him to the kitchenette where she washed most of him free of the Scalpie's blood and the scum that had sprayed everywhere from Nan's extermination of the Grimlings. Henriette had also discovered the telephone number for Christ's Church and had helped Father Touhey into a change of clothes while Mark and Nan had a few minutes alone. They had also washed their hands and faces in the kitchen sink, but they could find no towel to dry themselves off. They just looked at one another and laughed. Nan put her arms about Mark's neck. She lifted up her face and kissed him. "You were the real target—you know that?" she said.

"Maybe."

"We were a team."

"A pretty good team at that."

"The Grimlings were just a distraction."

"Some distraction!"

"The Scalpie would have killed you."

"We were lucky—we had Penny's help."

"Yes."

She kissed him again. "Oh, Mark, I sensed . . . If you had died . . ."

"We both would have died?"

She nodded. She hugged him fiercely, protectively.

It was a strange feeling, wonderful but also strange, to be kissed after fighting off an attempt at his life. As if the singleness, the oneness, of being had changed to something bigger, a duality of hearts and minds.

His fingers brushed her cheek. "Did it frighten you?"

"Half to death."

It was a joke. He chuckled, gazed into her dark eyes.

He had felt it exactly as Nan had. If one had died, the other would not have wanted to live anyway. That was as uplifting as it was disturbing, but it was also a thrilling discovery—an empowering one. Somehow it had everything to do with the fact that, unlike Alan and his First Power, they really did share the Third Power. This led them to a union of being; a oneness, that made them different. Mark didn't pretend to fully understand it, or what it was capable of, but it had certainly proved useful in fighting the Scalpie and the Grimlings. What else might it be capable of when they understood it better?

And now, studying the activities of the soup kitchen, he felt less than comfortable in a borrowed coat and baggy trousers in lieu of his leather jacket and jeans, which were being cleaned of the Scalpie's blood. He was beginning to wonder about the patterns of events in London.

From a brief conversation he had had with one of the pastors, it would appear that a legion of homeless—estimates suggested as many as half a million—lived on the streets. You couldn't walk a block without tripping over them, or being exposed to the begging hands or pans. And a more menacing legion of people—those Henriette had named Razzamatazzers—prowled the streets after dark.

Somehow, while he had been away on Tír, law and order in London had gone to pot. From what little he had been able to gather from talking to people, it had happened with surprising speed. Over no more than a year or two, Razzamatazzers were everywhere—addicted to looting and burning. Nobody really understood how, or why it had happened, only that normal policing had failed, leading to the rise of paramilitaries funded by big business. The role of the paramilitaries had mushroomed as the anarchy had spread, to the extent that they now provided a semi-official protective army. More sinister still was the rise of the leather-clad "Skulls," who were little better than professional thugs. Rumour had it they were exterminating the homeless and Razzers after dark and disposing of them like garbage. It was hardly surprising that many of the respectable population had fled the city for the Home Counties, or further beyond.

Patterns!

Mark also found himself questioning the hostility they had encountered. Was it a coincidence that the aggression shown by the homeless in the alleyways they had fled through, had progressed to a more calculated violence from the two thugs? Then, finally, on to the Razzers attacking the church and the attack by the Scalpie and his swarm of Grimlings? It seemed to Mark that there had been a definite pattern there. And patterns suggested organisation.

Somebody had put on cheerful background music—some ancient Bob Marley number—and the words "Everything's gonna be all right," floated through the space.

A loud chuckle and a voice came from behind him: "You t'ink everyt'ing gonna be all right, Mark Grimstone?"

Mark turned to face the towering black woman, Henriette. Back at the priest's lodgings, Father Touhey's housekeeper had acquired an ebony walking cane and changed her dress to something ankle length and coloured with all the shades of the rainbow.

"Hey—you were a great support back there."

"An' you haven't answered me question."

"No, Henriette. I don't think everything is going to be all right."

"Hah! No more I."

Her inflection, though it had the ring of a Jamaican accent, wasn't like any he had ever heard before.

"Where does your accent come from?"

"Belize."

Mark had to think a moment to place Belize in his memory—another West Indian island? Then he corrected himself. A tiny place in Central America. "Boleyn, is that a Belizean name?"

"Boleyn," she pronounced it Bow-laine, "French, originally, but now it belong to de Kriol people of Belize."

"How long have you been living in London?"

"One year, maybe two."

"Perhaps I should introduce myself properly."

"Dahlin," dere ain't no need. My question is not who, but what in de world you might be. Like de bwai, Robin Hood?'

Mark laughed. "I'm hardly Robin Hood." He was looking around for Nan, but he saw no sign of her.

"Your friend, she be okay. She washin' her hair."

"She'll be wondering where I've gone."

"She enjoyin' a cuppa comfortin' herbal tea."

Something deep within her laughing eyes alerted him. When he probed her mind, it proved unreadable. "What are you? Some kind of white witch?"

"Oh, hardly white!" She roared with laughter. "Not wid dese teeth." She grinned ear to ear. "But you hardly white yourself, despite appearances. You more of a piebald, like de black eye hidin' under your quiff."

He laughed at the thought of a piebald witch.

"Show me—let me see it—dis oder eye."

He let her examine his oraculum, her eyebrows raised, a slight frown showing her fascination.

"Ha! It like de window into your mind."

"I think it's meant to work the other way round."

Mark had the impression she was probing him, probing his loyalties as much as his story, for some reason of her own.

"What you say, we go out now, Mark Grimstone? We have a nice little stroll an' a chat."

"A chat about what?"

She chuckled, from deep in her belly. "About de Sword an' de Razzamatazz going on in dese streets."

"You've been talking to Father Touhey."

"Uh-huh."

Mark studied Henriette for a long moment. Who, and what, was she exactly? She looked both elegant and exceptionally fit, robustly built and not far off six feet tall in her flat-heeled shoes.

"How much do you know of what's going on?"

"I know de Reverend Grimstone's your fadah."

"I'm not really his son."

"Why den you claim to be?"

"He adopted me when I was a child—if adopted is the right term for what I've come to suspect was some kind of abduction."

"Dahlin', dat wouldn't surprise me."

"Really?"

"All dese people t'inkin dis de end of de world."

"Is that what you think?"

"More like de beginning of somet'in'."

He thought about that. He also thought about the fact that Father Touhey was Bridey's uncle. "What else did Father Touhey tell you?"

"He told me you have some great adventure in another world an' come back with a powerful weapon on your back. I'd like to hear more of dem adventures."

"You're unlikely to credit them."

She laughed again, from that place at the deep core of herself. "Let me make dis suggestion. You not ready to trust me an' I'm certainly not ready to trust you. So what you say, we take a stroll an' maybe we see some action?"

Mark still resisted her, gazing bemusedly at the growing mass of homeless people. "What kind of action?"

She lowered her voice, her eyes exactly opposite his own. "You askin' dese people about de Razzamatazz? You come wid me for your education. You ready to go find out what's really goin' on here in London through dat black eye in your pretty boy head?"

Entertaining as Father Touhey's Belizean housekeeper was proving to be, Mark was reluctant to leave Nan alone at the refuge, but he was intrigued enough to want to know more about the Razzamatazz, especially since Henriette had hinted that it had something to do with the Sword of Feimhin. Maybe he would even discover something about Padraig?

In the end, he acquiesced, resolving that their walk wouldn't take very long, and they exited the refuge into a neon-lit thoroughfare. Almost immediately, Henriette diverted him into a warren of unlit streets. A fine mist of rain was falling, but the rain did not trouble his companion. She had long legs and a surprising litheness and covered the ground with effortless strides. Within minutes Mark felt absolutely lost. Then, abruptly, she halted, with her hand on his shoulder.

"It is time you closed your blue eyes an' opened up de other one."

When Mark closed his eyes and looked out onto the same streets through his oraculum, he had entered a nightmare landscape. The lines and curves that made up the blocks and buildings were etched with a phosphorescent green light.

"Don't just scratch you bum. Look good."

He looked again, harder, deeper. Limned in that same phosphorescent light, the nightmare cityscape was inhabited by wraith-like beings, with shining eyes and smoke for hair.

"What in the world?"

"Clean your system out, Dahlin'. Look real careful at dis shit."

Mark refused to credit what he was seeing. Somehow Henriette had seduced him into a hallucinatory hell in which spectres of every shade and shape were creeping and darting everywhere within nib-scratched green lines that sketched the outlines of real streets. He and Nan had been surprised, reassuringly so, that their oracula worked on Earth, but there was something very different, something deeply disturbing, about the vision here. A biblical phrase crept into his mind: *like seeing through a glass darkly.*

"What are they—what am I seeing?"

"Like de boll weevil, lookin' for a home."

He thought about that. "What do you mean—they're parasites?"

"All drawn to de Sword."

A chill invaded Mark's being. "What did you say?"

"Not'in' wrong wid your ears."

Mark's eyes sprang open. But the strange visions pouring in through the oraculum refused to go away. It was as if the unearthly landscape were overwhelming his normal view of the shadowy streets. Henriette was in the act of turning around to face him. The tall black woman had been replaced by a wraith-like being, her own features limned by the green light, as if drawn by a green pen on a charcoal nothingness.

"My God—you're not human?"

"Mebbe I was once. De year 1633 comes into me head. De world was supposed to end den. But mebbe that too was just anoder beginin'."

Nothing seemed logical any more. Mark's senses were drowning in the vision. It was sucking him into its world, a world in which everything was curves and lines, and the disturbing limning green was the natural order.

"What are these? What are they doing here?"

"Huntin', of course."

"Hunting for what?"

"Dey have many appetites. Blood, meat, dreams . . . hopes."

Mark stared, horrified. "I see pinpoints of light everywhere. I think they're eyes."

"De Razzamatazzers."

"What are you implying? They've infested?"

"You remember—I told you. Like de boll weevil."

He saw something fly close by, a spectre the size of a cat, with wings. It resembled the Grimlings that had guarded the Scalpie, but it had a disgustingly insectile face with a human-type body. As he watched it, it pounced on something skulking in a drain—a rat or maybe a small cat. There was a loud screeching, then silence, punctuated by liquid sounds—the noises of feeding. The more closely he looked, the more horrific it became. Sinewy things, unlike anything he had ever seen, were crawling out of holes in the ground, insectile bodies with side-to-side jaws.

The closer he observed the nightmare landscape, the more he became aware of what might have been lines of force, dimensions within dimensions, etched in that acid-green phosphorescent light. He was reminded, in a way, of the strange lines of structure and purpose he had witnessed in Penny's mind. And everywhere he saw the wraith-like beings, the spectres that moved like ghosts in and out of the shattered doors and windows.

He saw alien shapes, slithering and slouching. He heard whispers; the faintest suggestion of communication. There were spectral horrors rising, slithering and flying in a three-dimensional matrix of dark energy—things with unbelievable shapes sucking, or fang-filled mouths utterly out of proportion to the rest of their bodies, like marine creatures hidden depths of the oceans appearing in the lights of diving craft.

Mark and Nan had returned to Earth with no real purpose other than to convince themselves they were still alive. When one had been consumed by Mórígán, the goddess of death—when you bore her trademark oraculum—it was somehow logical to do this. They had realised that Padraig was missing, along with the Sword.

Padraig was the hereditary keeper of the Sword. He knew more about it than anybody else. It was the importance of finding Padraig that had brought them here. But now they were here, now he knew that his native city was under such overwhelming attack by what he was now witnessing, Mark felt a rising urge to do something about it. But what could he do when he just didn't understand anything that was going on?

Now, more than ever, he was certain that there were bizarre patterns to everything that was going on here in London.

That's it. That's what Henriette brought me out here to see. But who, or what, is Henriette, and why is she offering to help me?

"Where on Earth are they all coming from?"

"No from de Earth, Dahlin'."

"From where, then?"

"All wheres an' nowheres."

Mark thought about what that ridiculously cryptic statement might mean. "Just how dangerous are they?"

"Hah!" She cackled. "Dangerous enough."

Mark felt gooseflesh creep over his entire body. Something gross, something monumentally terrible, was happening here. Had he not experienced life on Tír, he would have thought he was losing his mind, but now he knew better. He was being forced to perceive the city changing. The city of his birth was being invaded by what ordinary people would think of as monsters. It had become repulsively alive—a vast reptilian organism, all glittering scales and angles, flashing in a greenish threatening light.

He had no idea as to its nature, no knowledge of whatever he might do, even through the oraculum, to stop it.

"Henriette—you're telling me that all of this, this other place, these monstrous beings—it's all happening because of the Sword of Feimhin?"

"Dat's your name for it."

"If I understand you right, all of this stuff. These things. The Razzamatazzers. They're part of something bigger? They're gathering here for a purpose?"

"Dey waitin' for de comin'."

"The coming of what?"

"De comin' of de Sword."

She was her jovial self again, Henriette Boleyn—Bo-laine. Mark was conducting a mental exercise. He was taking not one, but half a dozen steps backwards. He was asking himself if this was real. He was asking himself if this would matter a month from now. He blinked and looked at Henriette walking by his side. He blinked again and stared at her statuesque figure that refused to evaporate into the air of fantasy. She was studying him back, with a knowing half-smile.

"Grimstone—he's behind all this?"

She laughed, showing her pearly white teeth. "You learnin', Dahlin'."

"Who do you serve?"

"De same dark lady as you."

"Mórígán?"

"Uh-huh." She pulled a blade out of the ebony walking stick and poked the sharpened tip among the charred rubbish to one side of a burning heap. The tip was steaming in the thickening rain. She spiked one of the diaphanous flying creatures. Sprite or not, it looked fleshy enough on the end of her blade.

"Grimstone," she intoned in a low-pitched hum.

"What about him?"

"He conjuring it all up."

Mark stared at her. He saw something deeper in her expression, an intensity. "What is he conjuring up?"

"Openin' doors into de dark." She seemed to caress the words with her mouth, her tongue, her lips, so he almost saw the syllables.

His thoughts raced. He was only beginning to grasp how it was all linked: Grimstone on Earth and the Tyrant on Tír. Grimstone was serving the Tyrant's purpose here just as his preceptors, his legions, served his purpose on Tír. Grimstone had always been serving that same purpose, even when he had adopted Mark and Mo as children. And that meant that anything Mark and Nan could do here and now to oppose Grimstone, might help Alan, Kate and Mo in their fight against the Tyrant on Tír. If only Mark could communicate with them.

"I need to know if Padraig is still alive. I need to know if he's here."

She laughed, burying the spiked creature in the red embers underneath the smoking ash. She held it there like a potato roasting on a stick, then brought it to her nostrils as if to smell the meat.

"Tell me how to find him."

"Dey's folks who can help you, folks who go up against Grimstone. Find de people who call themselves de Resistance."

"How do I find them?"

"You have a friend—an' I don't mean Nan. A being of magic who brought you here in his belly."

Mark was dumbfounded. "You mean the Temple Ship?"

Mahteman's Secret

The Gargs really did have a secret weapon up their sleeves: they could wear you out with tedium. The deliberate time wasting of King Zelnesakkk in arriving at any kind of decision with regard to Garg assistance was becoming increasingly stressful for Alan. And Qwenqwo appeared to be feeling the frustration even more than he was. "Wars," he laughed, "are said to be won or lost on the preparation." He took a swig from his flagon. "Methinks that was penned by the losers."

The dwarf mage's strategy was to ease his boredom by exploring the liquors of the Eyrie people. He was adept at it—trust Qwenqwo to discover that they enjoyed a wide range of alcoholic beverages, many of which, to his delight, had been woven into their fondness for ritual. Alan had even caught the Fir Bolg attempting to convince the cantankerous old Mahteman to partake in a pipe filled with baccy—to Mahteman's hissing indignation, whose use of the leaf was restricted to shamanic purposes. Qwenqwo then confessed to Alan that he was lonely, not merely for his own people but for the company of a woman.

"A woman?"

"Think you that I was not married some two thousand years ago, when the dark queen, Nantosueta, ensnared my people in the Vale of Tazan."

Alan was momentarily dumbstruck. He recalled, from the tales of his grandfather, Padraig, that the Fir Bolg women had fought shoulder-to-shoulder with the men. But it just hadn't occurred to him before now that Qwenqwo hadn't just lost his father and warrior companions, but also his wife and family.

"I'm sorry, Qwenqwo."

"Hah! Apology accepted."

It reminded Alan that he also missed Kate, even though their separation had only been for a week or two. What must it be like for the redoubtable Fir Bolg, whose separation had extended for thousands of years? Even so, he couldn't imagine what was keeping Kate from rejoining him. She had taken advantage of his exhaustion after the destruction of the Tower of Bones to take off on the basis of some utterly daft idea: the notion she could save the Momu and an entire doomed race. Over these days of frustration with Zelnesakkk, he couldn't help but think about that night when they had lain in the warmth close to the communal fire after they had returned from the meeting of the Momu. They had shared a blanket, and now, he thought, to wake with Kate's head on his arm, her warm presence pressed against him, her green eyes full of love, that was what he wished for more than anything. Instead, to add to his gnawing impatience with the Gargs, he found himself constantly fretting about Kate's safety.

<Kate!>

He called her now—he cast her name through the oraculum of the First Power embedded in his brow. But, as ever, there was no answer.

He felt the dwarf mage try to press a flagon of liquor into his clenched right hand. Qwenqwo was sitting cross-legged by his side and proficient, it seemed, at reading his mind. He whispered the words, "A man's balm," as he passed it over.

Alan shook his head and pushed it away. For his friend, baccy and liquor were the twin balms for every worry.

Below them, in the great sweep of the bay with its thousand islands baking in the sun, a proliferation of new sails were hoving to from Carfon, bringing gifts from Prince Ebrit for the Garg king and queen, as well as supplies of food and siege weaponry that could be employed straight off the decks. These included trebuchets that could hurl rock and blazing pitch for half a mile, blunderbusses that could shoot shrapnel capable of decimating any enemy foolish enough to poke their heads above defensive walls, and giant crossbows that fired steel-tipped bolts that would penetrate even the thickest armour. There were many other weapons he was less familiar with, the equivalent of the heavy artillery in the armies back home, he guessed. And then came the trained soldiers to man, prime and work them. Other ships had the sleek lines and banks of oars that bore the distinct trademark of the Shee, ferrying in yet more warriors to add to the growing army camped over many miles of shore.

This war, when it eventually came, would be vicious and bloody, and fought on both land and sea. *They're depending on me*, Alan thought. *And I've got absolutely nowhere in persuading the Garg king.*

Earlier that morning he had had his first sighting of onkkh: enormous flightless birds that would be deployed with their high-walled baskets of burden, to carry food and shelter for the marching army. The beasts were at least twice the size of the ostriches back home, with powder-blue heads and necks. Their scaly heads were crowned by a bony ridge that ran back from the root of the beak over the entire bowl of the skull, and the whole was crested, like the helmets of Romans, by tufts of golden feathers. The beak, if it really was a beak at all, was enormously thick and flattened at its working ends, reminding Alan of an old coal scuttle. No doubt it was an adaptation for feeding in the arid grasslands that were said to be the beast's natural home. The body was the only other part to be dressed with feathers, which could become haughtily puffed up, like a showy bustard, when the animal was riled. The whole of the beast was decorated with jagged greens and grey flashes, and scored with custard yellow. The heavily-feathered shoulders and chest formed a broad curve that ran back from the base of the neck to the huge rump, so dense with feathers they obscured any evidence of a tail. The onkkh, both males and females, had to be kept apart or they fought one another like overgrown fighting cocks. But the same toughness and endurance made them ideal for the arduous ascent and crossing of the Flamestruck Mountains, a formidable range that lay between them and the outer defences of the Tyrant's capital city, the infamous Ghork Mega.

Alan said, "Hey, Qwenqwo—is that flagon still on offer?"

He heard the dwarf mage's throaty chuckle as it was pressed back into Alan's hands, and this time he had no hesitation in taking a deep swig, feeling the fiery shock of it hit the back of his throat.

He was still worrying about a confusion of problems, when he became aware that the Kyra and Bétaald were closing on him, approaching from his left, while Mo and Turkeya were also heading his way, more distant yet hurrying with what looked like an equally urgent purpose.

He climbed to his feet, ready to greet the Kyra and her spiritual adviser, who arrived first.

Thank heaven for the shock of the fiery liquor; it helped Alan to abandon his frown and return the welcoming smile on Bétaald's handsome face. The soul spirits of the Shee were great cats and Bétaald's was surely a black panther, in whose sunflower eyes he saw the reflection of his own concerns. Of all the Shee, Alan respected Bétaald more than any other. Though she was, these days, a few inches shorter than Alan himself, he recalled how she had impressed him with her calm dignity and intelligence from their very first meeting.

Bétaald assessed him openly now, her nostrils twitching with the scent of the liquor, which would be all too apparent to her cat senses, her eyes lifting to the powerful pulsation of the ruby oraculum in his brow.

"Mage Lord Duval."

"Alan."

"Alan—I see that you are positively throbbing with anticipation of the coming expedition."

"More like my head is spinning with frustration at the many delays."

"An anxiety shared is an anxiety halved."

"I could certainly do with sharing a little of it. You're still confident about this landwards approach?"

"The Kyra and I have discussed it at length."

"I'd appreciate your reassurance."

"I know that you fear the mountain approaches, but we could not possibly attack Ghork Mega from the sea alone. The entire coastline within fifty leagues north or south of the city is massively fortified. The attrition would be terrible before ever we breached the sea wall defences—if it were possible to breach them at all."

"Landwards it's going to be a hell of an undertaking."

"One in which we must be sure of the help of the Eyrie People."

Alan sighed. "I don't know what more I can do."

"Then I would advise that you reconsider what we have learnt about the Eyrie people. They are surprisingly spiritual—and something else—a virtue perhaps that we witnessed even in the battle for Ossierel."

"What?"

"Have you ever seen fear in them?"

He shrugged. "No."

"Then fear is not what keeps them from helping us."

"What then?"

"Perhaps they need to sense something in you as leader—not power alone, but a sense of purpose they can identify with. A sense of destiny, perhaps?"

Alan wasn't quite sure what Bétaald meant by a sense of destiny, but even as he was thinking about it, Mo and Turkeya joined them. Mo was smiling but Turkeya looked flustered, irritated. Whatever it was, they could barely contain their excitement. Turkeya came up close then looked around, even though there was nobody nearby except a few urchins from the Olhyiu camp. Nevertheless, Turkeya spoke in a whisper. "We've made a discovery." He blurted it out quickly, almost silently, as if whatever he had to say must come first, before anybody else spoke another word.

Mo punched Turkeya on the arm.

Alan hesitated. There was such an intimacy to the act that it took him by surprise. He knew that Mo and Turkeya had long been friends, but he hadn't realised just how close they had become. This new Mo, a couple of inches off six feet, was still growing. She bore little resemblance to the Mo he remembered from their first meeting at Padraig's sawmill in Clonmel. She was also whispering now, breathless with excitement. "Oh, Alan, we have to keep it absolutely secret."

"What?"

Alan saw more than excitement in Mo's face.

"Something the Gargs have been hiding from us."

Her glowing hazel eyes met Alan's directly, impressing the importance of her words on him. And now she whispered urgently, her lips close enough to his ear for him to feel her breath. "They have a magician, who advises them. He's known as Magtokk the Mischievous."

"A magician?"

"Hush!" Mo tugged on his ear to bring it back to within whispering distance. "He's also known by other names. But the important thing is that Magtokk is hated by the Tyrant—so far as we could tell it's because of his magic, or his knowledge, or maybe both."

"Bétaald—did you hear?"

"I heard."

"Hush." Mo turned to warn Bétaald in turn. "Sorry. But we really do need to whisper the name."

"What's going on, Mo?"

But Bétaald halted the conversation with a gesture. She signalled the nearest Shee, who scattered the nearby urchins. One of them stayed and appeared to be deaf, but one of the others, a girl with sun-bleached bedraggled hair, dragged him away into the hustle and bustle of the camp, with its proliferation of crates and tents.

The company decided it best to move themselves, discovering a quiet little depression between some grassy dunes. They sat cross-legged in a circle, thirty yards or so from the surf beating on the fine white sand, blinking away the sand grains that were blowing into their eyes.

Alan looked at the shaman. "Turkeya?"

"Don't ask me—I don't believe a word of it."

Mo *tsked* at Turkeya. "The Gargs don't want us to know about Magtokk."

"What's so important about him?"

"He's very old—one of very few survivors from a race of magicians. The Tyrant feared their knowledge so much he had them exterminated."

Alan stared in bewilderment at Mo.

"Aye—and maybe it's a pity he failed," muttered Turkeya.

"Fortunately for us," Mo glared at Turkeya.

Turkeya muttered: "I can well believe that he is known as Magtokk the Mischievous!"

Mo dug Turkeya in the ribs. "He—if he really is a he—can take on whatever form he wants."

Alan didn't know what to make of what Mo was telling him, but Bétaald was nodding at him. He said, "Bétaald?"

The Shee adviser replied, "I had assumed such beings—Magtokk the Magician—to be no more than a romance, a whimsy of fables."

Mo said, "Take no notice of Turkeya. Iyezzz made a point of introducing us in secret as Magtokk has been tutoring him."

Turkeya wiped his nose on his sleeve and shrugged, still reluctant to believe anything about the magician. "I know that he bites."

"Mo—"

Turkeya interrupted. "Oh, he's a joker. He took the form of a monstrous monkey when we met him."

Qwenqwo was listening, enraptured, while lighting his pipe. "I, too, believed the legends of a wizard race belonged to fairy tales. Yet my father, Urox Zel, did talk of mischievous shape changers."

Mo shook her head, growing red in the face with frustration at their incredulity. "I think that Mahteman has been using him."

Alan put his arm around Mo's shoulders. "For goodness' sake, what does all this mean, Mo?"

Mo's eyes sparkled with excitement. "I think he's more than just a tutor to the Prince. He's magical and wise as well as mischievous. And the reason Mahteman has been keeping his presence a secret is because he doesn't want us to know what's about to happen."

"What is about to happen?"

"A solar eclipse."

"If you're stupid enough to believe it," piped in Turkeya.

Alan thought for several moments about what Mo had told them. "Mo, please explain?"

"It's true. And what's more, Mahteman knows all about it."

"My God! I'm beginning to understand. The Gargs are so superstitious."

"And that scheming Mahteman—he's planning to use it to his advantage," said Qwenqwo.

"So that's it! Iyezzz—he's been trying to tell me. And Shah-nur-Kian too. They've been hinting at some kind of omen."

Qwenqwo nodded. "If I know Mahteman—he'll have persuaded the King to wait for a sign."

Alan stared up into the sky. The moon was just about visible, even in daylight. It was what his mum would call an onion-skin moon. If the rumours of the eclipse were true . . . "An eclipse—God almighty! Mahteman has the King waiting for something really big—a sign that would frighten the Gargs out of their wits. He'll use it to dissuade the King from helping us."

The Kyra pressed Mo, "Did this magician tell you when the shadow will fall?"

"Exactly three days from now, mid-afternoon."

Bétaald followed Alan's gaze. "We need to be sure of this. Three days, Mo—you're absolutely sure?"

"I'm not, but Magtokk is."

The Kyra confronted Alan, the oraculum of Bree pulsating powerfully in her brow. "A living survivor from the Age of Magicians who fears our common enemy. This might be a useful turn of events."

Alan looked from the Kyra to Bétaald, then to Qwenqwo. "I have an idea—if Bétaald and Ainé are willing to go along with it. Maybe there is a way we could turn things to our advantage."

There was an unusual level of witch-warrior activity all throughout the shoreline camp as Snakoil Kawkaw performed a furtive reconnaissance of the area around the soup kitchen. This was the hideout of his detested fellow spy, Soup Scully Oops. And it was where he had recruited his own spies: the bedraggled urchins that came begging for food. He had warned the brats against coming to him with empty paws.

"*No news for me,*" he had impressed the mantra into their flea-bitten lugholes, "*no morsel for you!*"

Only two had returned to the vicinity of the two spies' tent, slumped with exhaustion and hunger, and one of them was that deaf cretin with the lousy hair. In fact, appraising the pair closer to, they looked alike enough, with the same tangled manes, to be brother and sister. Yanking them bodily to their feet, he hauled them behind the soup stand where they weren't likely to be overheard.

"Well? What have you got for me?"

"Please, Mister—we's starvin' hungry!"

"You'll gobble my blade if you've come here wasting my time."

"There is something—honest!" The trembling wretch of a girl had a red stye, exuding pus, in the corner of her left eye. A bubble of watery snot dangled from the nostril below the stye.

Kawkaw squeezed the nearby ear, wondering if he saw a louse jump to the black hairs that grew thick on the back of his hand. "I am running out of patience with you brats. Will you enlighten me before I explode?"

"She—the holoima, called Mo—an' the young shaman."

"Yes, yes—*yes*?"

"The Garg prince carried 'um up into the mountains."

Kawkaw saw the snot run down over her lip. He saw her tongue come out and lick at it, then dart back in. "And?"

"We waited an' waited."

He shook his hook, worn in place of his missing hand, and knocked the curve of it against her bony chest. "Must I hurry you with a clout?"

"They come back down."

"So they went up—and then they came down?"

"They looks different."

"Different?"

"They's excited. I see it on they faces, in they eyes."

"Excited?"

"Yeah."

He tapped the hook harder against the bones. "Tell me more."

Tears filled her eyes, running around the stye. "I dunno."

Kawkaw scratched his chin with the point of his hook. "The Garg prince—he took them up into the mountains. To show them something?"

"Then they comes down again."

"They must have said something. You must have overheard?"

"Ask 'im—me brudder."

He had no second hand to squeeze a second ear, so he lifted the point of the hook under the boy's dirt-caked chin, hauling his face up until he stood staring up at him on tip-toe. But the wretch just made some kind of moaning noise.

"What's this whining?"

" 'e's deaf."

"Well, what in a tart's kiss is the use of a deaf informant?"

" 'e can see they words—'e can tell me what 'em says."

"He can see words?"

" 'e can tell 'em me—so I can say."

"He can read their lips?"

"Is like I'm sayin'—yeah."

"What did he read from their lips?"

Her face contracted into an amazing myriad of wrinkles. "They was wisperin."

"But he—this wretch—he could still read their lips?"

"They run us off."

"They saw you listening to them?"

"They got them Shees ta scuss us."

"The witch-warriors shooed you off?"

"Go—git!" She made shooing movements with her hand.

"What did the cretin read on their lips?"

" 'e ain't stoopid. 'e's clever. Only 'e can't say it."

Kawkaw shouted into the ear that was now red raw from his pinching. "What in the name of a cleggyarse runt did he read from their lips?"

"They makes a discovery."

"What?"

"Wor he seen—wor they sayed."

"They made a discovery?"

She spoke to her brother. He mumbled something.

"A secret—he sayed."

"A secret? They discovered some secret?"

"Yeah."

"They discovered something—when they were carried up into the mountains, by the Garg prince?"

She spoke to her brother. Even Kawkaw could read the fact he was nodding his head. Within the tent, Sally Oops was stirring. Kawkaw couldn't have the bitch getting an earful of this.

"Aw, give us sum soup now, Mister?"

The moment he released the reddened ear of the urchin girl, the boy hunched down around her, with his bony knees upraised, and took her in his arms. Kawkaw stared at them, saw the fear in their eyes, their faces. They were right to fear—not just him, but the lady. *She'll kill them without a thought to ensure their silence.* It occurred to him that maybe he should kill them himself.

He held that thought for a moment, then ladled out a can of the thick, foul-smelling soup. He wanted them out of here, for at least a full day.

"You hear anything else? You tell me."

"Yeah, Mister!" The girl couldn't wait to scurry away with the soup.

He twitched his head, as if pointing to the danger behind him. "You listen to me, you little ratarses. You heard nothing about no secret. Got it? The witch-warriors scared you away."

She stared up at him, nodding.

"Now get out of here, if you want to keep your throats."

The Scalpie Dagger

Rain, rain, rain! It had soaked through the filth over the floor of what had once been some ancient kitchen, making them slippery as soap. Penny Postlethwaite's heart was pounding against her rib cage as she peered through narrowed eyes into the gloom of the alley ahead. The tarmac was so pitted with holes it was treacherous to walk in, especially in the dark, but it was the quickest way out of the ruins where she was hiding, themselves all that remained of a seedy hotel. Built out of rotting eighteenth-century handmade bricks, in daylight she would have been able to see the rising column of old fireplaces in the gable wall, one above the other, tottering into the heavens.

Stop! Look! Listen!

She did so, shivering, ignoring the downpour.

She knew they were still there. She could see the glowing ends of their cigarettes, three of them, performing a pantomime of moment from hand to mouth. She assumed that they were Skulls. They had made cat-like meowing noises when they were chasing her. Oh, how she prayed that they had given up the chase. But if so, why were they hanging around in the pitch dark, smoking their cigarettes?

They must know I'm here.

But she couldn't be sure of that. They might just think she'd be coming this way. Either way, she really had to think.

This late, and hanging around in the pouring rain, they must be drunk on cheap rum. Rum was the drink of the Skulls. Other gangs had chased her through the streets before, but that had been out there under the lights. All they had wanted to do was to frighten her, to humiliate her. But here—in the rain and the dark . . .

Penny was already close to home, close to Our Place, which was why she had come to a dead stop—she didn't want to lead them there.

She examined the tips of her knives, which she carried down the seams of her jeans, but she doubted they would do her much good against three well-armed Skulls. She thought about the thing in the box—the Scalpie's blade. Did the Skulls know she had it? She thought about hiding it somewhere here in the ruin, but she couldn't face the thought of parting from it, even though it was awkward and heavy enough to slow her down if she tried to run.

I'm being stupid, but I can't just leave it here, I can't. I just can't.

Gully had criticised her for things like this, again and again. He had warned her that she wasn't streetwise. "Penny, gel, you let things slow you down in the 'ead." Maybe he was right, but still she couldn't abandon the blade; it was too important, and too closely linked to what she had seen. It was somehow a part of the two aliens with those black triangles in their heads.

She had no control over the mixture of panic and exhilaration that made her heart swell so powerfully, shoving against her ribs with every beat. In her mind she replayed the scene around the coffin: the Scalpie kneeling before the blade, the Grimlings buzzing everywhere, then the explosion of power from the alien woman's head and the coffin shattering, venting forth some kind of whirling weapon covered with glowing runes, only for it to land in the fair-haired man's upheld hand.

Gully—you've no idea! The things I've seen . . .

He didn't believe her about the City Below—maybe he'd believe her now? But even if he did, how would he cope with the wonder of it?

Penny knew, now, that she had been right all along. The world wasn't like people thought it was. There really was a City Below. And it was hugely, monumentally, different from the city that people knew.

The glowing tips of cigarettes were moving. They were creeping closer to her, keeping to the shadows.

They know I'm here!

In her mind she saw the lines and curves and angles of the other lanes about her, all lost in the pitch dark. It was as if she were probing her surroundings with a personal radar. She scuttled deeper into the gloom and rain, her senses on what her father had called auto-pilot, slinking along through the mental labyrinths of recall, through jumbled ruin after ruin, in a deliberately haphazard trajectory aimed at confusing her trail.

Stop! Look! Listen!

Only when her nostrils were overwhelmed by the stink of the soot and ash from the underground car park did she finally pause to get a breather. Again she waited. She had to keep Our Place safe. She waited several minutes. She forced herself to stop, look, listen again. Again she waited: another minute or two, her heartbeat pounding in her hollow chest.

Coast clear.

Her spirits swelled with relief as she hugged the heavy wooden box close to her breast. The thing inside it was making noises. It wasn't just the beating of her heart against it, she could feel a vibration, like the ticking of a clock. It quickened as her own heart beat faster with excitement, until it overwhelmed her senses.

Like a heartbeat of its own!

She reached the airlock and rose through it, back pressed against the grimy wall of the lift shaft, her legs sliding her upwards with her precious burden. Then she was pushing the box onto the ledge in the great concrete abscess of wrack and ruin.

She could hear the muffled chorus of the dossers on the floor below; the cacophony of moans and snores, the farts and sighs. The one voice—always the same quavering male voice—screaming, over and over, like a demented mantra, "Shut the fuck up! Shut the fuck up! Shut the fuck up . . ."

She closed her ears to the vileness of it, closed off her mind.

In the deeper gloom Penny stood at the beginning of the I-beam, leaning with one hand on the cinder wall. She was listening to a deluge of rainwater, which had built up after hours of continuous rain and was now rushing and splattering to the ground. She was close enough to it to feel the mist on her face. She hoped that Gully would have collected enough to fill up the washing barrel.

She slid along the beam on her bottom, pushing the wooden box a foot or two ahead of her with each slide. Such was the buzz in her head she hardly noticed the time it took her to complete the crossing before she was standing, giddily erect, in front of the dolly with the box clasped in both her hands. She had to lift one knee to take part of its weight to free one hand and yank open the porthole, then, breathing hard, she hauled the heavy box up into the opening and shoved it out into the centre of the space. When that was done she stretched her shoulders, sighing with relief, and wriggled her shoulder blades to ease the ache in the muscles. She yanked, three times, on the cord.

But if Gully was home he wasn't answering. Gully Pockets was what she called him when she was mad with him, like right now. She could imagine him, those worried eyes behind the smudged glasses, the fingers that were never still, always fiddling with those bulging pockets.

"For goodness' sake!"

She hated having to leave the box inside the dolly. Nimbly, she wove her way back over the drop and searched with rising impatience for the knotted rope, then ascended ten feet or so to the engineers' ladder. As she emerged through the trapdoor at the top, into the map room, she took a good look around, fixing the remembered details that expanded into her creative world.

The signal that Our Place was safe was there in the half open door and the badly-chipped gnome that was keeping it ajar with its open arms.

She momentarily closed her eyes, comforted by the thought.

She hurried through the half-open door into the vestibule, noticing the puddles of dust in three places that marked new cracks in the ceiling, and a new scatter of raindrops from the leaks.

Gully was home, but nowhere to be seen. *He could only be up on the roof,* she thought. *In the dark, talking to his birds.*

She was glad about that because she wasn't ready to talk to him yet—she needed to be on her own. Pulling on the chain, she hauled the dolly up as fast as she could—she could tell from the weight of the dolly that the box was still there, but she didn't quite credit it until she had thrown open the door and lifted it out to hold it, once more, against her breast.

All of a sudden it felt too heavy for her to carry.

But carry it she did, through into the engineers' office that had become their home. She flopped down with it on the floor in front of the tiny window and pulled back the blackout curtains so she could press her face against the icy cold of the glass. Outside was a never-ending vista of twinkling streetlights under an inky sky devoid of stars. London was an enormous animal, squatting within its lair: a deceptively dangerous animal—never more so than when you dropped your guard.

She rubbed her left cheek against the glass, as if she were rubbing against its implacable fur. She heard it growl back.

Gully's voice was insistent inside her head: *"Just one light in that window, Penny, and Our Place ain't safe no more."*

She needed to examine her treasure, but she wasn't ready to shut out London.

Closing her eyes, she was back within the labyrinth inside her mind; the beautiful pictures sprouting and spreading until they became a maelstrom of moving shapes and lines and curves and angles, all coming together. The rounded knob of St. Paul's Cathedral was at the centre of it: the eye of her creative storm. The City Above and the City Below were assembled into a living, breathing whole. She sensed it within her picture-mind; she sensed it so perfectly she could inspect and trace every wrinkle of its skin, every crevice and hair follicle, as the great heart lumbered deep within and the great lungs sighed and breathed, the nostrils snorting.

The sounds of Gully's feet on the iron staircase brought her back to reality with a start. She waited for him, squatting cross-legged on the floor in the dark, with the box in her lap. She heard him draw the blackout blinds. When the light came on, rigged up from the battery he charged with the cycling dynamo, her eyes were momentarily blinded.

She heard his voice. "I got me a new one, Penny."

"Another injured one?"

"Nah—just 'arf starved!"

She looked over at him, to where he was stroking the bird; a striking squab, piebald as a jackdaw. Gully trapped birds to eat them, but this one he would feed and then let it go again.

"Look at you—you're soaking wet," she said.

"Bit a water won't do me no 'arm." He lifted the wire door on the keep and shoved the bird in before turning to look at her. “You’re wetter’n me, gel. You should take off them silver thingamabobs an’ dry yer ’air.”

“Maybe.” She couldn’t stop the wave of shivering.

He sat down next to her on the concrete floor. “Wot’s up with you?”

“They were hunting me, Gully.”

“Who was?”

“Skulls. I didn’t see them. Only the tips of their cigarettes.”

He had taken off his glasses to wipe off the rain. She watched him go through the routine of patting down his pockets, all six of them, the handkerchief emerging from the middle pocket on the right. “And they was huntin’ you specific, like?”

“I think so.”

“But you ain’t sure?”

“I—I am sure. They chased me. They were making meowing noises. And then they were hiding—hiding and waiting for me.”

“But why they got it in for you, gel?”

“I don’t know, but I was really frightened this time.”

Gully shoved his glasses back on his nose. His hands brushed through his sodden black curls. “Don’t make sense.”

“I think they might have been looking for this.” Penny’s eyes fell onto the polished wooden box that lay, heavy, on her thighs.

“Wot the ’eck is that?”

“Gully, I saw them—I saw such things.”

"Wot things?"

She was gazing down at the box, as if wondering at its presence, all of a sudden sensing the enormity of what she had done in stealing it and then bringing such a treasure back to Our Place. Had she placed both their lives in danger?

"I had to bring it back."

"Wot you got there, Penny?"

"Give me time, Gully. I have to gather my thoughts."

"Gather yer thoughts?"

She couldn't even begin to explain it all, not yet. She didn't know how to put it into words. She saw him, the young man, through the window of Oggy's Café, his face, his fair hair, his blue eyes peering out at her through the letters. She saw the thing in his head—in the girl's head too. She felt them reach out to her, their minds invading her mind, like two suns bursting into dazzling light. She knew then—she just knew for certain—that they were what she had been waiting for.

Gully climbed back onto his feet to shed his sodden denim jacket; the rain had just soaked through the hood. He gave it a quick wring, pattering water on the floor, then hung it on a screw that was sticking out of the shelves. Then he hauled out the cardboard box with their food in. He showed her the food he had bought from selling her sketches to the woman in the Post Office.

Then he glanced over at her, his face lowered, peering through the tangled bushes of his eyebrows. "You look 'arf starved, gel. You look worse'n the squab. You want me to make you a cuppa an' somefink to eat?"

Penny could barely nod back. She hadn't moved from her perch under the window, where she knew she was sitting in her own pool of wet. An excitement was growing in her, in her heart. She exulted in it. It was what had been promised her through all the pain. She whispered her triumph, feeling her cheeks glowing, into the gloom. "Gully, it's happening, it really is—it's what I've been waiting for."

She watched him use a cigarette lighter to ignite the blue flame on the Calor gas rings, linked with a red rubber hose to the cylinder.

"Got us two eggs," he crowed. "Wot about I make you a nice poached egg on crusty bread?"

"Sounds good." She nodded.

"Noffink like a nice poached egg an' a hot cuppa."

"Lovely."

She was wondering if she dared to think it all the way through. "I know that this is the sign, Gully."

"Wot kind of a sign?"

All this time waiting and now it was here she hardly felt ready for it. There was so much she still didn't understand.

"For the moment, I must keep it safe in its case."

"You talkin' nonsense, gel."

She couldn't make herself draw it, even though she so desperately wanted to right then. Her hands would shake. She laughed at the thought, a sudden explosive belly laugh. Then she saw herself laughing like an idiot, and imagined her teeth glinting whitely in her face.

"There you go, Penny." He was handing her the steaming mug of tea, so hot she had to put it down next to her on the floor. "One poached egg comin' up."

Penny nodded her thanks, but she couldn't stop herself trembling.

She stared at the cluttered austerity of the single room that was living room, kitchen, bathroom and bedroom for them both. There was no real furniture at all, only the two camp beds shoved against the opposing walls, the two gas rings, the basin on a piece of rigged-up chipboard that was their sink, and the circular iron staircase that went up to the roof. Everything was make-do, constructed out of salvaged crates and oddments of wood. The engineers' shelves—the only thing of theirs that had been left behind—were of brown-painted steel; shelf after shelf running from floor to ceiling, all packed with Gully's hoarded treasures. Her eyes turned to the door on her left, which led out onto the dolly cupboard and then to the other door, which led out onto the map room. She so wanted to go to the map room. She so wanted to draw the pictures in her mind that were screaming to be drawn, but she was too giddy, her hands too trembly even to think about it.

She said, "I might have to lie down, Gully."

"It's okay—eat yer poached egg first."

She accepted the egg, which he had covered with salt and sandwiched between two thick slices of buttered bread.

"Go on—'ave a bite!"

She took a bite.

"Good?"

"Delicious." She took another bite, her mouth dripping saliva. She'd had nothing else to eat all day and only then realised just how hungry she was. She took a swig of the tea and scalded her palate.

He was staring at her like he wanted to hug her. She warned him off with her eyes. Not another confrontation. *Not now!*

His voice was resigned. "Now, you gonna tell me about it?"

"There were two people—two beings. They looked like a young man and a young woman, but they couldn't have been what they seemed because they reached right into my head and tangled with my mind."

"Where's all this goin' on?"

"At Oggy's place."

"Wot you sayin'? Like they wasn't human?"

"They were looking for a church. I helped them. They were attacked by a Scalpie and Grimlings."

"Now you talkin' fairytales, gel."

"The woman, the one that looked like a woman, she killed the Grimlings. The man—he killed the Scalpie with some kind of magic blade."

Gully shook his head. Then he laughed. “You been out of your ’ead with nuffink to eat all day.”

Penny stared down at the wooden box. The trembling was so bad that her voice slurred as she spoke. “I stole it from the dead Scalpie.”

Gully reached out. He was going to touch it, to open the box and take a peek, but she held onto it grimly. He didn’t know how dangerous it was.

“They weren’t people.”

“Wot’s that supposed to mean?”

“They were aliens.”

He laughed. He almost reached out and hugged her, but her eyes warned him off again. “They had black triangles right there in the centre of their foreheads. They reached out with their minds and got inside my head.”

Gully snorted. “How could you tell they was aliens?”

“The woman—Nan, he called her—she moved her lips when she talked to me, but the words I saw on her lips weren’t the same words I heard in my head. She talked to me in her alien language, but I heard her words inside my head.”

“And the geezer—he talked alien too?”

“No, he spoke English like somebody who came from here.”

“So ’e wasn’t no alien?”

“He had a triangle in his head, just like she did.”

“So, what you reckon then?”

"Oh, I know exactly what he is. He's a warrior. And he's left-handed, just like me." Penny saw him clear as day in her mind. "The coffin exploded and some kind of weapon flew out of it. It spun through the air and landed in his hand. A weapon shaped like a stretched out letter S with blades like scimitars at each end. The blades were glowing with runes along their edges."

"Hot shit!" Gully screeched with laughter.

"I saw him, Gully. He called the weapon by its name—Vengeance. And it came to him right out of the exploding coffin."

Gully had tears of laughter in his eyes.

"I saw him kill the Scalpie."

"Strewth!"

"The alien woman—she did something magical too. There was lightning—not white, but a kind of blue-black—coming out of her head. She burned up the Grimlings with the lightning and the warrior chopped off the Scalpie's head."

"It's just them hunger dreams, Penny."

Penny couldn't explain any further. She lifted the lid off the box on her lap. "You can look for yourself."

He peered into the box and she looked with him. Something gleamed: the strange symbol, like a triple infinity, with three overlapping circles, glowed with a silvery light. He saw them pulsate and glow.

His hand reached down so fast she barely had time to slap it away.

"No touching it, Gully."

He was staring at it, disbelieving. Rivulets of green lightning were curling up over the wood. Penny slapped the lid back down over it, sealing it tight.

She could feel her skin tingle, right to the ends of her fingertips, where her hand had come into contact with the lid.

Gully wasn't laughing any more. His eyes lifted from the box to hers. She could see the fear in them.

"Oh, Penny, gel—wot you done?"

A Weave of Darkness

Kate had lost track of how long she had been comforting the Momu within the enormous roots of the One Tree. She was sitting back against one of the roots, with the roar of the ocean growing ever louder in her ears. How elegantly simple it had all seemed when she had journeyed here. And even after she had arrived and witnessed for herself all that was happening, a residuum of that hubristic over-confidence had remained right up to the moment she had demanded entrance here to the Momu's chamber. All she needed to do was to cure the Momu and the survival of her people—the Cill—would somehow be assured.

The seed of self-confidence had been sewn when Granny Dew had pressed the Oraculum of the Second Power into her brow. She had sensed its growing presence within her: a portal of enormous power, linked to the holy Trídédana and more specifically to Mab, the goddess of birth and healing. The portal, an inverted triangle of the purest emerald, had served her incredibly well, faithfully restoring life and fertility to the wasted lands of the Gargs. All she had had to do was to bathe the seeds, or the land, in its emerald glow and impart her desire through the oraculum.

The oraculum really was a source of magic. But that same magic linked her to an equally awesome and terrible entity the people of Tír called the Fáil, which the Tyrant sought to control. She had been able to do good for both land and people with astonishing speed and effect, but now, when she tried bathing the body and brow of the Momu in that same healing light, nothing happened.

A shiver passed through her.

What am I to do? Nothing in Kate's previous experience gave her the slightest inkling of an answer.

There had also been a sense, in her conversations with Alan, that an oraculum-bearer, such as he and she now were, somehow could not die. But that wasn't quite as comforting now: Ulla Quemar was a long way below the surface of the ocean and was being reclaimed by that deep and tumultuous tide. What use was immortality if you were obliged to live it out trapped forever amid the watery ruins?

She was forced to think more broadly—as her Uncle Fergal used to insist she do when he invited the younger

Kate to share a scientific dilemma. The key thing, he would patiently explain, would emerge from looking at the problem from a variety of different angles.

The problem facing Kate was assuredly big. She watched as a root slithered and curled its way around the Momu's left thigh, then burrowed back into the rock. Kate wondered at the implications. The dying body of her friend was being cocooned within an enormous shroud of roots. It was as if the One Tree was constructing a living mausoleum around her body.

Look at the problem from a new angle.

Could the failure of her oracular power imply that there was something different about the Momu?

Kate thought back to their first meeting—a true meeting of minds and spirits, as it had seemed back then—when they had reclined together within these same roots. The air had been filled with the sweetest scents, every nook and cranny vibrant with sea creatures.

She recalled her own eyes lifting to see that amazing face for the first time. It had shocked her to discover that it was much larger than any human face, and yet still delicate and slender—the face of a natural queen. The Momu had greatly elongated ear lobes widened to take ornamental spools of highly decorated ivory; the spools alone a full six inches in diameter. What a wonderful surprise to see those mother-of-pearl eyes for the first time, the irises performing a slow expansion and contraction that was a welcome in the culture of the

Cill. And the invitation, extended to Kate as she waded through the birthing pool.

Come—sit here beside me.

The Momu had looked at home among the roots and she had invited Kate to join her within the same embrace. Here, reclining together, the long webbed fingers of the Momu had extended to stroke Kate's cheek. And here, as if she had needed reminding, she had recognised that the Momu was not like any other creature she had previously seen. She was some kind of telepathic hive mother. A crystal of greenish-blue decorated the Momu's chest; an oraculum of sorts, in the depths of which motes of golden light pulsated and metamorphosed.

The Momu doesn't give birth to her people like humans do. Her spirit, her being, is unlike anything else. She draws the power she needs to nourish and protect the Cill through her crystal.

Kate remembered her earlier musings as she laid herself down among the same roots beside the dying body of her friend. She peered in, searching the web of writhing roots, and saw the gleam of the Momu's crystal. She probed it, quickly, pouring the strength and power of her oraculum into the shadows where it lay, and registered . . .

Nothing.

Even the Momu's crystal was not responding to her oraculum.

But what did it mean? She really had no idea, and the implications of her ignorance were truly frightening.

If the Momu was unlike any other being that Kate had come across in Tír, why shouldn't her death and the circumstances surrounding it be equally unique? The Momu's chamber—which she rarely left, even over the millennia she had lived there—was encased in the One Tree, but what tree could possibly grow to such an enormous size within a cave deep under the ocean? Kate recalled her awe as she saw it for the first time and had traced the boughs and branches that ramified all over the roof of the chamber. She had also marvelled at the roots, realising that they extended widely throughout all of Ulla Quemar. Even the leaves were not what she would have expected of a tree: they were curiously pink—fleshy. And now that tree, with its creeping and crawling roots, was growing around the dying Momu, strangling what was left of her life. It was as if the Momu were being taken back to some immense and unknowable place to be reclaimed by some alien and unknowable power.

How am I possibly going to stop this?

The Momu dying amid the ruins of her beloved city seemed so very natural. It also seemed predestined; so all-powerful it was almost a blasphemy even to consider interfering with it. But if she did not interfere, the Cill, those beautiful and gentle people, would be no more.

Kate didn't think she could live with that grief.

A thought—it didn't merit the word "plan"—was growing in her mind. It was such a desperate idea, but she couldn't think of anything better.

She wanted to stop the Momu being taken by the roots, but she had realised that she couldn't stop it by willing it so. The only thing left to her was to accompany the Momu. Wherever the roots were taking her, Kate would go, too.

The thought of doing this prompted a shudder of fear to ripple through her.

She looked around. The only light in the chamber was the emerald glow from her oraculum; an illumination—no matter how great the power within that mental portal—that was as feeble as a candle in the enormous gloom. She clenched her eyes shut as a renewed roar of the ocean burst upon her ears, a roar accompanied by the sounds of buildings tumbling nearby, the vibrations shaking the rocks that formed the floor of the chamber.

She had to grit her teeth to stop herself screaming as she lay down within the roots and allowed them to grow over her. She refused to think too much about what was happening to her, fearful that her innate cowardice would force her to flee. But she was unable to suppress a rising panic that she wouldn't be able to breathe. A strange unknowable darkness had settled over her, writhing, slithering, and coalescing around her body, around her limbs, about her breast and neck—her throat.

The roots!

Oh, God! Was it too late to escape?

She had to try to control her terror. Her desperate mind sought sanctuary within the oraculum, but the darkness was overwhelming her, body and spirit, like a tidal wave.

I'm drowning . . . I'm drowning . . .

She was lost in a terrible memory of a nightmare experience that had haunted her all of her life since. She had been just nine years old, and she had been drowning, deep underwater in the powerful current of the River Suir. Although she could swim, at least a little, she was too shocked and hopelessly lost in the murky depths, unable to determine what was up or down. The breath had burst from her mouth and nostrils because she couldn't hold onto it a moment longer, and there had been a tangible awareness that that was how she was going to die.

Yet the day had started out so happily. It was a Saturday morning and Kate had been returning home from the milk shed in the Presentation Convent. There, they still made butter the old-fashioned way. Kate had watched with fascination as the nun, wearing the white habit of the novice, turned the handle of the butter churn, a clod of butter slopping in the staved wooden barrel. The unwanted milk was what Kate had come for. Bridey had sent her to fetch a half-gallon of it so she could bake the soda bread that Kate loved.

In a strange pantomime of slow motion she did her best to hurry and keep up with her puppy, Darkie, swapping the half-gallon jug from hand to hand. She had been heading—skipping—for the hump of the second stone bridge.

The bridge . . .

She hadn't even needed to look over the bridge to her left to see the main body of the River Suir running south of the island, swollen from a week of storms that had filled it with uprooted trees and the bodies of drowned cattle. Nuala Farrel had been waiting for her on the bridge. Mad Nuala, with her wire-rimmed glasses with the sprung sides that wrapped around her ears. Nuala with her bully boyfriend Tee-Jay Flaherty, who had been wearing a Big Apple T-shirt and faded blue jeans. He had been pretending to fight with Brendan Logan and Micky Hoolihan, pushing and shoving and delivering fake kickboxing leaps.

It had been too late to head back to the convent and Darkie had scampered on ahead. Flaherty had whistled and called him, and then grabbed Darkie and lifted him bodily off the ground by the scruff of the neck.

"What d'ye call this, Nuala?"

"Sure, I don't know if it's a cat or a fish!"

The jug of milk had fallen in slow motion from Kate's hand, shattering against the pavement. The milk had been so white in the arc of its spilling, then it had scattered slow and sticky as blood over her birthday shoes, and sloshed down into the gutter before trickling down the slope.

"How do we see if it's a cat or a fish?"

Mad Nuala, squeezed the answer out through screeches of laughter. "We can test it—see if it will swim!"

Heart pounding in her chest, Kate had run, hurling herself into the mess of bodies and raining blows on Flaherty, who was reaching out his long skinny arm to dangle Darkie over the river.

"Stop it! Please don't!"

It was Nuala who grabbed her, twisting her arm behind her back and making her watch.

"Little rich girl Katie Shaunessy gets all she wants for Christmas!"

The glee on their faces and the mindless chanting of their taunts had been terrible. Then Darkie's body had been hurled into the air; a tiny ball of fur, spinning and kicking.

"Quick—the other side!"

They had dragged her across the road and rammed her face against the stone of the bridge, breaking her nose. Her fright was so great she clung to the wall with her fingernails and the nails cracked as her hands were torn away. The noise of their taunts rang in her ears, urging their leader, Flaherty, on.

Flaherty had hoisted her up onto the top of the wall and forced her to kneel on the big cracked stone. Nuala had laughed, but Flaherty was not laughing any more.

He was leering at her, with a sweaty look on his face. She had seen, with absolute clarity, where he had cut himself with his father's razor attempting to shave.

Her knees were bruised and her right ankle twisted. She had stared down into the rush of water far below, dark and swollen. Nuala shouted in her ear as Darkie's body emerged in the swollen stream, thrashing and whining.

"Ah, Jaysus—ye can hear it screeching!"

Even now, in her dream, Kate kicked back hard, just like she had done at the bridge. Her heel had smashed into Nuala's wire-rimmed glasses. She had freed her ankles, then her whole body as she jumped. There had been a terrifying fall then the almighty slap as she hit the water. An agony of pain blasted the whole front of her chest and abdomen, as if she had landed on concrete. The impact caused her to black out for a moment, until the deadwall of panic came and she fought her way back to the surface and tried to scream.

She tried to squeeze from her throat: "I'm drowning . . . I'm drowning." But nothing came out. The faces of her tormenters were looking down from a long distance away, pallid yet nervously triumphant. Then they were gone, leaving her alone to sink into the freezing silence of the water.

Kate remembered the darkness.

She had woken up in hospital. A fisherman had saved her—had saved them both, her and her beloved Darkie, but ever since then she had been haunted by the experience of drowning. Now it was happening again and this time she wasn't drowning in the River Suir, this time she was drowning in a more malignant darkness, one with a vast and terrible mind of its own. And the dreadful, terrible thing was that she was lucidly aware of what was happening, moment by moment.

She was lost in darkness that was blacker than the sky at night, darkness that was intent on robbing her of sight. It was also robbing her of her other senses. She reached out to touch it, but it swallowed her groping fingers and left nothing of her behind. It robbed her of hearing, of her sense of smell, of her sense of taste. The only way she knew it was there was through the absence of those senses, leaving her with the ghastly feeling of being swallowed whole by it until there was nothing left of her at all.

There would be no fisherman to save her here.

Kate felt, desperately, that she had to pit herself against it. She tried to outsmart it, she tried to beat it, she tried to slap her hand against some imaginary object—a wall, a floor—just to feel the pain. She tried to pull her hair, or even bite her tongue, but nothing happened. She felt nothing—just the endless darkness swallowing her up.

It was the scariest thing she had ever encountered—scarier even than the drowning. But she *wanted* to be scared. She held onto that scary feeling as long as she could—but even the memory of the scariness melted away and leached out of her mind to leave only the darkness.

Kate thought: *maybe I'm dead—really and truly dead?*

She hoped that she wasn't dead, but the fact that she was *hoping* she wasn't dead, told her that she wasn't—at least not yet.

I'm . . . I'm Kate Shaunessy. From the town of Clonmel.

She held onto that memory even as the darkness pressed in on her from all directions. It leached away at her senses, her mind and spirit, as if to prove that all there was was this terrible all-devouring darkness.

Instinctively her mind reached for her oraculum and it flared in her brow, filling her eyes with a blinding flash of emerald green light. But when her vision cleared it was not reassuring. She was still confined within the chamber of the Momu, supine within the roots of the One Tree. Still, the feeling of darkness and suffocation invaded and spread. It accompanied her imprisonment within the roots of the One Tree as if it were malignantly parasitic. Trapped and held in a growing lattice of roots encircling her body, she found her legs and lower body already half submerged in the freezing water.

With what little movement remained to her head and neck, she looked over at the unconscious and dying Momu. Her body was almost completely cocooned in roots, thick, gnarly roots that wove in and out of the long webbed fingers. Even as Kate watched, rootlets grew out of bigger roots, thickening and spreading over the Momu's head. Soon, not a part of her would be visible. Not even the half-closed mother-of-pearl eyes, which were fast disappearing in the slithering, extending weave.

THE UNEVEN HAND OF FATE

"AARGH!"

Snakoil Kawkaw tried to hold onto sleep as he was kicked awake, but his eyelids, caked with gunk, cracked open over gritty blood-shot eyes; the price of all that sand in the air. He pulled the thin, lousy blanket he had wrapped around his frozen body even closer—that was the difficulty of sleeping in a desert climate, it became as cold as an iceberg at night.

It was only just dawn in this shithole the Gargs called the Thousand Islands: an arsehole of festering sweat by day, and a scrote-shrinking icehole by night. That rat's dam of a preceptress must have a buzzing hornet in her bonnet, waking him at this hour. There she went, kicking him again, as if to remind him of his enslaved status, devoid of the dignity his poor, old, aching bones deserved.

"Yes, beloved Mistress?"

The small, circular tent was illuminated by the murky light of daybreak seeping in through myriad crevices in the sealskin patchwork that pretended to a weather-tight cover. The preceptress—vaunted priestess and the Tyrant's spy—was brushing her hair before a circle of burnished bronze. Kawkaw stood. His head pulsed with a venomous ague—a fit accompaniment to the nausea, which was the only result he could expect of the rancorous tipple he had stolen from a fish gutter last night. Dizziness caused him to totter into her stool.

"Clumsy oaf! Watch my dress!"

He failed to suppress a belch, grimacing at the utter foulness of what came up into his mouth from the burning hell of his stomach.

Clumsiness be blowed! He was hopping awkwardly from foot to foot because of the icy cold bare rock while, with her dainty feet protected by fur-lined bootees, she preened herself in a cloud of vapours.

"Mistress—you are celebrating?"

"My bridal anniversary, if you must know."

"What?"

"The celebration of my wedding to the beloved Master. What could a primitive like you know of such a wonder? It is the anniversary of the day I bathed in his radiance and was duly promised."

Holy boggardly shit!

Squinting in her direction—a furtive disbelieving glance—Kawkaw felt nauseated by the adoring expression lighting up her face. Rapture—could you believe it!

In spite of his discomfort he couldn't help but sneer.

In a thrice, the spiral blade was a hairsbreadth from his right eye.

"You would mock me?"

"A thousand apologies, comely lady."

"Many have I killed in my Master's name. You do him a grave disservice to mock the sacrament."

Sacrament!

A single bead of sweat erupted over Kawkaw's right eyebrow and trickled down over his cheek to the tip of his hairy chin. He saw it become the focus of her gaze. She watched its course towards his throat, as a cat watches a mouse, squeezing the handle of her dagger with a look of anticipation.

"I most humbly beg your pardon, Mistress. Please forgive what is no better than ignorance on my part. I know nothing of how our beloved Master might take himself a worthy bride. But now that you introduce the idea, it entrances the imagination."

She was hardly convinced. He watched her face as thoughts of strategy fought for supremacy over thoughts of murder. She withdrew the blade, though her eyes had not abandoned their fury. "To be selected is exaltation: the closest proximity to grace."

"I can scarcely imagine, my lady."

"Go ahead and mock what goes beyond your pathetic experience. But think you on this—darkness is as powerfully uplifting, maybe even more so, than the light."

"Forgive my lack of insight, loveliness."

She snorted with contempt. "How could you even begin to understand the bliss that comes with such limitless power?"

"How indeed?"

The danger had not entirely passed. He considered going down on one knee—never mind that, he considered prostrating himself—but he thought it more prudent merely to stand absolutely still. "I am lost in awe, Mistress." His imagination leaped at the very idea of such power. She had almost seduced him with the possibilities now gambolling playfully in his mind, and other regions.

"What would you, in turn, not give to be betrothed to a goddess? Oh, I warrant you, that in my master's palace there are many brides, but few have been granted the honour of serving him in the field."

This was the moment to bow his head. *Shit!* He fell to one knee. Let her savour his servile surrender.

She used silence to keep him abject for longer than necessary before turning back, without further word, to tinker with her execrable appearance.

He judged it prudent to maintain his genuflection a minute or two longer, but there was no doubt at all in his mind as to her eventual intentions regarding his life—especially now he had unwittingly humiliated her on what she clearly saw as her special day.

Was his fate not ever thus?

Kawkaw was reminded of his youth and Porky Larrd. *Alas—the late Porky Larrd, the heavens bless him! Poor old Porky ended up with the fate that the bitch-preceptor and her unfeeling master, intended for me!* Yet, such childhood memories had he of them both: the two outcasts of the tribe, always in trouble. Had they not shared the experience of fathers who beat their innocent sons senseless for nothing? In his case for the small indulgence of pride and the delights of larceny.

"You were out for half the night," she said.

He was racking his brains trying to remember anything of it. "I have been recruiting spies, my lady, among the rabble of urchins."

Surely she recalled the brats who took such joy in mocking her profession in soup-ladling.

"Ah, your mighty army of urchins?" On her painted lips the words embodied a whole new chapter of contempt.

"Urchins get everywhere. Nobody notices them. They feel hunger and they know the meaning of fear. They will prove useful to us."

"Then go frighten them some more."

"I—um—will meet with them presently."

She pointed a finger towards the flap of the tent. "Now!"

As he struggled to pull on his broken boots, he bemoaned the uneven hand of fate that had dogged him even in childhood, when the youthful Kawkaw had gazed on the beautiful Kehloke with the eyes of one peering at forbidden fruit. How could such beauty be living in poverty on her mother's boat? Working her fingers to the bone to gut fish and skivvy for a few coppers to make ends meet? A mere trinket would have seemed magical to her. *'Twas for you that I stole—at least that's how it started.* He had just wanted to see the light in her eyes when he presented her with some glittering jewel. *That day I saw you at the shingle, when the boats came in laden with catch. I saw that doe look on your face when that lumbering oaf Siam not only filled up your basket with plump catch, but handed you that bracelet of silver. No trinket of mine would ever be so adored on your slender wrist, not with the winsome looks you were casting at that brainless dolt.*

He cracked open the tent flap, then recoiled from the view.

"Scabrous perversity!" He exclaimed.

"What is it?"

"The place is alive with witch warriors. Some kind of military exercise."

"Well, you're going to have to go out there."

"Would you have them in here asking questions of you?"

She relented, without grace, to renew her veneration of the blade, kissing the sigil, even though it would burn the red paint off her lips.

Oh Kehloke, he reflected, *I was ever tongue-tied in your presence. And you, always polite with me—vilely, cheerfully polite. Did you know how your politeness cut me like a knife? Made the pain a thousand times worse?*

Was it his fault that she had spurned him when he would have loved and cherished her? He who wouldn't have had her wear her pretty fingers to the bone. *I'd have given you more than cheap baubles. I'd have given you my heart.* Yet, as ever, the mischievous devil, chance, had spurned him—spurned him as Kehloke did! And from that day, it seemed, it had ever been his lot to cheat and plot and squirm under the world's eye.

How many potentially great men, he wondered, had been dealt such a prejudiced hand as he? Who could blame him if, with the reluctant assistance of his boyhood friend, he had broken into her mother's boat and stolen the confounded bracelet? And who could blame him if the act had seemed so easy, so just, he had developed a fondness for it?

Kawkaw had worked himself into a temper. It was as well that the preceptress had eyes only for her reflection. He must learn to control his emotions in her presence. He knew his usefulness to her was limited and, when it was done, the dagger with the twisted blade would be the parting memory he had of her.

Loathing was not a strong enough word for his feelings towards her, but the opportunity to rid himself of her would duly present itself, of that he was sure. She would turn her back to him and he would take the chance to lunge at her with his knife. How he longed to do so. He dreamed of it, often. He felt the blade rub against the bone as he slipped it between her ribs, he heard the hiss of the parting flesh as he drew it clean across her throat; he savoured, most of all, the sigh of the point as it entered the small of her belly and then travelled up in a delicious sawing motion, his eyes on hers as her whole being was paralysed by the agony that he would give his good arm to inflict.

One day—one blessed day!

His teeth clenched in a rictus of triumph, he scratched at his stubbly chin with the point of his hook as he relished the thought. His opportunity would come and oh, how sweet it would be. And he would take it, and crow over her like a trumpeting cockerel.

He had spent an hour, maybe more, daydreaming when her hiss, up close to his ear, cut through his musings.

"There's something more than an exercise going on out there."

He was instantly alert. Had he muttered during his musing? Had he given himself away? His heart missed a beat, fearful, no matter how implausible, that she might somehow be able to read his mind.

"The Garg king, why does he hold out? He has already made an enemy of the master in helping the brat defeat the Great Witch. The master's revenge will be as inevitable as it will be terrible. Zelnesakkk has nothing to lose now."

Kawkaw's mind spun with alarm. The last thing he needed was to be right in the middle of it all when the

Tyrant struck. He recalled with a fearful lucidity how he had almost perished when he had been so foolish as to accept the deadly talisman from the Tyrant's spy, Feltzvan, back in Carfon.

"What would you have me do?"

"We have urgent need of information."

"Information?"

His lips squeezed out the word to convince her that he was listening hard, but he was thinking more than listening. Had not the preceptress made it clear to him that his life had no meaning in the machinations of her master? What could she have learned in her prostration before the black-bladed dagger? What madness was she about to unleash? And how was he to get out of it with his skin intact?

"Go find your urchins. Put the fear of your blade among them. Set the scum an example, just be sure to discover what's going on."

"I cannot move openly. It would be suicidal."

"Where is your mettle? Do you not understand? They plot and plan to attack my master—my husband."

"But, Mistress . . ."

"Desist from prevaricating. Are you not Olhyiu? Why, you even stink like the loathsome fish gutters."

"When you open the soup kitchen, the urchins will come to me."

"Now. This very instant." The dagger had returned to confront his face, its spiral blade—that poisoned tip—too close for his eyes to focus on it.

He snatched up the wide-brimmed hat he had stolen, pulled it down so it shaded his features, and threw on his coat, lifting the collar so it closed above his chin. He stuffed the hook that his left arm ended in into a capacious pocket so it would not be noticeable.

"Be off!"

"Mistress, I'm gone."

So it was that Snakoil Kawkaw, whose indomitable courage and resourcefulness counted for nothing in this world of schemers and liars and slime-tongued arselickers, was compelled to slouch out into the too-bright sunshine. And there exposed, blinking his red-veined eyes at the migrainous vision of black rock and searing white sand, he cursed her long and hard, fearing from moment to moment that it might be the ignominious end of his miserable existence.

The Memories of a Kyra

Alan was staring landwards at the encircling calderas where a sphere, illuminated from within, was floating gently down the slopes. It bobbed and twirled, so light it caught every whim of the wind, as if constructed from something as fine as gossamer silk. Yet, all the while it was descending, it kept coming towards him. He probed it with his oraculum and encountered only emptiness within, but he wasn't fooled by it.

"What the blazes are you?"

The voice that emerged from the sphere was deep and full-bodied, as if from inside a barrel. "It is I, Magtokk, come down from my mountain cave to observe the ceremony, if not in the flesh, at least in spirit."

Mo had told him about this magician called Magtokk. Now Alan stared at the sphere, which was about eighteen inches in diameter, which floated right up to him and hung, suspended by some innate buoyancy, in the warm noon air. But no natural force could have caused it to take up a position so close by them, giving it the ability to listen into the conversation.

"You—Mage Lord Duval—are distressed by the fact that that you cannot enter my mind?"

"You appear to have entered mine."

"That worries you."

"Should I be worried?"

There was a wobble within the sphere that Alan interpreted as a chuckle. "You are right to be curious. Please be assured that there is no cause for concern."

"I'd like an explanation."

"Explanations are so boring. Like your friend, the dwarf mage, I am very likely the last of my race. But we were never plentiful. The thinkers of long ago put it down to the fact we were too competitive to suffer one another's existence."

"What does that mean?"

"Yours is too focused a mind to be diverted by humour. I am confessing to a hereditary fault."

"I'm still not sure that that assures me."

Another wobble. "Oh, dear!"

"I don't trust a being I cannot see."

"Cannot see? Or should you say cannot *control* through that oraculum in your brow?"

Alan was about to speak his mind more directly when the sphere disappeared to be replaced by a large male orang-utan. The transformation was startling. The creature before him was a remarkably accurate representation of the animal, right down to the big floppy jowls and an incredible entanglement of hair that flowed over its feet.

"Well, well," said Qwenqwo, who had been observing the conversation with undisguised fascination.

"Enchanted in turn." Magtokk bowed low before the dwarf mage. "From the representative of one dying race to another, it is a delight to make your acquaintance. I have heard admirable tales of the brave Fir Bolg, but nothing would have prepared me for the youthful figure I now behold."

Qwenqwo cackled, his face creasing with delight at the thought that there was one among them who might be even older than himself.

"Come down to spy on us," the Kyra interrupted, from surprisingly close. Ainé could move both quickly and stealthily, as one might expect of a warrior with the soul spirit of a snow tigress.

"I doubt," said the orang-utan, scratching at its hindquarters with a broad, fat finger, "that any such transgression would escape those wonderfully attuned feline senses. And while I'm confessing to weaknesses, let me add that I would trade pleasantries aplenty for a snort of that flagon the dwarf mage is cradling to his breast—and for a pipe-full of that fine-smelling baccy."

Qwenqwo Cuatzel laughed with delight. Alan supposed that anybody capable of fencing words with the

Kyra was bound to intrigue his dwarf mage friend, who made no pretence to admiration of the Shee. "Sounds like the best offer I've had in two millennia."

Alan stared as he watched the orang-utan take a swig from Qwenqwo's flask. It looked like mischief in the making, but he wasn't yet sure which of the two red-bearded characters was the more capable. The dwarf mage stuffed two pipes brim-full of tobacco before passing one to the outstretched hand of the orang-utan, who joined him in puffing out clouds of smoke.

For all the jocularity, Alan still had no idea how trustworthy Magtokk the Mischievous was. He would have trusted Ainé, Qwenqwo, Bétaald, the entire Shee army—perhaps even the Garg, Iyezzz—with his life. But as to the magician—well, he would keep a wary eye on him and his tricks.

Bétaald was concerned with other matters.

"Would that you both understood the gravity of this venture. We are threatening the most powerful being in this world, other than the gods and goddesses. Do not fool yourselves into thinking that the Tyrant fears us. He regards himself as invulnerable. And with good reason."

"Perhaps he should fear us?" said Alan.

Bétaald shook her head. "Have you forgotten how powerful he is? You think he will feel threatened by our war on him? He will merely relish the challenge we represent. Perhaps he might resent our arrogance, being the paradigm of arrogance himself, but that will only add to his rage at our attacking his stronghold. And yet we foolishly arraign all of our forces within what is most definitely his sphere of influence. If, in the unlikely event that we should win, our world will be liberated. If, in the likely event that he should win, darkness will triumph throughout all of Tír." She narrowed her eyes, gazing from one of them to another. "Forever."

Alan nodded, feeling her warning in his gut. He spoke softly. "Is the Kyra ready?"

"All is ready," Bétaald said, then turning to Magtokk, she added, "But I will not allow any alien witness, whose mischievous presence speaks of nothing more than curiosity, to spy on the making of our plans."

"I'm sorry, Magtokk," said Alan.

"Please forgive me if my levity offended. I shall offer respect and empathy from a distance—in the good company of the dwarf mage here."

"So be it," said Bétaald. "For my part, I have no wish to offend a legendary magician whose counsel may prove useful in the difficult march to come. We'll need sleight of hand and every art known to us before we arrive at the gates of Ghork Mega."

"My feelings exactly," said Qwenqwo. "Our enemy will not sit and await our arrival. He will plot and plan—and my instincts suggest he will do so in ways we can not anticipate."

The ceremony was looming and Alan had no time to examine the magician further. But he did manage to prise Qwenqwo aside, if only for a moment or two. "Keep your eyes on Magtokk. Whatever you do, make sure he doesn't get anywhere near to the ceremony. It will be delicate enough without antagonising the spiritual adviser."

Alan turned to go, consoling himself with the thought that Qwenqwo was no fool. The dwarf might enjoy the camaraderie of Magtokk, but he was far too experienced to be taken in by any wiles or subterfuge. But he felt less than reassured when his departure was marked with roars of laughter and, glancing back, he witnessed the two red-bearded faces cloven by gleaming horseshoes of teeth.

Earlier that morning Alan had woken early from sleep, emerging from his tent to gaze out onto a misty ball of sun rising out of its own reflection on the sea. He had never seen the bay look so ethereal. It had deeply worried him, since he had witnessed days when that bank of mist had spread to cover the entire sky. But Iyezzz had reassured him that this was not going to be such a day; the mists would clear in plenty of time for the ceremonies that had been planned by both the Gargs and the Shee.

Iyezzz had proved to be right and now Alan stood perfectly still, gazing at the archipelago in the azure ocean, the air clear as crystal. He glanced up, through slitted eyelids, at the position of the sun, not far from vertically overhead. He could hear the tens of thousands of Shee humming.

Iyezzz had instructed Bétaald to clear the beach, and she had spread her instructions among the aides. Glancing to either side, Alan saw that everyone—the Olhyiu cooks and transport labourers, the supporting sailors and workmen who had arrived with the giant cargo ships of Prince Ebrit—had left the stretch of sand, to leave only the Shee warriors and Gargs.

He was also aware of sweeping movements taking place among the army of giant warriors: the aides were marshalling a gigantic spiral of attendant warriors around the Kyra in the centre. Alan watched and waited, alongside Bétaald and Ainé.

Over the distant headland, the tall, lean figures of Zelnesakkk, Iyezzz and his mother, Shah-nur-Kian, stood rigidly to attention, their wings folded tight to their backs. Mahteman also stood off to one side, his wings widely expanded, holding aloft an ivory sceptre. Beyond them stood perhaps twenty or so senior ministers of the Eyrie people. It was exceedingly formal. Behind the Garg hierarchy, tens of thousands of winged figures were rising into the clear blue sky.

The movements in sky and on land of vast numbers of Garg and Shee were curiously harmonious, a seamless and elegant choreography, mirroring one another just as Bétaald had intended.

At a command from their spiritual adviser, the Shee warriors raised their bronze shields to reflect the light of the dying sun as the eclipse began, fashioning a gigantic burnished spiral that twinkled and whirled as the warriors began to wheel, the pageant blazing with reflected light over several square miles of ground. In the sky overhead, an identical spiral of cruciform shapes wheeled on the breezes rising from the heated land, while balls of crystal, clasped in their clawed feet, magnified the sun's rays and caused them to fall in dazzling rainbows, which were reflected back up again by the shields of the Shee. Between the two very different races it was an awe-inspiring vision of reverence and union.

Union!

A high-pitched keening from above was the first intimation of the change. Alan looked at the Kyra and met her gaze eye to eye. The flat blue eyes of the tigress stared back at him, unblinking.

Now he had to speak. He hoped the tension didn't show in his voice as he, calmly and respectfully, addressed the entire group of assembled Shee, aides and Garg leaders in a voice magnified by the oraculum. "We are faced with a just and terrible war. To be victorious we need to be united in heart and spirit. For this purpose I must share a sacred memory with the Kyra. It's a memory that will be painful for me to recall and for her to witness. But it is also one that inspires new hope and courage in my own heart when I feel afraid—and I think it will be deeply meaningful to the Kyra herself."

The shadow on the sun was now visible to all: a narrow crescent was biting into its sphere. A new harmonious chanting erupted from the throats of the Shee, who were as superstitious in their way as the Gargs.

Alan's gaze continued to hold that of the young Kyra in the darkening light. Once before, on the beach at Carfon, he had offered this meeting of minds. But on that occasion she had reacted furiously against it, pronouncing it blasphemy. He spoke quietly to the spiritual adviser. "Bétaald—will you guide us both on what must be done?"

The dark-skinned spiritual adviser moved closer to the young Kyra. "It is a very strange and unusual request, but you are the Mage Lord whom we have all come to respect and trust. It is my counsel that the Kyra should place her trust in you."

"Thank you." Alan bowed to the Kyra. "I offer the sharing of one harrowing and very poignant memory. I understand the natural suspicion I see in your eyes, but I believe that you will take comfort in knowing how your mother-sister died."

With a flaring of her nostrils and a fierce glare in her eyes the young Kyra replied, "The Mage Lord is well aware of how I feel about this. Yet, based on my growing respect of his courage and honour, and given the counsel of my spiritual adviser, I would swallow pride and break with tradition. Yet if, even despite his assurances, I perceive the slightest threat of blasphemy, I shall halt the sharing of memory."

"Thank you."

A powerful communication, transmitted through the Oraculum of Bree in the Kyra's brow, spread as a command throughout the Shee. Even in the waning light, as the eclipse progressed to half light, the watching Gargs would have witnessed a fluidly coordinated movement of the vast army of warriors, fashioning concentric overlapping circles with their shields. Alan heard the melodious chanting of hymnal cadences that reminded him of the burial of Valéra, the noviciate Shee who had saved his life with the sacrifice of her own on the banks of the Snowmelt River. On that occasion, grief had been assuaged by the birth of Valéra's daughter-sister. Here, Alan hoped for a very different outcome.

He spoke softly. "I'm ready—if the Kyra is also ready?"

The Kyra was silent, but she appeared ready. Her face was expressionless. Her eyes never left his.

Gently, carefully, Alan turned the focus of his oraculum onto her brow, and the Oraculum of Bree. He was careful to minimise the power he now ignited in his own oraculum. He did not want the Kyra to think he was invading her mind.

"I will not violate your sacred trust, Ainé. All I intend to do is to open up a channel of communication."

There was a controlled explosion of power, linking oraculum to oraculum, in the falling dark.

Alan held out his hands, gazing into the huge blue eyes of the young Kyra. After a moment's hesitation, she reached out both her hands, claw-tipped and easily large enough to enclose his, so that they were physically united.

Alan spoke again. "I am going to recall when the former Kyra and I faced the Legun incarnate at the Battle of Ossierel. I ask you to witness what happened as I place the memory in your mind."

The young Kyra was silent, but her hands gripped his own a little tighter.

He found the place in his memories when the battle was going badly and the entire plateau was in tumult. A continuous rain of livid green missiles deluged the ruins of Ossierel from the legions on the surrounding slopes and every few seconds the shadows were lit up by explosive flares of foul livid fire as heavier missiles struck their defences. Even the sky around the perimeter of the island pulsated and glowed, as if illuminated by flickering searchlights.

In Alan's memory the former Kyra, the present Kyra's mother-sister, spoke with great urgency. "*Our cause is desperate. Our enemies outnumber us perhaps twenty to one.*"

In the same memory Alan wheeled about, taking in the desperate fight against overwhelming odds. The monstrous figure of the Legun incarnate reared in front of him, half emerging from the flames and ruin. A gigantic creature with the face of a skull, it sat astride a giant battle charger, with fangs for teeth and a frame armoured and powerful as a rhinoceros. Malice glimmered about the Legun as if a dark sun were continually reforming out of the voids of space. The Kyra attacked, but there was no pause, not even a shudder in her terrible enemy, her sword merely sliced through darkness with a blaze of green sparks. The Legun struck out with taloned claws while she was still in flight, catching her shoulder with an immense reach. Blood spurted from the previously healing wounds as the Kyra fell back against the wrack of bodies. The Legun picked her up by her tawny hair, dangling her body high above Alan as if she were a figure of straw, then cut deep with an extended talon, reopening the scars on the left side of her face.

Alan hurled the Spear of Lug, flaring Ogham runes, into the figure of darkness. With a roar the Legun dropped the Kyra. But, though Alan had attacked it with all of his power, he had not destroyed it and the Legun expanded even more until it became a thunderhead of dark power, devouring the light.

The Kyra clambered back onto uncertain feet, mortally injured, her right arm dangling uselessly by her side. "*There is little more I can do,*" she groaned. Then her blue eyes widened and a spark of awe lit them, as if from her inner spirit. "*Yet I thank the Powers that I should have lived to see the arrival of the Heralded One.*"

Her left hand moved to touch his brow and her oraculum pulsated stronger, taking power from him. "*Your duty is clear. You must support me in my instructions, Mage Lord Duval.*"

In his memory Alan looked into the eyes of the wounded Kyra. "*How can I help you?*"

He heard her, and Ainé heard her with him. "*Preserve these, my memories, for my daughter-sister.*"

Alan felt the squeeze of the Ainé's grip, so powerful it almost broke the bones of his fingers. His head fell. Only now, with the renewed chanting of the excited Shee, did he gently break contact, oraculum-to-oraculum.

The Kyra spoke softly, her own head lowered. "Her actions make it clear there is no blasphemy. Yet, I would wish to know what became of my mother-sister?"

"She asked me to let her draw on the power of my oraculum, to allow her a final blood-rage."

The young Kyra's voice was little above a whisper. "I sense that you are protecting me from what you imagine to be the pain of loss. I need to know how she died."

Alan closed his eyes. In his memory he heard the mother-sister demand of him, "*Give me this comfort. I would enter blood rage but my body is too weak. For this I must draw power from you.*"

He recalled focusing all of his power on the Kyra's oraculum of Bree and recoiled from the vision as he remembered the explosive union throwing them both backwards.

He saw his condensation of oracular energy strike the white tigress, the First Power turning her into a soul spirit of incandescent wrath. Each movement of her limbs caused arcs of lighting to spill onto the adjacent ground and her eyes radiated light, like miniature furnaces. With a roar that shook the ground, she pounced at the Legun, great jaws spilling lightning, her huge weight and energy tearing into its body, her maw directed at its throat while she retained the last vestiges of life.

The young Kyra watched with Alan, entranced and astonished. “She made her dying self into a living weapon.”

Alan nodded. “In doing so she saved many lives, including my own. She bought us time.”

As the moon fully eclipsed the sun, Ainé stood, still and silent, in the resultant gloom. It was as if the fighting spirit of the former Kyra, the mother-sister, still reared before them in the eye of memory, her soul spirit preserved within their shared minds.

The daughter-sister’s form began to change. Her clothing fell away from her and she became the great snow tigress that was her soul spirit. The encircling Shee began to sing a new hymn, closing in to fashion a protective circle around the central trio.

Alan murmured, “Bétaald?”

“The Kyra does you honour, Mage Lord Duval.”

Then Bétaald spoke gentle words of command, in a language that sounded older than the mountains. Alan stood still, his heart in his throat, as the snow tigress approached him, her muzzle brushing against his shoulder, her throat purring, so he felt the vibrations resonate in his chest.

He spoke again to Bétaald. “Is it time?”

She nodded. "The Oraculum of Bree must now be confirmed with the Kyra in her ancestral form."

Then he spoke the words that were obvious to him now, whispering them through the pulsating oraculum in his brow, which became the sole illumination in the darkened landscape, highlighting the figure of the gigantic snow tigress in brilliant rubicund light.

"I hereby return the memories that were entrusted to me by the former Kyra, who was my friend. I'm honoured to have been the carrier of this sacred trust. May it comfort and enlighten you, her daughter-sister, Ainé, the new Kyra."

From his skulking position in a shadowed crevice a third of the way up the cliff, Snakoil Kawkaw cringed before the thunderous detonation as the brat and the witch warrior made some kind of extraordinary contact. An eruption of red lightning broke out from the tiny cluster of three at the heart of the great gathering, catching the curves of shields and then radiating back into the sky, where the vast army of Gargs observed and wheeled.

"Odoriferous batshit!"

The hackles on his neck rose as the white tigress at the heart of it all lifted her enormous head and roared.

The blaze over the great spiral of shields coincided with the first brilliant flash of the sun emerging out of the darkness. Kawkaw's eyes lifted to the ledge high overhead and the figures of the watching king and the Garg high shaman, Mahteman. Kawkaw could see how the thunder and lightning must have appeared, to their superstitious eyes, as if the meeting below had re-ignited sun.

His guess was confirmed as a loud moaning issued from the gill-throats of the Eyrie people—a reaction to what they had witnessed.

"Execrable brat!" he muttered. He couldn't see how the lovely lady, for all of her face painting and celebration, could prevent the now inevitable union of the flying gargoyles with the witch warriors. They would march on Ghork Mega soon—a nightmare journey that he, no doubt, would be forced to join.

The Resistance

It took a few moments for Mark to become aware that he and Nan had arrived at their destination: a roomy windowless building that had once been industrial premises. In front of the broken bull bar of heavy vehicle, a figure was kneeling on an oil-stained fragment of carpet. The figure was that of a muscular male in jeans and a short-sleeved navy shirt, with an oxyacetylene torch in his hand. For another moment or two Mark was too disorientated to think clearly. He could hear nothing other than the roar of the torch.

Henriette had triggered it. He had no idea how. She had gathered him and Nan together behind the soup kitchen mission and she had sent them here, through the conduit of the Temple Ship.

<Nan!> He called out to her mind to mind.

<I'm here.>

The kneeling man, his face protected behind a visor, was still concentrating on the jet of flame, but it was no longer directed at the white-hot metal, which was rapidly cooling to brilliant pink. In the fraction of a second that Mark registered this, he saw the hackles rise on the back of the man's neck and he turned, lifting the visor, his thumb automatically brushing the knurled valve that turned off the flame. He dropped the burner onto the floor with a clatter.

In the man's mind, Mark registered the recognition that there was somebody else in the gloom; a stranger, with his face lit up. Shit—Mark was looking at his own face, looking like that of a ghost.

The kneeling man said, "What the hell?"

Mark glanced behind him at Nan and the blue-black zigzag of the lightning that coursed from her brow, lighting up her features. More of the tiny bolts ran in arabesques and rivulets over her head, coming together in a spider's web over her shoulders. The oraculum was pulsating strongly, aglow with a livid fire.

"Please—don't be alarmed. We mean you no harm."

He heard the man growl, "Shit!"

"My name is Mark Grimstone. My friend's name is Nan."

The man appeared to be transfixed with shock, but Mark thought that was hardly surprising. He sensed the prickling of gooseflesh that was running like a cold shower down the man's back. He read it in the man's mind that the building was a barn, somewhere in the rural wilds north of the M25, and that his name was Cal.

He said, "Take it easy, Cal. We want to work with you."

Mark was sensing three or four other presences within the barn. He heard a click and assumed it was the priming of a weapon.

Cal said, "What's going on? This some kind of a joke?"

"It isn't a joke."

"Tajh!" Cal shouted.

Mark held his hands out, to reassure all present that he was no threat. "I realise you weren't expecting us, but we're on the same side."

Mark sensed the sweat oozing freely from Cal's face, itching in the ridge across his forehead created by the strap. He felt him dump the headgear.

"Tajh—dammit!"

A woman spoke from surprisingly close, in a matter-of-fact Scottish accent. "Cool it, Cal. Let's hear what they have to say."

She was carrying a weapon. It must have been her priming the gun. She was close enough now to be visible. Mark saw that the weapon was a submachine gun and that it was pointed directly at his own chest.

"You must be Tajh."

"You say you want to work with us? You just turn up out of the blue to tell us that? Why didn't somebody warn us you were coming?"

"We didn't know how to warn you."

"You say your name is Mark Grimstone? You related to the Reverend of the same name?"

"My adoptive father."

Nan spoke, with icy calm. "You should tell Cal to bridle his anger. We have no desire to hurt you."

Cal hooted with laughter. "Shit! Shit! Shit!"

Nan spoke again, with the same cool authority. "If my suspicions are correct, there is good reason for us to combine forces. The danger facing you is far greater than you imagine."

"What's that supposed to mean?" That was another voice entirely, a male voice, from somewhere deeper in the gloom, close to where Mark figured the barn doors were. Tajh raised her voice to shout over her shoulder. "Sharkey—I know you're there. I don't want you do anything stupid."

Mark caught a glimpse of a tall, lean figure. He appeared to be unarmed.

"I won't, but I want to know what madam here means by all that stuff about danger."

"We arrived in London only a day ago, but in that day we have encountered strangeness beyond anything we expected: dark magic. In my world that would provoke suspicion."

"Dark magic?" The man called Sharkey was cackling with amusement.

"Indeed."

Cal said, "Bloody hell! This is bonkers. I'm telling you, the both of you, to cut the bullshit. How the hell did you find us?"

Mark thought it prudent to intervene. "That would take some explaining."

"That's it, Tajh, I'm not putting up with this."

Tajh motioned to Nan to come closer to Mark. That way she could cover them both with the submachine gun. Nan did so, but without any hurry. Mark could see that she was bristling with anger. Tajh must have noticed it too. "You'll forgive the fact we're all a little tense." She took a step closer, to take a good look at Nan's face. "What's that in your head? Some kind of jewel?"

Nan answered coolly, "It's called an oraculum."

Tajh peered more closely at Nan's oraculum. "My God, it's luminous—pulsating." Tajh blinked with astonishment, stepping back again, but she kept the submachine gun directed at Mark, who kept his hands wide in that same non-threatening gesture. She said, "You cool, Cal?"

"I'm far from cool!"

"Sharkey?"

"As the proverbial breeze."

Tajh said, "Okay. We all need to calm down." She threw Cal a towel to wipe the sweat from his face. "What's an oraculum?" The question was addressed to Nan.

"A gateway to power—it works through a crystal."

Tajh was shaking her head. “What—so you’re saying you and Mark here have crystals of power embedded in your heads?”

“Yes.”

“That’s the reason your hair’s standing on end full of some kind of electrical charge? Och, there are sparks in your hair—blue-black lightning running over both your heads.”

“It’s what happens when people aim guns at us.”

“I still want to know how these people located us,” Cal said. “How they found their way past Bull on security. What’s the matter with everybody? Don’t you folks understand the risks we’re running every bloody moment?”

Tajh sighed. “One thing at a time. What’s all this talk about dark magic and the danger being worse than we think?”

Mark shrugged, let his hands fall by his sides. “I could try to explain—but we’d need a deal of time and you’re unlikely to believe me at the end of it.”

Cal shook his head. “The crazy kind of stuff the guy is coming out with! And yet you’re just nodding your head, Tajh.”

Tajh frowned, ignoring Cal. “Tell me about this,” she pointed, “this axe strapped to your back—this is your weapon?”

“Yeah.”

“An old-fashioned medieval battleaxe?”

“A battleaxe, but it’s not medieval. It’s nothing like any battleaxe you know about.”

Mark caught the glance Tajh passed to Cal, who just stood there with frank disbelief written all over his face.

Cal said, "You know this is insane."

Tajh said, "You're right. It's insane, but insane things are going on in the streets of London right now. Things you and I just don't understand."

Cal had had enough. He grabbed the gun from Tajh and stepped up in front of Mark, training it into his face. "I don't know who you are. I don't know where you come from—or what you're doing here. I don't understand shit of what you're telling us. The only thing keeping you alive right now is the fact I need to know how the hell you found us."

Mark was aware of Sharkey moving around behind them as he and Nan took several more steps into the barn, coming within feet of the man called Cal. He kept a close eye on Cal, who appeared to be the leader of the group. Judging from his accent, he was likely to be London-born. Even in the gloom Mark could see that Cal was shaven-headed, his cheeks and chin stubbled with a two-day growth of beard. The woman, Tajh, was brown-haired, slightly gangly, with big silver pendants dangling from fleshy ear lobes.

Mark sensed at least two other presences, only one of whom had been identified: Sharkey. The other, a male presence, was creeping up on them. Mark wondered if it was the one Cal had called Bull. Mark kept the presence in his mind, deciding whether it was he or Nan that was the focus of the attack. He sensed rage in the attacking mind only a moment or so before the attack was upon them, then he froze the attacker, turning round to discover an extremely heavy-set man dressed only in boxer shorts. A heavy machine gun was clutched in his hands, with a belt full of bullets dangling over his left forearm. The rage Mark had detected in the man's mind was still apparent in his frozen eyes.

It was becoming increasingly difficult to inject any common sense into the situation. Mark watched Cal blinking. He was aware that the gun in Cal's hands had been primed earlier ready to fire. Sweat was once more running openly into Cal's eyes. Although Cal was unaware of it, a matrix of blue-black lightning focused on the submachine gun was subtly bathing him in electricity. Tajh had to be aware of it. Mark kept his eyes on Cal while appealing to Tajh. "Can't we just talk through this, coolly and rationally? Surely you can see that we're trying to be reasonable?"

Tajh went to Cal's side and threw her arms around him. Mark signalled Nan to make sure she didn't overreact.

"If you care for him," Mark told Tajh gently, "get him to put down the gun." He turned slowly, speaking to each of them. "I'm addressing all of you. I'm not expecting any of you to just trust us. All I am asking is we all take a mental step back. And could somebody please put some more lights on so we can all clearly see one another?"

A raft of lights erupted overhead.

Mark's eyes had been so adjusted to the murky dark it was like being caught in a searchlight. He let his hands fall by his sides, and saw that Nan did the same. Tajh was staring at him, breathing heavily. Cal was also staring at the both of them, his eyes moving from one to the other, but the gun had fallen to his side. Mark released the frozen man and he fell to his knees with a grunt.

Sharkey was standing several feet inside the doorway of the barn, next to the light switches. His hair was grey, tied back into a ponytail, and held with a Navajo ring. His face was so gaunt it resembled a mask, with a Zapata moustache dangling over his upper lip. His voice mimicked a sing-song Jamaican patois. "Before Babylon fall, jackals goin' raise their voices in falsehood. All af us done killin'. An' we lookin' to plenty more. But us also had killin' done to us."

"Then," Mark answered, "Nan and I find ourselves amongst friends."

Tajh squeezed Cal, as if to reassure him. She said, "Okay—my vote, if it comes to a vote, is we all sit down and talk."

Cal's voice was husky, low-pitched, his face lowered so Mark had to struggle even to hear him. "I'm talking to nobody. Not until they tell us how they found us. We're always on the move. So how the hell did they do that?"

Mark said nothing. How in the world could he possibly explain, in this fraught situation, how they had arrived here. He wasn't even sure where "here" really was, other than the fact it was somewhere rural, and a distance from London. The fact was, *he* didn't even quite know how such a thing could happen.

"You have special powers?" It was Tajh who came to his rescue.

"That's a good way of looking at it, yeah."

Mark watched Sharkey produce a spliff before lighting it off a butane ring. He took a puff then passed it on to Cal.

Cal smoked it automatically, just standing there, his eyes glittering. Tajh was slowly studying Mark and Nan with flickering movements of her eyes from one to the other.

Mark laughed softly. "Look—I can see that our arrival here has come as a shock. But we really mean you no harm. My name really is Mark Grimstone, but I'm no friend of my adoptive father's. Nan and I, we want to be your allies."

Tajh spoke quietly, urgently. "If only you knew, Mark and Nan, what we—the Resistance—have been through, you'd realise how hard it is for us to trust strangers." Her chin jutted out. "The Skulls murdered Cal's father and they murdered Sharkey's son."

"I'm sorry to hear that."

"The paramilitaries call us terrorists, but terrorists aim to victimise ordinary, decent people. We don't do that. We try to defend them."

"So you're freedom fighters?"

A dwarf in a wheelchair astonished both Mark and Nan by rolling out from the far side of the huge vehicle that Cal had been working on. Neither of them had been aware of his presence. He said, "Let me answer that. What we are is a crew—one small cog in the mighty Resistance."

Mark grinned. "Okay."

The dwarf grinned back, "Talking of cogs, I'm Cogwheel."

Nan, who was closest to him, shook his hand. "Glad to meet you, Cogwheel."

"Likewise, Nan."

Cal handed what was left of the spliff back to Sharkey. "What if these two lunatics have a truckload of pals out there? What if, right now, they're in the process of surrounding us while these two divert us with this crap?"

Tajh spoke tiredly. "Cal—think about it. Would they have come in openly among us if they were out to kill us?"

"It isn't that simple." Cal turned back to glare at Mark. "What the fuck are you people really up to? Why have you really come here looking for us?"

"Well, at least we're talking." Tajh put herself between Mark and Cal. "What do you say we all sit down and have a nice cup of tea?"

"A beer might be more conducive." Mark smiled.

"A beer then—boys?" She patted the shoulder of Bull, who now dangled the heavy machine gun across his thighs. "Okay?"

Bull shrugged.

She glared at Cal. “I hardly need to ask you—a beer?”

Cal snorted.

Mark glanced over at Nan, who shared his thoughts. It was going to take more than a beer or two to get Cal and his crew to trust them.

Suspicion

Awake soon after dawn, Mark listened to the sounds of restless activity around the camp. The crew had risen early, considering that one beer had become several the night before. It was perhaps just as well—sleep didn't come easy on the thin camp mattresses Tajh had provided them with, stretched out on the hard and lumpy floor of the barn. Touching minds with Nan, he found that she too was awake.

"What do you think?" she whispered.

Mark snorted. "We did our best to explain."

"I'm not sure that any of them believed us."

"No."

How could they expect the crew to believe their story? They had offered no convincing explanation of their arrival: a Belizean witch in London had arranged their trip through an invisible ship in the sky? Neither Mark nor Nan had felt able to offer that. All they'd been able to say in explanation was that it was "magic," which had provoked Sharkey into fits of laughter. "You sure you guys haven't been tripping on magic mushrooms?"

"I wish it were that simple."

"You really come from an alien world?" Tajh had looked every bit as incredulous as Cal.

"My world," Nan agreed. "One that has been torn apart by war for more than two thousand years."

"A world," Sharkey had difficulty controlling his lop-sided grin, "where you're a queen two thousand years old?"

"Queen of a sacred island only, The Isle of Ossierel. And I am now in—oh, I'm not sure whether it is my eighteenth or nineteenth year. I was frozen in time, and age, for two thousand years."

"Hey, that's cool, I'm into the notion of hobnobbing with royalty, however ancient." Cogwheel had joined them over a makeshift plank table, sipping beers. He'd told them he had achondroplasia, a cause of dwarfism, but that had been further complicated by an accident that had made him wheelchair bound.

Mark shrugged. "I don't blame you folks if you don't believe a word we're telling you. I'd be just as sceptical in your place. But you asked for an explanation and we've given it." He took a swig from his beer then continued. "Four of us went into Tír from Earth: Alan,

Kate, my adoptive sister Mo, and me. We were helped by Alan's druid grandfather, Padraig. From the moment we arrived there, we were caught up in that war."

Cogwheel whistled. "With an enemy who has lived for thousands of years?"

"A very formidable enemy indeed," Nan added. "One that cannot be understood in human terms. We know this enemy as the Tyrant of the Wastelands."

Mark emptied his bottle with one big swig. "I met up with Nan during a terrible battle to take her island fortress. She saved my life, but it was at a heavy price."

"Yes, it was." Nan nodded. "Mark was subsumed by the same power that had subsumed me two thousand years earlier, also during a terrible battle for that same fortress. And now you know how we came to acquire our oracula. We share the Third Power—the power of the goddess of death, Mórígán."

Cal snorted for the umpteenth time. "What I'd like to know is the relevance of this cock and bull story to what's happening here in London."

Mark looked over at Tajh. "Could you find a sheet of paper and a pen so Nan can draw the symbol of the Tyrant of the Wastelands."

Tajh provided a blank sheet and a black felt-tip pen, which Nan used to sketch out the triple infinity.

The crew stared at her drawing in bemused silence.

"But that's Grimstone's logo—the symbol of his church."

Mark let them think about it.

Cal exploded. "What are you implying? That just the fact they have some symbol in common we should all become buddies?"

"Before we crossed into Tír, Padraig, Alan's druid grandfather, took us to see a barrow grave. He, and his ancestors have been the hereditary guardians of the grave for thousands of years. Within the grave were the remains of a warrior prince from the Bronze Age. That prince's name was Feimhin. But what Padraig was actually guarding wasn't the barrow, or the remains, but the prince's sword—the Sword of Feimhin. Padraig told us that the Sword was the repository of a dreadful dark magic. While Feimhin wielded the Sword, it led to endless war, not merely in Ireland, but in all of these islands, and across all of Europe. So terrible was the potential of the Sword that Padraig's ancestors were commanded to guard it for all time. The same symbol that Nan has drawn, and the one you recognise as the symbol of Grimstone's church, is embedded in the hilt of the Sword of Feimhin."

Cal exhaled and turned his face away.

"I realise how implausible it must sound, Cal. But all Nan and I can do is to tell you the simple truth of what we experienced. You're going to have to believe or disbelieve it, as you think fit."

Sharkey reached out to brush his fingers over the inverted black triangle in Nan's brow. He had tattoos of what looked like dragons, witches and warlocks on his deltoids and forearms, extending onto his shoulder blades at the back and to his collarbones at the front.

"Hey, man—there really is a buzz going on here. That felt awesome."

"Knock it off, dopehead!" The beefy one that Tajh had confirmed as Bull slapped Sharkey's hand away.

Tajh took a swig from her bottle, deep in thought. "So—if I'm to understand what you're implying, and to answer Cal's question—you really believe that the Tyrant, on Tír, and Grimstone, here in London, are linked."

"We suspect that it goes deeper than that. We're beginning to think that Earth and Tír are linked because our oracula still work here. Don't ask us how, or why, because we don't know ourselves."

"And this enemy—the Tyrant—he's got hold of this magic whatyamacallit?"

"We believe he has access to the Fáil, yes."

"Which is dangerous"

"Which," Nan cut in, "is more dangerous than you could possibly imagine."

Mark agreed. "I think that the power of the Sword is also linked to the Fáil. It's the only thing that could make it so darkly potent. And given what Padraig told us about it." He paused. "Never-ending war has devastated Tír for two thousand years!"

Tajh was silent for a moment or two. "So, where is this magical sword?"

"We believe that Grimstone stole it. His followers burnt down Padraig's sawmill and they knew about the barrow grave. We went back there to find it vandalised and the Sword gone. We believe Grimstone has the Sword. We also believe that he has taken Padraig prisoner and that they are somewhere in London."

Cal sneered. "And you expect us to help you find them?"

Nan answered him. "It doesn't matter whether you believe us, or you don't. We offer an exchange of potential: we help the Resistance, you help us."

"What have you got to offer that we don't have already?"

"We might detect when you are about to be attacked. I have had two thousand years of experience in this. And as our undetected arrival amongst you has amply demonstrated, this is a telling deficiency in your defences."

Cal was chagrined into silence, which caused Mark to smile. Nan had taken advantage of a weakness in the crew to overturn a weakness in their own explanations.

Tajh asked, "Why's Padraig so important?"

Mark took advantage of Nan's ploy to press home their otherwise weak case. "Are you guys even beginning to realise the potential importance of all this? Grimstone is our common enemy. He has the Sword of Feimhin. He also has its keeper. If anybody understands the Sword's power and purpose it's going to be Padraig. We really have to find him *and* the Sword."

"You don't even know if he's still alive."

Nan said, "I believe we do know. Our power is the power of death. We believe that we would sense it if Padraig was dead."

"London is a very big place."

"Yeah—we know that." Mark fell silent.

Tajh helped him by changing the subject. "What happened to your sister, Mo?"

"She's still over there, on Tír."

"Aren't you worried about her?"

"Of course I'm worried about her. I'm worried about all of them, Alan, Kate and Mo."

Sharkey whistled through his teeth. "Hey—I don't know what you folks think about this, but I kind of believe them."

"Button it, Sharkey!" Cal finished his bottle with one swig and uncapped another one.

"No, I won't button it," Sharkey replied. "So, Mark, if I get this right, what you're saying is that whatever is happening right here in London is linked to the war and all that horror you encountered in Tír?"

"That's what I'm thinking. And now I'm wondering about something else—what if the best thing I can do to help my friends in the war on Tír, is to try to stop whatever he's planning with Grimstone on Earth?"

Mark gauged that Sharkey, like Cogwheel, couldn't possibly be ex-military. He looked and talked like a hippy. He was maybe six foot four and lean with a straggly moustache which merged with exuberant sideburns. He had gold studs in both ears and some of his tattoos, from what Mark could see, might have been Hindu gods. It was incongruous to Mark that someone with so peaceful a nature was also the guy who looked after the armaments of the heavy vehicle in the barn, the Mamma Pig. His weapon of choice was the submachine gun they had already seen, which he called an H-K MP5.

All of them, other than Cogwheel, were bikers. Mark had counted four heavy bikes within the camp: a Harley FLHTP and three BMW R1200s. According to Tajh, the BMWs were ex-police. The same model was popular with the Skulls, which might make them additionally useful if they were travelling in disguise.

Bull was built like the Hulk. He was extraordinarily broad-shouldered and was bald, with a few days' worth of brownish frizz over his beard area. There was a puckered scar on the left side of his face and the ring and little finger of his left hand were missing. His weapon was a belted machine gun called a Minimi, that was a lighter version of the Minimi mounted in the Mamma Pig. Bull rarely spoke. His eyes, which were blue and curiously gentle, never held Mark's for long. Mark doubted that Bull's silence was the result of shyness. The whole bunch of them were misfits—dangerous misfits.

In the morning, as Mark and Bull breakfasted on bacon and eggs and Sharkey and Cal were busy rigging something up in the adjacent field, Mark continued to probe for information about the crew.

"Tajh—is that her real name?"

Bull shovelled a forkful of bacon, egg and beans into his mouth, then shook his head, offering no reply.

"So everyone goes by a nickname?"

"Safer that way."

"Safer, how?"

"Safer for the crew—and safer for our friends and families. They get hold of one us, living or dead, they go hunting for contacts, relatives."

"Sounds grim."

"Uh-huh."

Mark digested that. "What's the story behind Big Ted?"

Sharkey had a teddy bear he called Big Ted. Mark had glimpsed it on his knee when he was listening to ambient music. Big Ted was a very small teddy bear with a tartan dickey around his neck. His fur was badly worn around what was left of his triangular snout and his left ear was partly chewed off. There were stains on the bear that could have been blood.

"You'd have to ask Sharkey about that."

With each answer Bull's eyes would lift to confront Mark's, then glide away from direct contact. Behind the banter, when Cal and Sharkey were also around, they and Bull seemed to have some unseen channel of communication. As far as Mark could see, their common interests were guns and bikes.

Mark stared at the nearby cluster of big bikes. "Bull—could you do me and Nan a big favour?"

"You can ask."

"We want to become active members of the crew. It would help if we could learn how to ride the bikes."

He laughed.

"Hah!" Cal interrupted the conversation from behind them. Mark hadn't even heard his approach. "Okay. You want to learn how to ride the bikes? First you get the chance to convince us of your trustworthiness."

Mark saw, now, what he and Sharkey had been doing in the field. They had set up three conventional targets perhaps sixty yards away, affixed to trees.

Cal handed Bull the lighter of the Minimis. "You want to show our friends what this baby can do without the help of magic?"

Bull climbed to his feet. He aimed and let off a rattle of fire that tore into one of the targets, scattering shreds into the air.

"Okay!" Cal said. "Now you go ahead magic man!"

Mark went back to the barn to get the Fir Bolg battleaxe. He stood in the same place Bull had. "It's a tiring thing to do and I'm half way to being exhausted already, but I'll attempt a single throw." He shifted his feet in a search of better balance and hefted the battleaxe in his left hand. Then he stretched back, taking a firm grip around the central stock. He focused on the distant target and his arm tensed, every muscle standing out. Then, in a streamlined movement that involved his entire body, he hurled the battleaxe, chanting a low-pitched mantra as he did so.

The battleaxe made a humming noise as it whirled, streaking through the air with astonishing speed. When it struck home the target disintegrated, as if struck by an explosive missile, but still the battleaxe continued to spin. It wheeled around in a wide arc and returned once more to Mark's upraised hand.

With grunts of awe, the crew gathered around him.

"I believe it is my turn," Nan spoke clearly.

If they expected her to borrow Mark's battleaxe they were mistaken. She confronted the third target, then closed her eyes for a moment. When she opened them again, her pupils and whites had expanded so her eyes were black, filled with tiny arabesques of silvery light that pulsated and changed.

"You had better step back," Mark cautioned the crew.

Nan's head and body were ensheathed in blue-black lightning. With a whip-crack detonation, a bolt of lightning burst from her brow and struck the third target, causing both the target and the supporting tree to explode into splinters.

Mark chuckled. "She's had a bit more practice than me."

Every member of the crew was staring at the target in astonishment. Mark heard Sharkey's half-hysterical bark of laughter. "Hey, baby—all hail! You guys got the magic. You want some bike lessons, first one's on me."

* * *

Nan hung behind when Mark went over to the bikes with Sharkey. Cogwheel, the only member of the crew still breakfasting, had come out to sit against the plank table in his wheelchair.

"What about you—what's your special role?"

"Me? Just the general factotum."

Nan heard an educated tone in Cogwheel's voice. "Factotum?"

"Driver, when they let me. Engineer—and inventor extraordinaire."

"What do you invent?"

"Let us say that I provide the brains, machine-wise. There's no shortage of brawn, as you have seen for yourself."

Nan smiled at him. "Would you care to show me?"

"If you wouldn't mind giving me a shove to that monster of a vehicle yonder, where I shall duly demonstrate."

Nan pushed Cogwheel through the open door and into the barn, past bench-mounted drills, lathes and other heavy maintenance machinery. She brushed her fingers over a narrow, high grille above the place where Cal had been welding the broken bull-bar.

"You have constructed this machine of war yourself?"

"Hardly—certainly not on my own. But I can claim some credit for the basic engineering and some of the add-ons."

"How enterprising!"

"Glad you think so. The truck started out more humbly, as a heavy duty Mercedes. We've been adding some interesting curlicues."

"Curlicues?"

"Making it our very own armour-plated personnel carrier."

"Armour-plated—ah, I understand."

"You're stroking 530 brake horsepower. Sixteen speed gearbox. Took us months to get hold of a European long wheelbase meant to pull twenty tons over the high passes in the Pyrenees or the Ardennes. The plating is half inch hardened steel—aimed to stop any shit except for armour piercing rounds. You're looking at fifteen tons and you can see it doesn't sit on the floor. Four by two, rigid axle base. And speed."

"Speed?"

"We disconnected the road speed limiter so it will top 70, downhill, with a following wind and despite its bulk. At low speed it would pull the front wall off a house."

Standing back, Nan admired the menacing vehicle, not that she understood anything Cogwheel had just said. With its steel walls camouflaged to look like some kind of official army ordinance and solid steel guillotine blades coming to a fearsome looking vee in front of the bonnet, it reminded her of the battering prow of a warship.

"Your idea?"

"My idea; Bull and Cal cannibalised the blades from a snow-plough."

"What do you intend to do with it?"

"Break through roadblocks."

Cogwheel used a remote to spring open the door on the driver's side of the cab, then used the same remote to bring a shelf lift down. He used his arms, biceps bulging, to transfer his paraplegic body to the shelf lift, then used the lift to ferry himself up to the level of the cab. Nan watched him transfer into the driver's seat, then shut the door. His grinning face looked down at her through the opened side window.

"You intend to take the fight to them?" she said.

"That's the plan."

"May I come up there to join you?"

"Be my guest."

She went around the cab and climbed three steps to open the opposite door. Cogwheel flicked a switch to illuminate the interior. There was more space in the cab than she had imagined and room enough to seat three people comfortably. The main body of the truck contained weapons and ammunition. He indicated the mounts, at the front and rear, for the heavy machine gun.

"The wheelchair—the accident was due to this war?"

"I wish. It was a road traffic accident, when drunk."

Nan leaned her left elbow on the dashboard and her head on the hand. She looked Cogwheel in the eyes. "Tell me about Cal."

He shifted uncomfortably. "Oh—pathologically anally retentive."

"What is this anally retentive?"

"You'd better ask your boyfriend."

"Tell me more about the enemy."

"The Goonies are light on brains. They piss around and murder people because the guys in power don't give a shit anymore."

"Goonies?"

"The paramilitaries and Skulls. They use roadblocks to control people. Stop and search so they can rob, rape, murder. With the Mamma Pig we can go looking for their roadblocks."

Nan blinked, thoughtful. She peered at three tiny human figurines sculpted out of papier mâché, and guessed that Cogwheel had fashioned them. "What do these represent?"

"Faith, hope and charity."

"What you call the three virtues?"

Cogwheel stared into space through the windscreen. "Not that I have come across much evidence of such."

"You are agnostic, I think."

"Takes one to know one."

Nan laughed. "And now—you can start her up?"

The cab vibrated with a powerful thrust, letting Nan know about it through the entire length of her spine.

"You feel that?"

She laughed, enjoying the vibration in her throat as she spoke. "But tell me about Sharkey. He seems different?"

"We don't ask too many questions here, but he claims to have some Indian blood in him. I refer to the country, India, and not the Native Americans. Different, you said. More like weird. He and Bull come as a package.

Those two gentlemen have been, shall we say, making havoc together."

"They are—how do you say it—gay?"

Cogwheel laughed. "Gay? I doubt it, in either sense of the word. More like natural born killers with good reason for their anger."

"Cal is a warrior?"

Cogwheel laughed at the term, toying with a spot on the windscreen. He spat on his finger and wiped it off. "No questions, remember. But you ask me, I'd guess ex-military, without a shadow of a doubt."

"So the answer is yes. He is a warrior?"

"If I'm right, most likely SAS. Which means he would be expert in stealth operations—operations behind enemy lines."

"And Tajh?"

"Our funky Amazonian woman?"

"Tajh must have a special skill?"

"Communications."

"So Cal's the officer. Bull and Sharkey—they're the warriors. You're the brains. And Tajh is communications?"

"Communications is a major problem. We have to be watchful, all the time. You don't know who to believe, what messages to trust. You get paranoid about the increasing number of crews being hit. You have to go on your instincts."

Nightmare Visions

Penny was staring at the Scalpie's dagger. She was sitting on the platform in the map room, her knees drawn up to cradle the case, rocking to and fro, her head clasped between her outstretched fingers. The platform was perched at an arm's reach from the ceiling, within easy drawing and painting distance. Her eyes followed the spiral blade, forged out of a black somewhat fibrous-looking metal she didn't recognise. She stared, her breath arrested, at the glowing symbol in the hilt. That the dagger was special—special and magical—she had no doubt. Who could have forged such a thing? Penny had no answer to that any more than she had the answer to an even more pertinent and scary question: why had the Scalpie tried to kill Mark?

Studying the dagger, immersing her being in its powerful presence, she was beginning to see through it to the underlying pattern. She was following the flow of it over the streets and underground.

Gully interrupted her musing. He was standing in the open doorway leading in from the vestibule. Penny made a pocket of her knees and her body, so he couldn't see she was examining the dagger.

"I got you some medical shampoo—an' a comb for the nits."

"Go away, Gully."

"Why you neglectin' yourself, gel?"

"Stop calling me gel."

"I know you been obsessin' again with that dagger."

She whined and squeezed down on her head. If only Gully would stop pestering her so she could sketch the ideas that were proliferating inside her mind.

"You're goin' cuckoo, Penny. You got to stop this."

"I won't stop it."

"Why not? Why won't you?"

"I just can't."

From the moment she had met Mark and Nan—from when she had seen the black triangles take fire in their brows—she had sensed the importance of their presence. She knew then, she just knew, absolutely, that she had been right all along. Something really cool was happening, something very exciting . . . and scary. The clue to understanding it was underground.

The pattern, the labyrinth, was there, if she could only figure it out.

“There ain’t no bleedin’ City Below. That’s just some kind of a daydream.”

“Shut up, Gully, please?”

“No, I ain’t shutting up. No way, gel.”

“You will if I tell you.”

“How you goin’ to make me then?”

“Oh, Gully, it’s not just a dream. It’s a labyrinth. I’ve been finding my way through it. I can see the way, inside my head.”

“Wot you talking about? It’s just them silly maps an’ things.”

“The maps are showing me the way.”

“The way to cloud cuckoo land.”

“You’re not helping me, Gully. I need to focus.”

“Only a month or two since you got that plaster off your arm. I can’t keep looking out for you, gel.”

“I’ll be careful. I won’t do any more climbing.”

“Just come down ’ere an’ forget about all that. I’ll brew us a cuppa.”

“Not just now. Gully, I can’t.”

“Why not? What’s the matter with you?” His voice was plaintive, pitiful. These days Gully sounded pitiful a lot of the time.

He reached up, as if to touch the back of her hand, but she withdrew it, her hand clawing up under its own will, like a crab retracting its claws.

"You're breaking the rules."

"Wot rules?"

She knew as she said it how it would provoke him, but she had to say it. "You mustn't touch me. You know I can't bear to be touched."

The hurt was plain on his face. "Can't bear to be touched!" He left her then, so she couldn't witness the tears in his eyes. She heard his voice trail out into the main room. "Them's your rules, Penny. Them rules is plain cuckoo."

Penny squeezed a fraction forward on the board, rocking backwards and forwards, blinking repeatedly. Why did he always have to go and spoil things?

When she climbed the awkward gantry it felt as if she were knocking on the door to heaven. Gully had constructed the gantry for her. He had put it all together so she wouldn't go falling off the steps again. Everything she needed was already up here, to help her capture her visions. The marker pens and crayons, the chalks and paints. Why then, after he had made the wonder possible for her, was he still moping about and upsetting her when she needed quiet and serenity to draw and paint? Why couldn't he accept that she was his friend? Why did he need to touch her? Touching was too close, too intrusive. Why couldn't he see that living together in Our Place was only possible if they allowed one another enough space?

She stared at the dagger in the box in her lap for several more minutes, breathing in and out through dilated nostrils. Even though she felt the need rising in her, she could only create in the stillness. She had to clear her mind of the confusion and upset so the vision would emerge. Arguing with Gully was so distracting. There were things she didn't understand about people—like that obsession with sex. Animals did not do sex, they rutted. Father had explained that to her, when she had asked him about it after the lesson at school. He had been annoyed that she had been subjected to the lesson without his permission. That was why he had taken her into his study and sat her down in the chair.

Sex, he said, was a thing invented by people for some peculiar and unpleasant purpose. She repeated his expression now, word for word, enunciating it clearly.

"For some peculiar and unpleasant purpose."

That was the trouble with people. They invented things for peculiar and unpleasant purposes.

Gully didn't understand. He had just got the idea into his head that he wanted to be like those unfathomable people and try the sex. What Penny needed was not the sex Gully wanted, but the exaltation of *being*. Even after she had stared at the dagger and fixed its image in her mind she had to close her eyes for several more seconds so she could assimilate what she had captured of the vision.

Gully had prepared the map room ceiling for her, over-painting the soot and water-stained surface with a thick and creamy magnolia paint. Magnolia was super. It meant she could highlight subtly in white. She could feel the rapture as her mind became one with the vision. She could see the places that were part of the vision clearly enough to begin to sketch them. Extracting the pens from the bag that dangled from a hook on the gantry, she began to apply the images with a confident hand, stroke by stroke, in true and perfect delineations. And so the map was extended. Her perspective varied because there were vignettes, particular buildings, or a frontage, or a feature—such as Cleopatra's Needle—which deserved to be captured in three dimensions, and sometimes even in full colour. In places she was obliged to show not merely the grandeur and the architectural artistry, but also the spirit of their beauty and essence.

That was what the City Above demanded of her. The people out there, the people Gully sold the sketches to—the lady vicar, Mrs. Patel at the corner shop, the woman at the Post Office—all those who bought her drawings because they liked them or they could sell them to their customers, they could see what she was trying to capture in the drawings. But they would be mortified if they knew about the other city; the City Below, that was entirely different. That was where the City Above concealed its secrets.

And now, with the dagger cradled in her lap, it was this darker animal, these sloshing guts and waterworks and liver and kidneys, that she began to fill in. She did so with the same dexterity and vision. It was as if her spirit had taken control of her fingers. She drew and drew, her eyes wide and shining. She could smell those vitally important innards, like blood and digestive juices. She could hear their gut moans, their contractions, their slivering, gliding movements over one another, their valves and sphincters opening and closing. The City Below was alive too, alive in a deeper and darker way than the City Above, powerful and vigorous. She had read about famous artists who had realised the same truth. Stubbs, who had discovered the soul spirit in his horses through dissecting them. And Leonardo da Vinci, who had also searched under the skin of humans, of men and women, even pregnant mothers with their unborn babies.

And then there were the spirits that roamed it, that lived in the tissues of the heart and lungs, the guts and the entrails. Dark spirits as might be expected to inhabit an underworld; hungry spirits that burrowed and gorged their way into the world of light; beings with wings, vast hordes of them. Through her pencils and brushes they came alive, sometimes partially concealed, or just emerging from the darker layers, and all in between. There were scaly-skinned males with white ovals for eyes; she saw one of them in the disgusting act of sex, reaching for the waist of a horned and winged woman. She saw others, their grotesque faces rising out of the carapaces of crabs, or insects, their expressions of need so very intense. And then the field of her mind simply filled up to capacity with shapes, too many to draw in a hundred years, swarms within swarms, massing, taking to the air, piping and wailing, others resembling a flock of misshapen birds, or monsters with the heads of fish and bodies of Venuses or Adonises, or the rush of scaly fanged demons out of a crack in hell's roof.

Something was calling them and they were responding, emerging in triumph, bursting through with the sheer pressure of bodies, urging one another out into the freedom of night so they could prey upon the blinkered, unheeding City Above.

Gully climbed the spiral iron ladder up to the roof. The concrete was skiddy because of the bird shit. Once on the roof, in the steady downpour and the cold, he scattered the corn. Night was falling and soon it would be a lot colder. It'd be a lot skiddier too because of the ice and maybe, judging from that sky, there might even be snow. That would make it easier to slither accidentally down the sloping roof and end up tumbling through that widening crack in the ceiling. He wiped his running nose on the snotrag from right pocket 2 and he watched the pigeons alight and take off again. They were so graceful he delighted in watching them, up here, on the roof of Our Place. He fed and watched them for several more minutes, his mind empty of anything except the ballet of them flapping their wings as they landed and making that knocking sound as they took off again.

He wiped his nose again, a good, long wipe, and looked up into the dark through the rain. "Poor little birdies. You ain't got much, but you got them wings and that's all as you need. You can fly away, and that's perfick."

Kneeling down in the wet, he set up a basket with holes in the side and scattered the corn under it, lifting it up on one edge, which he propped up with a piece of kindling tied to a string. Then he pulled back into the shadows of the stairwell and waited for Big Ben to strike. Up where he was, the sound carried for miles. As soon as the clanging began he consulted his two watches, one on each wrist. As he suspected, it was the left one needed correcting. It had lost two minutes and a bit in twenty-four hours. He had to hold the face up close to his eyes so he could correct it before checking the basket out. Two birdies—the blessing of patience. He hauled on the string.

Once he had captured the plumper one and folded back the flapping wings so he could hold it snug inside his coat, he let the other go.

"There you are!" he said, as he stared up into the rain, watching its flight.

Penny was daft if she thought he couldn't see that box in her lap. He saw it easy enough, and the way she was going to such trouble to hide it from him. That box, and that dagger—they frightened Gully. They scared him shitless.

"It's okay, me dahlin!" he whispered. "You an' me, we're still friends, but wot it is, you see, Penny 'n' me, we got to eat. I ain't about to hurt you. Honest."

After he had wrung its neck he sat on the iron steps for a while, just thinking on things, his hooded head poking up into the growing dark and the rain. He thought about his argument with Penny in particular.

Now just cause you're frightened of that dagger, don't you go back in there an' go pesterin' the gel.

"No! I shan't."

But he didn't rightly know if he could stop himself.

You're lucky—you know that?

"I know."

You don't deserve 'er.

Never in his life would he have had the courage to befriend a real live gel like Penny by himself. Gels was so different.

You just can't tell wot they're thinking.

Smoke was rising through the ruin from the dossers on the ground floor far below. It was swirling up through a crack before being blown away by the wind. Out there it became lost in the darkening sky. Gully could hear shrieks in the distance. Another Razzamatazz. Soon there would be even more smoke, lots of it, and billowing flames lighting up the sky.

In bright daylight there would have been the tiniest glimpse of St. Paul's in the distance, just one piece of its bowl-like roof. Gully had seen the ghosts and wraiths that Penny had drawn all creeping and crawling around the cathedral, another of her nightmare imaginings in the smoky, uncertain air.

"Instead of criticising me, you should be helping me," Penny would say.

"I would if I knew how."

"Oh, you're so useless, Gully."

"I ain't allitrack."

"You're not literate just because you can print your name."

"That ain't fair."

"Why didn't they teach you at school?"

Gully hadn't learnt much at school. The fact was he hadn't seen much of school, not with his junkie mum. He remembered being hungry and the drunkenness and the beatings. Care, the people called the new place he went to when they put her in jail. Care and foster homes. But there hadn't been much care or much fostering in neither. There wasn't no memories there he wanted to revisit. The only thing he wanted to remember was his nan, who got him away from them when he was twelve. She was the only one called him "dahlin." She had tried to explain the readin' an' writin' before she got this teacher in, an' he told her he had that condition called dyslectrica. It was one a them words that put a fine end to things, that put you into a hole and covered you up, like leprosy, where you rotted away an' your nose and your fingers fell off.

That was why he couldn't help Penny. The dyslectrica, but she stayed friends with him in spite of it. They lived together, in Our Place. An' there was ways in which she wasn't so clever herself. Streetwise ways she was kind of dyslectric. An' that meant he had to take care of her.

Deadly Intentions

Kate wasn't quite sure if she was dreaming or if she was experiencing visions more dangerous than a dream. Her body, her entire being, felt weightless, borne along in a thick drifting ether. In this dream, or vision, she was meandering through an eerie landscape constructed out of crystals resembling black ice, passing through streets that didn't run true but wandered about in the organic ways of streams or tracks made by animals in a wilderness. But wilderness was too benign; these streets and the buildings that lined them with their scratchy-edged darkness, had an overwhelmingly threatening feel to them. Her every movement through this landscape violated her being, as if she were being forced to do it.

I'm lost, Kate thought.

Her last memory was of lying down next to the Momu within the entwining roots of the One Tree. But this was a different place entirely. Wherever and whatever this place was, there was a dreadfully cold and calculated quality to it, as if it were the territory, deliberately planned and constructed, of a hostile mind. A trap—a trap as deliberate and deadly as the web of a spider. And its intention, she sensed, was equally dreadful.

<It is the Land of the Dead.>

"What?" she whispered, uncertain who, if anybody, had spoken to her.

<It is the Land of the Dead.>

Kate looked around, but the words had come from nowhere. The notion of such a place and the sense of grief and hopelessness that those words carried, struck Kate like a physical blow. She shivered. How was it possible that she could feel herself shiver, when she knew she had no physical substance here? She looked around again, but there was nobody close, no presence she could see that might have accounted for the voice. She was no longer sure that she had heard it. The silence was unnerving. A sense of threat clutched at her heart.

At first she thought this new creepy city was uninhabited, but then she began to see figures, or imagined she did. They looked so wan and pale, little more than skin and bone, their clothes hanging from their wasted limbs like the wind-blown rags of scarecrows.

She was blinking rapidly, as if she were waking up after falling asleep for a while, or perhaps she merely imagined it.

Kate didn't know if it were possible to sleep, but she was aware, somehow, of the passage of time. During the time she had arrived and the present, a shade had come to stand before her. The shade had a slender feminine shape, as grey as a shadow, but with a definite face in which two almond-shaped eyes, black and liquidly glistening like bubbles of tar, were regarding her. Her clothing, including the hood that enfolded her head, was filmy, like cobwebs, with an uncertain separation between material and the underlying flesh.

"Who are you? Was it you who spoke to me earlier?"

"I am all that remains of a poor succubus."

Kate studied the creature's pallid blue and grey face, struggling to find any focus in the amalgam of planes and angles it presented. Open wounds of some past injury were livid scarlet lines on the flesh.

"You're what? Did you say succubus?"

"A truly undeserving creature was I. Punished for my imperfection."

"What do you mean?"

"I was blemished by kindness."

"You were punished because you were kind?"

"My Mistress—the Great Witch—she would test us, examine our faces, our bodies as we developed, our voices, our reactions. We were created to seduce. When she discovered one that was imperfect, she drove the flawed one out of her tower. Out into that terrible place."

Kate's heart fell. She remembered the dreadful hinterland that had surrounded the Tower of Bones.

"But men—they would have been attracted by your kindness."

"Men were attracted to me. I was a most diligent succubus, but I could not hurt my prey. Such was my flaw."

"What happened?"

"I was expelled and hunted by the stealers of souls. I tried to save my soul from them, but then she punished me further—I was condemned to become what you now see of me, a wraith, haunting the Land of the Dead."

"Do you remember dying?"

The tormented spirit shook her head. "I have no memory of the actual moment—only of waking to find myself here."

"Then you don't really know if you are alive or dead?"

"I know this is the Land of the—"

"Dead." Kate interrupted her. "So you say, but perhaps they only intend for you to believe that. How do you really know you're dead?"

"I don't recall . . . only my name, Elaru."

"Elaru?"

The spectre blinked.

Kate reflected on this for a moment. "My name is Kate."

"Kate." The shade smiled, a haunting wisp of a smile, as if it were the most precious thing in the world merely to exchange names. "Have you, Kate, looked around you? Have you seen what place this is?"

"It could be designed to mislead—a trick."

"Can you remember your journey here?"

Kate didn't need to think about that. "I have no memory of it at all. All I can recall was that I was lying in the roots of the One Tree."

Kate was now suspicious. Elaru was a succubus—a being who would make a sly use of her wiles. Was this so-called blemish of kindness a trick intended to ensnare her? She said: "But I know I'm not dead."

"You think not. And yet you find yourself wandering through this terrible landscape, as if lost. It is not safe to wander in this place."

"Elaru—what are you, really?"

"You mean, what have I become? I fear I am a phantom."

"But here, what is your purpose here? Why have I met you? Are you some kind of spirit guide?"

"I might be, if you so wish. You drift into danger even as we speak. The shadowed doorway, which beckons you, Mistress, it is not a place you should enter."

Kate's breath caught in her throat. She realised that the succubus was right. She was being drawn towards the enormous arched doorway of a cathedral-like edifice in the distance. She sensed danger emanating from it; a dreadful malice.

"Oh, Mistress—you must be newly dead."

"I'm not dead."

This provoked that haunting smile again, a rictus on those fissured lips in the ravaged face.

"Why else would you be here, in this terrible place?"

Kate felt her heart miss a beat. Was she dead? How could she feel things so physically if she were dead, like the succubus? She summoned up her courage, willing her heart to beat normally.

"Did somebody send you to find me?"

"I . . . I do not know."

"Is there somebody—some being—in control of this dreadful place?"

"I cannot explain."

"You cannot, or dare not?"

The lips of the succubus trembled. "It is not safe to ask such questions here."

"Why not?"

"Be wary, Mistress. Oh, do be wary. I have learned—and 'tis a lesson learned from the bitterest of experiences—that tormented though one's existence might be, it might become more terrible still."

A wave of fear moved through Kate's breast. She considered what the succubus was telling her. "I'm looking for a friend."

Her words provoked a ripple of emotion in the damaged succubus. "Such devotion, if you speak true! To pass through death's portal for the sake of a friend! Would that I had such as you for a friend!"

Was Elaru playing a game with her? Kate wasn't sure. Elaru spoke as if she were terrified even though her eyes were utterly flat, unchanging. It reminded Kate of the time she had seen a dead lamb in a ditch back home. Its face was crawling with bluebottle flies but, being dead, it did not flick an ear or blink. There was that same lack of reaction on the succubus' face; as if all interest in the world, all curiosity and all feeling, had been abandoned.

"This friend I'm looking for isn't dead, or, at least, I don't know if she is dead or not. She was taken—absorbed—by the roots of the One Tree."

"I know nothing of such things."

Kate looked at that ravaged face again. She wondered what those all-black eyes had seen, what strange and frightening things. She guessed, for no rational reason at all, that Elaru's eyes might have been a pearly grey in life. And since succubi were, by birth, both beautiful and deceptive, Kate had to guess that those grey eyes would have been well practised in reflecting emotions not actually felt. This unfortunate being had been designed to be cruel and devoid of empathy for the men she seduced—but she had crossed the paths of a being much crueller still.

"Please—will you be my guide? Will you help me to find her? I must save my friend. A whole people, a whole civilisation, depends on it."

"What do such considerations matter here?"

"Perhaps you might direct me where to look?"

"What would you do for me in return?"

"I can't promise anything."

The spirit of the succubus smiled again with a terrible twist of her charcoal-lined mouth, exposing black fangs.

"I have nothing to give you. If I had I would."

"I cannot help but notice that bauble in your brow. Why, it appears to glow a perfect emerald. How beautiful it is, how lovely. It's the only thing of loveliness in this cheerless place."

Kate shook her head, or thought she did so. "With or without your help, I'm going to search for my friend. Come with me, or don't bother. If you won't guide me I'll find her on my own."

She was lost—*lost!*

The feeling of desolation had returned the instant she discovered this. Kate was angry with herself for engaging in argument with the succubus. And now, dear God, she had no idea what trouble she was in. It felt as if the prevailing darkness had swallowed her whole. As if . . . No—she refused to be cowed.

I demand to wake up!

There was a pinpoint of light that expanded, within the splinter of a moment, into a figure she recognised. A kneeling figure that might be female, or one that only appeared so in her mind, one whose eyes reflected a nacreous opalescence inside a veil.

A keeper.

<Nothing here is ever quite as it seems.>

"I'm just beginning to realise that."

<There are powers that fight without cease.>

Kate became aware of confrontations and enormous rivalries all around her; the slithering movement of titanic powers embracing, or fusing with another, or maybe slithering by one another. Powers belonging to beings of such magnitude they were unknowable. Kate felt ordinary and defenceless in such proximity. She felt humanly vulnerable, and alone.

She felt impelled to explain herself.

"The Momu asked me for help to save her world. I refused to help her because the safety of my friends came first. So I blame myself in part—I contributed to the ruin of the Cill's last surviving city. I feel obliged to make amends."

<In what way would you make amends?>

"I must save the Momu. Save her people, the Cill."

<For such a lofty ambition you will have to be one with the mysteries.>

Kate thought: *What was it Elaru said about asking questions in the Land of the Dead?* "I'm not a deity. I have some power of healing. How then am I going to achieve that?"

<You have naïve notions of good and evil, of life and death.>

"Why don't you put me right?"

<Through your love of the Cill and your respect for the Momu, through the power that was bequeathed to you and through the guile of your human imagination,

you can look for understanding. And through understanding discover the grace to allow Life to beget itself again.>

Kate blinked, exhausted. Why was the keeper telling her these things? She wasn't sure that she understood any of this. Did the key to the great mysteries lie in the ordinary?

"Why would a keeper help a mortal?"

Her question provoked a lengthy silence from the keeper—one in which Kate imagined those reflecting eyes change. For a moment they became blue-black; mirrors of darkness, seeing through her.

<Our being, from time immemorial, was created to observe. To do so, truly and objectively, we are obliged to be neutral. Yet there is one who would subvert that sacred trust.>

"What do you mean? Oh, I imagine you are talking about the Tyrant."

<Do you have any idea of the danger here?>

"Can you not advise me?" Kate looked around her, but still there was nothing solid to use as an anchor. She was engaged in this perplexing conversation in a place that, seemingly, did not exist.

"You said I was being too naïve."

<Do you imagine you can create a new world without the immensities?>

Kate was startled into thinking about what that might mean: good versus evil, life versus death? She didn't know what to think.

“Please help me. Tell me what to do.”

<The Witch wraith would have you believe that this is the Land of the Dead. Where then is the beauty within?>

Those auger-like pinpoints of darkness penetrated the opacity of that terrible gaze again.

“I don’t understand.”

<Understand, then, that a succubus, even thus reduced to spirit, might yet retain the art of deception.>

“But they are all dead. Their mistress, the Great Witch, is destroyed. I saw Alan destroy her with my own eyes.”

<Succubi are enchantresses. I have witnessed one bewitch a lion, so it consumed its own mate.>

“But even so . . .”

<Prudently, you were suspicious from the first moment that you encountered this spirit. A spirit of an enchantress consigned to the Land of the Dead—even as she was consigned to extinction by her creator.>

“What are you implying?”

<I do not imply, any more than I advise. I merely record.>

Kate tried to figure out what the keeper was telling her. Was the succubus still guided by her instinct to seduce?

“I give up. I’m too stupid to understand.”

Was there something else, something important, something so slippery that she was failing to grasp it in her mind? She tried to get her confused thoughts in order and readjust her focus; to look with new eyes on all that she had witnessed in the Land of the Dead.

Did she imagine it or was there a sigh of vexation from the keeper?

I have to understand. Everything depends on my understanding what is happening here.

"Granny Dew!" She shrieked the name, hurled it into the confusion in which she whirled and spun.

<I cannot help you here. You must think harder, child.>

<But think of what?> Kate spoke to Granny Dew mind to mind.

<Consider the forces that seek to outwit you.>

<The Witch is gone. Only the Tyrant remains.>

<The Tyrant indeed.>

<What are you trying to say? That in rescuing the Momu I am opposing his will? I might be helping Alan's purpose in defeating him?>

<Is this not your destiny?>

<Yes, but how am I to oppose him?>

<Remember the immensities!>

Setting Out

Straightening his back, Alan clung to the saddle that was perched between the powerful shoulder humps of the onkkh. The Garg king rode beside him, having taken Alan by surprise earlier when he offered to accompany him to the outer reaches of the city. Zelnesakkk was similarly mounted, but even with his wings folded, he still crouched like a tensed spring, ready to launch himself at a foe. Alan couldn't imagine the High Shaman, Mahteman, suffering the heaving and rolling of the ugly bird for the sake of etiquette. The King was gazing out to his right, to where the last battalions of the Shee army were pouring out of the transport ships into a choppy ocean, grey as slate.

"Never have I witnessed such a war fleet, in all my years of existence," Zelnesakkk said.

Carpeting the waves as far as the horizon, the accumulated fleet appeared to fill the ocean. A good third of the fleet comprised carriers, already preparing to set sail, with the objective of rejoining the war at the walls of Ghork Mega after disgorging themselves of the food and provisions that would be needed for a hungry army on the march. Those provisions were now packaged and strapped onto the backs of thousands of onkkh. Other ships in the fleet were cannon-bedecked fighting craft that would come into play when they laid siege to the city. It was an army calculated to bring an end to a war that had devastated Tír for more than two thousand years. Alan had learned much from his time in Tír and he now knew when to withhold his opinions and listen. He turned to the Garg king. "You have wisdom, and its equal in experience. Do you have any advice for me in the war to come, Sir?"

"Can you imagine how irksome it might be that one who has brought such grief to my heart would now ask my counsel?" The king's words emerged with a ratchety rattling of the gill-like openings on either side of his lengthy throat.

Alan stared ahead in silence.

"You were cunning with the eclipse. Did my son assist you?"

"We had warning, but not from Iyezzz. We have adepts of our own."

"If Mahteman spies are to be believed, even the queen has been assisting you."

"You are mistaken, Sir. The queen allowed me to witness a beautiful ceremony—but nothing more than that."

It was hard to concentrate when the retching induced by the rise and fall of the beast was worse than the rocking of a boat at sea. The onkkh were the most ungainly animals Alan had ever seen, like a cross between an ostrich and a camel, if twice as big as either animal. How long was it going to take him to get used to this rocking and pitching? He dreaded riding the beast for the nine-hundred miles that lay ahead of them. In any case, he was far from sure it was truly a bird, in spite of the feathers; the scaly skin of its neck and head and the thick muscular legs with their flared three-toed feet more resembled a lizard. And no ostrich sported the retractable claws that sprang out of those toes when the beasts became riled—or took to their poisonous spitting. And the onkkh riled and spat very readily.

Thankfully, those enormous claws, retracted to suit the sandy beach surface, would be handy in the ascent of the Flamestruck Mountains that lay, like crouching predators, across the landward horizon. He also had to admit that the onkkhs' muscular shoulders—like the humps of a camel back home—made excellent baggage carriers, with many baskets made of whalebone and webbing hanging from them. It was an amusing thought that Qwenqwo, Mo and Turkeya—and maybe Magtokk too, although currently invisible—were similarly mounted within this ungainly baggage train.

Zelnesakkk growled, "I am not sure I believe you. For reasons that escape me, my son has befriended you. I cannot fathom how one properly learned and devoted to Eyrie lore and traditions could bear to be close to your human stink. Yet I must remind myself that your companion, Greeneyes, made fertile the land and restored hope to my kingdom. It is in recognition of this alone that I help you."

Alan was too nauseated to reply immediately. As if to add insult to his silence, the onkkh chose this moment to fart long and loudly.

The king turned his head to confront Alan eye to eye. "This war you undertake would daunt the most adventuresome of warriors. Do you consider yourself invincible?"

Alan said, quietly, "The Tyrant of the Wastelands killed my parents."

"Ah." Those reptilian eyes widened. "It is comforting to know that you, too, suffer inconsolable loss."

"Sir—I respect your grief and I regret the part I played in it, yet your son died in battle fighting for my enemy, and you know, in your heart, that he is your enemy too. Do you have any more helpful counsel?"

"Mahteman is right, you are insolent beyond endurance. Perhaps I should be content that you face certain death."

Zelnesakkk was probably right, but how could Alan mitigate such a threat? Every time they had challenged the Tyrant he had responded in a way they had not anticipated.

The bitter king had fallen into silence.

Gazing out over the bay, with its sand dunes and protrusions of black volcanic rock, Alan saw that it was now dense with Shee, still humanoid in shape, but robed and uniformed to accommodate Garg sensibilities. Though the Shee homeland of the Guhttan Mountains, in the far northeast of continental Monisle, remained unconquered, they had been preparing for this day for generations. He wondered if the martyred high architect, Ussha De Danaan, former ruler of that continent, had foreseen this final stage in a two-thousand-year war.

As the spiritual leader of the continent of Monisle, the De Danaan had been the nemesis of the Tyrant. Yet she had allowed the Tyrant's forces to take over great cities such as Isscan, on the confluence of the rivers Snowmelt and Tshis Cole, and prevented the Shee from opposing his army as it overwhelmed the spiritual capital, Ossierel. There, the Tyrant's forces had massacred her ruling council and sacrificed the De Danaan on the fabled silver gates. The high architect, from what Alan had come to understand, had developed a final desperate plan that went beyond her own death. For an ordinary guy like him, coming from Earth, the idea of having plans that went beyond death seemed bizarre, but this was no ordinary world where logic reigned. This was a world where magic was paramount. Here, there was a power that ruled above all—a power that could even destroy demigods—and De Danaan's plans had included Alan and his friends. It had been Ussha De Danaan, last high architect of Ossierel, who had brought the four friends here.

A discordant blaring, deep and plaintive, brought his attention back to the departure. A band of Gargs were performing a ceremony of farewell within a grove of trees. Alan wondered whether it was in honour of the war ahead, or in relief that such an enormous force of former enemies would soon be leaving their capital city. He looked inland, across the shore with its dunes of sand as white as bleached bones, to the grove of strange trees with leaves of glittering silver. The fact that the Gargs were deeply spiritual had been a revelation—one that shamed him now when he looked back at how he had first regarded them. The foliage of the trees tinkled with a chime-like music that reminded him of the dream journey Qwenqwo had conjured up for them, taking them back to the fall of Ossierel. But unlike the musical trees he recalled from Ossierel, this was strange, discordant music. In the rising cliff of rocks that formed a crescent behind the trees, Gargs were opening up natural tunnels to capture the powerful inshore breezes. In the mouths of the tunnels they had set up a strange woodwind orchestra, a miscellany of interesting driftwood shapes: hollow logs with fibrous strings stretched across them, reminiscent of harps, or banks of gourds of varying sizes arranged like the pipes of organs. The assemblage captured the wind, amplifying the sounds of nature in a bizarre counterpoint to the tinkling of the leaves. Arriving at a suitable headland, Alan hauled back on the reins, arresting his beast. He looked around at the winding column of onkkh below him, four abreast and miles long, that led north along the Jourlanaaa River's valley. Then he turned to the sky where hundreds of high-flying Gargs were advancing with them; the proffered allies and scouts led by Zelnesakkk's son, Iyezzz. He narrowed his eyes to pick out the Garg prince himself at the forward tip of the huge vee formation, almost invisible against the changing light where narrow strips of clouds captured the rising sun along their edges.

Zelnesakkk, who had also halted his beast, held his silence.

What a glorious sight the prince will behold in the march ahead, Alan thought. The great bowl of calderas that, while impressive in themselves, were merely the foothills of the mighty Flamestrucks, reflected many shades of blue, grey and violet that enveloped the tidal estuary on which the city had evolved. He realised that the Garg orchestra was now humming—a wordless lament to be added to the natural sounds of the wind blowing through the caves and trees.

A mile wide at this point, the Jourlanaaa snaked down into the bay following the contours of the foothills. Perhaps the most amazing feature of all was the greening that proliferated over its banks, swarming over the surrounding foothills. Alan could see how Kate had impressed Zelnesakkk and his people: the whole area had recently been desert and was now a swarming density of vegetation.

All Kate's work.

It amazed Alan to witness her influence still operating here, changing things for the better. On a day of frantic preparation, this healing of a wounded land affected him deeply and made him love her all the more. Where was she? What the hell was keeping her from rejoining him on the march? He was still thinking about Kate when Bétaald approached, her dark-skinned face aglow with anticipation. It was Bétaald who had bade the Kyra and her army delay the transformation of the Shee until they were beyond the city boundaries. Her bow was addressed to the silent Zelnesakkk, who did her the honour of alighting from his onkkh. Even then, the Garg king was a good two feet taller than Bétaald. He returned her bow, but did not speak—neither was fluent in the language of the other. Instead he turned his face to the sky where his wife and Iyezzz's mother, Queen Shah-nur-Kian, was swooping down to alight by her husband's side. Within minutes they were joined on the headland by their son.

"I hope you have had sufficient instruction with the onkkh?"

Alan smiled somewhat ruefully at the Queen. He had had no more than an hour's instruction from Iyezzz, but even in so short a time he had discovered how different an onkkh was from a horse. One had to perch in the space between left and right humps, legs stretched out on either side of the creature's neck—and a scaly neck at that, as rough as the skin of an alligator.

A trumpeting from the river valley evoked an answering call from the Kyra, who was standing on a nearby headland.

Alan allowed himself a final glance out to sea at the extraordinary panorama of the great ships, many with sails unfurled, making ready to depart. The ceremony on shore had been timed to take advantage of the tide. His attention moved back to the foreshore, as a new command, mind-to-mind, came through the oraculum of Bree on the Kyra's brow.

The huge army began to loosen ranks, fanning out to flank the onkkh columns, the shifting of so many heavy feet provoking a billowing storm of sand. The band of Gargs blew on conches while others among them were hurrying to and fro as if in anticipation. The aides, small, intense women who assisted the Shee in organising and planning, walked alongside. They were experienced with both the manufacture of weapons and all of the complex logistics that war involved.

The head of the column had reached the outskirts. The sight of a hundred thousand marching Shee was breathtaking—and for Alan, somewhat heartbreaking. He wondered how many of them would survive. What arrogance entitled him to expect such life-or-death loyalty from so many brave souls? If he had ever thought it, now he saw it before his eyes on this beach: they were heading into what, for Tír, was a world war.

Only when he could control his emotions was Alan able to turn back to express his gratitude and bid farewell to the king and queen. There was no question of an embrace, or even a handshake.

"Sir—despite our differences, I would like to thank you on behalf of the Shee army for suffering our presence here in your beautiful capital city. And most respectfully and humbly, I thank you with all my heart for providing the onkkh and the Garg scouts for our impending march."

"You can thank my son for all of it."

"Yet without your sanction, and that of your graceful lady queen, it would not have happened."

The king spoke curtly. "You cost me my eldest son. If you would offer gratitude to myself and the queen, do so by returning our youngest son to us."

The angry king looked to the skies, his gaze finding the Garg lookouts that now wheeled and soared high above, already watchful for danger or attack, even at this early stage of their adventure.

"Sir, Madam—be assured that we'll keep you informed of our progress through messengers among your scouts."

At a command from the Kyra's oraculum the metamorphosis began. Alan watched the thrilling spectacle unfold. The Shee flowed like a living stream, with its own powerful movements and rhythms, in a continuous undulation of massed muscles, sinew, claws and fangs. He saw huge columns of tigresses, lionesses, cheetahs, panthers, ocelots and many others, under a variety of coats and markings. Their movements were graceful, unhurried, their multitude so huge it seemed to take forever for the movement to ripple from the lead to the rear.

Alan reflected on how complex the task of the Kyra must be—to bring them all together in a battle situation. The Shee were aware of Alan's attention. He saw in their eyes the clarity of intention, the coldness, the purposefulness, as, in passing him by, they found his own.

With a bow to their royal presences, Alan left the anxious king and queen on the headland and descended to take his place beside the Kyra, now in the form of a huge snow tigress. The march was underway.

A Voice from Nowhere

Pausing within the entrance of the deserted Tube station, Penny listened carefully, paying attention not just to what sounds she might hear, but also to sounds that were different from what she might expect to hear.

Listen carefully—then listen carefully again!

She was alert for the absolute silence that would tell her if the animals, who had eyes and ears even better than her own, had detected an unwelcome presence.

She had discovered the ghost Tube station on one of her trips to Piccadilly Circus. There she would admire and sketch from different angles and in different levels of light. On several occasions, at dusk, she had seen bats emerging from a cleft in the soot-stained stone wall of the station. They had wheeled and skimmed through the narrow deserted side street, heading for the huge open space with its mighty lions a hundred yards riverwards. But bats didn't make nests in clefts, they had to get inside and roost in the spaces that would let them fall into flight. There had to be a way in through the cleft.

It involved a bit of a climb. She had to tie her trainers around her neck and carry the dagger in Gully's old denim backpack, first making sure the stitching would take the weight and that the box would fit. It also meant breaking her promise to Gully, but that had only been half a promise, the sort you were only half obliged to keep. And although she had never climbed a sooty old wall like this before, she was confident she could climb it with ease by inserting the tips of her fingers and toes into the cracks where the mortar had decayed. Inside she found a cluster of thick black cables snaking down the cobwebby walls, supported at intervals, by iron brackets. These ran conveniently down the walls and into a box-like enclosure on the floor. Within seconds she was landing in thick dust in the station atrium.

"Don't you do nuffink stupid, gel!"

She pictured Gully's brown eyes looking up at her on the gantry, through the thick eyebrows that were like knotted string.

"No more broken arms—I promise!"

There was no hurry, now that she was in.

He had tried to dissuade her from exploring the Tube tunnels. *"People's talkin' about something goin' about killin' people. Honest to God, Penny. There's some kind of bogeyman roaming about down there."*

"Bogeyman?" She couldn't help laughing.

Gully didn't like her to talk about the City Below. He didn't understand it and that was why it frightened him. And now he was trying to frighten her, trying to stop her exploring by talking about monsters.

Penny didn't take Gully's fears seriously. He was very superstitious: OCD, plus plus plus. That was why he carried a watch on each wrist and carried his stuff in strictly different pockets, and why he touched wood and counted to twenty when worried. His upbringing had done that to him: his druggie mum and dad, and the demon drink. But underneath the OCD, Gully was smart. He was street smart. He was a survivor. And he liked to think that he took care of her. He liked to think that she wasn't street smart enough, that she needed him to look out for her.

She felt guilty about breaking her promise to Gully, even if it was only a half-meant promise. She had even thought about telling him where she was going, but she just hadn't been able to do it.

No telling. No touching.

"*You stay here,*" she had insisted instead. "*You stay here and take good care of your pigeons.*"

And now she was picking up faint rustling and a distant, very soft ticking: the deathwatch beetles in the timbers overhead. All the while she was standing still and listening carefully, her eyes were becoming accustomed to the gloom. It wasn't pitch-dark; there was a trickle of light coming in through dust-grimed windows set high in the walls. Nevertheless, she would have to use the torch. Slipping the backpack off her shoulders she popped open the side pocket and took it out. She checked the torch with a quick flick of the switch. How piercingly bright it was! So bright she waited a minute or two longer, worrying if it was safe to use it. Then she thought of a trick that Gully had taught her and she wrapped the torch in a piece of tissue she would otherwise have used to blow her nose.

It worked.

The light from the tissue-covered torch was much less bright, yet still enough for her to make out her surroundings.

She was standing in what had been the Tube station entrance. It was much pokier than she would have expected. The lower half of the walls were tiled in a creamy white, streaked in places by a rusty brown. Lines of tiles, the colour artists called Pompeii red, broke up the creamy monotony into oblongs and diagonals. Ahead of her was a winding staircase of grimy steps that led downwards in a spiral. She was inhaling dust with every breath; it painted every horizontal surface and powdered the murky dome of ceiling. On the staircase she read fading letters painted into the plaster above the tiles—TO THE TRAINS—a somewhat unnecessary instruction accompanied by an equally unnecessary long slim arrow that pointed downwards.

There would be no trains today. There had been no trains through here for tens of years.

Placing the torch, still wrapped in the tissue, on the dusty floor at the top of the stairs, she opened the main pocket of the backpack and lifted out the heavy dagger, still safely secured within its box. Hugging the heavy object to her breast, she thought about what she was doing. She closed her eyes.

Was it her imagination or could she feel a slight vibration from within the box? She placed the question mark shape of her ear against the lid.

I do feel it! As if it were calling me.

All the time she had been drawing the labyrinth over the ceiling—making sure the streets were at the right angles to one another, that the landmarks of the great city were each in their exact place, drawn with a perfect accuracy from the elevation that she most liked to draw it—she had been certain that there was a purpose in it. She knew that, she had sensed it absolutely, even though its purpose had been clouded in mystery. Solving the mystery that lay hidden within the labyrinth, that was the key to everything. And when she had first seen the Scalpie's dagger, with its strange spiral blade and the glowing symbol in the hilt, she knew that it was a vital clue. All that had happened—including the arrival of the alien man and woman—had been an integral part of the plan. She had seen the identical jet-black triangles in their brows. She had been thrilled to look deeper into the pulsating arabesques within them, knowing she was gazing through tiny windows into their alien minds.

That sense of revelation had been confirmed by the ease with which Mark had destroyed the Scalpie. And it had been further confirmed when Nan had destroyed the Grimlings without needing a weapon. It was as if she had simply thought them dead and the crystal window in her brow had made it happen.

Like magic!

The strangeness of that! The wonder of it! The fact she had been drawn into it as their guide! And then the dagger just falling at her feet . . .

That the dagger was both mysterious and powerful, she had no doubt, but she also sensed, strongly and absolutely, that she mustn't attempt to hold it by the hilt. It was why she had brought the heavy glove Gully sometimes used to hold troublesome pigeons. For the moment she refused to hold the dagger, even when using the glove. She figured that if she just kept it at a slight distance, if she kept it within its box, it would lead her to what was calling her. Only then would she understand the powerful sense of destiny that was troubling her in every waking moment and tormenting her sleep. She would discover the City Below. This would enable her to put the two halves of the great mystery together—the linking truths that made an extraordinary whole of the labyrinth: the City Above and the City below. She would discover whatever part she was destined to play in this extraordinary mystery.

She returned the dagger to the backpack and picked up the shaded torch, then descended the dust-caked staircase and stopped on a landing with a claustrophobic cluster of rooms. In one of them there was a toilet, with a broken wooden cover, and two sinks side-by-side and black with dirt. She could hear water running down the walls and dripping onto the floor somewhere to her left. The ammonia stink of decades of bat droppings was almost unbearable. A small head was poking out of a hole in the floor immediately ahead of her. It was twisting around, like a glove puppet, sniffing at the air. It was a rat, although for a moment, she imagined that it was a Grimling.

Fright was making her imagination run away with her. She readjusted the heavy backpack to make it more comfortable, and listened carefully again for anything out of the ordinary. Her footsteps were the only sound.

As she moved through the rooms, she found an even narrower tunnel, so narrow her shoulders almost brushed against the walls as she walked through it. It followed several acute bends, until she came to some cast iron signs in lime green that were rust-speckled but still perfectly legible: BEWARE—ELECTRICITY. BEWARE—TRAINS. She chuckled again. The electricity she understood, but why would anybody descending into a tiny Tube station need to beware the trains? Surely they knew to beware the trains? Even as she pondered the incongruity she saw, through the gloom ahead, the unmistakable dark mouth of a tunnel. It was on the other side of a rusted steel mesh fence enclosing a padlocked, ironwork door. A long dead pigeon, rotted to bones and a couple of feathers, poked out of the claggy dirt inside the gate.

She tested the padlock.

It looked as old as the station itself, but it was large and forged out of solid steel. Pulling at it and shaking the ironwork door only raised clouds of dust and made too much noise.

Penny slid the backpack to the floor again, took out the box and opened the lid. Donning the heavy leather glove, she stared for several seconds at the dagger, its triple infinity sigil glowing like a silver jewel embedded into the hilt. She took the tissue off the torch so it provided some light when she placed it on the ground, then she closed her gloved hand around the hilt of the dagger.

A tingling sensation travelled through her hand, making the muscles cramp up hard. Sweat erupted on her brow and she panted for several moments, waiting for her heartbeat to normalise. The dagger was too heavy for her to lift with one hand. She gripped it tightly with her gloved left hand, then wound the fingers of her right hand around the glove so she could two-handedly lift it out of the box. Blinking her eyes to try to clear the sweat, she struck the padlock with the spiral blade.

There was a brilliant flash of light.

She blinked furiously, half blinded by the glare, then urged herself on before her courage failed her.

You have to do it again! Do it, right now!

She struck out again, clenching her eyes shut as the heavy blade made contact with the hook of the padlock. She saw the glare even through her clenched lids and heard a sharp explosive crack, loud as a gunshot. For the briefest moment, in the illumination of the glare, she thought she saw something very strange, something as huge as a train carriage in the tunnel to the left. She was so shocked she dropped the dagger and heard it clang against the dusty floor. When she opened her eyes again the padlock dangled brokenly from the door, its hook snapped in two, with the fractured ends blue-black as if they had been scorched.

With her heart in her throat Penny retrieved the dagger, her left hand juddering even within the steadying support of her right, and placed it back in its box. She was shaking so badly she couldn't close the lid; she left it open, with the dagger and its symbol glowing within. The trembling threatened to spread and engulf her entire being. She copied Gully's mantra and made herself count to twenty. She closed the lid, clumsily forced the box back into the backpack, then held the bundle against her breast.

Oh, God—Oh lord!

Had she imagined it?

She didn't know what to think. She felt for her claws only to realise she hadn't brought them. The torch was still shining in the dust-carpeted floor. Now she clutched at it, clumsily, hitting the floor and scraping the skin off her knuckles in her haste. She flicked off the light, then she just stood there, not daring to move, struggling to think.

She heard her father's voice, speaking clearly and calmly in her head. "*There is always an element of logic to any situation. What we have to do, what we were put on this Earth to do, is to follow that logic to its natural conclusion.*"

It was one of those times when Father had invited her into his study. She liked to think of it as his brown study. It had a brown desk and wooden chair with brown leather upholstery and straight ladder back—the chair of reason she had come to label it—in which she would sit opposite him and be instructed on how to follow the thread of logic to its natural conclusion. After these lessons in the brown study she would ask his permission to go out into the garden. She would make straight for the summer house. Neither Father nor Mother liked to sit in the garden and so she knew she would be alone. When she needed most desperately to think, she imagined herself back in the summer house. She imagined herself there now and pondered the direction that the element of logic was pointing her in.

I saw something.

She thought back to Gully's warning. Could Gully be right? Was it Gully's monster she had glimpsed in the flash of light? An amorphous thing that moved like a giant amoeba through the tunnels, hunting for prey—hunting for people? A ghoul that devoured people, that ate them alive?

No! It couldn't be. Such things were impossible.

But then why was she so frightened?

Stop, look, listen!

Penny did so. And she thought she heard something: a slithering movement followed by a faint rattling of the rusty iron grill. Then a pause, as if something were . . . were testing, peering in through the grill, already aware of her footprints in the dust, sniffing, trying to catch her scent.

Shaking with fright, Penny lowered the backpack to the floor. She took a firmer hold of the unlit torch, forcing her unwilling hands to point it out into the tunnel. Her thumb refused to press the switch. She felt spasms crabbing in her hands.

What if the monster was real?

Don't be ridiculous.

She pressed the switch.

A face was staring back at her. It was a man's face, long and grey, poking out of a thick vaporous cloud. The face appeared to be detached from any body, as if floating on the cloud. There were horn-rimmed spectacles askew on its nose. Two brown eyes, behind the spectacles, were staring back at her.

"Hello there!" The lips moved as it spoke. "What you up to? Come for a little nibble?"

As Penny froze, paralysed with fear, the cloud turned and she was suddenly looking at a very different face, the face of a fox. Its amber eyes reflected the light back at her, its whiskers twitching. Then the cloud began to roll, with one human face after another coming into view to stare back at her in the light of the torch.

One of Penny's legs was juddering like a drumstick against the floor. Both her arms were trembling, her fingers going numb.

<You cannot stay here, Penny. You must flee.>

She had no idea where the voice came from, other than it was inside her head. She wanted to run, but she had to lean against the steel mesh to stop herself from fainting.

<Take one step, then another.>

"Yes," she whispered. "I should take one step . . ."

Even in her panic she had the presence of mind to pick up the backpack, awkwardly, by one shoulder strap. Then, with her throat as dry as the dust under her feet, she was slipping and sliding back along the filthy tunnels. One step, then another step, then step, by step, by step. She didn't know how she would find the courage and strength to climb back out of the ghost Tube station and return to the sanctuary of the City Above, to find her way back to Our Place, to her one true friend, Gully.

The Beast Beneath the Skin

A DRIVING RAIN SPATTERED THE VISOR OF HIS helmet as Mark stared to the west where, no more than three hundred yards away, a gasometer was exploding. He blinked in amazement as great arcs of blue and orange flames erupted into the evening sky, curling back on themselves like the flares surrounding sunspots.

They had extinguished the lights on the bikes, but such was the glare from the distant blaze that Mark could read the CLOSED sign on the door of the defunct filling station where they had gathered for a final evaluation. They had swung in there assuming they would find some concealment as well as a respite from the rain before heading deeper into central London. But the roof of the overhang where the pumps had once stood had been largely ripped away, and what little cover they had was spoiled by copious leaks.

"Razzers," Cal said, kicking in the glazed door to the reception.

Like the others, Cal was dressed as a patrolman, wearing a Scorpion helmet, yellow heavy-weather jacket with glow strips and black trousers. Mark, Nan and Sharkey followed him into the reception area, which stank of piss, leaving the four bikes outside on the forecourt. With their blue on yellow, hatched Battenberg markings, they remained easily visible beyond the grimy glass. They sat down on the floor in the driest corner, removing the heavy helmets and unbuttoning the flak jackets to expose the Kevlar vests.

Cal's face was briefly lit up as he checked his mobile phone.

Mark's eyes found Nan's. He'd have preferred her riding pillion on his bike, but she would have none of it. He'd forgotten her love of horse riding from back in her own world, even if that had been two thousand years ago. And now, given the chance of riding again, albeit a machine rather than a horse, she was in her element. Already there was nothing anybody could have taught her about what she now called "her favourite mount," the Harley FLHTP sitting next to the three BMW R1200s outside.

Disappointed, Cal slammed the phone down on the floor then took to fiddling with the safety on the MK-5.

Mark tried to relax. He and Nan had been hard-pressed to take in two days of instruction and practice on how to ride the heavy bikes. Sharkey had worked them hard over the rough terrain around the seaside camp, then out onto the narrow country roads at night until, like the knights of old, they were expected to become one fighting machine with the steed between their legs. Nan had undoubtedly been the star of the show, a natural rider.

And now Nan was comforting him, protecting his injured pride. He could smell her soaped-clean skin under the smell of rain-soaked leather.

Cal growled. "Knock it off, love birds."

"Ignore him," Nan grinned. "He's just jealous."

Mark was reminded of his first meeting with her: the conjured-up image of the girl in the nemeton brought into life by Kate and her crystal. What a different person she was today from that vision of the dark queen in the battle for Ossierel. He had been on the threshold of death at the moment of consummation with Mórígán. The way he recalled it, it was hardly a romantic high. They had become one in the embrace of Mórígán's dark power, the power of death. The experience had been so overwhelming, so extraordinary, that he had never really understood it. And yet, from such a terrible first meeting, their love for one another had been born.

He pressed his lips to her ear. "You rode as if you were born to that saddle."

"Is this a prelude to tonight?" she whispered back.

They were all a bit high with pre-battle anticipation. The potential for violence exuded from Cal's sweating face. Mark couldn't deny that he sensed it growing within himself, like a contagious fever. Nan hardly needed the warrior-to-warrior contagion. Violence was an integral part of her nature. Ossierel had been proof enough of that.

Mark didn't know how they had come through the journey from the camp in one piece. It had been a continuous nightmare, particularly the M25, littered as it was with wrecks and abandoned vehicles, some still burning. The hard shoulder and slow lanes had run with filthy streams of water in which rainbow-hued reflections told of spilled petrol and the potential for conflagration. The havoc of the Razzamatazzers was worsening day by day, with nobody interested in towing the wrecks away. Emergency vehicles had streamed by them on both sides of the central reservation: ambulances, police, the grey-with-camouflage uniformed paramilitaries, heading for who-knew-what trouble. The cop uniforms had probably saved them. They had been Tajh's contribution, though it was a mystery to Mark how she had found what looked like real police leathers, helmets and vests.

More evidence, perhaps, of a link to an organised central authority? It wasn't the first time that thought had crossed Mark's mind.

The uniforms, coupled with the heavily customised bikes, made them look like they were on some kind of emergency duty. Plus they drove fast enough, but not so recklessly as to attract attention to themselves.

They had prepared throughout the day, checking every step of their plan and, keeping to it, had come off the M25 after just fifteen miles or so, heading into a sector of the outer city that was only scantily lit with a few surviving street lights. The road surface had been treacherous in the downpour, with water-filled holes and murky and silent buildings. Twenty-foot high mounds of black rubbish bags littered the streets, spilling out into the roads, uncollected in months, and the stink permeated everything. The noxious reek of leaking sewage penetrated even now into the junk-scattered reception of the filling station. The sun was setting somewhere behind those rain-laden skies, making the air smoggy and dank. Headlights gleamed sickly on the road.

Now, as they were waiting to set out, Mark recalled the earlier conversation they had held with the group about the mission the Resistance had been given.

"This woman we're looking to protect."

"She's called Jo—Joanne Derby."

"Okay—these people are planning to kill her."

Tajh shook her head. "I wouldn't imagine they'd just kill her. That would be too overt. It's more likely they'll arrest her under some ruse."

"Don't kid yourself. They'll kill her on the spot if they bloodywell feel like it," Cal said. "Even if they take her alive they'll just grill her somewhere else, and then kill her. These guys are not interested in hostages."

"I hope they're interested at least in one," said Cogwheel.

"You can hope, pal."

"You saying they don't even care about witnesses?"

"Not a jot—not any more."

"What do you think, Tajh? Up to now, Grimstone's people wouldn't do something as brazen as that, surely. Not murder a respectable woman right out there in the open."

Tajh had lifted her eyebrows in Cal's direction, shrugged.

Now Mark glanced over at Cal, hearing the mobile chime. Cal pressed it against his ear, his eyes narrowed. He gave them the thumbs up.

"That's it. She's arrived."

Joanne—Jo—Derby hitched her spectacles a half inch higher on her long, narrow nose, gathering herself before the lectern in the theatre at King's College. A tall figure, close to six feet in her sensible one inch heels, her copper-red hair was fixed in a coil on the back of her head with a green enamelled clasp—a family heirloom inherited from her Scottish grandmother. Her audience, maybe sixty souls in a theatre that would have accommodated three times as many, shuffled in silence, giving her the impression her own tension might have been catching. It was rare these days that she was invited to lecture, and she had hesitated for a week or more before she had accepted. It had been eleven months since she had taken part in any function relating to her senior lectureship in sociology and politics at the LSE.

Before setting out she had glanced at herself in the hallway mirror. Her face had startled her with its haunted look. Make-up had become essential, even if kept to a minimum, and jewellery to plain gold studs in her ears. She was still in two minds about whether to go or not when the door com sounded and she heard the driver's firm but courteous voice. "Miss Derby—we're running late."

And now, after an unsettling journey through rain-battered streets, she felt so jittery it threatened to freeze her mind. She worried that it was a mistake to come. Had it not been for the name on the invitational letter—Will Johnstone—she wouldn't have dared to respond. She had never met him, but he represented an opportunity to make a point with a senior university authority. There was a craggy, bearded man with sticking out ears sitting in the second row—he resembled Abraham Lincoln—who might've been him. But if it was Johnstone, why hadn't he welcomed her on her arrival?

She exercised her jaw to try to wriggle loose the stiffening muscles, covering it with one. She took a deep breath before she could bring herself to speak, then began, a little too hurriedly, as if her haste was capable of banishing the fears that preyed upon her mind.

"Nobody could have foreseen the anarchy we face today on the streets of this city. I know that London is not unique, but it is the worst affected in terms of riot and violence.

"Over the course of the last year or two we have seen how this . . . this miasma has spread, undermining the stratagems of weak government. For reasons that are utterly incomprehensible, we have witnessed the wanton neglect of the infrastructure that maintains a city of this size and complexity."

She didn't want to deliver some preachy sermon on morality. At the same time she desperately wanted her audience to grasp what was happening, to understand the nightmares that were disturbing her sleep and very likely theirs.

And yet their faces remained blank as sirens sounded loudly in the streets beyond the domed glass windows. Their curious lack of affect baffled her. What was the matter with these people? Did they want her to rant and shout that the world around them was going to the dogs? Not just in London, but all of Britain's big cities.

"Water and electricity have come to be regarded as luxuries. There are many streets, just a few hundred yards from here, that are too dangerous to walk by night—and some even by day. The collapse of public services has resulted in a wave of anarchy and consequential overreaction from those who feel themselves threatened. The response of the authorities has been increasingly disordered, increasingly brutal. There is little in the way of organised health care any more, and a progressive atrophy of public education. It's an anguish to witness society degenerate into the naked expression of Darwinian survival of the fittest. Middle class residents in wealthy neighbourhoods hire armed garrisons to make fortresses out of their apartment blocks. Criminal gangs roam the streets, provoking a mushrooming of private security forces, with sickening reputations for brutality."

Her words were provoking some kind of reaction. There was a murmuring, perhaps an intake of breath.

"I . . . I'm afraid that it has been, at least in part, the predictable response to such predation that sections of the working class have fought back, forming guerrilla groups and arming themselves as best they can."

She looked over the scattered pond of bland faces, trying to figure out the strange, somewhat sullen, expression most of them were sporting.

"You don't need me to tell you that this is a desperate situation. All that a decent human being can do is struggle to hold onto an increasingly tenuous thread of normality. Tolerance and caring about the society in which you live, work and worship, is slowly disappearing. People inevitably look to the authorities. And their answer, increasingly, has been the paramilitaries."

It was then that the bearded man stood up and stared at her in a thoughtful silence.

"You disagree?" She asked finally.

"Chaos certainly reigns on our streets. It's popular in some quarters, Doctor Derby, to blame those who are attempting to return the city to order, but the paramilitaries did not create the disorder."

"Perhaps you will tell us what did?"

"The evil that is prevalent in the hearts of men and women."

A chorus of "Amens" rippled through the audience.

"Evil is a rather abstract concept in this modern world."

"Do you think so?"

"My goodness—who could blame you if you are frightened?"

"We're not frightened."

She stared at him, then returned her attention to the increasingly restless audience. She had come across doom-laden assessments before, even from sociologists—as if a profound worry buried deep in the collective subconscious were surfacing. Warnings of apocalypse were popping up even in professional circles.

The bearded man spoke again. "Oh, there's nothing abstract about evil. And I very much doubt that I am alone here in believing this. Cruelty—sadism—has for years been promoted on television as entertainment."

She was surprised to hear laughs throughout the audience.

Jo Derby had the strangest sense of dislocation, as if the perceptions and reactions within the hall were decidedly off-kilter. She peered down at the man's face, wondering if perhaps she recognised him after all. He looked vaguely familiar but she wasn't sure where from. She noticed that he was wearing a pin with the triple loop logo in his lapel.

"I see that you are a member of Grimstone's church?"

"I am."

There was the sound of raised voices somewhere else within the building. Jo struggled to regain her focus. "I can't agree on such an abstract explanation, though I readily understand the fears that provoke you to say it." She nodded towards the audience. "I have serious concerns about the paramilitaries. They are not answerable to the electorate. Just who are they answerable to?"

There was a noise she didn't recognise at first, perhaps because it was so incongruous, so shocking. Her audience were rapping their feet against the floor. It had begun with one, but soon many were following, all rapping in unison, so the noise became as regular and loud as drums.

It was a very intimidating sound.

The bearded man had not joined in the thunderous percussion. He was watching her calmly. She paused, swallowing hard against the dryness that was gathering in her throat.

From somewhere within the building she heard what sounded like gunshots. Automatic fire. It seemed outrageous to her, but somebody was firing a weapon within the confines of a famous university college. The tension rose in her again, suddenly, screamingly. She knew now that her fears were realised. It *had* been a mistake to come. Her jaw clenched and she found she couldn't speak above a whisper. She watched as the bearded man crossed over to the doors and shot the bolts, locking them in. She assumed that he had done this to protect her, and her audience, from whatever was happening elsewhere in the building. He remained by the door, standing guard.

But he looked altogether too calm. The shocking thought occurred to her. Maybe he was part of it?

Jo Derby spun to face the audience with their pallid sweating faces, thunderous mocking feet and their cold eyes. Perhaps the bearded man was waiting by the door only to open it again.

There was a loud commotion in the corridor and the sound of much closer gunfire then running feet. The bearded man was reaching to slide the bolt back when the doors exploded inwards, crushing him against the wall to their right. Two figures rushed in wearing the uniforms of police motorcyclists, including helmets. One of them, tall and moustached, was directing a belted machine gun into the lecture theatre. The other, shorter and built like a woman, was hurrying to the podium where Jo was standing. The audience were on their feet. Their faces had become ugly with hate, their lips drawn back into a common hissing. The tall figure fired the machine gun into the ceiling, a thunderous detonation in the close confines of the lecture theatre. Joanne felt close to fainting.

"Miss Derby—you must come with us."

The shorter of the two police riders had approached the podium and was speaking to her. The figure had a woman's voice and, from what Jo could see of her neck and hands, a bronzed complexion. As she pushed the visor on her helmet up, her eyes startled Joanne. There were no irises or whites—her eyes were all black.

Jo barely recognised her own husky croak. "Who are you?"

"Friends."

The young woman smiled, but there was a frightening quality to the smile on that face with the all black eyes. "Your life is threatened. We don't have time for explanation. You must come with us."

To her right, the tall man was firing his machine gun again, lower this time, barely above the heads of the audience, keeping them at bay.

"Quickly—you really are in danger."

Jo allowed herself to be hauled off the podium and rushed through the splintered doors, where she had to step over one of the trailing legs of the bearded man, his grey trousers pulled up halfway up his calves, exposing a fawn-coloured sock. Behind her, she heard more shouts, then several deafening rounds of the pistol were directed away from them, down another corridor, where figures were diving, or possibly falling. On her other side, Joanne allowed her arm to be taken by the woman.

"What's going on?"

"We mustn't stop. We need to hurry."

She was being hauled across a landing dead bodies lay. The floor was slick with blood.

She cried, "I don't believe this is happening!"

The tall man running alongside them grinned, a peculiarly toothy grin from what little Jo could see through the visor, framed by a straggly Mexican-style moustache. "Lady, it's real as fucking rain. You were just minutes from being dead."

"For pity's sake!"

"Not much of that round here."

Nan grabbed hold of the arm of the tall red-haired woman, who was fumbling with her spectacles, removing them from her nose and shoving them deep into the breast pocket of her bright green jacket, as if they were as needful of saving as she herself. "Keep close to me. We'll shelter you."

As they emerged into the street and the pouring rain, Cal joined them from where he had been guarding their escape. He roared, "Watch out!"

Nan looked in the direction that Cal was pointing. The paramilitaries had created a barrier of vehicles that extended wall-to-wall across the T-junction with the main street. Gunfire erupted from the barrier from at least half a dozen different points. The oraculum in her brow flared and a bolt of blue-black lightning exploded against the barrier, electrifying bodies and burning out vehicles. Within moments the barrier was a wall of flames.

"What now?" the woman asked.

"We run." Nan could feel the woman trembling as she hurried her down to where Mark was guarding the bikes. Nan slapped the saddle of the Harley. "Here—climb onto the pillion."

The woman was still dazed, so Nan shoved her onto the seat, sprang into the saddle and immediately started up the engine, kicking back the strut and roaring out towards the lightning-ravaged T-junction. She heard the roar of Mark's engine, then Cal's and Sharkey's behind her. Arriving at the rubble-strewn T-junction at the top of the street, she took the right hand fork, where she received a flash of communication mind-to-mind. Nan saw what Mark had spotted: an armoured vehicle with a field gun on a rotating turret was wheeling into position on the roundabout ahead. The turret was swivelling around to face them as all four bikes roared towards it.

Mark and Nan's oracula erupted simultaneously and two bolts of blue-black lightning exploded into the armoured vehicle with ear-splitting detonations, ripping the roof from the vehicle.

As Nan screeched around into a U-turn, she caught a glimpse of the detached turret with the huge gun still attached, flying through the air, then crashing into the tarmac of the road surface and skidding towards them in a shower of sparks. It ground to a halt just a dozen yards from the bikes, now wheeling around to head left along the main street.

Nan looked around, searching for an alternative escape. Buildings had caught fire from the exploding vehicles and the glazed façade of a six-storey office block was in the process of disintegrating, with glass and debris showering down over the pavement and road.

"We're trapped," Cal shouted.

"Not yet," Mark called back. "Look for the Tube."

"You're bonkers."

"Do you have a better idea?"

Ignoring the small-arms fire splattering out from behind the blazing barriers at both ends of the street, Nan throttled towards the protruding sign of red circle bisected by a blue horizontal—a closed Underground station.

She burst through the boarded up entrance, switching on the headlights as she did so, then juddered down a flight of seven steps into what had been the main ticket concourse. Directing the bike through the wider gates intended for wheelchairs she faced three escalators, all defunct. A sign overhead signalled the Northern Line. The others were close behind her, the bikes spreading out to take all three escalators, rattling down what seemed like a hundred steps through an accumulation of discarded rubbish. At the bottom, all three paused to recover their breath before following the signs once again for the Northern Line.

Nan heard Cal's husky whisper, "Let's hope the bloody line isn't electrified."

Then it was Mark's voice, full of alarm. "We've got an even bigger problem." He directed the beam of his headlight onto the tracks to reveal the deep central pit, too narrow to fit a bike.

"Not so!" Nan shook her head. Mark underestimated the power in his brow. Through the oraculum of Mórígán, a cyclone of blue-black lightning ripped into the buried floor of the pit and forced it to erupt, rising level with the steel tracks. Nan laughed as she drove the machine-steed over the edge of the platform, landing with a slithering bounce onto the now-level ground between the tracks, then accelerated through the vaulted tunnels and roared ahead, with Jo Derby holding onto her for dear life.

It was Nan who first felt the alien power in the tunnels as she roared on through the dark—something immense and frightening.

She mind-sent her message to Mark. <You sensing that?>

<Yeah—I'm sensing it.>

The Cathedral of Death

Kate floated between whirling galaxies of raw, immensely beautiful, colours. Broad, pure planes of blue, yellow, red were suspended at their intersections, flaring into rainbows of every subtle shade in between. But they were hallucinatory distractions. Oh, if only in attempting to save the Momu she could do something that might oppose the Tyrant's will and so help Alan!

"Remember the immensities!"

But how?

She knew she must search for the deeper truth behind the legendary stories of the One Tree and the serpent-dragon that was reputed to inhabit the roots.

The Momu, and Driftwood too, had talked about such mystical things as fate. Kate was too common-sensical to allow the mystical to carry her away, but in the lengthy and only half remembered conversations at their first meeting, the Momu had talked about how fate and mystery were intrinsically linked to the everyday world. The Fáil was, perhaps, the most mysterious entity of all. She had also talked about the great richness of nature. The One Tree was linked to this holistic way of seeing things, to the cycles and balances of the terrestrial and oceanic worlds and the interactions of all that inhabited them—which were not and could never be benign. To accept nature, to truly understand it, you had to understand the need for its gargantuan cruelties and see past them, to grasp their quintessentially amoral nature. There were rules that governed life, and they applied throughout all of nature from the simplest of beings to humans—or the many different types of people and beings that inhabited Tír.

Rules!

Could it be that the One Tree had something to do with the deeply embedded rules that governed the great cycles of life?

The Momu had made this vision into the mysteries possible, and through it Kate saw how critical the sense of balance was. Her very power—the power of healing—was linked to such cycles and balances.

Kate felt that she half understood something that was at once exhilarating and terrifying. Birth, life, death—these were the immensities. And the One Tree and the serpent-dragon that inhabited its roots had something to do with them.

With a shiver Kate remembered the terrible place she had only recently fled: a landscape cold as space with jarringly angular buildings made of black ice, the Land of the Dead. That place was still perilously close, a dimension just a faltering thought away. Death was one of the immensities and death was certainly involved in this battle. It sought to consume the soul spirit of the Momu, but this was not the everyday death of Tír, the death ruled over by the goddess Mórígán, this was the death beloved of the Great Witch—and of that other even greater malice, the Tyrant of the Wastelands. Was it possible that the Tyrant ruled here, in the Land of the Dead?

If so, what purpose did it serve him?

Could it be that the Tyrant had something to do with the spirit of the succubus, Elaru, whose every word was probably a lie? Kate just didn't know what to believe.

Think back. What else did the Momu try to teach you?

Kate recalled her time with the Momu within her natural chamber in Ulla Quemar. She remembered looking up into her enormous, gentle face, astonished at what the Momu was attempting to explain to her.

"This gift—will you show me how I'm supposed to use it?"

She recalled how the crystal on its chain about the Momu's neck took fire. The explosion of light had filled the chamber. She saw the effort of will it took for the Momu to stay calm. *"Greeneyes—child! Your naïvety leads you to flaunt such a temptation before me."*

"But it's a power I don't understand. I don't know what's expected of me."

Those enormous mother-of-pearl eyes had drawn so close to Kate's own it felt as if the Momu were becoming one with her mind. She had watched, bewildered, as the Momu reached down with one great webbed hand and explored the base of the tree of life—the One Tree, whose fleshy branches, leaves and roots ramified everywhere within the chamber. She recalled the palm of the Momu as it was brought up under her chin, how she had stared at it, wondering what it was that the Momu was showing her. Decay! The heart of the great tree was rotten.

"Beloved Greeneyes—now do you understand?"

She had seen that same decay in the houses and streets throughout the beautiful city of Ulla Quemar.

The Momu had blinked, as if to confirm Kate's observations, and put her arm around Kate's shoulders. *"Nidhoggr, the serpent, fertilised a seed of the Tree of Life. That seed grew into the One Tree in whose roots we converse, a chimera of magic and being. But the One Tree is dying, and with it my beautiful Ulla Quemar. I, the first born of that chimera—who am almost as old as the One Tree itself—am dying with her."*

The Momu was born from some interaction between the Tree of Life and the serpent-dragon Nidhoggr. That interaction had given rise to the extension of the Tree of Life, the One Tree that filled the chamber, and whose roots ramified throughout the city of Ulla Quemar.

Kate thought hard. She considered what the Momu had shown her. There had been a reason she hadn't quite understood at the time, but she felt much closer to understanding that reason now.

She heard the Momu speak, words that praised her resurrection of the dragon Driftwood—a resurrection she felt no pride in, since the fossil of the dead dragon had spontaneously revived while Kate slept.

She had asked the Momu for an explanation.

"You have a very great power. The gift of life, of rebirth."

Why then couldn't she use this gift to cure the Momu, who was dying? What if the Momu had not meant to ask Kate to cure her? Kate considered the memory again. The One Tree was growing within the chamber of the Momu . . . What if the corruption extended not merely to the seedling, but to the great mother tree, the Tree of Life itself? What if that was the real explanation behind the decay of the city and the death of the Momu?

What if I am expected to cure the Tree of Life itself?

Even as she thought about it the realisation loomed, immense in her mind. A message had been carried to her in her memory of the Momu's words: *"Nidhoggr, the serpent! The serpent-dragon that coiled about the roots of the Tree . . . Nidhoggr, who gnawed at the roots of the world and fertilised a seed to give birth to the Tree of Life itself."* Understanding struck her, swelled in her, filled every one of her senses. Nidhoggr gave birth to the Tree of Life. The same Tree of Life that was essential for the wellbeing and health of the Momu, of her people, the Cill and of her beautiful city, Ulla Quemar!

Nidhoggr and the Tree of Life are dependent on one another.

She must have fallen asleep—or something deeper. But now, as if her new understanding had sounded a shrill alarm throughout her being, she was waking. Her imagination was filled with vague black shadows, like the scatter of arterial blood over a field of virgin snow. Only this blood was black—thick, curdling, threatening black. And even as she watched it continue to spread, the pattern of it altered shape and the clots assumed the form of a human; a tormented body rent into huge disjointed chunks. Three quarters of a head with half a jaw formed, then a brow with a chisel-shaped chunk of it missing; then one arm severed at the elbow, and half the neck, which dissolved into the leprous white of the snow, as if invisible shark-sized jaws were biting. They tore and devoured, ripping away the left hip and the left leg from the knee down, all eaten away.

A warning? But a warning of what?

Kate had no idea what it might mean. Only that it frightened her deeply.

Even as the visions slowly faded she saw that she was back among the glittering black ice monstrosities that were the architecture of the Land of the Dead.

"No!"

Had her realisation about the potential meaning of the Tree of Life and the serpent-dragon Nidhoggr drawn the attention of some malignant intelligence? Had that malignant presence gained access to her mind? Had it warned her off with the dreadful evolving patters of black clots against virgin snow? Was this why she found herself back here, in this terrible land of hopeless spirits and gaunt places with their spindly Gothic shapes and overwhelming sense of malice?

Kate heard her own voice tremble in her ears: "Whoever—whatever—you are, leave me alone. I don't want to come back here!"

<It is I, Mistress, who called you back. Please forgive me. It was selfish of me to have prayed for your return. But I felt so lonely.>

"Elaru—I am not your friend."

<Oh, please? I have prayed for a thousand years that I might find a friend. Would you please be my friend—even if just for a short while? You may feel free to abandon me at any moment.>

"I can't trust you."

<Who indeed can trust any other? And yet there is need. Is not need close to friendship? Is it not part of what might grow to something more charitable than the horror and dread that surrounds us both here?>

"It isn't nearly enough."

<There is the lingering scent of the flesh about you. There are those who would savour even the ghost of life. They will smell you and hunt you.>

Kate looked down at herself, at what passed for her body. There was no true body there. Driftwood had warned her. He had warned her and she had taken no notice of his warnings and now she was reduced to what? A fleshless soul spirit?

"Where is my body?"

She was panicking. She realised that she had abandoned her body in the drowning city of Ulla Quemar. It was devoid of nourishment. How long had she been adrift of her body already? Would it simply starve to death, or drown? Was that what this vile and terrifying imprisonment was meant to achieve? Parted from the body she needed, the body that should protect her just as she had a duty to protect it, her physical being would perish and then she really would be lost forever in this monstrous world.

"Do you know what I am really doing here?"

<I assume that you have come to witness.>

"To witness what?"

<Why—your friend's death.>

"I didn't come here to witness the Momu's death. I can here to save her, and to save her people."

<But, Mistress, I thought you knew. None can recover their mortal being from this place. None ever has—since the world began.>

"Take me to her."

<Oh, Mistress—my friend, if only you would permit me to be so—let me counsel you against such madness as to go there.>

Anger at the presumption of this deceptive spirit consumed Kate's mind. Anger, mistrust and a growing, creeping dread all came together in a dizzy, terrifying crescendo, overwhelming her senses, her mind. And then, in the time it took to blink, Kate recovered her equanimity and control of her senses only to find herself drifting towards the building that was the source of the pallid light that illuminated the entire Land of the Dead. Although she resisted, she could do nothing to divert her path from the menacing Gothic cathedral, constructed out of glimmering black ice. It was so tall that the apices were out of sight in the gloom overhead. In the age it took her to approach it, it appeared to grow taller still. It flickered from within and twinkled and blurred, as if constantly reforming the dully-glowing needles of its construction; shimmering black crystals that were minuscule from a distance, but were miles high now.

When she finally stood before the entrance Kate felt utterly dwarfed by it. It was a portal so vast that its roof was lost in the gloom overhead and yet still it was only a minor arch against the vast and beckoning chamber within. A distant sound came from that chamber, faint but striking against the silence of the landscape without. It took another age for her to pass deeper into the building. She felt herself shrinking smaller and smaller, in being and courage, until she felt no bigger than a grain of sand. An eerie light swept upwards from the floor, pervading the lower portions of the encircling walls so that they positively glowed; the glow fading gradually as the walls soared to dizzying heights. The walls were so tall they became invisible and disappeared into pitch-black shadows overhead. The light was strangely iridescent with beautiful rainbow hues, like the colour that glimmered around the carapaces of black beetles or the scales of dead fish. That eerie light moved, diffusing down the chamber like the fall of snowflakes.

Surely light in itself could not fall? It had to be something else; a never-ending drizzle of millions upon millions of weightless motes that reflected the light. When she reached out and allowed a few to land in her hand, she saw that they comprised needle-like crystals which glowed with that same rainbow-coloured iridescence that coloured the black ice surrounding her.

The crystals were the source of the light within the gigantic chamber. It was their glow that illuminated the meandering streets outside. Their eddying cascade was accompanied by a high-pitched keening sound, like. . . *like millions of tiny cries!* Kate thought, as they dropped to become one with the floor.

Kate gazed at the light as it fused with the substance on the floor around her feet. She saw there was no accumulation as there would be with snow. Instead, the crystals fused with and became the actual floor, continuing the same twirling, spiralling patterns of movement she had seen as they fell. It was a constantly metamorphosing carpet of ice, like a moving sea of diamonds, which twinkled and flowed away to meld with the walls, and then to rise again. It was breathtakingly beautiful to behold. But utterly cold, so cold it caused Kate to shiver.

The entire cathedral is recycling.

She sensed a force of malice as unquenchable as it was pitiless, which drove the gargantuan edifice to grow ever bigger, taller, more awesome and terrifying. A dread grew in her heart once more.

The vast structure—which utterly dwarfed any notion of life—the keening cries and the source of the light—every aspect oppressed her spirit. She was numbed by its grandeur and scourged by its cold, though she should have been impervious to such feelings since she had no flesh. She began to feel exhausted again, though she should have no muscles to register exhaustion.

I sense . . . despair.

She felt as though she was encased in despair—a despair so debilitating her mind began to freeze, her thoughts getting slower and slower.

Only now, thoroughly frightened, did she register the presence of the keepers. They knelt with bowed heads at the five apices of a pentagon fixed within the crystalline metamorphosis of the floor.

A pentagon!

All five of her senses were overwhelmed. She perceived the true nature of the background sounds: a screeching, moiling symphony of groans, whines, screeches and ear-splitting high pitched whines.

"Elaru? Where are you?"

The plaintive voice came from a few steps behind her. <I am here, Mistress.>

"You seduced me into coming here, didn't you?"

She could see the ghostly creature, cringing—trembling. How could a soul spirit tremble like that?

<N-no, Mistress. A thousand times no.>

"It was because of me? You were spared just long enough to mislead me—to trick me into coming here?"

<Did I not caution you to avoid this place? Did I not beg you to stay away?>

"Yes," Kate murmured. "Yes, you did. But perhaps it was just part of the seduction, a trick of suggestion."

<There is time. You must abandon the search for your friend and use your portal to escape this sepulchre. Quickly, before you are subsumed.>

But it was already too late. Kate blinked slowly, or thought she blinked with whatever ghostly eyelids a soul spirit might possess. Then she blinked more rapidly, until it became a fluttering of panic. The succubus had tried to warn her. She recalled her precise words: "*said to be the Land of the Dead. Said to be . . .*" But of course it wasn't the Land of the Dead. It was something closer to hell. She looked back at the keepers.

The soul spirit of the Momu hung suspended at the centre of the pentagon, semi-transparent, like smoke. Kate saw the elongated face, so slender and caring, with those great mother-of-pearl eyes half closed in the repose of impending death. She felt the rush of tears come to her eyes and realised that, back in the chamber of the Momu, she was truly weeping. The Momu's flesh was fading. Iridescent crystals were invading her spirit where it hung suspended, swirling through it without resistance or interruption in their inchoate flight. Within her chest, back in Ulla Quemar, the Momu's heart must have been beating very slowly, so slowly Kate was unable to detect any associated movement within her spirit. Her breathing was also suspended. Neither movement nor sound came from her etiolated figure. Even the image of her crystal was dimming, its light pulsing slowly within an invading ulcer of the verdigris. And even as Kate looked at it, she saw how the same verdigris was beginning to move into the surrounding chest.

<Such entertainment have I created in the spirit of enlightenment.>

Kate spun around to find a spectre gazing at her. The face was made up of the same metamorphosing crystals of glowing green that were the structure of the cathedral, but the eyes were irredeemably black.

"You—I know who you are. You're the Tyrant."

<Right now your beloved Alan plots and plans to destroy me. He has invaded my world with an army of witch warriors. His intention is to make war on me. It's as contemptible as it is risible.>

"You delight in tormenting people. That's why you're doing this—what you're doing to the Momu. What purpose could this possibly serve you?"

<Greeneyes—that's what they call you, is it not? You affect to restore the blighted lands. You have learnt a little of nature, but you have not heeded the deeper lesson.>

"What lesson?"

<That there is no more sentiment in death than there is in life.>

This was the being that had killed her parents and her brother, Billy. He—it—had killed them in the attempt to kill her. Kate felt a wave of shock pass through her. What had she been thinking in coming here so unprepared? Everybody had warned her: Alan, Driftwood—Granny Dew. How could she have failed to realise that the Tyrant was behind her torment here. Of course he would now be focusing not only on Alan, but also her, and Mo and Mark.

Her heart was faltering back in Ulla Quemar. Here, in the so-called Land of the Dead, her spirit was also faltering. She was panting, struggling for breath. "You will not subvert me, any more than you subverted Alan."

<There will be no further offers of mercy for you and your insufferable companions to decline. I shall not merely defeat your purpose—that would be simplicity itself. The arrogance of your attack upon my continent and capital city offers me an opportunity. I shall

exterminate you in such a way that will provide sport for me and an example for others.>

"You will not win."

<Why, then—use this power of the witches to cure this creature you so care about. I should be impressed to witness such a deed. But you know, as I do, that you cannot cure her. And with her death this creature will be incorporated into the architecture of this place. Her soul spirit will become part of the creeping floors, the rising walls, to scream and fall in the eternal cycle of torment from which there will be no respite.>

Only then did Kate truly understood the nature of the landscape, of the streets and buildings. "The falling crystals—the light—dear God—they're the soul spirits of the dead? You've trapped them all here. Millions and millions of dead? They're—they're the molecules that make it?"

<It is your destiny to become part of the same construction. It pleases me to contemplate this end for you and your friends.>

No! Kate did not accept this fate. The Momu was not yet dead. If she had been dead, this monster would have gloated about it. He would have compelled Kate to watch it happen—the wonderful being, and all hope for the Cill, transformed into a mote of glowing ice. The Momu had survived this far and that meant that the Tyrant could not be the only source of power in the Land of the Dead. The Momu still relied on her. She was depending on Kate to save her people, just as

Alan's purpose would be helped by her opposing the Tyrant's will.

The cry came out of the heart of her, out of her very soul spirit, rising to become one with the terrible, soulful keening of the tormented dead.

"Granny Dew! Take me out of here!"

Hoovering Up

"Normally we'd do it back at maintenance, but this one ain't for moving unless we sort her out first. We've got to take a look under her belly." The speaker was a stout and jocular man wearing a navy peaked cap and an orange vest with grey vertical stripes. He was explaining the ropes to his teenage apprentice. The train had stopped about thirty yards down the tunnel from a Tube station, whose lights Penny could see in the distance.

She watched the emergency team that had come to fix the train blocking the tunnel, peering out through a cast-iron grill that sealed off the older tunnel she had previously discovered.

Penny had surprised herself by returning to the ghost Tube station. And she had surprised herself even more in returning to explore the tunnels so soon after her fright. Gully accused her of being addicted to it, but she didn't think she was addicted, she just knew she had to be brave; she had to take risks if she was to discover the City Below. But this time she hadn't brought the dagger with her. This time she wasn't going to draw attention to herself with explosions of light and bangs. Even so, she still lacked the courage to explore the tunnel to the left. That was where the monster had come from—if it truly had been a monster at all and not a hallucination dredged up out of Gully's myths and her own morbid suggestibility.

If anybody was going to draw attention to themselves it was the emergency team, who were carrying inspection lamps that cast them in brilliant arcs of light, like actors highlighted on a stage. The girl apprentice had a pointy, nervous face, with short cropped dyed blonde hair. She was wearing cleanly washed overalls, with a spotless orange vest. The stout man, whose overalls were already dirty, had just taken a quick look under the front end of the driver's carriage. His voice had an archly humorous tone to it, which he was putting on for the girl. "It ain't just the one engine, you see. Every carriage has its own engines tucked underneath. Our job"—he said, wiping his sweating face with the back of his hand—"is to check it all out, see if them brushes needs changing."

He had a grey moustache and beard that, when highlighted by the glare of his light, made it look like he had a brush right there on his chin.

Penny chuckled at the idea.

She was glad that she had found the courage to come back to the tunnels. She was thrilled to be spying on these people—watching while they were unaware—and comforted by the calm, resigned way the maintenance people worked—it reminded her of Mother.

"I heard," the girl said, her voice curiously high pitched, "that there was a woman last week walked out onto the track."

"Jumped more like."

"When she knew the train wasn't stopping."

"We call them 'one under.' "

"Oh, that's creepy!"

"It's creepy for the team that's got to scrape 'em up."

"You're scaring me. Don't tell me any more."

Penny was scared too. She didn't want to hear any more about scraping people up.

She could see the expressions on their faces with exceptional clarity in the bright light of the inspection lamps. The contrast between the brilliant light on their brows and cheeks and the surrounding shadows was what painters called chiaroscuro. Maybe she would sketch their faces on her ceiling in chiaroscuro?

"Nah—don't you worry, sweetheart! You think that's frightening? You heard the talk about the bogeyman?"

"Don't!"

The fat man's belly wobbled as he chuckled. "Nothing to be frightened of."

"Leave it out. You'll give me nightmares."

"Good thing I'm down here with you, then. You'll be all right with me. But you know there's talk about it, there are some who think he lives down here—they say he eats people alive. Honest to God! Them old tramps who kip down here. Sucks 'em up, blood and gristle, teeth and bones."

The girl's mouth turned down. "Yukk!"

The fat man laughed out loud, smacking his lips. "Mmmmmmm!"

Penny felt a chill creep slowly over her skin from the nape of her neck and down her back. All of her newfound confidence drained right out of her. She recalled the monster she had seen in the torchlight: the vaporous cloud studded with living, talking faces. She recalled the sound of it in the dark, the slithering amoeboid movement, the faint rattling of the rusty iron grill. And then the horror of something hunting her, sniffing . . .

Was Gully right? Was she being crazy coming down to the tunnels again? She really had had to force herself to come back. She'd had to block out the fear in her mind at every step as she had followed the tunnel to the right, with its single set of tracks set in tarry wooden sleepers. The fact it was a single track said a lot about how old the tunnel, and the ghost station, likely was. But now she had come to the end of the right hand tunnel only to find that it terminated with a brick wall, hoary with soot and dust, surrounding the iron grill she was now peeping through. Logic dictated that she must now explore the left-hand tunnel.

You're not going to be a scaredy cat—are you?

But now the fat man was frightening her all over again with what he was saying to the girl apprentice. Penny watched, with her eyes open wide, as he clapped the shoulder of the skinny girl and laughed. "You know what, sweetheart? There's some who think it's the bogeyman hoovering up the place."

Penny bit down on her quivering lower lip. He had used exactly the same word for the monster as Gully—bogeyman.

Oh, Gully!

She had never really had any friends before she met Gully. Mother did try, once or twice, to have some of her classmates around to the rambling old house, with its neglected gardens, but the noise of the children nearly gave Father a nervous breakdown.

"*For heaven's sake, Rowena!*" he had said.

So Mother had to promise to desist from such foolishness. Penny had been secretly relieved.

When she complained, soon after that, that the other children didn't seem to like her, Father told her it was because she was special. She couldn't expect the other children to understand that because they were ordinary.

At the age of seven her mathematical skill was at the level of a seventeen or eighteen year old; she didn't know why they made such a fuss of something so simple. But that wasn't all. They did tests on her eyesight and her hearing, with electronic instruments to measure her acuities, to discover she was in the top

0.5 percentile. Penny Postlethwaite was also top of her class in science at school. The teachers had been impressed, but they didn't really like her. It was almost as if they feared her. And the other girls and boys made rude jokes behind her back.

"Does your mummy kiss you at Christmas?"

Penny shook her head. "We don't celebrate Christmas."

But when she saw the other mothers and fathers kissing or hugging their children, she told herself that they did this kind of thing because they were ordinary, and not special like her.

They didn't have television at home because Father frowned upon the idea of celebrity and thought it was the death of culture. But Mother insisted on her Radio 3 and 4 programmes, which played classical music and operas, and gave the serious news. Art, the only subject that Penny loved, was dropped so she could focus on the sciences. She complained to Father that it was the only subject where the teacher, Miss Warren, liked her. But Father was not impressed with Miss Warren. Penny overheard the argument when Miss Warren had tried to stop the headmaster agreeing to Father's wish to stop the art class for good. Miss Warren, who was usually very quiet, so quiet she hardly raised her voice in the hour-long lesson, had shouted at the headmaster that it wasn't right, but as usual, Father had had his way. In tears, Miss Warren had later given Penny a plastic shopping bag with half-a-dozen books on art—books that had Miss Warren's own name written inside the cover—which Penny hid in the greenhouse and read over and over.

Her performance in maths and science led to her being tested for an Oxbridge University entrance when she was twelve years old. She had to sit in a room with older boys and girls and answer some trick questions, called progressive matrices. She passed the test—Father said that she had sailed through it with flying colours. He was beaming with pride as he sat her down opposite him in his ladder-backed chair.

"For you, my girl, things are going to change."

That night she had climbed out of bed, fully dressed, at three in the morning. She had already borrowed Mother's debit card, together with an envelope, ballpoint and postage stamp from Father's desk, cashed the maximum she could obtain from two closely located ATM machines, and posted the debit card home. In the same rebellious act she had abandoned her surname, which would be too easy to trace, and became just Penny, as she sneaked out of her bedroom window and, like the once-upon-a-time mayor, Dick Whittington, headed for London, though not on a stagecoach but the early morning train.

Now, back in the abandoned Tube tunnel, a less-than-confident Penny watched the maintenance gang getting ready to leave. A driver was climbing aboard the train. She would have to make her way back to the ghost station and head for home. She had explored the right-hand tunnel as far as it went, but it wasn't the place she was looking for.

She thought again about the left-hand tunnel. The idea of exploring it was very frightening. She didn't know if she could do it. She'd have to go back to Our Place and think about it some more.

You're not going to be a scaredy cat, are you?

The River of Bones

For days, as the Shee army approached the lower slopes of the Flamestruck Mountains, they had been harried by hot, dry winds. The landscape around them became arid, with desiccated spinneys of gorse and shrub, littered with the bones of animals. But, since they had woken that morning, they had been able to see a valley up ahead. As they drew closer, they began to see that a winding river ran through it, and could hear the lowing and squealing of vast herds of animals on the bank, desperate to get to the greenery of the mist-laden foothills across the river.

As evening closed in, the true number of the animals became breathtaking; there must have been millions, perhaps tens of millions of the creatures, wheeling in confused and agitated herds, like clouds blown about in a tempestuous sky.

The Shee constructed a shield wall around the more vulnerable load carriers and camp support staff. A saddle-weary Alan approached the shelves of black rocks that poked out into the stream in staggered ledges and halted his onkkh in amazement. With horror he saw that the white gleam they had seen from further away, which they had assumed was the foam-crested tide of a wide and fast-flowing river, was in fact a monstrous torrent of bones. He stared at the spectacle flowing through the valley as a major river would. It was a good half a mile wide, curling away into the distance on either side. The air was filled with the roaring of its currents, the shearing and tearing of bones sliding and grinding and fracturing against other bones—vicious and intimidating, unbearable to behold.

He dismounted, lost for words.

He could hardly walk, with his blistered backside, and it was agony just to stretch his aching back, the result of being rocked and jolted on that miserable onkkh over nearly a hundred and fifty miles. And now he felt numbed with shock, gazing out over the abysmal scene, his eyes lifting beyond it to the soaring peaks of the Flamestruck Mountains lit by a fiery sunset.

He heard Qwenqwo's approach, his boots grinding over the gravelly beach behind Alan's back. The dwarf mage looked equally overwhelmed.

"I suppose that the multitude of bones over the approaches was hint enough—though I would never have dreamed of this."

Alan shook his head.

They were joined by Mo and Turkeya, and then by Ainé and Bétaald. Together they stared out into the awful abyss.

"It's beyond cruelty," Turkeya said.

"In more ways than are apparent," Bétaald added.

Alan looked at the Shee adviser. "You have any idea as to what's going on here?"

"These herds of beasts—they are every bit as dismayed as we are."

Qwenqwo agreed. "They're too terrified to ford the river."

"Indeed so." The hissing voice of Iyezzz announced his arrival, sweeping down to land within feet of the small group. "Instinct dies hard. And their instincts tell them that once this was the mighty Neirann. In the old dialect of the Eyrie people, the word signified bounty. The Neirann gathered the mountain streams into a single torrent, its flood plain bringing fruitfulness to the now famished lands between here and the mighty Jourlanaa. Back then these banks were verdant with life; the greenest prairies ran all the way from the Flamestrucks to the Thousand Islands. Great herds roamed in their millions and there was food aplenty for all."

"Until the Great Witch came," Bétaald sighed.

Iyezzz shook his head. “Not so. Spiteful as she was, she lacked the power to subvert such a mighty river.”

“The Tyrant’s work!” Qwenqwo slumped down on a ledge of rock. “But how, why would he conjure up such a monstrosity?”

“I think we need to ask my mentor,” said Iyezzz.

Mo looked up at the Garg. “You mean Magtokk?”

“If you know where to find the charlatan,” said Turkeya.

“I think what Iyezzz implies,” said Alan, “is that Magtokk is here right now, and listening in to this conversation.”

“Clever Mage Lord!” The orang-utan manifested twenty yards from where they were standing, performing a series of somersaults to land within two feet of Qwenqwo, and causing the nearby Shee to metamorphose to cats in alarm.

“So you have been listening?”

The orange-bearded face with its heavy dewlaps of cheeks widened to a grin as he bowed before Alan. “Listening and observing, both.”

“And your opinion?”

“If you ask me, I would agree with the consensus. This is the work of the Tyrant.”

“But why? To what purpose?”

“The River of Bones is a most effective barrier—you could regard it as an outer moat of Ghork Mega.”

“What could possibly make it flow?”

"That I know not, but I fear we have only just begun to probe its unpleasant mysteries. No doubt there will be more to discover."

Alan shook his head, irritated by the riddles. The grating and grinding, the cracking of bones as they sheared and broke, was so deafening he could hardly hear himself think. "If this is a moat, how far are we from Ghork Mega?"

"Approximately eighty to ninety leagues, as the Garg prince flies."

Alan translated in his mind: about 240 miles. That was some moat. "How are we to get across, or around, this thing?"

"May I speak to you in private?"

As Alan walked downstream he saw there were numerous small islands in the river. They looked like stony outcrops resistant to the stream, their surfaces worn to spiky hummocks by the grinding passage of the bones.

"Hideous as the spectacle is, I am of a mind to consider it a manifestation of his humour," said Magtokk.

"Humour?"

"A dark and exceedingly cruel humour, I grant you. But this monstrosity—is it not a message as well as a warning?"

"What message?"

"The River of Bones. Is there not subtlety of a kind here—beyond what might be needed for a barrier?"

Alan blinked. He had been staring out at one of the stone outcrops only to find it had disappeared. "I don't follow you."

"The Tyrant enjoys playing games."

Alan stared at another of the many islands. "You think he's playing games with me, personally?"

"You think not?"

A thought, a memory, came to Alan. "Is it possible that he fears us?"

"I doubt he fears you personally. He has access to the Fáil. The goddesses who have empowered you, when you consider it, are powerless to destroy him. Why else have they not done so already?"

Magtokk's reasoning was more than a little disturbing.

Alan saw that the island in the stream had disappeared. He stared at the spot where it had stood. "Is this leading somewhere?"

"What I am suggesting is that in examining his patterns of behaviour you might look for signs of weakness."

The memory nagging at Alan was the moment when the Temple Ship had come to rescue him at Carfon. At the time he had assumed he was about to die. He knew nothing of what Mark was thinking or how he was about to use the Temple Ship to intervene. In that same moment Alan had sensed fear. Had the Tyrant revealed his own fear at the arrival of the Temple Ship?

The island had reappeared. It was hard to see it clearly in the waning light and against the obscuring cloud of bone fragments, but Alan thought the island had moved against the stream. And then, abruptly, it was gone.

He returned to the conversation. “Maybe you should enlighten me?”

“We might begin with an attempt at understanding the Tyrant’s aims and motives. Where you value goodness and life, he venerates darkness, death. Understanding this, he provokes you into violence, so you forego your moral nature.”

Alan watched another island while considering what Magtokk was saying.

Long ago the Tyrant had provoked Nantosueta to condemn the Fir Bolg to an eternity of death in life. He had provoked Alan and his friends at Ossierel, where the lessons of the first battle had not been learned. *We were consumed by anger, hate, as well as fear for our own survival. We killed a lot of people. Half the army of the Gargs died there and a whole army of the Tyrant’s legionaries.*

Kate—Kate might have been the only one to understand. But Kate had been kidnapped, taken, so she could play no part at Ossierel. Had that been a deliberate part of a bigger plan? In the Forest of Harrow—the trees tried to kill but they couldn’t help it. Okay—so the Tyrant had a grim sense of humour, but maybe Kate had instinctively understood. When Alan had destroyed the Forest of Harrow, she had then healed it again.

Alan stared at the moving obscenity in front of him. "So he enjoys playing grim games with us."

"Indeed he does. But let us examine it further—how did you come to engage with him?"

"To hate him, you mean?"

"If you like."

"He killed my parents."

Magtokk blew out his cheeks until they looked like inflated balloons. "Can you think of any other wile that would have better engaged your attention?"

Alan felt his temper rise. "You're telling me the murder of Mom and Dad was an opening gambit in his game?"

"Perhaps another power had already chosen you. Perhaps the Tyrant decided to make it more interesting—from his perspective."

The second island had also submerged; there could be no doubt about it. Alan frowned. He returned his attention to the orang-utan. He had to suppress his irritation at the calm, sly intelligence he sensed in that face, those eyes. The big wide tongue emerged to lick over the tombstones of teeth.

"You think his arrogance is his weakness?"

"Don't you?"

Magtokk the Mischievous took the opportunity for another somersault, landing with surprising lightness on those hand-like feet at the end of his short but powerful legs.

Alan paused, trying to get a firm control of his emotions. "You really believe he killed my parents just to get my attention?"

Magtokk scratched his bearded chin. "I would surmise that was part of his intention. It is no shame to suffer grief and hurt in such circumstances. Yet emotions are antipathetic to reason."

Alan had to pause again to think. He breathed out slowly, feeling his exhaustion, his many aches and pains. "But none of this explains the River of Bones—or tells us how to cross it."

"That we need to ponder afresh—after a good night's sleep."

If Alan had thought he would get some rest overnight he was disappointed. Worry about the barrier that faced them, the thunderous grinding of the bones and the lowing and screaming of the multitude of tormented animals, all kept him tossing and turning. And now, at first light, there was the sound of sharp cracks and detonations, like gunfire.

Alan dressed hurriedly to observe the obscene river again, feeling the frustration of the animals that bayed and wheeled about in seething masses of agitation. Some among the herds resembled giant zebras, with coats of brown and tan stripes. Others, much faster moving, were flightless birds about a third the size of the onkkh, and possibly related to them. They lacked the brilliant colouring of the scales about their heads and necks, but they had the same shaggy bodies and long feathers; their wings, though too small to enable flight, flapped as they ran, like overgrown chickens. Other beasts looked too strange to compare with anything back home. And then there were numerous smaller creatures, moving among the restless giants.

Lightning balls were forming over the nearby slopes, crackling and exploding like pricked balloons. These were the source of the gunfire-like cracks that spooked the animals, causing them to panic.

"You really have to pity them." Mo had appeared by his side, soon joined by Turkeya.

Alan *did* pity the unfortunate beasts. Many had wasted to skin and bone, starved because terror forbade them to cross the river, though they could see and smell the food on the distant banks: a tempting landscape of lush grass and shrubby trees fed by the streams coming down off the foothills of the Flamestrucks.

Mo spoke his mind. "If only Kate were here. She might have worked her miracle and greened this desert."

"Why hasn't she returned, Mo? Why am I still unable to contact her, no matter how hard I try?"

"Something has delayed her. It must be something important. You have to trust her. Kate is smart—and resourceful."

"Still, she was only meant to be gone for a few days, not weeks. Where's that dragon that's supposed to be her friend?"

The aides, assisted by the small party of Olhyiu cooks, prepared and served the morning meal. They were now limited to two meals a day; morning and evening. They ate the food sitting on flat ledges of rock, or patches of shingle, and talked about every possible way of circumventing the river.

The Gargs had shown that they could fly over it without a problem, but for a few hundred Gargs to attempt to ferry the entire Shee army—and the loads borne by the onkkh—across the river would take weeks.

Alan asked Iyezzz, "Is there any other way around it?"

The Garg shook his head. "There is no passable route. The river twists and winds for fifty leagues to east and west."

"I'm beginning to think that Magtokk is right. The Tyrant is playing nasty games with us."

Qwenqwo agreed. "He harries us even while playing games. He's playing for time."

"Magtokk?" Alan had now come to assume that even if the magician was not visible, he would inevitably be close.

"If you please, Mage Lord." The voice sounded from a short distance away, close enough to listen to the conversation, yet on this occasion the magician deemed it unnecessary to materialise.

"May we have your advice?"

"I must agree with your advisers. The Tyrant amuses himself, meanwhile he weakens your army by attrition. You cannot circumvent this barrier by moving around it. But I have been observing the maddened beasts. Can you not sense how, in their agitation and movement, they are gathering the courage to attempt a crossing? Cruel as it might seem, I for one would be most intrigued to observe what happens when they do."

Alan shook his head. "I think the surrounding landscape of bones has already answered that."

"Maybe it has, but perhaps not quite as you think. Is this not a migration of a kind? We must presume that the River of Bones has been here for centuries, and it must have seen many similar migrations. Had the migrations failed, the beasts would have been exterminated long ago. Yet here they gather, in their millions."

"I don't think we shall be kept waiting long." Iyezzz stared up into the sky, where fireballs were crackling and fizzing with increasing force and frequency as the heat of the morning scourged the parched landscape.

The Garg's words were prophetic. The first major lightning strike came out of the blue, setting fire to the desiccated gorse and shrub a few hundred yards from the perimeter of the camp. The tinder burned with a fierce crackling as flames danced from spinney to spinney, provoking clouds of sparks and spreading rapidly. The aides rushed about taking down tents and covering belongings with sand while the Shee distributed themselves around the perimeter of the camp with blankets to douse any spread of the flames.

Within an hour the land all around them was aflame, with fire devils rising hundreds of feet into the air. The screams of the herds rose to a crescendo. The heralded stampede announced itself with a deafening thunder of hooves. It was led by the zebra-like beasts, which charged in a solid wall of flesh and tossing horns, trampling smaller creatures under their hooves as they thundered straight into the obscenity of the river.

Bétaald and Ainé took command of the protective wall of Shee, stabbing and slashing with javelin and sword, keeping the perimeter of the camp safe as the landscape turned to bedlam around them.

Alan roared above the din, "Mo, Turkeya, keep an eye on those rocky islands in the stream!"

"Why—what are they?"

"For sure they're not islands."

Then Mo screamed.

What resembled spiky rocks, each perhaps forty or fifty feet in diameter, yawned open to reveal blood red mouths, ringed by enormous fangs. Huge diaphanous shrouds like gaping nets shot out of them trapping several of the terrified beasts at once and dragging them back into the rending jaws.

Turkeya's voice shook with horror. "I think those shrouds—"

"Are stomachs," Alan agreed.

"Ugh! The poor things are being consumed whole!"

Still the stampede forged out into the blood-drenched stream, so those at the front were pushed relentlessly into the waiting maws. Hour after hour the frenzy continued. The screaming of the dying was continuous, the fountains of blood had grown to a red cloud that hung over the carnage, and everywhere the vast proliferation of mouths gaped open, fangs ripping.

"You were right, Magtokk," Mo whispered, her voice filled with tears. "It is a dreadful kind of ecosystem, based on agony and blood."

It was many hours later when Turkeya hugged her to him. "Look, Mo! The river channel—it's filling up with the bodies of the dead."

At last the giant carnivores became sated. They could consume no more. Their bony shells that had appeared to be islands of stone, were closing, the spiky domes submerging. But still the stampede continued with wave after wave of the herds breaching the blood-drenched stream and crossing the bridge made of the bodies of the dead. The River of Bones struck the dam and, with a torrent of water, it began to flow outwards in a vast encircling tide, to become a flood plain of blood and ravaged flesh and bones.

"Make ready!" The Kyra's command ran throughout the Shee. Trumpets sounded and the huge camp woke in a flurry of preparation.

Alan climbed back onto the shoulders of his onkkh. The columns formed again and the army was once more on the move. They started out across the horrific dam, the onkkh sure-footedly picking their way over the packed flesh and bones with claws extended, following the stragglers of the herds. Alan's eyes fixed on where they were heading: the looming foothills of the Flame-struck Mountains and the beginnings of what promised to be an arduous and hazard-filled ascent.

Trapped Between Opposing Forces

Kate knew that Granny Dew was nearby. She could sense her heavy head nodding, those all-seeing eyes staring down at the stupid girl whose eyes were caked shut, ensnared within the roots in the Momu's chamber. Kate heard a heavy bare foot stamp against the floor of the chamber and that growly voice rise in fury.

"Foolish child!"

"I'm not foolish. I'm doing what I have to do."

"What madness possessed you?"

"The Momu is dying."

"What is this obsession?"

Kate heard the roar of frustration and the thunderous detonations as the wooden staff crashed against the stony floor. The impact echoed and eddied around the walls with their proliferation of trunks and branches. Kate felt the force of the blow vibrate the cage of thick, fleshy roots that enclosed her body, leaving barely enough room for her chest to expand so she could breathe.

"They're all connected: the Momu, the Cill, the One Tree, the serpent-dragon, Nidhoggr. It's all part of what the Tyrant is doing. All part of some kind of labyrinthine plan."

"Gullible heart! And how easily led is the mind that guides it. Little good would you do this confounded Momu, whose life you consider more precious than your own, with such a threat to your mortal self."

"My mortal self?"

"See how the roots have gathered you up. The tree you thought to cure is now infesting you."

"Infesting?"

"Never will it release you from its fastness—not willingly."

"But the tree is dying—and the roots . . ."

"Pah! I know not if it is dying. But ravenous it most certainly is. And you have become a meal to its hunger."

The idea was too frightening to bear thinking about. Kate's eyes struggled to break open, but the lids were sewn up tight with gritty crud and she couldn't free her hands. She fought to break one eye open a slit, but the effort utterly exhausted her.

"What's wrong with me?" Her voice was the tiniest whisper. "What's happening to me?"

"When did you last taste a morsel of food? Or a sip of water? Have you entirely lost your wits, child?"

"I—I just lay down here."

"And where, pray tell, is here? Look around. Look within and without."

"I'm imprisoned by the roots. I can't move a muscle."

Kate caught a blurry glimpse of Granny Dew through the slit of the one eye she had managed to open, her brooding face silhouetted against a flickering light. As she fought again, squeezing her eyes shut, then haltingly, agonisingly, forcing the lids a fraction more open, she saw the brooding figure squatting down in the dirt; her grey hair a flood that overflowed to the floor, the red pin-points that were the eyes of the spiders glinting in her dress. She felt the movement of the spiders as they forced their way in between the mesh of roots to wrap Kate's shivering body in a weave of cobwebs.

"Thank you. I knew you would save me."

"Ach—foolish girl!"

With a prolonged litany of curses, Granny Dew tore the roots from around Kate's face and body, those powerful fingers freeing her left hand so she could rub at the caked eyelids. The roots provided kindling for a crackling fire in the dirt.

"As the roots will never cease in their efforts to consume you, so shall the fire never cease to draw off them. It is all I can do for you. Ach, so must these opposing forces battle on if you are to survive. Simple warmth will you need—and sustenance aplenty. Can you not feel how you are wasting away even as we speak?"

"The Cathedral of Death—I know it's the Tyrant's work."

"Pah!"

"I sense it. The death of the Momu—the destruction of the Ulla Quemar—the end of the Cill! It means something to him. It is all part of his plan."

"You sense nothing."

"I know that I sense it. Just as I now realise that I have to stop him. I sense it, overwhelmingly, that it is my purpose in coming to this world, just as the war against Ghork Mega is Alan's purpose. Poor Alan, who will be pining for me all the while I've been here."

"She worries over others. When her concern should be herself."

"But it's true. I think I understand it better now. All of us—we were brought here by Ussha De Danaan, each with a specific purpose, but always to oppose the Tyrant."

Granny Dew's all-black eyes regarded her for several moments in contemplative silence.

"I—I'm reminded of something the Momu showed me, something she warned me about when I first arrived in Ulla Quemar."

"Speak no more of the Momu, or Ulla Quemar. The Cill and their city are lost to this world. We must ensure that you do not follow their example. And that risk to you is growing moment by moment. These are not the roots of any ordinary tree. This one is needful beyond your ken. It will be all that I can do to delay its devouring you. Did you not consider your so-called purpose when you lay down here? Had you no thought in your head as to your mortal—aye, and spiritual—danger?"

Kate blinked her gritty eyes more fully open. She did her best to wriggle what she could of her arms and legs. What she felt of her body, her limbs, terrified her.

Her voice had never risen beyond a whisper. "I'm so thin."

"Skin and bone is what you have been reduced to."

"Can't you help me?"

"Alas, and witless also!"

"Help me. Help me, please?"

She attempted, with every fibre of her being, to engage the oraculum of power in her brow, but there was barely a flicker of a response.

"What's wrong? Why won't my power work here?"

"Can it be that she still fails to understand?"

The old woman's head lifted as if she were sniffing the morning air. Her eyes, black as a robin's, reflected the flickering flames of the fire. Her tongue, green with mould, licked over black tombstones of her widely spaced teeth. Kate heard the rattling sound of her breath emerge from deep in her chest. Only then did she notice the black pot simmering over the flames of the fire.

"Cha-teh-teh-teh-teh-teh!"

A thrill of fright swept over Kate's body. She knew what that strange expression meant. It was Granny Dew's word for danger—danger in the extreme.

"Cha-teh-teh-teh-teh-teh!" she warned Kate again.

A vision flooded Kate's mind. She saw millions of tiny threads, rootlets so fine that they were invisible to her ordinary sight, invading her skin, slithering down her nostrils and throat and poking into every other orifice, sucking the life forces out of her.

"What's happening to me?"

"The One Tree has you in its thrall."

She began to realise the enormity of what that meant. Not just her flesh and bone and blood. "It's feeding off my spirit too—my power! The power of my oraculum!"

"There is mystery here—mystery aplenty. You are right in your conclusions, and it is a lesson even to me, but why should it suffer such insatiable need?"

Granny Dew was stirring the stew with her elongated index finger. Kate could smell the contents of the pot by now. An acrid-smelling gruel with the strangest medley of smells, mushroomy, fleshy, spicy.

"You have the arrogance to think you could heal the Tree of Life?"

"I never attempted to cure the Tree of Life."

The black teeth bared in a throaty cackle. "Where did you think to lay yourself down? Whose offspring is the One Tree of Ulla Quemar?"

Kate attempted to shake her head. "I was thinking only of the Momu."

" 'I was thinking only of the Momu,' " Granny Dew growled. "When the truth is she was not thinking at all."

"I *was* thinking. Please don't tell me otherwise. Maybe I don't fully understand what's happening, maybe you understand it much better than I do, but I know it is part of what is expected of me. Please don't scold me, Granny Dew. Can't you just free me?"

" 'Oh, pity me! I don't understand. Oh, please, free me!' So does she beg. She who has laid herself down in a bower of teeth and claws and given herself body and spirit to a dying world."

"I was trying to help."

"Hark at she who has exposed her very soul to the hunger of Nidhoggr."

Kate wept with terror. "Well if you can't, or won't, save me, save the Momu. Save her dying people."

Granny Dew ripped out more of the roots around Kate's head to feed the flames, all the while stirring the pot with her elongated finger. The crooning stopped. The heavy face, as lined as a walnut, lifted so her basilisk eyes reflected the roaring flames. "Hmmmm! A conundrum has her witlessness provoked. A purse of tidbits will hardly suffice. Small creatures come! You who would be the sole survivors of this doomed city. Come—come quickly! Hear my call."

Kate looked around in horror. She beheld columns of creeping and crawling things. Sea creatures such as baby starfish, sea urchins, baby periwinkles and cockles slithered and wobbled out of the birthing pool behind the fire, making their way into the waiting hand that was feeding the pot. Other columns were skirting the fire and the heavy figure that squatted by it, heading onwards towards Kate herself, still trapped amid the roots.

"What are they doing?"

"Eat!" The old woman growled, reaching towards Kate with an arm that seemed to elongate, forcing a fistful of the living ingredients between her chattering teeth.

Kate wheezed. "Stop it. I'll choke. I—I can't even chew it."

"Eat!" The old woman insisted again, shoving a second fistful into the back of Kate's throat, a finger pushing the piping hot wedge of food down.

Granny Dew continued to push food into Kate's throat, forcing her to swallow it down without chewing until the pot was empty. In spite of the hot food, Kate's entire head drenched in a freezing cold sweat. The feeding had utterly exhausted her, but the old woman took little notice, rocking backwards and forwards and crooning to herself.

"Ach! No matter if she feeds and feeds, the roots will leech off her still."

The soup was reviving her, if slowly. Kate felt an increase of vigour in her muscles and limbs.

"I . . . I saw the soul-spirit of the Momu. He—the Tyrant—is holding her in the Cathedral of Death."

"Pah! So stubbornly naïve still. And all the while the seeds of chaos are flowering. Soon—soon enough—the consequences may be too grievous to bear."

"Why do you talk like this? I'm doing what is expected of me. Why won't you explain what's wrong in words I understand?"

"She would understand? How could she possibly understand?"

"Please try—do try to explain."

The old woman's head fell so that she became a squat triangular shape, indomitable as a mountain. "Methinks," she growled, "there is another player in the game. A cunning trickster, who has already engaged her naïvety. I would protect her, foolish as she is. But even I am constrained by the opposing forces."

"For heaven's sake—what opposing forces?"

The growling continued while Granny Dew mused aloud. "Surely her life is now one with the Tree. She must solve the riddle for herself if she is to escape the trap she so foolishly fell into."

"Help me to use my oraculum—the power of the goddess."

The triangular shape was rocking to and fro by the fire, her humming interrupting the grumbling soliloquy. "Ach—she must be fed, continuously, if we are to compensate for such hunger. She must consume, as she is consumed, in flesh and in spirit."

"Oh, Granny Dew—why won't you answer me?"

Kate had already exhausted what little strength she had regained from the gruel. She knew that Granny Dew was furious with her, but was also attempting to assist her.

Trying to assist me, Kate made herself believe.

But her thinking had become increasingly hazy. Her thoughts were dissolving into inchoate fragments in her mind. Whether it was the gruel that Granny Dew had fed her, or some stupefying effect of the myriad rootlets that were invading her body, Kate felt sleepy, intoxicated, as if her consciousness were melting away into a world of dreams in which these hordes of little creatures were coming to her aid, building a cocoon about her.

What's happening to me?

A residuum of her need, her restlessness, quivered about her lips, but she no longer had the capacity to speak her thoughts aloud.

<You must discover how best to resist the seduction, child.>

<To resist . . . resist the seduction?>

<Your body ebbs strength. Your heart grows weak. While you chase ghosts in these shadow lands, your purpose is lost.>

Kate roused herself a moment. How had she allowed her eyelids to close? She had to force them open again.

<Let the creatures of the oceans feed you. Let the dew of the deeps moisten your lips and tongue.>

No! She tried to clench her mouth closed against the squirming, wriggling things that moved through her lips and into her throat. Others were invading her nostrils, her breathing passages. She should gag, choke—if only her body was not too weak to react.

Yet at last she understood some small part of it. Granny Dew would not allow her to starve. The little creatures, which felt so like worms, creeping and crawling and slithering grotesquely inside her—they would feed her, keep her alive, at least for a while. A war was taking place between opposing forces and it was an integral part of that war that the little creatures would do battle with the invading roots. As the roots sucked her strength and the power of her spirit, the little creatures would fight back by nourishing her in equal measure. Oh, yes—Kate understood this small part of some bigger picture in which she was caught up. The fight would endure while her strength remained. Only thus trapped between the opposing forces would she be allowed to travel further and enter the dangerous portal she had discovered.

The City Below

Penny paused at the rusty steel mesh, her torch illuminating the door leading out onto the narrow railway platform and the ancient single carriage rails running to the right and to the left. She had improved on the dimming after Gully had produced an "almost perfick snotless noserag" from one of his pockets. It had been raining hard and persistently for several days in the City Above and fresh rivulets were running down the walls, following the older stains she had seen before. Squeezing through the half-ajar door she examined her own, earlier footprints leading along the station platform to her right. They were preserved, as if frozen in virgin snow. She only realised that she was holding her breath when she released it with a sigh of relief. There were no other prints, nothing to suggest that any other feet had added to her presence. Yet she felt the need to be still. Even though there were faint sounds coming from a distance, probably carried along through the tunnels for miles, there was nothing else to suggest a presence nearby.

You see it's fine. No need to be a scaredy cat!

She had suffered nightmares thinking about the tunnel to the left. She just couldn't help feeling jittery after that time when she had, perhaps, imagined something monstrous coming up to the mesh. But Penny wasn't altogether sure of anything any more. Not now. Not here, in the City Below. Things that might appear to be logical and reasonable in the City Above might not apply down here. Here, a different set of rules applied.

Gully had been driving her mad. She had been adding the two turrets to the Church of St. Mary Woolnoth on the ceiling map, when he had invaded her space. The churches were some kind of loci, or so her instincts suggested. Could it be that there were loci both in the City Above and the City Below? She had been trying to think this through when Gully had begun whistling, making her unable to concentrate. Gully could be very irritating with his serious whistling. He was just letting her know that he was wound up tight, but he had been wound up tight most of the time recently, which made it very difficult for Penny to do her work.

"Them tunnels is dangerous."

"Everywhere in London is dangerous."

"Why won't you listen to me, Penny. I'm tellin' you there's a . . . a thing down there. It's eating people."

"Don't be ridiculous."

"Will you come down off there an' we'll 'ave us a nice cuppa an' some bread an' butter?" He hadn't pronounced it "butter." He pronounced it "buhher." "Will you come dahn an' 'ave a cuppa an' a bit a bread an' buhher?"

"I haven't got time for this, Gully. I need to complete my maps."

"You an' them maps—them maps is drivin' you bonkers."

"You don't say that when you take my drawings out to sell them."

"They ain't drawin's. Them's just pictures. They ain't even pictures, to tell the truth—them's more like scribbles."

When he wanted to hurt her, he dissed her art. "What would you know? You wouldn't know a drawing from a donkey," she had replied.

His eyes showed his hurt in return. And then she was sorry she'd said that because she knew how sensitive he was about his lack of education. It was why he never talked about his parents. The only family Gully would talk about was his nan. He had cared for his nan, doing all the shopping and cleaning and cooking for her when she had suffered a stroke. Then the council had thrown him out when she died.

"You should stop this, Gully."

"Stop wot?"

"This is not about tunnels or maps."

"You won't never come close to me—why won't you let me touch you?"

"You know why."

"I been takin' good care of you. I been gettin' the food. I been taking chances for you. I made that gantry thing so's you could put your pictures up there on the bleedin' ceiling. But still you go lookin' right through me."

"No I don't."

"Yeah—you ruddy well do. You don't even see me here. I been tellin' you for ages about that stuff. Anybody could see that it's jus' natural, exceptin' you."

"No."

"That's all you ever say—no."

"You know that I can't bear to be touched."

"Can't? Won't more like. I mean, why? I mean, wot've I done to you, gel? I don't think it's me at all. Maybe it was your da. I mean, I'd understand it—I would. I mean, my own da was a crock a shite an' worse."

She stood still, feeling the increase in her heartbeat even now, just as she had when she lay there on the gantry.

"An' I got you out of that squat. All of them idiots was there. You've got no idea wot might've 'appened. You was 'eadin' for bother."

"I know."

"It was me found Our Place. I brought you 'ere. I did it all, I did everything for you." His hurt struck her, like a punch in her guts. She didn't want to hurt Gully. She really didn't. She felt for him. She liked him.

Closing her eyes, she tried to shake the memory of Gully from her mind. She had to focus on the present, the small dusty platform in the ghost Tube station and the leftwards track, which led centrally, to the ancient heart of London.

She reopened her eyes, sat down on the filthy lip of the platform and, shoving herself off with her hands, hopped down onto the track. She waited for the cloud of dust to settle. She patted the ground with the tips of her trainers to locate the first of the wooden sleepers, all the while directing the torch ahead into the pitch black tunnel. Finding her rhythm as she stepped between sleepers she moved forward, making her cautious way into the gaping mouth of the leftwards tunnel.

The moment she entered it she felt something, a prickly awareness that was both scary and thrilling.

She had moved ahead several hundred yards when she was forced to call a halt to have another think. It was obvious that this line was more damaged than the rightwards one. She had passed stretches where water pattered down in silvery droplets from holes in the arched roof and now the track had disappeared into a pool of stagnant water that she would have to cross if she was to explore further. For a minute or two she just stood still, peering into the darkness ahead. Then, on a whim, she extinguished the torch and waited until her eyes became accustomed to the dark. She saw a faint bluish light. It reminded her of descriptions she recalled from books: the light sailors described in the dark of night coming up out of the oceans. She struggled to remember the word, and then she thought of it—phosphorescence.

But phosphorescence was a natural light and she didn't think this was natural. It wasn't coming off the walls, it was coming towards her through the air, from some definite source somewhere in the distance. Her torch reignited, she sat in the dirt and removed her trainers and socks, hanging her trainers around her neck by the laces. She rolled up the legs of her jeans so she could wade into the pool, sliding her feet forwards rather than stepping to get a better impression of the bottom. She watched out for hidden traps or drops while she tried to keep her stride paced to the safety of the drowned sleepers. It took her fifteen minutes to negotiate what was probably only thirty yards. As she was drying her feet with the socks, which she discarded now they were soaked, she felt a definite movement in the air, like the faintest gust of wind. And then, while slipping the trainers back onto her feet, she heard the whisper, however distant, of running water.

The rail track ended with the pool, but the tunnel continued, though the walls looked rougher, perhaps older, or merely unfinished. The fanning movement of air became stronger as she moved on and the sound of water became louder. After about half a mile she was astonished to find that the tunnel opened out into a huge enclosed space, with a gaping hole to one side of its floor. She was breathless with surprise at her discovery.

She had to be very careful now, with that hole in the ground. She removed the handkerchief from the torch and shone the bright light in great wide arcs, discovering layers in the walls. There were broken red bricks on the floor and a shiny white piece of porcelain that could once have been part of a loo. The space was wide, perhaps eighty feet or more, and the roof was just as high. She wondered if it might be a bomb site, left over from the Second World War, but when she inspected the walls in more detail they were too worn and natural, too cavern-like. Shining the torch over the floor she saw a great heap of rubbish that must have fallen into it from above, piling up to make a slope. She peered up the slope into the roof of the cavern. Wherever it had come from, that was the hole the draught was blowing in from. Maybe there was a way out that would save her retracing her journey back to the Tube station.

She turned her attention to the hole in the floor. When she dropped a pebble into it, it fell for four or five seconds before splashing into water.

Gosh!

She took several steps closer to the place where she could hear the sound of running water. She paused next to a big crack in the wall where the sound was loudest. She turned the torch off.

"Oh my God!" The blue light was all around her, as if a tide of ghostly luminescence were flowing into the cavern.

She kept absolutely still, listening hard and looking in all directions, attempting to figure it out. As she did so she heard a sound like the fluttering of a large bird's wings. An owl perhaps? But what would an owl be doing in this strange cavern under the ground?

Then she saw two beams of light, like tiny red searchlights. They were moving through the air. And something was caught in the focus of the searchlights. Penny saw a mouse hesitate against a dark, shadowy stretch of wall. She could just about make out its eyes, which were pinpoints in the darkness. Penny jumped as a dark shape pounced on the startled mouse. She caught a glimpse of a terrifying imp-like face. The searchlights were rays of light emerging from the creature's eyes.

A Grimling!

The temptation to switch on the torch was overwhelming, but Penny resisted it with all of her might.

I must be absolutely still, be careful to make no noise and not use any torchlight—nothing that would attract its attention.

She watched in the light of the Grimling's own eyes as it devoured the mouse whole like an owl, the head first, then with a series of gulps, the body, with the tail slithering away between its razor sharp teeth.

Then the Grimling vanished.

Penny waited several moments before she dared to move. She thought about what she had just seen. It was possible that the Grimling could switch off the light emanating from its eyes, but it was more likely that there was a simpler explanation. Edging closer over the rubble-strewn floor of the cavern, she reached out with her right to touch the wall, at the place she thought the Grimling had vanished. She felt the draught at much the same time that she found the gap—a cleft just a few feet high and barely wide enough for her to squeeze her head and shoulders through. And then she almost squealed with fright.

She saw creatures—enormous creatures—the strangest, most alien of creatures she could possibly have imagined. They were constructing things—huge and complex things, structures that were glittering in the gloom.

She withdrew her head and shoulders, trembling with shock.

There had been more than one type of creature. She had seen lots of Grimlings there, but they had just been buzzing around the huge creatures, like bees buzzing about a hive. What in the world did it mean?

Oh, Gully I was right. I knew I was right. I knew it all along—there's a second city, an alien city, below the London we know.

The City Below!

It was at once breathtaking, wonderful . . . terrifying.

Penny hardly recalled how she found her way up the rubble slope to the surface, her heart pounding, her mind and senses overwhelmed. She just welcomed the cooling feel of rain on her face as she emerged into the street. She had scrambled to the roof of the cavern like a monkey, clawing with hands and feet, following the downdraught of air to emerge into the ruin of a Victorian terrace. Just another burned-out street, with most of the neon lights vandalised. Turning through a circle to orientate herself, she was greatly relieved to see St. Paul's Cathedral no more than two hundred yards away. It confirmed her suspicions that the important structures of the City below were linked to the sacred buildings in the City Above. She slumped down on the wet pavement against a derelict garden wall, exhausted by her journey through the tunnels and breathless from the climb.

What have I found?

She was certain that there would be other tunnels, leading to more discoveries—truly an alien City Below that was growing directly beneath London.

"Hush!"

She jumped as a voice sounded from directly behind her. An elderly man, small and neat with a white beard, was standing in a gutted doorway behind the wall. He was wearing a navy cloak with curiously roomy sleeves that glistened with rain. He put his finger to his lips.

"Please—don't hurt me."

"I wouldn't dream of hurting you, Penny."

He spoke with just a trace of an accent, waving her to her feet, then ushering her back around the wall.

"How do you know my name?"

"It's the easiest thing in the world to decipher names. But there is no time to explain. We must hide and keep very quiet and still. There's something rather intriguing going on out there."

Penny looked at him more closely. He was an inch or two shorter than herself, and his skin looked a shade of bronze in the neon light, with features that could be Asian, or even South American.

"What is it?"

"Hush now! Whisper if you must. But you can see for yourself, over there."

Penny saw an abandoned camper van perhaps forty yards along the rubble-strewn street. It was close enough to a functioning street light for her to make out an amorphous mass squeezing out through the van's side door. She watched it expand into a huge, malformed shape as pallid as a cloud.

Penny darted her head down under the wall. Her lips were trembling, so it was hard to whisper. "Oh, shit!"

"Hush!"

Penny didn't want to look at it, but the bearded man bade her lift her head again. Together they peered over the lip of the wall, ignoring the rain that was running unchecked over their faces. The old man, whose face was remarkably unlined for his age, whispered into her ear, "I doubt it is interested in you or me, but still we mustn't draw attention to ourselves."

Penny couldn't have moved even if she wanted to. Her muscles were frozen with terror. "Who are you?"

"My real name would sound altogether foreign to your ears," he whispered. "But they call me Jeremiah at the mission."

"You work in a soup kitchen?"

"I'm a lay brother. We try to help those who cannot feed themselves. We give succour on a more spiritual level too." He smiled an apologetic smile. "I came to see how my friends, the itinerants, were getting on. Then I saw this curious thing happening just as you emerged from your crack in the ground."

Penny studied him; his straggly white hair was plastered to his scalp and he had rounded cheeks. Rain drops glistened in his white moustache and beard. His speech was quaintly formal, but he seemed so gently spoken that she didn't feel threatened by him. She blurted, "I saw it before—in the abandoned Tube tunnel."

"You did?"

Penny looked sideways at Jeremiah. There was a strangeness about him, proven in the fact he knew her name.

Jeremiah's hand waved her down again just as the thing turned to look in their direction. There had been the impression of faces around the edges of the cloud. She recalled the bespectacled face of the man and the fox's head, but it seemed just as impossible now as it had before. How could anything have more than one face? And yet she was sure that she could see different faces studding the surface of the monstrous thing as it twisted and bulged in that slimy amoeboid crawl.

"What is it?"

"It's a very ancient being. Its name is Shedur."

Penny cowered, the name sent fear through her heart.

He said: "Ah! Something new is happening!"

Penny darted her face back up over the wall to see. The thing was breaking up. It was the most terrifying spectacle she had ever seen.

Jeremiah actually chuckled. She thought he did so to reassure her because she was shaking with fright. Penny couldn't stop herself staring at the monster, which was fragmenting into many smaller bits. And each bit . . .

Oh, my God, there's a different face in every bit!

Penny's whole body was trembling. Still she couldn't help looking over the wall. She saw each of the smaller bits of the monster take on a life of its own. They were spreading out, taking on vaguely human shapes to move away in awkward staggers, each one of them heading in a different direction.

A jolt of panic swept through Penny. She wanted to find somewhere to hide. Somewhere to creep into and hide forever.

"I think it's safe for us to go to them now."

"W-what?"

"We should go to see them—the people who live in the camper-van."

Penny felt sick to think there might be people living in the van, the same van the thing had just come out of.

"I—I think we should stay away."

"Oh, I think the danger is past. Shedur has gone away."

"I want to go home."

"Don't you think we should go and see if they're all right? Shouldn't we find out if they're hurt—if they need help?"

"I can't—oh, God—no!"

He almost patted her shoulder, but stopped his hand an inch away, startling her not with the motion but with the fact he stopped. "There's no need for you to go at all. I'll go on my own. You may stay here—watch out for me."

Penny felt guilty, cowardly. Didn't she need to know about the thing? Hadn't it frightened her half to death down in the tunnels? And had already determined on going back again to the City Below.

She thought, *I can't. I don't dare to.*

He had already started out on his own.

"Wait, I'm coming with you."

"Well now." He turned around to look directly at her with those kindly eyes, the brown of mahogany. "You are a determined young lady, but we should be careful still and keep close together."

He led her to the camper van. Its tyres were flattened out like melted candle wax. The rubbish all around must have belonged to the people who had lived there. There were hundreds of bags with the name of a nearby supermarket amid a small hill of discarded bottles.

"Why do you care about them?"

He ran a hand, shiny with rain, through his beard. How calm he was compared to her. There was a neatness, a precision, about him that reminded her of Father. "I care about people."

The single chamber inside was also full of rubbish and horribly smelly. There were clothes strewn over the floor and bundled in the corners. Amid the clothes, there were bottles and crumpled plastic bags that contained the dog ends of cigarettes. Penny saw one of those machines that people used to roll their own cigarettes.

She whispered, "There's nobody here?"

"Not any more."

"What?"

"You should look more closely."

Then Penny realised that the clothes piled on the floor, or against the walls, weren't just rags. They looked suspiciously abandoned—as if the bodies within them had been sucked right out.

"Your eyes do not deceive you."

Penny couldn't get enough of air into her lungs to breathe. She thought again about that overheard conversation at the broken down train, the repair man's jokey expression: *"Hoovering up."*

A Deepening Peril

It was late evening under an overcast sky. The crew were sitting around an open fire next to the Mamma Pig in a state of shock. Mark watched Cogwheel rolling a cigarette. He was talking, in between spreading the tobacco into the paper, about a time when he would have liked to have been alive. "It's a thing I dreamed about at college."

Cal was drinking whisky from the neck of the bottle. "What college?"

Cogwheel squinted in the direction of his miserable companion through the rising pencil of smoke. "The College of Experience."

Cal tossed the bottle to Bull, who took a swig in silence. Cogwheel waited for the bottle to do its rounds, via the itchy, restless Sharkey, and finally to him. He took a drink, coughed into his fist, then returned to rolling the cigarette. "Back there in the historic Sixties there was another kind of underground."

Mark glanced over at Nan, who shrugged, put a finger to her lips. He was only just coming to realise how much she liked to observe people.

Tajh had grabbed the bottle from Cogwheel and confiscated it. "We need to stay alert. After today, the likelihood of an attack is going to be heightened." Bull grabbed the cigarette roller from Cogwheel and headed for the Mamma Pig without a word. It was his turn to be look out.

"This isn't fair," Cogwheel said.

"You were talking about another underground?" said Cal.

Cogwheel grumbled. "Shit, shit—and more shit." He accepted a lit cigarette from Tajh and took a drag. "Okay. If I can recapture my thoughts. I was talking about a more spiritual kind—in a cosmic sense."

"You mean comic?" said Cal.

"I mean there was a movement back then, one that advocated a laid-back alternative. Those people interest me—the people they called Crusties."

Cal snorted. "Named after the clagg around their unwashed arses?"

"Gentle folk who were into meditation, vegetarianism, mandalas, pacifism." Cogwheel puffed contentedly on his cigarette, then continued. "A philosophy very different from the more militant aspects of the prevailing underground."

Sharkey grinned. "Hey, that's us, folks."

Tajh laughed too. "Oh, come on, Cogwheel—you and your Crusties! You imagine yourself as some kind of post-apocalyptic hippie."

"I can think of worse things." Cogwheel's eyes wandered around the circle, attempting to locate the confiscated whisky bottle. "I truly would love to understand that long-lost philosophy of life."

Cal yawned. "Dead and buried, you ask me."

Cogwheel spoke though a cloud of smoke. "I mean, if they lived today—and you know, maybe they do, somewhere—they would be implacably independent of any of society's social structure."

Mark followed Nan's gaze. She was looking across the fire—fuelled with timber they had collected from the surrounding woods—at the tall, slim figure of Jo Derby, who might have perked up at the mention of society, but was otherwise still lost in the stunned silence she had fallen into after her rescue. Mark saw that Tajh was also keeping an eye on her.

Cal flicked a cigarette from a pack and caught it in his mouth. He lit it. "I'm beginning to think like a Crusty myself."

"Well, at least you're thinking." Cogwheel grinned. "It seems to me they were thinking ahead. They were very pure people in their way. They believed in what they were doing."

The whole conversation was aimed at lightening the tension around the silent Jo Derby. Sharkey was beginning to get the idea. "And what, exactly, did they believe they were doing?"

"They perceived themselves as different—certainly. They opposed any conventional stereotype."

Cal belched. "So they definitely wouldn't be up for an honest day's work?"

"Hell, no! That would undermine the aspirational apathy of what they were about in the first place."

With the air of assumed innocence Nan turned to Cogwheel. "How, then, might such a Crusty earn his living?"

"As lazily and as independently as he could."

Sharkey winked at Nan and said, "Hey, Cogwheel, what does this Crusty music sound like?"

"Maybe like a clock ticking, or the sound of rainfall, or birds twittering, or a waterfall, or a stream—or the sea. I think they might have called it ambient. You could see it as a kind of poetry in tune with nature. You might listen to it and imagine the song of lovely cotton-wool clouds in the blue summer sky."

Jo Derby's shoulders shook as she began to weep. Tajh crossed over to sit beside her. She put her arm around the woman's shoulders and lifted her eyebrows at Cogwheel. "It sounds very relaxing."

"Kind of like an electronic sedative."

Nan followed the whispered conversation of Tajh and Jo Derby. She saw how Jo took a deep breath, then slid her spectacles further up her nose. Tajh called over to Cogwheel. "I'd like to hear it. Do you have anything like that you could play for us?"

"Oh, I think I might be able to lay my hand on something."

Cogwheel played the ambient music and they lay back around the fire and listened to it, enjoying a few minutes of comradely contemplation. Nan rested her head on Mark's shoulder, watching the sparks rise up into the dark. "I presume," said Cal, "that these Crusties had no objection to getting money off the State?"

"Ripping off the system was socially acceptable."

Cal started to laugh again, and once started, he was unable to stop. Perhaps, Mark thought, it was the need to save them all from more of Cogwheel's ambient music that induced Jo Derby to speak. "Thank you, all of you, for saving my life back there."

"Think nothing of it," said Cogwheel.

"This from a guy who wasn't there," said Cal.

"Thank you, anyway—all of you."

"Me too?"

"I'm sure if you had been there, Cogwheel, you'd have fought every bit as bravely as your companions."

A grin split Cogwheel's face from ear to ear.

Cal spat into the fire.

Jo shrugged. "But now, Cogwheel, I'm going to have to spoil the party, because this point in time is where your Crusty dream would end."

Mark looked over at the woman they had rescued, hearing the tremble of fear in her voice. "What are you saying, Jo?"

"There are no state handouts today and nothing for the seventy per cent of people marooned in London; those who can't escape the city. There are no jobs and the bulk of the population are devoid of any form of income."

"But what can they do—all those people?" Mark asked.

"Go to hell—or the soup kitchens!" Tajh said.

"Or bloody well fight," said Cal.

"But why isn't the State doing more for them?" Mark asked.

"What is the State any more?" Jo's voice had a tone of exasperation. Her face was still pallid with shock. Cal offered her the bottle of whisky but she shook her head.

Tajh said, "I'll get you a mug of tea, if you like."

Jo nodded. "Strong, please."

Mark couldn't get his head around what he was hearing. "I was away from London for just a couple of years. All of this has blown up while I was away. How could everything go to pot in such a short space of time?"

Jo looked as if she couldn't believe she was sitting around a fire with a crew of resistance fighters. She took a shaky breath. "I don't think it happened in the last two years. Things were going bad under the surface for longer. I think, perhaps, the conspiracy was active for years, maybe even decades. We were too complacent to notice. We were all preoccupied with our own small worlds. We took normality for granted—the fiscal system, law and order, every other facet of what we would call the civilised society. We went out to work to generate income. We paid our taxes, so the State could function. The schools, the health services, the social services, the army, the police, the folks who collected the rubbish from our streets—these were the real pillars of society. And when they began to fall apart, there was some sort of domino effect. When one pillar fell, the strain of it provoked cracks in the other pillars. And all the while the underlying conspiracy was undermining everything from within."

"What conspiracy?"

"A deliberately stoked culture of selfishness coupled with violence. It undermined the morality that lay at the heart of it all. I'm a Methodist. I was brought up in a religious family. I can see, now, where religion might have come into it. Might have done more to expose the spreading rot. But Grimstone subverted that. Oh, I realise now, listening to Mark, that must have been his role all along. Grimstone was somehow, everywhere, at the very root of it."

"Well," Mark nodded, "I can confirm that he's been spreading the word—his version of it—for many years. And you're right. It was never the Holy Word of God, at least not any kind of Christian interpretation of it, as far as I or Mo could see."

"Tell me what you remember."

"I was adopted here in London by Grimstone when I was a baby. I know nothing of my mother. I believe my father may have been—or now I see the situation, may have become—a traveller." Mark hesitated. Then he showed her the harmonica. "It's all I have of my father."

He explained a little more of what he knew.

"Now I'm no longer sure about anything. I talked to my adoptive sister, Mo. She was born in Australia. Her mother was part, or for all I know, wholly aboriginal. But now I think maybe there was always more to it—the adoptions I mean."

"What do you mean?"

"I think—I don't really know for certain—but I think our parents may have been . . . heck, I don't know . . . somehow special."

"What do you mean? You think your birth—the births of all four friends—were preordained."

"I wouldn't say it was anything in any religious sense, but I think our births were predicted. We were picked out very early, for some reason."

"But why—you must have some notion."

"I really don't know, but what if there were some way of predicting the future—of selecting individuals on the basis of such a prediction?"

"Fate?"

Mark's turned to Nan. Fate was what the word Fáil meant on Tír. "Something like that, yes."

Nan stared into the fire, cradling the mug in her hands.

"I know how it sounds, but on Tír we saw a lot of things that would make no logical sense here. It's weird, really. The two worlds seem to be linked in some ways, but in other ways they follow different rules."

Jo nodded. "It's an extraordinary story."

"I know it is. But what if beings on Tír, long ago—a very long time ago—knew more than we know on Earth today? What if they had a different kind of learning or knowledge? What if they had a deeper level of understanding of what makes up the universe?"

Mark was thinking back to the words of the dying high architect. The Fáil had been constructed by a race of magicians called the Arinn. He explained what little he knew of the Fáil.

"It's a fucking fairy story," said Cal.

Jo spoke quietly. "I saw Nan's eyes, Cal. And we both saw what Mark and Nan did to the roadblocks—the lightning that came from those things in their brows. I'm struggling to come to terms with it too, but I can't deny what I saw."

Cal sighed. "But you can't explain it, neither."

Jo shook her head, staring into the fire.

"It's bonkers," Cal muttered. "You all know it is. There just has to be some ordinary explanation. Maybe it's some new kind of weapon."

"I'm every bit as shocked as you are" Jo said. "I'm even more shocked to consider what it might mean."

"What might it mean?"

“I thought I understood. I thought I had figured it out. But, if what Mark and Nan are telling us is true, the real explanation runs much deeper and the danger is much worse than we imagined. Please, Mark, go ahead and explain what you and Nan are trying to do. This magical sword you’ve been talking about.”

“The Sword of Feimhin.”

“You believe this sword is somehow connected with what’s happening here in London?”

“Once you understand the connections, it does have a logic of its own. If the Tyrant is connected to the Fáil, and if Grimstone is his disciple . . .”

“Tell me more about this man, Padraig,” said Jo.

“Padraig is Alan’s grandfather. We believe that he is some kind of druid. The hereditary keeper of the Sword.”

“Tell me more about Alan—the other friends.”

“Alan and Kate made up the four with me and Mo. We were drawn into Tír from Earth. Alan’s grandfather, Padraig, was the only one who had any real understanding of what was happening. He told us he was the guardian of the Sword of Feimhin. He showed it to us and warned us how dangerous it was. I don’t think the Sword is just a weapon. As far as I know, Feimhin was a warrior prince from the Bronze Age. I don’t know if he actually came from Ireland, or if he just ended up there, but once he got hold of the Sword, the world became a nightmare of bloodshed and destruction. Padraig described an ‘Endless war.’ But he did more than just talk about it; he showed us the Ogham—a kind of Celtic rune system that covered the walls of the barrow grave where Feimhin had been buried along with the Sword. Padraig's ancestors had been guardians of the grave for centuries, maybe even millennia. He was afraid of it because he feared what would happen if the Sword fell into the wrong hands. He feared its capacity for malice. I'm not sure I believed any of it at the time. I was pig-headed and thought he might be making a romantic yarn out of it. But never-ending war was what we encountered when we arrived in Tír."

"A war brought about by this Tyrant?"

"On Tír they call him the Tyrant of the Wastelands. His symbol is a silvery triple infinity. You find it everywhere there, just as Nan and I have been finding it everywhere here in London."

"And this is the same symbol as on the hilt of the sword?"

"And on the hilt of the Scalpie's dagger."

"The Scalpie you killed in the church?"

"Yes."

"There is more," Nan said. "This dagger, with its twisted blade—the dagger removed from the church by Penny—is the same type of dagger that is wielded by preceptors back on Tír—a vile priestly caste that travel and fight with the Tyrant's Death Legion."

Jo Derby shook her head. "It all sounds so preposterous. Yet here you both are, with Mark claiming to be Grimstone's adoptive son. You have this whole extraordinary, fantastical story, and the more we examine it, the more links we find to things that previously didn't make any kind of sense."

"But," Mark said, "you've been studying Grimstone. You've been looking at how he works. You might be able to help us locate Padraig—and the Sword."

"Oh, Mark. Things are changing so rapidly. We have been seeing less and less of Grimstone publicly for the last few months."

"We think Padraig is the key to what's happening. We're sure that Grimstone's people took him. They took risks and torched his sawmill. We also know that they found the grave of Feimhin and we know that they stole the Sword."

"When did you say this happened?"

"Maybe three months ago."

"I suppose there could be a connection. I don't want to make too much of what may be nothing more than coincidence."

"Go on."

"But I have to admit that in these last few months the problems in London have become worse. The chaos has escalated."

Nan asked, "Could it caused by the presence of the Sword?"

"The timing might make sense." Jo looked at Mark. "This sword—I know how preposterous this sounds, but could it exert some kind of mind control?"

Mark looked at Nan. "I don't know. What do you think, Nan?"

"Maybe it can draw on the Fáil?"

"But how can this make any kind of logical sense?" asked Tajh.

"What if Tír and Earth are connected?" said Mark.

"How connected?"

Mark and Nan exchanged glances. He said: "We don't know."

He did his best to explain things he didn't fully understand himself. He told them how they had been returned, in some kind of dream journey brought about by Qwenqwo Cuatzel, to witness the death of the last high architect, Ussha De Danaan. He described the terrible scenes of plunder and killing throughout the ancient capital of Ossierel. He told them what he recalled of her dying words, which had explained something of the Fáil.

"She told us that the Fáil had been constructed by a race of magicians called the Arinn. She called it a malengin. She said they created the Fáil to give themselves immortality, but what they had actually achieved remained a danger to Tír—and maybe now to Earth."

"How dangerous?"

"She said there were three portals. We understood that a portal meant a way in to gain access to its power. She told us that the Tyrant had gained at least a partial access to one of those portals."

"Making him all-powerful?"

"Yes."

The crew looked restless, uncomfortable. Cal was drinking steadily, chortling to himself in a derisory way. He said "Then how the bleeding hell did you get back here to Earth?"

Mark became angry. "You want me to show you how?"

"No!" Nan put her hand on Mark's shoulder. "Let him doubt us, but do not be tempted into a display of power. Think back to the rescue of Alan at Carfon. They would not welcome the arrival of the Temple Ship."

Jo smiled at Nan. "I saw what I saw and that's enough to convince me there's something deeper going on here. What we need to do is find a way to get you two closer to Grimstone. You say you can read minds. Get close enough and maybe you can get all you need straight out of his head."

Nan nodded. "Can you do this—can you get us close to him?"

"There's a major gathering planned—something he calls a Confirmation of the Faithful. It will take place at Wembley Stadium. Maybe we can find a way to smuggle you into there."

Hobson's Choice

<I can't go back there . . . Granny Dew, I can't.>

In her mind, the answering voice was implacable. <The choices, Child, are ever yours.>

<Choices!> Kate groaned. <What choices do I have? I'm trapped here, caged by the roots. My mouth is barely free to speak. My throat is full of wriggling things, offering their bodies for food and I am probably only imagining the voice that speaks for me in that place. I have no choices. Or else it's only Hobson's choice. I dare not rest or fall asleep, or I'll become lost and purposeless, drifting to that grotesque cathedral.>

<Then call your dragon.>

<I will. I'll call him right away. I've done everything that I can here. I can't do any more. Surely nothing more can be expected of me.>

But then she remembered the despair of the Cathedral of Death, its pitiless cycling of life, the keening cries.

<I want to run away, but I can't abandon the Momu. If I abandon her now she'll become one of those poor tormented souls. And—oh, Granny Dew—I know that I will also be failing Alan, Mark and Mo.>

<Then your choice is made.>

As she closed her eyes she felt her spirit departing the chamber. It was a feeling of weightlessness and a dizzy, endless falling. She recalled what Granny Dew had told her. She must search for the serpent-dragon, Nidhoggr, in the roots of the One Tree—the so-called Tree of Life.

<But where am I to find the Tree of Life?>

Granny Dew had snorted a reply, as if the question were so childishly naïve, it hardly merited an answer.

<In Dromenon of course.>

Kate was becoming all too familiar with the disquieting world of the dead and the power of her oraculum that allowed her to separate her physical self from her soul spirit in this way. She was also becoming familiar with the concept of Dromenon, an in-between world. A domain where magic, dark and light, ruled. It was a place that didn't physically exist. It was more a landscape of the spirit, capable of being modified by powerful forces—and an exceedingly dangerous landscape. Of course, it made perfect sense that if the Cathedral of Death existed anywhere, it must be in Dromenon. <How, once there, do I find the Tree?>

<Pah! Has not your guide already found you?>

<The succubus—Elaru?>

<A spirit that is not necessarily friendly, perhaps. Yet a spirit that has the knowledge to aid your quest.>

Kate recalled the tormented face of Elaru and her sad entreaties. <I know that she prevaricates. I can't even be certain that she was spurned by the Witch.>

<Yet, did she not warn you to avoid the Cathedral of Death?>

<Oh, sacred mother of mercy! What am I to do?>

<In Dromenon even Fate is said to conspire. You must discover how to confront cunning with more cunning.>

<How?>

<Believe nothing you hear. Question everything you see. When all your faith and trust says true, look again—probe with your oraculum.>

Kate had no confidence in her cunning—or her oraculum.

<You must never forget that a goddess empowers you.>

The same words as the Momu had spoken.

During the time she had been forced to lie still and allow the bizarre nourishing of her trapped body, she had alternated between panic and refusal to give up. Even now, as she tried to imagine the place into which she was descending, she knew that whatever she did, whatever happened to her here, would have consequences in the real world. That was an intimidating thought. And others, perhaps more powerful and dangerous than she was, even with her oraculum, would be capable of seeing her, confronting her and hurting her—and that hurt would also be real in the same way. With a heavy heart Kate called the presence of the succubus into the full light of her oraculum.

The shadowy figure squirmed before her, and Kate once again looked on all-black eyes in a face of splintered flesh, bruised and bleeding; a mask of torment constructed out of clots of suffering. Elaru did not appear any more pleased than Kate to meet again. She struggled as if determined to escape her grip. Then she shrieked and Kate witnessed a bizarre and astonishing change. In Elaru's place was a flamboyantly feathery creature, its plumage a piebald melange of dazzling white and deepest black, puffed up with umbrage and as tall as a Garg. Two malevolent black eyes glared down at her from a vulture's head.

"What in heaven's name are you?"

"Urale—who else, dearie!"

"Urale—but that's . . ."

In Kate's imagination the being metamorphosed to Elaru, then changed back to Urale again.

A caution came to mind: *If Elaru is female and friend . . .*

Kate's eyes widened with astonishment. "Urale is . . . is male and enemy?"

A screech pained her ears, a sound that was a discordant mix of opprobrium and anguish. "Elaru—Urale! You takes your pick and you makes your choice."

"Is this some malicious game?"

A sigh that was also, somehow, a cackle. "Ooh! She is observant, is she not? Some game indeed. Oh, no. Oh, dearest Mistress!"

"Stop this—stop it this instant!"

Urale clacked his cruel beak. "Such penetrating insight! We cannot bandy irony with this one."

"Are you some minor deity?"

"Minor? Would you care to kiss these raptor lips?"

"Would you like to kiss my green fire?"

"Touché!" The vulture-being bowed mockingly low. "I present myself, grandson of Loki the fickle, born of a conjugal dance with the goddess Hel of the nine worlds who was cast by Odin into the deep sea of Nifelheim. There she brooded, acquiring the graces of slovenliness, famine, cold and hunger. Skills calculated to vaunt her ambition of the goddess of misfortune."

Kate hesitated, unable to make the slightest sense of it. "You are—what? The offspring of some goddess of misfortune?"

"Oh," he coughed into a fluff of fanned feathers, then wheezed what might have been a dramatic overture. "The Mater is the most venerated of what you so disparagingly referred to as the minor divinities. Many indeed are the supplications to visit bad luck hither and thither in liberal measure."

"To visit bad luck?"

"Would it be too odious to pray for someone to lose a bet? Or more odious still," he cackled, with a heave of feathered shoulders, "that a certain nuisance should forfeit a limb? Or, to raise the stakes a mite, that a rival should forfeit life, or a treasured offspring? How popular do you now imagine my dearest mamma! Cast your imagination a smidgin further. What prayers might emerge from bended royal knee for the gift of plague and pestilence at your service?"

"Your mother sounds perfectly odious!"

"How kind. But pray tell me, have you been so fortunate that you have never been insulted, beaten, slandered, raped—or otherwise traduced to an extent so grievous you would not treasure vengeance?"

"Oh, I think . . ."

The memory of Flaherty invaded her mind: that mocking gap-toothed sneer as he looked down off the bridge to relish her drowning in the Suir. Maybe, in that moment, or in the shocking recall of that moment . . .

"I need to know more about you. Were you sent to spy on me?"

Those vulture shoulders shrugged. "A trifle melodramatic, dearie. I may have inherited a weakness for theatre, but is not the most celebrated of actors the most sublime of deceivers? I so treasured my role of poor little succubus. Did you not relish her flaw of kindness?"

"It wasn't altogether convincing, but I need to know your purpose here. Are you—and Elaru too—are you servants of the Tyrant?"

"Oh, bless you, dearie! Tyrant—Great Witch—I'm anybody's friendly little goblin. Ever willing to strike a bargain. Even the ignoblest minor divine has its needs."

"What needs?"

"Why, the need to please oneself. Is there ever any gratification more unctuous than serving oneself?"

"Then you must be selfish in the extreme."

"Why, thank you, my luscious."

"It wasn't meant to flatter you."

"What could be more gratifying than the exercise of power? Why, would you pretend to claim no pleasure in exercising this bauble welded to your brow? Have you not gloried behind the camouflage of those caring green eyes in wielding the green fire to inflict pain and damnation on those who most deserve those afflictions, while affecting such gentle benevolence on the poor and deserving?"

"No! I mean . . . that isn't . . ."

That insidious cackle came again. "Oh, come, come, now. There—in the Cathedral of Death—surely you bathed, as we all did, in the reflected glory of that deceitful lord. Such a brazen splendour! Why, the exaltation of darkness still provokes the old feathers to a quiver. Did not a tiny part of you thrill to think: thank the powers it isn't I who cycles here?"

"How I must disappoint you."

"Must you deny the most interesting facet of your being, the part that skulks in the deepest, most secret, crevice of your soul?"

"Why did Elaru try to dissuade me from entering the Cathedral?"

He—it—yawned. "Did she truly, dearie?"

Kate hesitated. "I think she did. So perhaps in some crevice of your alter-ego, there is some potential for good?"

"How dull you would traduce me! Yet now it is time to choose. Call back that mediocre factotum. Or trust in me?"

Hobson's choice, she reflected again. Choose between Elaru, who pretended to want to help her and Urale, who openly admitted the opposite. "Then I will choose to have you both as guides, since it would appear that I cannot choose one or the other."

That sneering squawk of a laugh again.

"By all means, let us go."

She blinked, awaiting her fate. And then, in a great sweep of plumage and claws, Kate found herself hauled into the air by her hair.

"You may scream if you like."

Kate wanted to scream; she wanted to scream her lungs out if it would calm the rising fear that filled her being.

In moments she found herself entering a threatening landscape, green-tinged as if putrescent, inky black but with salient features etched in maggoty white. A great leafless tree stood in the far distance at the end of a dreadful valley of jagged tors and meandering rivers. Kate shivered, *the Tree of Life*. The rivers, as they soared closer to them, became as wide as oceans, while under their glimmering silvery surface they moiled with desperate movement. As they neared the Tree it became too gargantuan to encompass, its branches streaming out to infinity in the black of sky.

In a moment they were plummeting, like a stone cast over a precipice.

"What game are you playing now?"

"Even a mind as prosaic as yours must savour the melodrama. There is ecstasy even when tragedy prevails. What is the loss of a friend, a city, a people when compared to the dying of a universe?"

The screaming of her senses, even in soul spirit form, was altogether too in tune with the mad glee of Urale's spiral. They fell faster, more terrifyingly by far than the frantic descent to Ulla Quemar on the back of Driftwood. The distances through which they plummeted felt cosmic: never-ending voids of space between whole galaxies of stars.

"You may open your eyes."

Kate hadn't realised that terror had clamped her eyes shut until she had to overcome that same terror to open them again.

Roots!

Like everything about the Tree these roots were vast, even from a distance. They were not still, but constantly moving, sliding and slithering over one another, twisting about themselves—writhing! The more she examined them, the more she realised that the word movement was inadequate to describe their slithering. They were constantly changing within themselves, as if refashioning their essence over and over, desperately metamorphosing from moment to moment.

"You are, perchance, awed?"

She was dumbstruck by the colossal wrongness of what she was seeing, by her utter ignorance of what it might all mean, and by the likelihood that her mission would fail.

The roots were vast, much broader in girth than even the mightiest tree on Earth. They were fleshy rather than woody, and malodorous with rot. It was impossible to assess their extent since, wherever she turned, they appeared anew, as if manifesting out of some stygian darkness. They confused her senses so she had no idea whether she was moving up or down or across in any dimension. The roots were a maze so vast that they created innumerable secondary ecologies within them, evolving into other worlds, other universes, as many as there were imaginations to inhabit them.

A maze she now had to negotiate, and she could not trust her guide—or guides—one iota.

"Wakey, wakey!"

"What is it?"

"Your first challenge, dearie."

"What challenge?"

Again she heard that infuriating cackle. "Did we imagine that entry to the labyrinth would be unguarded?"

"You will stop this nonsense at once."

"Oooh, masterful—or should we say, mistressful!"

She was looking at two beings who had twinkled into the air immediately before her. They looked like non-identical twins; one male, one female. They were squatting, naked other than their elaborate headdresses of enamelled gold and chunky plaited collars of many woven colours. They had elongated heads, like those of horses, and vestigial limbs. Their skins were a uniform copper in colour. Their faces bore grave expressions despite childishly plump cheeks, broad lips, snub noses and bulging chestnut eyes that looked peculiarly vacant. The reason for this, Kate noticed, was that there were no pupils. She knew, instinctively, they were not to be trusted.

"Who are you?"

The male replied, "We are the Yoolf."

The female said, "We do not answer questions."

"We ask them," the counterpoint continued.

"And woe betide those who fail!"

"Or falter."

To Kate, the Yoolf resembled the ultimate spoiled brats. They were bobbing slowly up and down in empty space against the background of endlessly writhing roots. Her eyes lifted to see that she was still suspended by her hair from the horny claws of the vulture-being, Urale.

The male spoke in a malicious monotone. "What is the direction of time?"

The female added, "The direction here—not there."

"What is the direction of time—but only here?" Kate asked.

"We ask the questions."

"And woe betide—"

"Those who fail—I know," Kate said

They stared at her, blinking slowly in unison.

Kate heard Elaru's whisper enter her mind: <Upwards, Mistress.>

But could she trust the alter ego of the obnoxious vulture?

She said, "Upwards."

The two chubby faces looked at one another, their features creased with rancid displeasure. Their mouths gaped, exposing rows of sharp fine teeth.

"Wrong!"

"Doubly wrong!"

<Beware, Mistress—they cheat.>

Elaru was right. Kate knew from their wrathful expressions that her answer had been right. The questioning began again.

The male and female alternated:

"What is right when wrong?"

"And wrong when right?"

"A parody of truth?"

"When seen, a delight?"

Elaru's whispered answer: <Irony, Mistress.>

"Irony," Kate said.

The male screamed, "Wrong, wrong—a thousand times wrong."

The female screamed, “Bite it—rend it! Cast it into the yawning void.”

“Oh, Elaru.” Kate felt nips of teeth on her arms and legs. “What are these little monsters doing to me?”

But it was Urale’s voice that answered: “Poor darlings—they cannot help lying and cheating.”

Kate’s heart was full of dread as the interrogation began again:

“What is a song without voice?”

“Hera’s torment?”

“Zeus’ delight?”

“An answer without question?”

“As here to there.”

“As darkest day to blessed night.”

Kate felt a fury of nipping and biting all over her arms and legs. The Yoolf had multiplied. She struck out with her oraculum at the hordes of brat faces with their myriad snapping teeth.

“Help me, Elaru.”

Elaru’s voice whispered so quietly that Kate could not hear the answer. The snapping grew rapidly worse. Although she had no flesh here, the Yoolf gorged on her spirit and were intent on devouring her.

“I can’t hear you.”

<Eeecho!>

“What?”

Then she realised what it was. She screamed it, at the top of her voice. “The answer, you miserable wretches, is echo!”

"Wrong!"

"All wrong!"

"Wrong from start to finish."

"And from finish to start."

"Consume her."

"Devour her."

"Nnnngg! Toothsome."

"Nnnnngg! Bloody."

"Liars!"

Kate's oraculum erupted. She tore herself free from the claws of Urale.

"Liars! Cheats!"

She plummeted through the void, her auburn hair flapping around her face, twirling and twisting in the bottomless abyss.

But the fall came with a sense of liberation. She screamed to her twirling, falling self, "I am free of them."

There was a second being, broken free, detached from Kate's own spirit, a figure of smoke with a tormented face, twirling and spinning beside her. Kate turned, to hold the figure steady.

"Thank you, Elaru—for helping me."

"Oh, Mistress."

"We're certainly in a pickle. And I don't quite know how to get out of it."

"Then we are lost. We shall plummet into the abyss forever."

"Not if I can help it. Your alter-ego has wings. From what you say, he made you. But then you allowed him—Urale—to control you. You allowed him to entrap you, make you dependent upon him. You must break free."

"But how can I do so? I exist only as a manifestation of him."

"He created you. And he's a god, even if only a minor one."

"I do not understand your reasoning."

Kate chuckled, though she felt curiously dizzy, almost inebriated. "I'm not quite a goddess—but a goddess certainly empowers me."

"Oh."

"I still need a guide."

"Oh?"

"He was you—and you he. You must, somehow, abandon his control."

"But how?"

"I don't know. But we'll find a way."

Abomination

Smoke was curling into the sky from several different directions as Penny emerged from the fire-blackened wound of St. Martin's Lane. The Razzers were everywhere. She heard the sirens of dozens of fire engines and stared with sad concentration at the ruined front of one of her favourite churches: St. Martin-in-the-Fields. There was a thickening veil of smoke in the air as she backed away into the open space of Trafalgar Square.

She had been so furious with Gully because he had refused to capture some live pigeons for her.

"Why're you rabbitin' on about it? What do you want with a live pigeon? You know I can't go with that. It's cruel, Penny. Catchin' one an' puttin' it in a bag would frighten the life out of it."

"You're the one who wrings their necks."

"But that's a kindness, gel. They ain't no hurtin' in that. I do it so fast they don't even feel it."

Gully was staring at her through the smudged lenses of his glasses. He pushed the glasses up the bridge of his nose. "Aw, Penny—don't you go out right now. Them streets ain't safe no more."

Now Penny stared up through a tangle of razor wire around one of the giant bronze lions. The authorities had fenced them off to stop the Razzers from spraying them with graffiti. She felt the breeze blow on her face, coming up from the river. Raising her hood she squinted at the glare of the late afternoon sun, feeling the lancing cold cut straight through her clothes. Her breath steamed from her nostrils. She couldn't afford to hang about. There were Skulls and paramilitaries among the crowds. Still, she loved to look at them, the lions and the soaring Nelson's column.

Hurrying on, she pulled up the zip on her parka as high as it would go, heading for the Embankment and the rain-swollen current of the river that Gully called "the Old Man o' London Town." The wind roared through the sparse foliage of the plane trees over her head, while their ball-like seeds gambolled and whipped in its current. She had to press her body forward against a spree of autumn leaves that bowled along the pavement, battering against her jeans and jacket, adding their resistance to the wind's.

She didn't like travelling in the City Above during a Razzamatazz. Maybe if Gully hadn't got her so mad she wouldn't have chanced it. What was more, the argument had caused her to forget her claws. But there was no going back, not now. She knew she had to return to the left-hand tunnel, no matter that she was terrified to do so. She remembered the underground river falling down in an amazing cascade. Her heart beat faster when she thought about what else she had discovered: an entrance into the City Below. She had glimpsed constructions of some sort, glittering things, fantastic and wonderful, but she hardly dared to consider the implications.

She had figured out that she could probably get past the Grimlings if she could distract them. If only Gully had done as she asked of him. If only he had got her some live pigeons.

"I don't want to harm them. I just want to let them go."

"Wot—down there? In them 'orrible tunnels, with them Grimlings an' all you been talkin' about?"

Penny's memories were scattered by three different sirens—police, fire engine and paramedic—all hurtling past. They were fewer these days, with the authorities not bothering to respond very much any more. The noise was so distracting that it was difficult to keep hold of the train of her thoughts.

Resolve and fear were fighting inside her head. *"I have to examine it—the City Below."*

"Why?"

"So I can picture it, Gully—so I can draw it on the map."

"You've gone bonkers with them pictures. You know them pictures is driving you crazy, gel."

"You must help me, Gully. Or . . ."

"Or wot?"

"Or so help me, Gully, I'll leave you."

There it was. She really had said it to him. And he had stared back at her, lost for words, his glasses sliding down his sweating nose. His owlish brown eyes had blinked frantically behind the smudged-up lenses.

"You know I mean it."

His face had gone pale. He looked about to cry. *"Wot? Leave all a that scribblin' up there on the ceiling?"*

A shiver had invaded her then. She had begun to tremble.

He reached out, as if to hug her.

"Don't touch me!"

"I know how you feel—about that stuff. Them maps!"

"You know nothing."

"I know you're jolly well goin' bonkers, Penny."

"I am not."

"Yes you are. You're stark ravin' bonkers—that's what you are."

"I will—I'll leave you, Gully. If you don't get me those pigeons."

* * *

As she reached the Embankment, the evening sun had begun to glimmer red on the muddy water. A mist of rain hung in the air, aglow with sunlight and permeated with smoke from the burning streets. Soot was smudged on her clothes and skin. She stared at the fires, which seemed to be everywhere. Smoke was rising from half-a-dozen places south of the river—big billowing stacks suggesting whole streets ablaze, or major buildings. She felt a choking sense of sense of fear just looking at the chaos, which was getting so much worse day by day. The globular lights on their intricate bronze stands flickered on as she reached Cleopatra's Needle, illuminating a ragtag bunch of drunkards fighting with one another on a muddy patch. She saw bodies on the ground, writhing and groaning. She glimpsed flashes of knives, which made her want to run.

Somebody behind her was shouting. When she turned her head she saw that a tall, bedraggled man was calling out to her. Staggering drunk, he was dressed in old army fatigues, with a heavy beard on a deeply-lined face. He wanted to know what she was carrying in her backpack. As he took several steps towards her she increased her pace to a trot. He was far too drunk to catch her. Nevertheless, she had taken a big risk carrying the dagger so openly and so far. But she felt she had to do it, an inner voice told her that it was time she put her theory to the test.

There were Skulls everywhere. Big groups of them, all wearing long black leather jackets, were crossing over the four lane road, heedless of the fact they were interfering with traffic. Just a few years earlier the streets would have been clotted with red double-decker buses, but nobody would risk such open transport any more. Most of the traffic was taxis; the drivers sealed within their cabs by reinforced steel walls and bullet-proof glass. But even then they weren't safe, according to Gully, because the robbers could knife or shoot them through the back of the seat.

Paramilitaries, in their grey camouflage uniforms, were sitting in a minibus immediately opposite her. A Skull was speaking to the man in the front passenger seat, through the gaping door. The man wore a neatly tailored suit. He looked like a God-botherer from Grimstone's church. As Penny hurried by, just feet away, he looked at her. She met his gaze, puzzled by the familiarity of his face. Penny had a very good memory for faces. She realised she had seen him standing beside the Reverend Grimstone on the posters that were all over the city, on Tube station walls, on billboards and on the pamphlets they distributed throughout the streets. She turned and glanced back at him a second time to be sure. He was staring back at her. She trotted quicker.

Up ahead was the Blackfriars underpass. She had to cross the road but was worried by the possibility she would be held up at the lights. Before she had travelled more than ten yards there was an explosion in the side street opposite to the river and a building big enough to take up a whole block burst into flames. Razzers were screaming with triumph, emerging from the doors. Penny blinked several times, fixing the scene, and all the maniacally jubilant faces with their tattoos of spirals and stars and the rings through lips and nostrils, in her memory. She hesitated, then turned to look back at the minibus. The paramilitaries were emerging from their vehicle, looking to join the Skulls. They were carrying guns. Penny heard shots almost immediately. They were shooting at the Razzers. She searched among the paramilitaries for the man in the suit, but he had disappeared.

When she looked again she saw the suited man talking with two of the armed paramilitaries. He was pointing in her direction.

Penny started to run. Glancing over her shoulder, she saw that they were running after her.

She stared ahead to where she glimpsed the rounded dome of St. Paul's Cathedral in a gap created by a demolished row of buildings. The sight spurred her on. She couldn't afford to wait for the lights, but ran between the traffic, ignoring the screaming horns. She was still running when she crossed the road immediately opposite Blackfriars station, tearing through the traffic again, only slowing down when she reached a maze of winding streets.

A greenish glow was pervading the late afternoon sky as she entered the circular space around St. Paul's between the heavy railings that surrounded it. Some had been hacked away around the front, the missing railings replaced with steel mesh and posts fixed into the paving stones with ugly blocks of concrete. In front of the cathedral, unprotected by the mesh, was the statue of Queen Anne surrounded by mythological figures. The figures were vandalised and had missing heads and limbs. Penny had no idea how anybody could have got to them; the authorities had surrounded the cluster of statues with razor wire seven feet high.

She headed for the entrance to the cathedral. There were ten black granite steps, a marble inlaid platform, then another fourteen grey marble steps to the main entrance. The big central doors were shut, as usual, but the side entrances were open. She headed for the door on the right, drawn by the friendly light inside the entrance hall through which a small rush of people were emerging, heads down. The women's faces were obscured by scarves and there was a single man with a wrinkled bald head. There were cigarette butts scattered over the tiled floor. Inside, the giant nave was completely empty.

When Penny had drawn St. Paul's, she had inserted something extra to it—a kind of three-dimensionality. Gully was always pestering her to put in some people.

"No people."

"Why ever not?"

"People spoil things."

That was exactly what they were doing. They were spoiling everything—everything that she loved.

Penny assumed it had been the sounds of gunfire that had frightened the people away. Given the open doors the great church was hardly a refuge. There were people out there with no respect for churches.

She drew back her hood while thinking of where to go. She headed left, across the black-and-white tiles of the floor, and passed by the monument to the Duke of Wellington. She was heading towards the little chapel at the far end of it, immediately to the left of the high altar and the painting of Jesus as the Light of the World. When she got there she stood underneath the picture, in which the face of Jesus was in deep shadow. She readjusted the straps of the backpack and moved into the American Chapel.

In the light of dusk she stared up at the triptych of stained glass windows showing an image of Cain and Abel, the Washing of Feet and the Nativity; the central showing the Crucifixion, the right, the Entombment topped by the Resurrection.

The dagger was rattling inside the backpack.

"I knew it," she murmured.

She was directly over the spot where she had seen the alien beings and the Grimlings through the fissure in the underground chamber.

The big cave is under St. Paul's Cathedral!

But what did it mean?

While she was thinking about it, she heard the crash of one of the side doors slamming shut. It caused her heart to rise into her throat. There was a second crash—the other door shut and bolted.

Somebody had followed her in here.

Penny headed into the shadows to the right of the main altar, past the white marble effigies of heroes and luminaries. Her feet clattered over a huge circular brass grid, which allowed heat from the basement to come up into the chancel. She heard a sound behind her—boots treading quietly.

She pulled the backpack down and hugged it to her breast.

There was a side entrance, which was very close. She ran for it only to find a heavy oak locked door barring her way. The big iron key was in the lock. She was afraid that it would be hard to open, but it turned easily in her hand. She pulled open the door just far enough to allow her to slip out into the gloom. Dusk had fallen, but the street lights had failed to come on. She found herself in an overgrown garden with neglected shrubs, small trees and a dark patch of lawn.

Desperately she searched for an escape, but the garden was completely surrounded by high iron railings. She darted into the shadow of a bush and fell onto all fours beneath it, hoping that her pursuer would not find her. She screamed when a hand dragged back her back by the hair.

A blade was pressed against her throat. *Skulls carry knives they call sharps.*

A deep male voice whispered wetly into her left ear, "A single peep and I'll slit you—in more than one place."

Oh, God—if only she had brought her claws!

Though she resisted, he easily threw her onto her back. The hand that had been yanking her hair now moved to her throat. Her right hand broke free and she flailed it at him, clawing at the shaved dome of his head. He grabbed her hand and shoved it behind the small of her back. He used the blade to cut open her parka, then the belt of her jeans. She felt its cold sharpness slide inside her underwear and rip it open.

"If you're nice to me—I won't cut you."

He kissed her, pressing his tongue between her lips, deeper between her teeth. She felt a wave of revulsion that brought sick into her mouth. She tore her mouth away and twisted her neck around so that her mouth was half in the dirt.

"You stink."

Her face exploded with pain as he punched her, hard into the centre of her face, breaking her nose. She could no longer breathe for the blood filling her nostrils and the back of her throat.

"And you smell sweet, like a virgin."

"Cut me then. Kill me. I'd rather die than be raped by you."

"Wishing is becoming."

"Do it!"

He was fumbling with his clothes. She felt something obscene touch her. *Abomination!* She was breathing in and out so fast she felt dizzy and faint. She was blacking out with disgust and loathing of what he was doing.

But then a voice entered her mind:

<The dagger is lying on the ground, close to you.>

I can't see it. I don't know where it is.

The voice came back into her head. <Call it! Bid it come into your hand.>

What?

Her mind was reeling with the revulsion of his fumbling down there. But still the calm, logical part of her brain questioned what was happening: whose voice was it that was speaking to her? It sounded like the voice of Jeremiah, the man who had shown her the monster.

<Jeremiah—help me!>

<Call it!>

In her turmoil she willed the dagger to come to her with every fibre of her being. The Skull was no longer interested in what she was doing with her hands. She reached out her left hand, holding it up into the freezing air, and screamed for the dagger to come to her. And then she felt something strike the palm of her hand, like a heavy blow from an iron bar: the hilt of the Scalpie dagger. She screamed aloud, swinging her hand down at him, stabbing him again and again, in the shoulder of the arm that was choking her.

Penny sat up, tears welling into her eyes.

She had killed a Skull. They knew her. They had seen her. They would hunt her down until they caught her.

Then she would be dead. She didn't know what to do. She didn't know where to run.

<Leave no trace that will betray that you were here.>

"Why me? Why did he try to rape me?"

<Pick up the dagger, Penny.>

She returned the bloodstained dagger to her backpack and strapped that onto her back. One of her trainers had been ripped from her foot by the violence of the attack, but she knew that the voice was right: she mustn't leave anything of hers here. She picked her way around the dead man and the growing pool of blood to pick it up. She had to hold up her jeans as she moved, weeping openly as she did so. Blood ran down from her nostrils over her lips to drip from her chin.

She lifted the hem of her parka to staunch her bleeding nose.

<Why?> she screamed in her mind. <Why?>

How strange that it was the soft voice of Jeremiah she still heard within her head. <You are very naïve> he whispered.

"I . . . I don't understand."

She had to go back through the interior of the cathedral, then through the winding streets to Embankment and the river. Instinct bade her throw both her trainers into its muddy stream. She descended the metal steps of a tube escalator in her bare feet at a run. She vaulted the ticket barrier, so fast nobody could stop her, then hid in a crevice and waited for the station to close. In the gloom, she curled up and cried. Her heart was beating so hard and fast she couldn't fill her lungs to breathe.

She closed her arms about the backpack and the dagger inside it—the blade that had saved her. She listened to the meaningless sounds of the station, her body shrinking down into itself, her mind a blank.

A False Prophet

"The Islington Church of the Saved is truly global."

"Really?"

Mark paused mid-stride before walking on again in the company of Jo Derby, Sharkey and Nan. They had separated into two groups, each made up of male and female pairs; the other group consisted of Cal and Tajh. The followers of the Islington Church almost invariably travelled in male–female pairs and they didn't want to stand out in the crowd.

"Grimstone's church militant has seen phenomenal recruitment over recent years. So much so that the mainstream churches—indeed, various arms of the establishment itself—are in awe of it."

Mark considered the implications of what she had said—the church militant! "But from what I know about Grimstone and his church, they don't share much in the way of their beliefs with the other churches?"

Jo inclined her head. "There's no real crossover with other faiths, that's true."

"Because Grimstone's way of seeing things—his purported theology—has little to do with traditional Christianity?"

"That may be putting it simply, given the warring history of Christianity. But, basically, you're not far off the mark. He quotes the Bible, especially the Old Testament, but you know you can argue just about anything from the Old Testament."

They were heading for Wembley, where Jo had got hold of tickets for the meeting of the faithful. They had parked the bikes a good distance away, guarded by Bull, and walked about two miles to the gigantic arena. No need for sign posts; they just followed the crowds all heading in the same direction. Jo had also taken the precaution of laying her hands on the Church's book of prayers, and badges for their lapels to get them through the gates, which would probably be manned by disciples. They could also expect a heavy security presence, she said, if only to keep the Razzers at bay.

"You're expecting trouble?"

"Grimstone's meetings attract them. They won't be allowed to enter the main arena, but you can expect hordes of them."

Mark squeezed Nan's hand.

"That's bizarre, don't you think?"

"What isn't, these days?"

Grimstone had left the running of the original church in Islington to subordinates. The adjoining small detached house, where Mark and Mo had grown up as children, had been converted into accommodation for visiting dignitaries from abroad, confirming the global reach of the Church. These days Grimstone needed big stadiums to accommodate the crowds mesmerised by his message.

Nan spoke to Mark, mind-to-mind. <We must keep our ears, and minds, open. We may learn something important about Padraig and the Sword.>

Mark also planned to keep a close watch on Jo.

Back at camp he had been observing her, especially her relationship to Tajh and Sharkey. They had quickly arrived at some common understanding. After her rescue, Jo had spent a long time sitting in the Mamma Pig, receiving signals through the rooftop receiver. Once she had emerged, he had seen Tajh make a beeline for her. He had already begun to suspect that a higher authority was regulating and supplying the crews. If that was true, was Jo linked to them? And did she know who the authorities were and what they might be planning?

He said to Jo, "I keep asking myself what Grimstone is really up to."

"You and me both."

"If he's linked to the Tyrant, it's likely to be dangerous."

"You're right. Even I hadn't realised just how dangerous it was until you rescued me from the lecture. It isn't just how people behave. It's what they feel—what they think. I'm more and more convinced that there's some element of mind control."

Mark saw Jo Derby look at him out of the corner of her eyes, though she continued to press forwards. They were now approaching the feral mobs that were attracted to the periphery of Grimstone's events.

He knew exactly what she was now thinking and agreed with her. Mind control was what Grimstone's church was all about.

She added: "Well, certainly these people—these so-called Razzamatazzers, and the Skulls too, even the paramilitaries—appear to have lost any sense of moral compass. They don't care about what was socially unacceptable just yesterday. They're prepared to kill with impunity. They die themselves, as we have seen, and still they just don't appear to care. That's worrying."

Was Jo allowing him some insight into the thinking of his presumed higher authority?

Although they had no idea whether or not Grimstone would be able to detect them, Mark and Nan had decided that it was best to suppress their oracula entirely while they were attending the meeting.

As they approached the arena Mark saw that Jo's presumption was confirmed: it was a place of pilgrimage for the Razzers. So many of the surrounding streets had been gutted that it suggested a deliberate, ruthless planning. As far as he could make out, the entire periphery of Wembley for a distance of several hundred yards, had degenerated into shanties and hovels teeming with thugs: the Razzers had created their own wasteland in the ruins. It was similar to what had happened in the city of Isscan on Tír, and Mark wondered if it was in Grimstone's interest to encourage this ruin. His flock could then contrast the orderliness of his services with the anarchy that surrounded them.

They followed the faithful into the arena, gaining entrance without any difficulty. The stadium was approaching full—over 90,000 souls. At the centre of the grassy oval of what had, until recently, been a national football arena, Mark saw two senior church figures—deacons or dignitaries of some sort—wearing white togas with hoods pulled forward over their faces. There must have been several hundred in the larger, outer crescent. He wondered if Grimstone's wife, and his own adoptive mother, Bethal, was among them.

"Why the cowls?" He spoke quietly to Jo.

"Presumably they don't want to be identified. There's a great deal of secrecy to the inner workings of the New

Islington Church. We believe that they include eminent military representatives, politicians and billionaire businessmen."

Mark had caught the expression, "*We believe . . .*"

"Impressive."

"Your adoptive father is nothing if not charismatic."

Mark thought again about what Jo had said before: was that what Grimstone was after—*mind control?*

In the inner crescent, closer to the speaker's podium, a smaller cluster of figures, probably all men, were robed and cowled in black. *If Grimstone's church is global,* Mark thought, *are they the equivalent of archbishops—leaders of the overseas branches?*

An uncowled choir of men and women dressed in flowing robes of powder blue filled a sector of the stands. They rose to their feet and sang a hymn that Mark recognised from many makeshift church meetings he had been dragged to by Grimstone: *Soldiers of the New Risen Christ.* A deacon climbed onto the podium and spoke before the table being used as an altar. At its centre was a plinth bearing a twisted cross.

"What avails a world that has descended into the adoration of Mammon and machines?"

In unison the crowd responded, "Nothing."

"Behold," he spoke, "he comes with clouds, and every eye shall see him. And all kindreds of the Earth shall wail because of him."

Jo whispered: "From the Book of Revelation."

"I am alpha and omega, the beginning and the end. I am what is, and what was, and that which will come to be."

The audience roared, "Amen!"

Mark wondered about the apocalyptic tenor of the words. Whatever was being proclaimed as coming, he very much doubted that it was the risen Christ. Was Grimstone referring to himself, to the triumph of his rising church—or to something else entirely?

The choir sang again, a rousing hymn about cleansing fire, and the hope and certainty of the new world that would follow. As they sang Grimstone made his entrance, emerging into the arena from the tunnel out of which football teams once appeared. He strolled forward with a confident step to climb the podium and take his place before the cluster of microphones. He was dressed in a dove grey linen suit over a black silk shirt, with a white dog collar. His long black hair was neatly coiffured and streaked with grey. The blue of his eyes shone like lasers over the huge expectant congregation.

A woman began screaming hysterically. Mark caught the words, "Where's my son?"

Grimstone waved to the stewards to bring her forward. She was ushered down one of the radial aisles and brought over the central oval to the podium, where Grimstone dismissed the stewards. He took the woman's face in his hands and spoke softly to her, but his words, of course, were carried by the microphones.

"Blessed are they who mourn"—the crowd rippled—"for they will be comforted."

The woman collapsed into Grimstone's arms.

Mark whispered to Jo, "Looks contrived."

"Oh, I think it's more ambitious than that. Grimstone is setting himself up at the very least as a prophet."

It was hard for Mark to see the violent bully he recalled from his previous home life in this gentle pastor with the caressing arms and the greying hair. Grimstone waved at the stewards to come and help the woman back to her seat. "Take care of this troubled soul. Treat her gently. Show her the comfort of grace."

Mark sensed a contagion of adoration running through the crowds. He saw it move through their postures, the expression on their faces.

Grimstone addressed the congregation again. "This unfortunate soul is not alone. Many are lost. I wandered this confused world for a generation and everywhere I encountered the same desolation of spirit, the human soil waiting for the seed of redemption. We need only look around ourselves in this stadium, or further to the streets of this great city, to witness it day by day: the cancer of despair in the hearts of decent men and women and the fear that comes with a world that has lost its way. Is it any wonder they feel abandoned?"

Shouts from the crowd, "No, Lord!"

"Blessed are the peacemakers."

"For they shall be called the Children of God!"

Grimstone lifted the cross from its plinth, brought it to his brow and then to his lips, so he could kiss it. Mark had seen him kiss the same twisted cross many times during his services, in houses seconded as makeshift churches. But the cross was not a cross at all. It was a dagger with part of the matte black spiral blade broken off. The top limb of the cross was actually its hilt, with the glowing sigil of the triple infinity embedded in it. The memory of the dagger-cross was so stark, so creepy, that Mark could smell the sulphurous stink of burning as the glowing sigil made contact with Grimstone's lips. He felt the enormous wave of power that radiated out from the distant grey-suited figure and the dagger he was holding to his mouth. It was vastly more powerful than he recalled. He wondered if this came from the proximity of the Sword.

Mark felt what the congregation felt: the desire to offer oneself to this man who wielded so much power. He felt the thrill of being consumed and becoming part of the greater whole. The rapture.

The figures that Jo believed were high-ranking military, the civic leaders and the billionaire businessmen, all knelt before Grimstone with deeply bowed heads. Mark could see how the vast gathering had been enchanted, lost in the rapture of Grimstone's promises, their eyes glazed.

Mark's eyes met Nan's. "Do you feel it too?"

She nodded. "It's as if an oraculum has opened."

Grimstone replaced the dagger on its plinth. He addressed the multitude, his arms widespread. "I thank you all for coming here. Look around you when you leave. You, my beloved brethren, have been brought close to the lost on your journeys here. Please do not abandon these unfortunates, who merit and need our help."

This charitable sentiment evoked a muted applause.

"As unto the angel of Ephesus, I say to you: I know how you have laboured, I know your dedication, what you have endured in holiness and patience and all that you have borne for the sake of goodness and kindness. Yet you have still offered charity in hard circumstances of crime and poverty. I thank you for your generosity from the bottom of my heart."

The applause thundered out again. Mark was impressed. Grimstone was capable of manipulating the mood of his entire flock on a whim.

"We look with new eyes on this harried country and this great city—this city we all love—and what need do we see?"

The crowd intoned, "Be watchful and make strong the things that remain, those of us who are ready to die, for they are not perfect before our God!"

Grimstone picked up the twisted cross again and held it once again to his brow. Mark felt another wave of rapture pass out through the multitude. He whispered to Nan, "Where's the Sword?"

Nan shook her head. "I don't know."

It was difficult to think clearly through the noise of over 90,000 voices raised in acclamation.

"What if Grimstone doesn't fully understand how to use the Sword?" she asked.

"It might explain the need to question Padraig." Mark nodded. "But, from what I know of Padraig, he wouldn't give in—not even if it cost him his life. He was a cantankerous old devil. He'd likely hold out."

"If you're right, his cantankerous nature might have kept him alive."

"I really hope so."

Mark thought back to the Tube tunnel after they had rescued Jo from the lecture. They had sensed a great power somewhere underground and had reached the same conclusion: it had to be the Sword.

Somewhere underground.

And, if he was right in his thinking, all they had to do was to find the Sword and Padraig wouldn't be far away.

Nan whispered, "But we still don't know what Grimstone is planning."

"I'd say something big."

"What should we do?"

"Grimstone didn't come here by road. There has to be an underground link to here—somewhere that allowed his entrance into the oval. It's got to be a Tube line, maybe one reserved for his private use. If we could only find it while Grimstone is still talking."

"That would be dangerous, with the security everywhere."

"Yeah, but it's mainly aimed at controlling the gates."

"And looking after Grimstone himself."

Mark nodded, thoughtful for a moment. "But not at controlling the congregation, especially now that Grimstone is getting into his stride. I think we should have a nose around underground."

Grimstone intoned, "Blessed are they who thirst for righteousness."

His flock replied, "For they shall be satisfied."

"Yes, indeed—they shall be satisfied. My brothers and sisters—my beloved brethren—you and me, we will be satisfied."

"When?" the congregation cried.

"Soon—I make this solemn promise."

"Amen."

Mark and Nan whispered their intention to Jo and Sharkey, suggesting they meet them and the others later on at the place where they had stowed the bikes. Then they slipped out of their seats, taking advantage of a renewed wave of rapture. They made their way back along a radial aisle to the enclosing wall around the arena. Two stewards looked over at them. Quickly, Mark pretended to support Nan while she slumped back against the wall. Lifting a placatory hand he signalled that she had fainted and began fanning Nan's face with his hymn book.

The stewards looked back towards the podium.

"What now?" she whispered.

Mark continued to fan her face. Over at the edge of the crowd, the mother who had heckled Grimstone was still weeping as two muscular young men in neat suits ushered her forcefully through twin doors not more than thirty yards from them. Where earlier he had thought her cry some contrived interruption, now he was no longer sure.

"I'd like to know where they're taking her."

In the central arena Grimstone was walking along the columns of elders, touching their brows with the twisted cross. Taking advantage of the new wave of excitement, Mark led Nan along the radial wall to the twin doors. When they tested them, they discovered that they were unlocked.

Mark could see no guards in the gloomy corridor within, just some surprised disciples. But there was something else; a palpable sense of threat that caused Nan to clutch at his forearm as they used their oracula to stun the few disciples they encountered into unconsciousness. The tunnel led to a very ordinary looking lift marked "STAFF" and an adjoining staircase. They followed the winding stairs down two floors to emerge onto a private underground railway platform. Mark and Nan hung back within the doorway, gazing out at a two-coach Tube train, pristinely white, that stood next to the platform. It bore no markings or designations, but Mark could not see any other vehicle that would have brought Grimstone and his inner coterie to the arena. The big question was: where did it lead?

Peering around the opening, Mark saw that the train was guarded by a small army of paramilitaries, who stood rigidly to attention at the front and along both sides of the carriages. A strange blue light permeated the walls and the air of the tunnel. The sense of threat was overwhelming.

Mark was stunned to find Grimstone's voice sounding from behind him.

"Did you hope to discover something to your advantage?"

He spun around to discover his adoptive father just twenty feet away. The sense of shock and of evil at having Grimstone suddenly so close caused Mark's heart to quail. Even now that he was grown into a man and armed with the oraculum of the Third Power, Mark felt an overwhelming nausea. He threw a protective arm around Nan's shoulders.

Grimstone sneered at his reaction. He was standing next to a smiling woman—the mother who had been creating a fuss about her son. Mark understood now why there had been no guards in the tunnel at the top of the stairs. It had all been a trick to draw him in.

"I gathered that you were back in this world—my useless son and his black-haired bed warmer. Knowing your arrogance, it was altogether predictable that you would come here to confront me."

This close, Grimstone looked a decade older than the man Mark recalled. But the glare of hatred in those blue beacons of eyes was all too familiar, as were the powerful muscles concealed under the pastor's clothes. But something had changed. There was a new power about him, a menace that had no fear of Mark's and Nan's oracula. Mark noticed the glowing symbol of the triple infinity that was embedded in the centre of Grimstone's brow. *Embedded!* That was new. It resembled a sinister oraculum of Grimstone's own—an exceedingly powerful one.

From above, though faintly, Mark could still hear the choir singing. The ceremony above was continuing. Grimstone must have left his deacon in charge and made some excuse for an interval.

"I see that you have noticed I don't need the cross any more to communicate with my beloved master. I am one with him at all times."

Mark's oraculum flared, and he sensed Nan's do the same. "I'm not a child that you can hurt or bully any more."

"No—you're an ingrate, with ideas above his station."

Instinctively Mark put his left hand above his right shoulder. But of course the Fir Bolg battleaxe wasn't there. "I warn you. Don't even consider hurting me or Nan."

"You think you can threaten me? This is no game we're playing. You imagine your scheming will undermine my work? You think your little bauble will defeat the will of my lord and master?"

"I know you have Padraig. You need him to understand the Sword."

Grimstone laughed. “I could deal with you now, effortlessly, but that would be too easy. It’s not a fitting punishment for your disloyalty.”

“What are you planning? What are you doing in London?”

Grimstone’s voice oozed with triumph. “Oh, I think you, being so smart, must have worked that out for yourself.”

Mark stared at his hated adoptive father, his eyes bright.

Nan tugged at his arm.

“I think you should pay heed to your trollop. You should take the opportunity and run.” Grimstone’s voice rose to a roar. “Run! Like the scared rabbits you are.”

Mark was about to turn his oraculum on Grimstone when Nan whispered to him through her oraculum, <Don’t do it!>

<Why not?>

<Expose neither your mind nor your power here.>

<What is it?>

<A furnace burns in him, the like of which I have never witnessed. It is a malignant sun.>

The choir above was coming to a climax, their voices sweet; the harmony of angels. Grimstone’s laughter followed them up the stairs.

“I sensed no human in him any more, Nan. What the hell is he—what has Grimstone become?”

“A Legun incarnate.”

The Search for Nidhoggr

Before Kate's startled eyes, even as they tumbled headlong through the abyss, Kate saw the succubus attempt to detach herself from the vulture. She was demanding a separate existence, a will of her own. The ravaged face drew close to Kate's and she whispered urgently, "There is great danger here," Kate heard the whisper like she would a swirl of wind.

She summoned her courage to face a major new uncertainty: "I must know—are you Elaru or Urale—or both?"

"Oh, Mistress—I truly am Elaru, your humble and devoted servant—I most sincerely assure you."

"How can I be sure that you could possibly become independent of him?"

"He's a god, however mean and cruel. Through slight of cunning he created me. But once created, I do have some rudiments of free will."

The vulture god chuckled: "And if you believe that, dearie . . ."

"For goodness sake, Elaru. What am I to think? I suppose I have no option other than to trust you."

Trust you perhaps one quarter of an inch, she thought.

Granny Dew's voice inside her head was now whispering to her. <Darkness grows. The usurper of the Fáil, feeling threatened, will now attempt to assert his power. The peril will increase a thousand-fold because you threaten him directly. But through the power you already possess I can implement some succour. I will stay by your side in the trials that lie ahead.>

"What do you mean?"

<Nothing here is truly as it seems.>

"The Tree of Life?"

<The maze in which you are falling headlong.>

Kate considered this. "I'm right, am I not? Whatever is happening here, in this part of Dromenon, in the roots of the Tree of Life—it's all somehow linked to the Tyrant's plotting? I really can help Alan if I can weaken the Tyrant's purpose here."

<Think carefully, child.>

In the short time that Kate's attention had been distracted from the succubus, Elaru had paled until she became little more than a wispy outline. All three of them were spinning and spiralling in their never-ending descent.

"Mistress, heed! I may become subsumed again."

Kate thought, *No! Granny Dew has cautioned me. Nothing here is as it seems.* She said, "I'm sorry, Elaru. I think I understand now. I must keep your existence constantly in mind."

"Do not be sorry, sweet Mistress, you treated me as a friend. When I was created to . . . intended to . . ."

Kate issued the command, with all of her might, through the oraculum: <I will stop falling!>

The headlong descent halted immediately.

The vulture cackled a laugh, lifted one leg high into the air, then scratched at its beak with a fearsome-looking talon. "Bravo! I thought myself incapable of surprise. Yet here we still are. And you are allowing yourself to be taken in by an exceedingly stupid, if tiresome, creation of mine. You can't win, you know."

"I'm tired of your tricks."

"By all means, discharge me of my services to you, dearie. But consider then that you will be obliged to solve the mysteries of the labyrinth alone."

"Elaru stays."

"If I go, she goes."

"Elaru—is he right?"

"My existence is dependent, yes."

"You mean, he could erase you—your existence—because he gave rise to it in the first place?"

"Alas—I suspect so."

"That's hideous."

"If erasure is my fate, so be it. At least you would retain me as a memory of friendship, Mistress."

Urale preened. "Oh, how delightful—I have sprung an offspring with the winning wiles of a minor seductress."

"You might yet save me, Mistress."

"How?"

"The power of a goddess illuminates your brow. Take what is left of me. Let me be one with you rather than my creator. Do it quickly, if you are of a mind to. There is very little time left."

Up in the Momu's chamber, within the cage of roots in which myriad tiny forms slithered, Kate's eyes opened wide with shock. The idea of subsuming Elaru intrigued her. Immediately, she focused her whole being on the act of subsuming Elaru. Even if she had the power to do this, which was far from certain, she had no idea what to expect if she were to succeed. Were succubi real people—or at least real life forms? Would such a subsummation change her?

"Oh!" Kate felt the ghost of a life enter her, like an ethereal expansion within her mind, within her spirit.

<Thank you, Mistress!>

She felt a curious flush of warmth spread throughout her being.

Kate had no idea what had just happened, or how it had happened; oracula had powers beyond logic. But had she done the right thing? There was so much she failed to understand. *I was no longer really human anyway,* she thought.

Did it matter? Was her humanity so important?

<Beware, Mistress! They will attempt to delay and distract you in this place.>

Kate was more confused than ever. *Who were they? Were the Yoolf still playing their tricks on her?* She must stay focused. She must hunt down the serpent-dragon in the maze of roots under the Tree of Life. It was only natural that Elaru would want Kate to take her with her; she wanted to escape from the Land of the Dead.

<Mistress—I beg you.>

Kate didn't know if the succubus possessed any really helpful knowledge, but if she had spent as long as she said in Dromenon, it was likely that she did. "You must give me a hint, a clue, as to what I must do."

<You must consider the colour blue.>

What in heaven's name . . . ?

Kate reached out through her oraculum and filled her senses with the purest, primary shade of blue, the blue of the sky in the sunniest day of summer. She willed herself to dissolve into that sky, to become one with that soothing shade. A feeling of tranquillity suffused her being. Shades appeared in swirling movements, then came the shimmering arrival of other primary colours and a fusion of colour with colour, expanding the glorious creativity so that she was witnessing the primordial beginning of a creation. But what could it mean? How could it possibly help her in her search for Nidhoggr?

She began to understand—not rationally but through intuition.

"Well, if you're right, the colour blue must represent something important. And this mystery has something to do with the roots of the Tree. But that's a puzzle in itself, because if I am correct we are still in Dromenon. The Land of the Dead is certainly not on Tír, or Earth, and that means the roots of the Tree must also exist in Dromenon. But what could possibly feed it here?"

Elaru sounded equally excited. <As you say, Mistress—you face a very great mystery.>

Kate had never considered colour as a source of creation before. But she recalled Uncle Fergal explaining how insects saw colours differently from people. He had shown her beautiful pictures of flowers, both how people saw them and how insects saw them, and it had been a revelation. Insects were guided by colour to fulfil an all-consuming instinct—in human terms a passion—to find the nectar. Yet, in doing so, nature determined that they also pollinated the flowers. The passion of the insect was driven by a pure colour. Kate deliberately imagined that she was placing windows of clear blue in front of her eyes, then looked through them into the surrounding Dromenon.

She glimpsed something fleeting, but the picture faded almost immediately.

<Think harder, Mistress.>

"My oraculum sees better than I do." Using her oraculum, Kate Shaunessy looked once more through the imagined windows of purest blue, opening her mind onto a wonderland.

The roots of the Tree of Life were not made out of wood. They were constantly being reborn of swirling clouds of . . . of matter. She could think of no better way to describe what she was seeing. They were clouds of *being,* within which matter, the essence of substance, twinkled in and out of reality. The roots extended to infinity amid the galaxies, nebulae, stars.

Kate recalled what she had seen when the demigod Fangorath attacked the Third Portal of the Fáil. He had shown this same twinkling essence of being. She held onto that mind-blowing thought: *The universe also constantly twinkles in and out of being in Dromenon.*

"Oh, my goodness." Kate looked around in wonder.

She heard the growl of outrage that was Urale. "Betrayed! I am betrayed by my insubordinate self. I am doomed—the Master will punish me."

She ignored the hysterics to recall the advice of the dragon, Driftwood.

"*Remember what you saw in my dreams.*"

She hadn't understood him at the time. But now she remembered entering the soul-spirit of the dragon when she had used her power to restore his wings. Through the reawakening of his memories she had experienced what it was to soar through air and ocean on dragon's wings. She had felt the enormous heart of the dragon contract within her own chest and the golden blood pulsing through her arteries and veins. Within the exquisite joy of communion, she had felt her soul drift further to a time before people, a time of beginnings . . . a time that belonged to beings resembling angels: ethereal creatures that existed in perfect harmony with nature, devoid of ordinary mortal needs.

The Arinn.

She recalled the ecstasy that had filled her being.

What she was still gazing on within the prisms of blue windows took her breath away. "It's beyond anything that could be described as beautiful. Oh, Elaru—this has to be something to do with the Arinn. It's what sustains the roots of the Tree of Life and the serpent-dragon, Nidhoggr. It's something to do with the Fáil."

"Pah—you may search until the ends of time, dearie. You will discover no logical answers here."

<Mistress—through his wiles, my other self seeks to distract you still. He would complicate that which you envision.>

The vulture croak rose to a scream. "I will kill her, rend her, pick at her bones—she who, through her imbecility, subverts my every scheme."

<Ignore his wiles, Mistress. There is another prism of view—a window that opens on the most implacable darkness.>

Kate ignored Urale's tantrums. She was so thrilled that she had been privileged enough to glimpse the working of the Fáil: the way of light, which was inextricably linked with its opposite, the way of darkness. The shrieking of Urale was enough to warn her that her situation had grown more dangerous. Was Elaru telling her something important and new? Desperately, Kate asked herself: *how can I possibly look through a window that is the very absence of colour?* Again and again she was confronting beings, entities, concepts that went beyond her simple human logic to understand.

Still, she would have to make herself understand.

She poured every last ounce of concentration through her oraculum, melting away the blue, all colour, until she was looking into Dromenon as through a glass darkly.

She perceived.

"Oh, my God!"

Against the renewed wrath of Urale screaming with fury she saw the explanation for everything, the decline of Ulla Quemar, the dying of the Momu and the rotting of the One Tree . . .

Where Ya Hidin', Penny?

Gully talked to himself as he searched through the maze of West End streets leading eastwards of the Razzed-out St. Martin's Lane. "Hellfire, Penny, even the weather's gone bonkers on us. 'Ail stoning down thick as snot one minute and then rainin' like a bleedin' river."

He stopped himself, peering down at paving stones slick with filthy water. He had slipped already and his knees were bruised. He sniffed, screwing up his face. "This rain ain't for stoppin'. Them kerbs is runnin' like Ol' Man Thames!"

Crowds jostled him in Piccadilly Circus, their hats pulled down and collars pulled up, causing him to blink owlishly through his rain-spattered spectacles, avoiding any kind of eye contact. He sloshed though icy streams.

"Listen to me, Gully Doughty. Listen to me, will you? You don't do nuffink wot makes you stand out from the crowd."

Turning left off the Circus, he hurried along rubble-strewn back lanes heading for the market.

"I got to find somefink to eat!"

He had to sacrifice a few minutes at the wheelie-cart market haggling over two sausages at ridiculous prices. Stuffing the greasy package into Pocket 2, he patted at the shapes in Pocket 5, comforted by the feel of a nylon climbing rope he had acquired. He pulled each of his sleeves in turn so he could check out the watches. *Twenty-five minutes to four o'clock, the same on each—perfick!* Give it half an hour, it'd be falling dark. He sniffed again, thinking hard, and wiped his nose on his left sleeve.

He counted to twenty, listening to the pouring rain beating down on his hood. There was that bleedin' noise again, like a roaring inside of his brain. "Now look wot you done to me, gel! Where ya hidin', Penny?"

He had lost track of where he was exactly, scurrying through the downpour in a frantic rush. Taking his rain-spattered glasses off his nose he wiped them on a snotrag, staring ahead into the boarded-up Kingsley Court. He slid the glasses back on and slunk along in the shadows up the narrow Beak Street, looking to find Oggy's Café. That was where it had all begun: where Penny had seen them aliens. What he saw there stopped him dead in his tracks and caused him to slide into the shadow of a doorway. Gully squinted his eyes and tried to make out what was going on. Yellow light from the wire-screened window of the café was spilling out onto the pavement, illuminating two bikers, dressed in leathers, sitting there in the rain. They was watching the café like they was waiting for someone.

"Blimey!" he said. He had this real strong feeling about it.

"Got to be that geezer wot done for the Scalpie! An' the woman wot done for the Grimlings!"

He needed to get closer to them, close enough to see if they had the things stuck in their heads, but he didn't dare move any closer. Gully was pressing himself so hard against the doorway the powdery plaster was coming off onto his shoulder and sleeve.

"You got to check it out, mate," he said to himself.

One of the leather-clad riders had to be a woman—he could make out tit bumps. He couldn't make out her hair or face, what with the helmet. And them Skulls, they didn't take no women. Yeah, for sure, the two of 'em was just sitting there in the pouring rain like they was waiting for somebody to come along.

Somebody like Penny . . .

He drew back into the crumbly doorway, sniffling the snot back up into his nose, trying to get his brain to work through the panic in his head.

He recalled Penny looking really scared. He recalled her whisper, *"I know that this is the sign, Gully. This is the sign I've been waiting for."*

He had seen how she was trembling. Her eyes was all over the place. His hand reached out, just like it had with the cuppa in it. "*There you go, gel!*" He handed her the cuppa he had made for her. An' the poached egg on a bit of toast.

She had told him about the man and the woman. Them bleedin' aliens with the triangles stuck in their heads.

"*They tangled with my mind, Gully!*"

"*Where'd this 'appen?*"

"*At Oggy's place.*"

"*How come you're so sure they was aliens?*"

He remembered Penny looking up at him, her grey eyes wide. She'd told him about the black triangles, stuck into their heads.

He stuck his head out to peer at the riders again.

"Yeah—them's tit bumps all right."

But it was impossible, what with the helmet, to see if she had something stuck in her head or if she didn't. He felt a prickling in the skin at the back of his neck. He was still trying to figure it out when a voice caught him unawares.

"Hey, Pockets! Where's that crazy gel a yours?"

Gully squinted behind him at a rat-faced kid with a ponytail. He knew him from a knick-knack stand further down the street. Only a year ago he had been on nodding acquaintance with Sadiq Khan, the man who had owned the stand. Sadiq had always moaned about the fortunes of Millwall football club. Gully didn't know if Sadiq had been murdered or what, only that he hadn't seen him around for a while.

"You got somefink to say?"

"That gel—you got more'n one?"

Gully looked into the pasty-white face of a crack-head. Gully knew he had also been dealing drugs from the stand to his fellow crack-heads and sofa surfers. Right now, though, he was dialling a number with his thumb, mouthing the numbers to himself. Gully heard him refer to "Cat," which was what the street dross called Penny. At the top of the street Gully caught a glimpse of two new figures wearing black leather jackets. Rain was running over the tattoos on their half-shaved heads. They were looking in his direction.

"That Cat—she done for a Skull, mate."

"Wot?"

"You 'eard me. The Skulls is lookin' for 'er."

"Shi-it!"

Gully ran.

He tore right past the figures waiting on their bikes. A glimpse—it was all his panic would allow him—but he saw how sharp they looked at him. They watched him run by, water from the puddles sloshing around his trainers as he skidded and bumped into some old basket case standing there wearing "Rapture" boards, proclaiming the coming of Judgement Day.

Gully shoved past the old man. He kicked in the flimsy door of what looked like an abandoned office and ran through the debris-strewn building, finding a rear door standing ajar. He emerged, in the falling dusk, into a tiny closed-off yard.

"Arseholes!"

This wasn't familiar territory to Gully. He clambered up onto a hillock of rubbish piled in sacks, hauling himself up a red-brick wall. He vaulted the wall to find himself in a second, bigger yard, crammed with skips the Razzers must have set fire to at some point. Everything was ashes and soot. The cindered remains of twin loading doors gaped onto a concrete loading bay. Gully stumbled awkwardly through, fell, then rose again, already running. He picked out the wreckage of a staircase leading into the gloom of the floor above and headed for it. He didn't need to look behind him to know his pursers had followed him into the yard. He heard at least one of them stumble at the same awkward space between the loading doors. He heard the metallic click of what sounded like a weapon.

"Shit, shit, shiiit!"

He took the darkened staircase two treads at a time, learning, after he had taken several splinters, to avoid hand contact with the banister. This situation was bad. Gully was afraid of the Skulls chasing him, but he was even more afraid for Penny. It was Penny they were really looking for. He had to find her. His head was so agitated he couldn't get it to work. He counted to twenty.

Pockets—Pocket 6!

On a turn, three-quarters the way up to the first floor, he found the double sided Sellotape roll and stuck lengths of it over two successive treads, close to the edge. It didn't matter that his glasses were smudged to shit, since the staircase was pitch dark anyways. From the same pocket, Pocket 6—T for Traps—he extracted a fistful of marbles. He did it all in the dark by feel and touch, pressing the marbles down onto the sticky tape, covering the treads. Didn't matter that two or three of the marbles went pattering down, tapping their way down every step. The operation was done and dusted in thirty seconds. He barely had time to hop awkwardly over the trap before he heard the clatter of boots on the treads at the bottom of the staircase.

Gully hurried on up into a cave of charcoal—a big open space now razzed to rubble. He moved in a zigzag over the space, feeling his way past broken shelves, putting what distance he could between himself and the landing. He halted before a plate glass window, three quarters shattered, with rain gusting in.

A howl from the stairs told him that one of them had found the marbles. He heard the tumbling and cursing that meant he had a few more seconds. The glow of a torch was now leaching out from the head of the stairs. The torchlight flickered on and off in spurts, illuminating first one area then another. His hunters were taking their time now. They had figured that he had no place to run.

Gully peered out of the big gap in the glass and saw the woman on the bike down below. She must have followed him from Oggy's. And there she was—just sitting on her bike and waiting. But how had she figured out he was right above her?

"*They tangled with my mind, Gully.*"

The hunters were so close, he had to trust his instincts. Pocket 5! Gully opened his jacket, released the nylon climbing rope and ran it out through his fingers. There was a problem with the broken glass in the lower edge of the window frame.

You ain't got no time for dithering, mate—ya got to take your chances.

Crossing the Peaks

Alan had been observing how the aides made use of the plentiful flat pieces of rock on far side of the summit; fashioning them into horseshoe-shaped shelters of stone as breaks against the icy wind. The continuous clattering of stone against stone was rhythmical. The sky overhead was a jade green. All the while, the cold was searing through their clothes. Alan's breath emerged as white fog to be torn away by the wind, which howled between the soaring fangs of the mountain tops. Two-thirds of the huge army had already managed to cross over the razor-like mountain crest; their numbers were so large that the aides could not construct the shelters fast enough. Huge numbers of Shee hung about with little to do, blowing into their furry hands in the freezing air. It was so icy Alan had long lost any feeling in his face, and a numbing chill was seeping deeper into his nostrils and airways with every breath.

They were about halfway there, in their march on the Tyrant's city of Ghork Mega, and if the aides could rig sufficient shelters, they would be able to rest their exhausted limbs overnight before beginning the descent.

The way he looked forward to the smallest pleasures was laughable. He longed to just fall asleep and dream ordinary dreams, especially his favourite dream about Kate.

He had enjoyed that same wonderful dream, over and over, a hundred times or more. It was actually a memory that had become a dream. In it, he was waiting for her to emerge from the gates of the Doctor's House in the small Irish town of Clonmel on a beautiful Sunday morning. He saw the small door built into one of the two gates opening and then, as if in slow motion, her bike roll through as she held onto its handlebars. He saw the excitement in her eyes—the excitement that mirrored his own. He had kissed her on the lips for the first time. After that, it seemed as if his heartbeat had never quite managed to slow down again. More than anything he longed for the realisation of that dream, when Kate would come back to him and his heart would beat crazily again in that impossible, unstoppable tide of love that made everything else hollow and meaningless.

The sound of a drawn-out animal scream woke him from his reverie. He spun around, his breath caught in his frozen airways.

It was another of the onkkh in trouble. The enormous bird was twisting and tearing at the retaining ropes, its panic threatening the security of the aides and Shee to either side of it.

"Damn."

They had lost something like a hundred Shee in the climb, and perhaps half as many aides. He didn't want to lose any more, not when they were so close to finishing the ascent. Alan peered down into the convoluted lattice of mountain ranges that fell away below them. The furnace black of the rock gave the mountains their name—the Flamestrucks. The drop was immense, more than ten thousand feet. The zigzagging shoulders and peaks rolled away, becoming lost in the cloud that swirled and eddied around the panorama of peaks and valleys, a hundred and fifty leagues distant from the Eastern Ocean, where their climb had begun in the arid beauty of the deserts and islands of the Garg Kingdom.

Alan thought, *No—no more losses*. And Mo! Mo was not yet across—and nor was Qwenqwo.

The steep escarpment was crawling with figures, thousands hauling themselves across a carefully constructed framework of ropes, the makeshift spider's web spanning several-dozen strata of treacherous ledges, perhaps a hundred yards or so across and only a few hundred yards below the wind-buffeted summit. It was the last step in what had proved to be a tortuous crossing through the moraine traps of narrow valleys. They had been devoid of any natural path or easy climb and the army had struggled for days to negotiate a few miles of passage. The rolling pebbles had broken ankles, and traps of quicksand had swallowed up at least half a dozen of the burdened beasts, their screaming beaks the last to disappear as their desperate struggles just hastened the end. And it had all been accompanied by a flaying chill that cut through furs and skin, and bit deep into bones. The Tyrant had no need for defensive ramparts here: the treacherous mountains, and the inclement elements, would have been more than enough to defeat any ordinary army. But this was no ordinary army. This was an army of battle-hardened Shee. Still, even the Shee would have struggled had they not benefited from the advice of both Qwenqwo and Magtokk and the Garg scouts braving the icy climate and perilous winds to help them negotiate the hazards. And here was the final hurdle in a march that had looked impossible—the passage of an army of a hundred thousand Shee, with aides, assistants, cooks and baggage train, across an almost sheer cliff face in temperatures twenty degrees below zero.

It had taken them several days just to plan and organise the crossing. Gargs had carried the first light ropes to straddle the mountainside and axes had broken the cliff face to create a series of ledges, and then more lines of ropes and iron tethers had been slung between the lines, creating the handholds and toeholds for ten horizontal columns of Shee and aides to make the crossing. The scourging wind had torn at ropes and ties, handholds and footholds, ripping garments out of belts and fastenings and cracking the frozen coverings like whips. Alan could feel his hair blowing horizontally as he shouted encouragement and warnings.

The screaming of the troubled onkkh was being taken up by others. Alan looked across at the agitated bird, which was snapping its powerful beak at everything and anyone in its vicinity. Its clawed legs, strong enough to break a Shee's arm, were kicking out at the ropes, threatening to rip the tethers and guidelines out of the rock face. Alan could see no way out of the situation other than to ask the Gargs to risk flying out into the tempestuous air and cut the bewildered beast free. Within moments, Iyezzz had volunteered to do so.

With the warning of Zelnesakkk about his younger son's safety uppermost in Alan's mind, he watched with trepidation as Iyezzz made several attempts to cut the rope, each time being caught up by the tempestuous wind and hurled towards the abyss. But on the fourth attempt Iyezzz managed to grab hold of the rope with one of his feet and, with the razor-sharp claws on the other, cut the beast free. Alan watched the unfortunate bird plummet away into the distance, its limbs clutching at the air and its vestigial wings flapping, until it had dwindled to a speck above the clouds wheeling over the lower slopes and ridges.

But it was too late to prevent the panic from affecting the remaining onkkh. Alan heard a call from the Kyra, mind-to-mind, and he turned to witness the sacrifice of several-dozen Shee who had severed sections of rope where the panic was no longer containable. With horrified eyes Alan watched the falling figures, many still tethered to beasts or to one another by stretches of rope, until they too became flailing dots against the moiling clouds far below.

He was joined by the Kyra, who looked at him, her cat-eyes slitted against the wind. No words were exchanged, but her look was sufficient: the danger had not gone away. A third of the army still needed to cross the treacherous cliff. What could they possibly do to prevent more losses?

He was worried that any attempt to use the First Power in this hazardous environment might put the trapped warriors in danger. He recalled what had happened when he had used it to save them from the Forest of Harrow: it had destroyed everything, turning the landscape to ash. *What if I turn it against the elements here and destroy the entire mountain face?*

He struggled to come up with a solution. Where was Iyezzz? Could he possibly work with the Gargs in some way? But he had already seen how difficult it had been for the Garg prince to sever a single section of rope. The ferocious winds would blow the Gargs about like rags tossed into a maelstrom.

Mo—*Mo!* He guessed that Mo was somewhere out there with Turkeya. He could communicate with Mo, mind to mind.

<Mo—do you hear me?>

<Alan—I've been trying to communicate with you. We haven't moved more than inches in the last hour or so. Our hands and feet have lost all feeling. We're barely clinging to the rock.>

<Do you have any suggestions?>

<My companion thinks the stones might be useful.>

Mo's companion?

Alan had forgotten the magician, Magtokk, who was keeping his existence a secret. An orang-utan might have held his ground better in the ropewalk crossing than most. *But why would he suggest the stones might be useful?*

Alan turned around to where those aides that had already managed the crossing were constructing the horseshoe-shaped shelters out of flat stones. He looked down the slope onto the extensive scree of similar stones. The screams of panicking onkkh were rising even above the screech of the wind behind him.

He had to shout to Ainé, who was only twenty yards away, so he could be heard beyond the screeching of wind and beasts. "Have the Shee and aides collect together big flat stones that would make a path."

She stared at him. "A path?"

"I have an idea. I may be able to use the First Power to lay a path leading out across the cliff face. I don't have time to explain."

As the Shee and aides laid out the first half-dozen flat stones, each perhaps a yard or more in length and width, Alan put all of his concentration into the oraculum of the First Power, the Power of the Land. He willed the path to shift until it was under the feet of the nearest struggling group, straddling the cliff face of the mountain. As he did so, the stones moved and assembled, with no visible support against gravity.

"Get them to test them," he shouted to the Kyra.

She issued the command to the threatened Shee through her oraculum. Alan saw the panicking group discover the steadying stone path beneath their feet. He watched them test the firmness, the reliability, of what should have been impossible. The tiny section of path held.

The Kyra's order alerted large numbers of Shee and aides already watching from the scree-covered ground. More and more figures began to haul big flat stones into the path before Alan, and as quickly as they laid them he shifted them, with a command through his oraculum, to construct a gravity-defying path along the most troubled sections of rope guides extending across the mountain face.

He passed his message to Ainé. "Get the people gathering the stones to hurry."

Already the first of the rescued Shee, aides and beasts, were being assisted off the makeshift path, which floated on thin air and was impervious to the wind. The panicky cries of the onkkh were quieting and the columns stabilising. Alan built a second path across the mountain, and then a third and a fourth, until all eight of the rope crossings had been underpinned with stone paths, snaking around the irregular buttress of the cliff face, all suspended above the drop by the power of his oraculum.

For the remainder of what would prove the most intractable day of the entire climb, Alan worked tirelessly, extending and strengthening what he had already constructed, while the Kyra and the growing army of Shee now ferried to solid ground helped the rest of the army and the baggage train across. All day, and even through dusk into night, the excruciating effort continued, with no possibility of rest until the entire army and their beasts of burden were safely escorted onto the rock-strewn ground, and then led to the shelters. As he saw the final stragglers safe, such was his exhaustion that Alan could hardly stand. He was glad of the steadying arm and shoulders of Qwenqwo as he allowed the First Power to release the stones, watching in a numbed awe as the strange paths of his own construction lost their anchorage on nothingness to clatter and tumble away into the abyss.

At last, with small central fires to warm them against the cold, the army bedded down for the night in the thousands of horseshoe shelters that had proliferated over the mountain top. While trying to find some comfortable position for his many aches and pains, Alan sat among his friends in one of the larger shelters, ignoring the wind that still shrieked around its stony walls. He was grateful to the aides who massaged his aching muscles. He was also very glad of the flask of healwell pressed against his numbed lips, and although it was difficult to persuade his reluctant throat to swallow the burning liquid he appreciated its comforting warmth as it spread out into his belly and heart.

Most of the Shee had adopted the body forms of great cats for the night, their pelts better suited to the cold and wind than bare skin. The Gargs had also settled into their own shelters. Though many in the camp must have welcomed the chance of sleep, others remained awake and busy: aides released burdens of tents and provisions from the onkkh, others were already at work on a nourishing and sustaining breakfast for the coming morning. The bedlam of the settling camp was, in itself, a cheering sound and, with the healwell coursing through his blood stream, Alan could already feel his spirits rising. Qwenqwo was sitting to his left in a contemplative mood, nursing a flagon of drink, his jaws were clamped around his unlit pipe; he was forbidden to smoke in such an enclosed space.

"Magtokk—are you here?"

There was a rising cacophony of grumbles as the bulky body manifested among the crowded company, taking up the space of three, his arms extending around the shoulders of Mo and Qwenqwo, between whose shuffling bodies he squeezed his shaggy bulk with a grin.

Alan smiled across the fire at the orang-utan. Magtokk's dark irises reflected the flames, the lids drooping as if he, too, was longing for sleep.

"Thanks—for the idea." Alan said.

A nut was flipped into the air by a grey thumb and caught by the cavernous mouth. "Think nothing of it."

Mo was snuggling down inside the cosy cradle of Magtokk's right arm. Sleepily she said, "Alan's right. It was brilliant to think of the stones."

"Mine was a mere thought—the power and deed were Alan's."

Mo's eyes drifted closed. She looked dead to the world.

Alan was close to dropping into an exhausted stupor himself, but he was already thinking of the next day. "What," he asked Qwenqwo, "can we expect up ahead?"

Qwenqwo took the pipe from his mouth and contemplated its empty bowl. "We have made important progress. The peaks were the main barrier that had to be crossed. Methinks, for all of today's tribulations, we may be cheered by the fact we have completed the most difficult half of our march and still have the bulk of the army intact. But we must still make the descent, which will take at least another week. At the foot of these slopes we will then face the first of the defensive fosses that guard the Tyrant's city."

Alan glanced from Qwenqwo to Magtokk, who was poised to flick another nut. "How do you think the Tyrant will react to our progress?"

Those eyebrows lifted, deepening the trapezoidal depression that took up the centre of Magtokk's brow. "From what I have seen thus far, the Tyrant is paying remarkably little attention to our progress. He appears content to leave it to the landscape to slow you down."

"What do you make of that?"

"It would suggest that delaying you is sufficient for his purposes."

Alan fell silent. What Magtokk said made sense, but it still left him wondering what longer game the Tyrant might be playing.

The dwarf mage took a swig from his flagon, belched, then laughed, waving it between Alan and Magtokk as if asking which of them wanted it most. "A toast, then, to courage—and to victory over the elements!"

Mo roused herself at Qwenqwo's toast. Though still sleepy-eyed, she laughed at the bright expression that creased the dwarf-mage's red-bearded face. "Oh, Qwenqwo's surely right. We've crossed the peaks. Hopefully that will be the worst of this journey."

"Aye!" Qwenqwo roared. "Sup up and be merry. Tomorrow we shall face the day refreshed with food and rest."

Alan toasted that thought with the flagon before passing it on to Magtokk's outstretched hand. He thought about the slope of freezing shale they would soon be descending. He wished that he could share Qwenqwo's and Mo's optimism. As the burning liquid set fire to his heart, he couldn't help but wonder about his absent friends. Looking with affection on Mo's sleepy but contented face, he asked himself: *where is my Kate and your brother, Mark? What dangers are they facing? Is the Tyrant playing that waiting game with us while he focuses all of his malice on Kate and Mark? Is that why we haven't had any word of sign from either of them for such a long time?*

He saw Mo's face lift towards him: he saw how fright had scared the sleep from her eyes.

Nidhoggr

Kate was staring, wide-eyed, at a monochromatic landscape. All essence of *being* was black, but its darkness did not derive from a complete absence of light. It was more like entering the world of a photographic negative. She had no idea why colours were so important, but in this strange perspective of the world, the roots had assumed a powerful solidity. They ramified everywhere, seemingly to infinity. They were trails that blazed through the heavens, like nebulae. She also realised how shrunken and shrivelled up they were; as dry as the husks of insects her Uncle Fergal had shown her, in places where once-living creatures had abandoned their skins. But there had been no metamorphosis here, no change from one living form to another. She heard a booming sound—oh, merciful God—the sound of a great heart pulsing a single heartbeat. A struggling heart, fighting for its existence.

<Explore!> She heard the voice of Elaru inside her mind. <Use all of your senses—so that you may distinguish truth from falsehood.>

Kate was so overwhelmed with the horror of what she was sensing it was difficult to focus on it anew. Perhaps she should close her eyes and try another sense, like hearing, tasting, feeling . . . Oh, lord, she didn't know if it would make a jot of difference. Yet, now she did feel something new, a pattering, like the sensation of rain falling upon her naked skin. She heard it too, now that she was aware of it: a continuous, liquid rushing. And she smelled it: a foul, obscene deluge, as if she were being showered in a cascade of filth.

The feel, the sound and the stink of it overwhelmed her senses, but she couldn't afford to be squeamish. It had to mean something, but what?

Through the oraculum she opened all of her senses at once.

And saw the truth.

Her heart almost stopped with the shock of realisation: the roots were black not because they were dying, but because their surfaces were completely submerged in a teeming infestation of parasites; a vast proliferation of black worms, each worm gigantic, yet minuscule against the scale of the roots. They were packed so tightly around their prey they completely obscured its substance, gorging unceasingly like a monstrous brood of insatiable leeches. Everywhere the parasitic worms fought one another to pry open a space for attachment. Now she had seen the worms, she urged the power of her oraculum to bring her closer. Kate saw that the worms had no head other than a gigantic ring, like the sucking mouth of a lamprey. In battling one another for space, they ravaged each other's flesh with the fangs that lined their sucking mouths. Their slimy bodies were contracting and expanding as they sucked and filled themselves with the sap of the roots. The sap inside them then moved in peristaltic waves from mouth to anus. The obscene shower was the rain of their excrement, deluging out into space and time, spreading their putrefying filth and stench into every avenue of the living universe.

"I don't think the Witch could have done this."

<No, Mistress!>

"Oh, Elaru! This means that the wasting lies much deeper than the tentacles of the Great Witch; she was controlled by Fangorath, but the Tyrant must have been manipulating them both."

Kate felt faint with shock. She could hear the thunder of lapping sounds made by millions upon millions of feeding worms and the continuous squelching of their excretion. How could she not have heard it before? Now that she was aware of it, it was omnipresent and utterly deafening.

"But how can I stop this?"

<Are you not the healer? Do you not carry the power of a goddess in your brow? One that venerates life—the wonder of birth?>

Kate thought back to Granny Dew, of her own feeble body trapped in the roots within the Momu's chamber, still being fed by a host of tiny creatures. Where was she going to find the power to undo this obscenity?

"If only Alan were here, with his Power of the Land—or Mo, with her Torus."

<There is one—a potential ally.>

"Who?"

<Nidhoggr himself.>

"What do you mean?"

Kate sensed a weakening in Elaru. Though she was determined to help, Urale was equally determined to silence her. The message was weakened to the merest whisper: <The great serpent-dragon that lies coiled within these same roots—the black worms take what is rightfully his.>

Kate thought about this. "Quickly, tell me, what's the relationship between Nidhoggr and the Tree of Life?"

<In nourishing Nidhoggr, the Tree bears fruit.>

"How? What fruit does it bear?"

<The . . . the Circle . . . >

"Elaru—you mustn't fade now, I need your help. I need you to explain more of this to me."

<The Circle . . . Life . . . >

Kate was only beginning to sense a deeper meaning to all that was happening. A meaning that might fit with what she had learnt from the company of the Momu. "But where can I find this serpent-dragon?"

There was no reply, only an ominous silence.

Kate turned her oraculum inwards, searching for the soul spirit of the helpful succubus. She discovered a wisp of being, as insubstantial as smoke. She poured what was left of her strength into it, saw it thicken and strengthen somewhat, then assume the familiar shape.

<Mistress—you must look to the senses again. Continue to unpick truth from the web of lies.>

"I feel lost. I just don't understand."

<Did you not restore another dragon from a stony grave?>

"What . . . Another dragon?"

Kate was dumbstruck for a moment. Elaru could only be referring to Driftwood. But Driftwood was more obviously a dragon than anything she detected here. She had met him as a baby dragon. Though he professed a fondness for eating her, she had been confident in ignoring his childish threats. Here, with Nidhoggr, she had no such confidence. And if she had learned anything from her dealings with the maturing Driftwood, it was that she knew little to nothing about dragons. But it was also true that she had restored him to life from being long dead. He had been no more than a black fossil buried in the rocks of the island.

"I wasn't aware of reviving him, Elaru. It happened when I was asleep—when I was too exhausted to have been aware of what I was doing."

<Yet it happened.>

"Yes." Kate reflected on what little she could recall. "I was carried to the island by a wolf that had the soul spirit of a man. I fell into a stupor with my head against the black rocks. Later, after the dragon was reborn, I noticed that the black rocks had disappeared. I assumed that they must have been fossils—the bones of the dragon fossilised into stone over time."

<You revived him.>

"But how did I do it?"

<Something innate in the power.>

Kate's soul spirit brought her hands to her lips and her brow furrowed. She was thinking the impossible, of something Alan had said as he held her in his arms on their first night by the fireside, after they had been reunited in the City of the Ancients. Kate had been unconscious when she was taken prisoner by the Gargs at Ossierel and carried across the Eastern Ocean to the Tower of Bones. She hadn't witnessed what had happened to Mo, but Alan had told her about it in an awed whisper. Mo had saved them all at Ossierel. She had delayed the Legun for a precious while, but at terrible cost to herself: the Legun had ravaged her soul spirit. Mo had been deeply unconscious, unresponsive even to Alan's oraculum. In desperation he had joined spirits with the Temple Ship to call upon the Goddess of the Second Power, Qurun Mab, to help

Mo. The Goddess of the Second Power—Mab and her daughters—had actually manifested and it had taken her to heal the ravaged soul spirit of Mo.

Kate felt an urge towards caution.

Both Driftwood and Granny Dew had warned her to be careful. To call upon a goddess—she hardly dared even to think what that might mean. She was just an ordinary girl. And she was all too aware that the succubus whose advice she was listening to was the alter-ego of a malevolent minor god, currently implanted within her own soul spirit.

Yet if I fail here, not only will the Tree of Life be consigned to rot, but the Momu will die and the Cill will be lost.

How she wished she had been there to witness Mo being healed by the goddess. But hadn't Alan explained to her, how he had engaged the help of the Temple Ship and then, jointly, they had pleaded with the goddess.

I don't know how to call on the Temple Ship—if ever it could hear me from here. But I do have a friend who might hear me.

"Driftwood!"

Kate allowed her desperation to overwhelm her heart and mind as she called out his name—her friend, the King of Sea Dragons, who was revered as a living god by the Gargs.

It couldn't work. She felt exhausted by the effort; it was asking for the impossible. Her spirit flailed, sinking into the hopelessness of her situation in this dreadful corner of this impossible spirit world.

<Kate . . . girl-thing!>

Was she dreaming? She sensed something enormous—a soul spirit utterly unlike herself—swell into being close beside her.

"Oh, Driftwood—if you are really here, please help me. The Tree of Life is being sucked dry by these horrible worms. I must stop them, but it's beyond my ability. I need to revive Nidhoggr."

<Do you know you what you would ask of me?>

"What are you afraid of?"

<I fear nothing for myself but everything for you. I would warn you that the soul of Nidhoggr is chaos.>

"Life, it seems to me, is nothing other than chaos—and that's certainly true if what I saw in the black cathedral is the Tyrant's vision of order."

<You must understand how dangerous this might be.>

"There is danger everywhere I turn. But there's so much at stake—not just the Momu. These black worms are vast and there are millions upon millions of them. They're sapping the life out of the Tree. I dread to think where this might lead."

Kate hesitated then, sensing how even the great dragon shuddered.

<What would you have me do?>

Kate recalled Alan's words about the healing of Mo: *"As far as I could see, no ordinary healing could cure Mo. The Legun had hurt her too deeply. The damage was spiritual."* Alan had explained how the ship had shared a communion of spirit with him. He had told her of the golden heart he had discovered in the inner chambers of the burned-out hull. It had helped him enter into a consummation that then enabled them to call upon the goddess.

"I—I wonder if I should call upon the goddess, Mab, the Second Power, whose crystal I bear in my brow."

<The goddess is the spirit of life and healing. You may yet have need of her. But your goddess is not the spirit to invoke here.>

"What then? Will you help me?"

<To discover this force you may wish to enter consummation with me—a second consummation, if you recall?>

Kate could no longer speak. Mentally and spiritually her arms reached out to the giant presence that she sensed nearby. She was aware of the sigh of awe from the succubus, Elaru, and the curses of Urale as she turned the power of her oraculum inwards. She sensed her union with Driftwood: one soul spirit minuscule in scale, but brilliantly radiant, the other enormous and darkly powerful. The fusion resulted in one gigantic source of power, like a waking sun.

"Now what are we to do?"

<Nidhoggr has been rendered insensate by the Night Hag's bane greatly strengthened by the power of another. Once seduced into slumber he was rendered emasculate, so that what remains is no more than the shade of what was.>

"Then it's already too late?"

<Not so. A dragon god cannot be entirely extirpated from being, not in worldly reality and not in Dromenon. You proved this to be so in my case, why can you not see it in these perilous circumstances?>

"Open my vision—let me see."

<All that is necessary is that Nidhoggr should awaken.>

"But how can I wake an almighty being, a dragon, when I can't even see him?"

<Have you not harkened to his shade in every sense and moment since you entered these roots?>

"I don't understand."

<Nidhoggr is omnipresent in this place.>

Kate struggled with the vagueness of this explanation. Was Driftwood asking her to grasp the concept of a universal being? She wasn't sure she was capable of understanding all that he was telling her, but perhaps she understood enough of what it implied. She focused on the healing power bequeathed to her by Granny Dew. She let it flower in her now—let it be through feeling, instinct, caring.

<Kate, Greeneyes—now do you see?>

She saw nothing at all, at first. Her vision was too focused, too local. But when she opened her awareness through the oraculum, she saw the astonishing nature of the being that was Nidhoggr. His soul spirit seemed infinite, but she saw how emaciated his physical being had become. He had shrunk to little more than a diffuse shade of scarlet, like watered-down arterial blood that was wrapped and coiled around every visible root, at one with the vast proliferation of the One Tree throughout all worlds. He wasn't a sea dragon, like Driftwood, with the golden blood of magic circulating through his heart, but a serpent-dragon, with the carnal sap of Life circulating though his being.

<Do it now! Be one with the soul spirit of Nidhoggr!>

To escape the limits of her imagination, Kate closed her eyes and wished that it be so through her oraculum. She wished that the power of the goddess Mab and the Daughters of Mab should bathe the roots, all roots, through all dimensions of time and space, through all worlds.

The violence of Nidhoggr's awakening swept through her like a lightening strike, forcing her eyes wide open.

Kate's vision, her every sense, recoiled from the immensity of the killing as the worms were annihilated. It was as if, with a single great swallow, Nidhoggr had reversed the flow of their parasitic infestation and sucked them all dry. The parasites were reduced to feather-light husks that blew away in the fire of his exhalation to become dust, and then nothing at all.

Kate was still marvelling at the healing vision when she heard the thunderously deep voice of her friend Driftwood. <I must now abandon you to another's keep. Be warned! Nidhoggr is ever jealous of his domain. And war between dragon kings is not what you would choose to countenance here. Yet you should

mark well my warning. You have loosened chaos into the world.>

"Thank you, Driftwood."

Kate needed time to gather her thoughts, but she wasn't allowed any. A great fury of change was manifesting about her. She knew that there was something important she was still missing—something about the nature of Nidhoggr. Driftwood had alluded to it, but she hadn't really understood him.

Consider Nidhoggr to be omnipresent.

Was the serpent-dragon a metaphor for something more abstract, more nebulous by far? Something more powerful and dangerous than she yet realised . . . perhaps more dangerous than she was capable of realising? A presence was invading her mind, erupting through all of her senses at once:

<I see you—she who profaned my slumber.>

"I think that you are mistaken in describing your former state as slumber. You were tricked—duped—into abandoning your duty."

Her senses were overwhelmed again by the assault of the dragon's reply. *<What duty would I, Nidhoggr, have other than my needs?>*

"You abandoned your needs. Those worms were feeding off the roots of the Tree of Life. They had sucked the Tree dry, and you with it. They had"—she thought of the expression used by Driftwood, a good word she decided—"rendered you emasculate." She hastily added, "my Lord."

<Emasculate?>

She recoiled as the enormous dragon, even worn away to a ghost, roared.

"If you do not believe me, open your eyes and look around."

Kate's vision, that blackly negative perspective of the world of Dromenon, was drowned in carmine light. It was as if a megastar had exploded, turning night into lurid, bloody day. Change, enormous, and shocking, erupted through all of Kate's senses.

"There is no time to be lost. I need your help in return."

<You expect a favour of me?>

"No—I appeal to our common interest. Would you have the Tree of Life die? Would you have the Momu, who supported your world, and would support it in the future, be destroyed by your common enemy?"

<What is any of this to me?>

There was an impression within the chaos that spawned around Kate of a great head turning and a great maw opening, with fangs that would have dwarfed mountains.

"You drowsed, if my guess is correct, for tens of thousands of years."

<Your notion of time is meaningless here.>

"Then come with me. Take me out of here to the Cathedral of Death, where the Momu lies on the cusp of extinction. There she holds onto the last gasp of life so that her people, who venerated you, might not be lost forever."

<I have no knowledge of such a place—a Cathedral of Death. Should I be curious to know of it?>

"Why not go there and see for yourself?"

<If I should discover this be a confabulation, I shall devour you, power and all.>

"You're not the first dragon to fancy gobbling me up, but I might not prove to be all that digestible."

<Woe betide you if you indulge in mischief.>

"Woe, indeed!"

Warriors

Mark and Nan woke in the dark, aware that something was amiss. For a moment they stared at one another in the pulsing light of their oracula, as if astonished by their appearance; the evening before, in the interests of hygiene in the squalid conditions of the camp, they had shaved off each other's hair, rendering them crew cut. In the next moment, the same cry came from both their mouths.

"We're under attack!"

They threw on clothes and trainers and Mark grabbed the mobile he had kept switched on around the clock in the hope of a call from Gully.

Nan had ferried the frightened youth to the St. Martin's Lane exit off Piccadilly with Mark covering her tail to make sure they weren't followed. It was still raining heavily, but there was no place they could find shelter. It was important that they had the opportunity to talk with him.

"It's okay. Nobody is going to hurt you. All we want to do is to talk to you. What's your name?"

"Gully."

Gully had already wriggled off the pillion of Nan's bike. He looked ready to run. Mark put a hand on his shoulder. "You're a friend of Penny's, aren't you?"

"I don't know nuffink about no Penny."

"We know you're friends. Just tell me the truth, Gully."

"Don't you go jangling with me 'ead."

"Time's short and we don't have time to explain it all, but we're your friends. We know about Penny, we know she's special, we know you want to protect her—we can protect you and Penny."

Gully had torn himself out of Mark's hands. He was shaking his head, as if unable to believe he had been so stupid. "You don't get it. I got to find 'er."

"You're both in a lot of bother, Gully. The paramilitaries and the Skulls are looking for you."

Nan motioned Mark to hush. She put her hand lightly on Gully's shoulder. She looked him eye to eye. "It's really important we talk to Penny."

He shook his head. "Uh-huh."

"She really is in danger."

"Wot you want to talk to Penny about?"

"She knows something of what's going on. We know she's been drawing a map. We're looking for a friend who might be somewhere underground."

"How do you know about her maps?"

"Because we saw them, Gully, inside Penny's mind. That time when we met her—when she helped us find the church."

"Bleedin' 'eck!"

"Penny helped us—she knew we were on the same side."

"Nah. I don't believe you."

"It's true, Gully."

"Let me see 'em. Let me see them fings in your 'eads, wot Penny told me about."

They showed him their brows, then Mark had spoken. "I'm Mark—and this is Nan."

Gully had stared at the oracula through his rain-spattered spectacles, muttering their names.

"It's just like Penny told you, isn't it, Gully?"

He said nothing, but his silence was enough confirmation. Nan had patted his shoulder, gently, comfortingly. "It's grown really dangerous, Gully. You and Penny—you're not safe any more."

"It'll blow over—always does."

"No, Gully, it won't blow over. Those people are looking for you and they'll never stop looking until they find you."

"Oh, Penny—Penny, gel!"

Mark handed Gully a mobile phone. "All Penny needs to do is to call me. We'll help you—we'll protect you. Just call me."

Gully's eyes had opened wide as saucers, staring at the mobile phone. "It's a trick, innit?"

"No—it's no trick. You keep the phone. There's a number preset into speed dial 1. Find Penny. Even if you can't find her, call me."

A confusion of emotions had swept over Gully's face. There was a lot of fear in him as he wiped his nose with his sleeve then shoved the mobile phone into the top right-hand pocket of his rain-soaked jacket.

That call had never materialised and it was very likely it never would. Mark no longer had time to worry about it. They were springing out of the tent and sounding the alarm through the camp in a moment, alerting the others to the fact they were under attack.

"How the hell do you know we're being raided?" Cal demanded, in the pandemonium of getting ready to run.

"We both sense it—it's coming."

"What's coming?"

"We figure there's a truck full of paramilitaries out there, but they're holding fire, or else they're circling around us."

The camp had been on continuous alert so there was little in the way of packing to do. Bull was already mounting guard on the bikes and Cogwheel was hoisting himself up into the cab of the Mamma Pig. Cal and Sharkey, who had armed themselves with an RPG and the smaller of the Minimi machine guns, were debating a plan of defence when Nan interrupted them. “There’s something else.”

Cal glared at her, looking impatient in the freezing rain, the weight of the RPG yanking at his arms. “What?”

“Listen—listen carefully.”

The two men listened. Sharkey had the better hearing. “A chopper!”

“Incoming,” Mark agreed.

Cal shook his head. “Shit and piss! It’s an Ugly.”

“What’s that?”

Sharkey spoke softly, tapping the barrel of the machine gun against his bony knee. “That’s heavy-duty shit—a battlefield hunter-killer. We try to run for it and we’re done. They’ll pick up the heat of the exhausts like they’re beacons. The Mamma Pig will be a sitting duck.”

Cogwheel cursed out of the window of the Pig.

Cal said, “It’s even worse than that. The paramilitaries don’t have Uglies, it’s the regular army.”

Mark was reminded of the hooded figures at Grimstone’s meeting at Wembley, one of whom, if Jo Derby was right, was a field marshal.

Sharkey gripped the machine gun between his legs in order to free his arms. He tied a red bandana around his head to contain his straggle of greying hair. “Now we know what’s killing off the crews: we’re looking at a wipeout strategy. They truck paramilitaries in, but they don't attack right away; the heavy ordinance does the hit. Then the truck comes in to finish off and record."

"Sounds organised," Tajh called down from the passenger window of the Pig. "What do you reckon, Cal?"

Cal had put down his weapon to slip an MK-5 up to her through the open window. He picked up the RPG again, weighing it thoughtfully with both hands. "I agree with Sharkey. It's professional—regular forces."

"What's the plan?"

"They know by now that we've heard their approach. They're out there watching us on infrared. They're expecting us to run."

Sharkey muttered a whole string of curses.

Cal shrugged. "You ask me, we might as well stop and fight. At least we can take some of 'em out before they take us."

Mark shook his head. "Nan and I will see what we can do."

"What can you do?"

"We can give you people the chance to clear out. Save the Mamma Pig."

Cogwheel was shaking his head at them through the open cab window. "You expecting us to just drive out of here in the dark? We won't know where we're going—no lights in that downpour!"

"You know your way well enough around here. You could maybe get a mile or so clear before you need lights."

Cogwheel started up the heavy motor. “Come on, Tajh. You’re going to have to navigate.”

“Shit—okay!”

Cal motioned with the barrel of the RPG. “Bull—you ride shotgun with the heavy Minimi. Cogwheel—head south, but keep off the proper roads if you can. Sharkey and me, we’ll cover your arses.”

Mark saw Bull grunt, then climb into the back of the pig where he could fit the belt-driven machine gun. Cal turned to face him and Nan. “I want to know—what are you planning?”

Mark took a BMW and Nan had mounted the Harley. He heard her start her bike and Mark followed suit, free-wheeling around to face the opposite direction to the Pig, which was now revving up. “We’re better equipped to take the fight to them. We’ll deal with the chopper.”

The sound of the rotors was growing louder.

“Are you guys insane?” Cal said.

Behind him, Mark heard the Mamma Pig rising through the gears. As he was sliding the Fir Bolg battle-axe into its harness over his shoulder he saw Sharkey stuff something into his backpack. In the poor light Mark couldn’t see what it was, but through the assisted vision of his oraculum he saw a small, fat sausage shape poking out from under the flap: the frayed leg of Big Ted.

Mark nodded to Cal. “Good luck with the truck. Nan and me—we’ll do what we can to give you a little time with the chopper.”

“Even without lights they’ll pick up your exhausts.”

"That's what we're hoping, but we'll give them lights as well for the time being. Just to make sure they spot us."

All four waited until the Mamma Pig was lost to sound. Then Sharkey pushed the safety button on the heavy machine gun. "Better hang fire a minute or two." Mark said. "Me and Sharkey will head out on foot. That way we'll fool them into thinking we're travelling with you."

"Sounds like a plan."

Sharkey came alongside so he could high five Nan. "I like the thought of them lazy bastards hanging fire out there thinking we're sitting ducks. But instead of waiting for the chopper to hack us to pieces, we become the hunters."

Nan was grinning in Mark's direction. He caught the gist of it: she thought that Sharkey fancied her.

"Okay, we'll catch up with you later."

Cal grinned. "Maybe."

Mark waited until the two men had faded into the shadow of the trees before he spoke to Nan. "Got your homicidal tendencies in gear?"

"I'm looking forward to it."

"You're one bloodthirsty queen."

"Affirmative."

Mark barked a laugh.

"There's a small hill in the direction they're coming. We can take advantage of it to use our lights to get as near as we can."

“The ground in between is covered with scrub—and trees.”

“We’ll have to cut through it as best we can. Use the oracula to burn through it if necessary. We’ll let them see our lights—so they think we’re coming right down their gun barrels, then cut the lights when we climb the hill.”

They waited until they were at least a hundred yards from the campsite before roaring through the rain-filled darkness with the bikes’ headlights on full. Mark found himself heading straight into an oak coppice. He swerved, his right foot tearing through the rain-soaked ground, to avoid the collision, then he was side by side with Nan, tearing through brambles and nettles, jerking and bumping over uneven ground scored by rocky outcrops.

Nan’s voice came mind-to-mind: <You hurt?>

<Nah—managed to avoid the bigger branches.>

The truth was that his right hip and thigh stung like shit. The heavy fabric of his coat had saved his upper body, but his jeans felt shredded and his knees and thighs were laced with scratches.

They sensed they were maybe 200 yards from the hunter–killer, which showed no lights, but made the air throb with the clatter of its rotors.

He directed Nan. <Don’t think we can wait any longer. You cut your lights and head off at ninety degrees to the left and I’ll head straight on to the summit.>

<The Powers preserve us!>

The throbbing of the heavy rotors was closing quickly, the noise became deafening. His headlight burned a tunnel through the trees. It would be a beacon to the incoming pilot. A hail of machine gun fire ripped through the foliage only feet to Mark's left. He cut his lights, swerving to his right. Nan had to be a good thirty yards away by now. They would have followed her on their infrared, but he had given them such an easy target he could assume they were specifically targeting him. He slid to a halt under the dripping cover of a hawthorn cluster.

Mark stared up into the night sky, feeling the downdraught from the rotor blades on the skin of his face. The hunter-killer was directly overhead, but was still almost invisible. He revved up the throttle, then slotted the gears into neutral and let it run before hurling himself out of the saddle and letting gravity take the machine down the slope on the other side of the hill. He pressed his head and body down into the muddy ground, the smell of mulch and grasses filling his nostrils. He could hear, and sense, Nan closing down her engine at the same time. She was, maybe, a hundred yards away. He saw the trajectory of the missile as it struck the bike, which was wobbling perilously, but still rolling, maybe twenty-five yards from where Mark lay panting amid the scrub. The night exploded. He could hardly breathe because of the sulphurous hot gases and the stink of high explosive. The chopper was still hovering perilously close to him, the cockpit now illuminated, but hopefully they'd assume he was dead. They were operating something on board: a belly-mounted camera swivelled, capturing the carnage around where the heavy bike had been blown to smithereens. Mark figured that he had maybe half a minute before they turned around and searched for Nan.

Mark climbed to his feet, reaching over his shoulder as he did so. He hauled the Fir Bolg battleaxe into his left hand. The oraculum pulsed strongly in his brow. For the first time since he had pledged his life to the Third Power and goddess of death, Mórígán, he called on her for help. <Save us—me and Nantosueta—right now. And while you're at it, charge my blade.>

With the chopper beginning to move off to his left, Mark stared up, looking for the cabin area that contained the pilot. He glimpsed a blurry triangle of white—the pilot's face—through the windscreen. Less clearly, but still obviously enough, he could see the gunner, his head bent over the machine gun with its circular metal sights. Mark brought down the power from the oraculum into his shoulder and then let it flow into his arm and out into the blade. He felt the intensity of it build. Where the Fir Bolg runes should have been glowing, white as molten iron, it was the blade that now glowed white while the runes flashed black, the promise of death.

Mark drew back his arm and, with all of his physical strength, he hurled the twin-bladed battleaxe at the cockpit. It spun as it lifted with a low-pitched hum, then struck with an explosion less loud than the earlier missile strike, but deadly with dark energy. The sky above Mark became brighter than day for several seconds, aflame with a crackling fireball of blue-black lightning. The pilot was dead. Mark crouched down in the small coppice, watching the pilotless machine shoot off at a crazy angle, then spin out of control and hurl itself at the dark mass of the ground, maybe sixty yards away. The returning battleaxe struck his uplifted hand just as he was forced to duck from the explosion of the crash of the chopper. The conflagration was so fierce there would be no survivors.

He sensed Nan's return and saw the headlights of the Harley cut through the smoke and confusion. He heard a more distant explosion, followed by the unmistakable sound of automatic machine gun chatter: Cal and Sharkey firing the RPG and the Minimi. He doubted that the paramilitaries would win that one. This was one crew that was determined to survive.

A Disturbing Communication

Alan stared up into the green late afternoon sky to watch Iyezzz swoop down with what looked like a sense of urgency. There was no need to alert Aíné, Mo and Qwenqwo, who were already hurrying over to join him, all of them sensing, even from a distance of a hundred yards, that the Garg prince was the bearer of news. It had taken the army three days of grindingly slow progress to make their way this far down the steep moraine of slippery stones and treacherous gullies, where any temptation to hurry could lead to a broken ankle or worse. They had lost three of the supposedly sure-footed onkkh, but the Shee and aides had suffered nothing worse than a single broken wrist and half a dozen sprains. Although they calculated they were halfway down the northern face of the Flamestrucks by now, the air remained so thin they still felt breathless. It had stayed frigidly cold, but that was bound to change quite soon as they descended. They could already make out drifts of snow below them on the lower slopes. But for now, the attacking wind and lack of moisture still prevented any snow this high. They hurried to where Iyezzz had alighted, his taloned feet skidding over the scree that still extended ahead of them. The scree led into a valley that ran between charcoal black rocky foothills.

The gill-like slits in the Garg's throat gaped with his efforts at breathing. "You head into a strange valley, still dry as any desert, but with signs of intelligent life."

"What sort of signs?"

"Pyramids of skulls."

Alan hugged his gloved hands under his armpits, trying to warm them. "Have you seen anything of the people who made them?"

"Nothing."

"We've already crossed a river of bones. I don't think we need to be overly worried about pyramids of skulls."

"These are not skulls I recognise."

"You mean, they are not the skulls of people?"

"Not Eyrie people, nor Cill nor humans—those I would recognise. Nor are they the skulls of any beast I recognise. But then, what possible creatures could inhabit these inclement valleys?"

"Do you think it a warning?"

"I do not know, but it is something meaningful, a declaration of territory, perhaps."

Alan looked first at Ainé, then at Mo and Qwenqwo. The gathering was accumulating small clouds from their exhaled breaths.

"We have little choice other than to proceed."

"Then do so with due caution, Mage Lord. You may be heading into a trap," said the Garg.

An advance party of Alan, Ainé, Bétaald, Mo, Turkeya and Qwenqwo, flanked by guardian Shee, moved ahead of the main army. Because of Iyezzz's warning, Alan made certain that Mo and Turkeya kept close to him, and where Mo went Magtokk wouldn't be far behind. The increasingly close relationship between Mo and Magtokk was both intriguing and disconcerting. But for the moment Alan needed to concentrate on whatever mystery and danger might lie ahead. After two hours of steady advance, they arrived at the first of the strange monuments.

The structure really was a pyramid, ascending into the air through a series of platforms of decreasing diameter, tapering to a point thirty or so feet above the base. But Alan could see what had rattled Iyezzz. The basic building blocks were skulls, many hundreds of them, all carefully knitted together with what looked like limb bones and ribs, so that the pyramid held fast against wind and weather.

Alan approached it cautiously, wary of the possibility of traps, but found that he could touch it without mishap. Iyezzz alighted and watched from nearby as Alan looked closely at the individual skulls.

"Whoever—or whatever—these creatures might be, they're huge."

Alan reached out a gloved hand to feel the strange shape of the skulls, which were as big as the skulls of some dinosaurs he had seen in museums. But their shape was different. They were elongated front to back and the projecting jaws were mounted side to side, with curiously incurved canines that met in the middle, sharp as needles. The eye sockets were unusual—grossly oversized even for the size of the skulls.

"You see for yourself," Iyezzz huskily insisted. "Not Eyrie People, not Cill—and certainly not human!"

"I agree." Alan took a few steps back to look again at the pyramid as a whole. "From what you say, there are more of them?"

"Many hundreds."

"All the same?"

"All similar—as far as I could discern from the air."

"It suggests that the creatures who built them must have lived here for a very long time. Yet I assume the Eyrie people have no knowledge of them?"

"None."

"But what do they mean? Are they totems of identity—or meant to frighten strangers off?"

"It is hard to believe that their makers expected to encounter any strangers in this inhospitable land."

Alan looked at the dwarf mage, who was standing to his right, his protuberant nose and broad cheeks purple with cold. "What do you think, Qwenqwo?"

"Who knows how ancient these landmarks might be? Is it not possible that their makers are long dead and gone? Perhaps the pyramids are a relic from a time long ago when these slopes were less arid and forbidding."

At a signal from Mo, Ainé gestured for them to be quiet. "Hush a moment—we should listen."

Alan hushed. There was a sound coming from somewhere, a buzzing sound, almost like a choir humming a tune. But now that the Kyra had drawn his attention to it, Alan could even feel the humming as a vibration through the rocks under his feet.

"It's coming from the pyramid."

As he stared at the structure in bafflement, there were cries from a party of Gargs further ahead. A group of them had been probing another pyramid, but now they were scattering, hurriedly taking to the air, while smaller, flying bodies buzzes around them, like a swarm of extremely large and disturbed wasps.

"We'd better go see what's going on."

Alan and the other leaders moved cautiously forwards, to observe lids of rock being thrown back to expose holes in the rocky ground. It was from the holes that the swarms of wasp-like creatures were erupting into the air. Closer to, the creatures were unlike any he had ever seen before. Their wings were more insect-like than those of the Gargs, yet the bodies of the creatures, only a foot or so in length, were humanoid with disproportionately large heads. Their eyes were bulbous and glaring and their mouths held vicious fangs.

"Methinks these look like a hybrid of wasp and goblin," said Qwenqwo.

"Don't harm them!" Mo was hurrying forward, her cry echoed by Turkeya.

"Tell the Shee to hold off." Alan waved a cautioning hand to the Kyra.

"Stay back," the Kyra commanded.

"What is it, Mo?"

"I think we should observe and no more."

Some of the attackers were forming a protective swarm around the disturbed pyramid. Other creatures, much larger than the attackers, were issuing in twos and threes from the holes in the ground. These slug-like creatures, about the size of a hippopotamus, were more lumbering. They were heading for the disturbed pyramid. As Alan and the others watched, they began to repair the structure, restoring the skulls and knitting them back into formation with elaborate care, using a glittering thread-like material which they manipulated with the same incurved canine teeth that Alan had noticed in the skulls.

"The skulls—they must be theirs!" Alan said to Mo, who was sticking close to his side.

She nodded. "I don't think they mean to harm us. The pyramids must be totems. Altars to the dead. But these are the first living creatures we've come across since we left the Garg homeland. I, for one, would like to know more about them."

Alan didn't know what to make of the pyramids, or the creatures. "Okay, Mo. We'll explore a little, but keep our distance."

The Kyra was unmoved. "Mage Lord—we mustn't forget that this is the Tyrant's land. We should stay alert."

"Have the Shee stand by. I'll get Iyezzz to calm the Gargs down. We need to see if it is possible to communicate with them."

"Mage Lord Duval!" Alan turned at the call from Magtokk. "Before you attempt any form of communication, I beg to speak to you."

Alan turned to observe the orang-utan squatting with his short legs criss-crossed before him in the arid dust. His coat, enclosing his immense bulk, looked even thicker than usual, maybe a response to the biting cold.

"Ainé—is there any possibility of a windbreak—or a fire?"

As the Kyra signalled the aides, Alan made room for the dwarf mage to take a position by his side. He almost envied Mo when Magtokk wrapped an arm around her. Turkeya took a seat on the opposite side of the circle from Magtokk. Alan sighed, lifting an eyebrow to Qwenqwo, who hissed when his ageing buttocks made contact with the icy ground, huffing and puffing and tamping a couple of pipes against the heel of his boot. *If ever there was a time for that warming flagon of liquor to make its appearance,* he thought, *this has to be it.* He half fancied one of Qwenqwo's pipes full of red-glowing tobacco himself, if only to cradle the piping hot bowl in his hands.

Instead he had to wait for Qwenqwo's quasi-ritualistic performance of stuffing the bowls with baccy for Magtokk, whose eyes crinkled with delight over the red-glowing bowl, before they would condescend to grace them with a word of advice.

Alan said pointedly, "Go ahead."

"Look around you," Magtokk said. "Look hard at the land itself. What does it remind you of?"

Alan cast his eyes around the settling camp, witnessing a ravaged wasteland over which the fierce wind blew the stink of sulphur. Here and there he saw mirrors of icy reflection and rock scorched to malignant shades of orange and red, like the ghosts of leviathan furnaces. Some of the rock had melted to a watery smoothness. He couldn't recall ever seeing a more devastated and tormented world. Other than the winged creatures and their equally strange allies there was no sign of life, not even a bird or an insect or a stain of lichen coating the rocks.

"It looks like hell."

Magtokk asked him: "Do you not have landscapes such as this on Earth?"

"Only in the worst pits of industrial damage—or what remains after nuclear weapons testing."

"Ah!"

At last the flagon appeared. The dwarf mage was generous enough to pass it to Alan's half-numbed hands first. He took a gulp, coughed, then returned it to its master.

"What point are you making, Magtokk?"

"This is the Wastelands—the Tyrant's domain. And throughout the Wastelands, the only communities allowed to survive were those enslaved to the Tyrant or his allies."

"Okay, but I still don't get the point."

"Do you see evidence of enslavement here?" Magtokk puffed on his pipe. "If this is a place despoiled by mining, where are the taskmasters?"

Qwenqwo joined Magtokk in puffing on his pipe, the two of them billowing out fragrant smoke. "My thinking exactly," Qwenqwo said.

Alan thought some more about it. He could feel the warm, welcoming fire of Qwenqwo's liquor spread through his belly.

Magtokk lifted the pipe from his mouth. "I would dearly like to study these creatures to discover how they have managed to survive here."

"In other words, you don't know the answers to this mystery any more than I do," Alan said.

Mo said, "Oh, Alan—let's do it. If ever there was a reason why Turkeya and I came with you on this journey, this might be it."

"I don't know, Mo. The wasp goblins are aggressive little brutes. Look how they drove off the Gargs."

"But the Gargs were damaging their pyramids. The creatures were only defending what precious little they have."

"I think," Qwenqwo said, "there may be something in what Mo suggests. I have been observing these pyramid builders now that the Gargs have withdrawn from poking around in the bones. They have done nothing other than meticulously repair the damaged piles. They are withdrawing underground as we speak without further ado."

The Shee adviser spoke. "If I might be permitted to comment?"

"Go ahead, Bétaald."

"It is well known that the Tyrant laid waste to this whole continent to pillage and plunder, annihilating or enslaving all that lived here. Yet our historians, most notably the last high architect, the venerable Ussha De Danaan herself, saw a purpose, however sinister and corrupt, in his actions. Everywhere he tore and ravaged the land, as if searching for something that would aid his purpose. Is it not possible that these curious survivors may have long ago served the Tyrant's purpose here? A purpose designed to exploit these lands, no matter how inclement? It would explain the ravaged nature of the landscape. If this is true, then we might discover something of his purpose in these creatures."

Mo clapped her hands. "Then all the more reason why Turkeya and I should explore this further."

"I hope you're not suggesting what I think you are? Mo—don't tell me you're thinking of going down into those holes?"

"I sense no threat from these creatures. I sense only fear—directed towards us." She was fingering the Torus hanging on a thong around her neck.

"Mo, we have no idea what you might encounter. We know nothing at all about these creatures. You might be venturing into a wasps' nest, one in which the wasps are as big and fierce as hawks."

Mo looked distracted. "Oh, Alan!"

"What is it?"

"I'm getting an urgent message from the True Believers. Oh, my word! Ignore what I just said; we are all instructed to stay away from the entrances to the labyrinth."

"Labyrinth?"

"The rock below us is honeycombed with tunnels. They run very deep—for miles. We're sitting over an incredible labyrinth of tunnels and . . . and chambers."

Alan looked at Mo, eye to eye. He saw the rising excitement there. "Hey, Mo? What is it? What's really going on here?"

Mo hesitated again, her eyes closed. "I'm trying to understand . . . I'm getting message after message. There's so much coming through, it's confusing. I think . . . I believe that I'm getting an important communication—a message, a warning, I just don't fully understand as yet, but it's coming from the True Believers. We should do nothing to upset the Akkharu."

"The Akkharu?"

"That's what the True Believers call these slug-like creatures."

"In legends," Magtokk spoke, with his eyes wide with interest, "the Akkharu were exquisitely skilled craftsmen—the weavers of the gods."

Mo said, "The True Believers warn against disturbing them. They say that we mustn't interfere with them."

"Are they—the Akkharu—even aware of our presence?"

"Yes, they know that we're here. They're deeply disturbed by our presence in the valley. I'm getting that message overwhelmingly."

Alan looked up into the falling dusk. The sky was cloudless and a deepening shade of green in which the first pallid stars were beginning to appear.

"I don't get it, Mo."

"No more do I, but I get the impression it has something to do with me—with my Torus."

"Can we communicate with them in some way? Reassure them we mean them no harm?"

"I'll try again."

Mo closed her eyes again for a minute or so. "From what I gather, it isn't possible to communicate with them in words."

"Well then, how are we going to communicate?"

Ainé was clearly vexed by the rising confusion. "Mage Lord—we have an army halted in their march. Surely this is another of the Tyrant's tricks? Another delaying tactic?"

Alan agreed with her. "Mo, you have to press for more information. We need to know what's really going on here."

Mo nodded, her face turning up to the rapidly darkening sky. There was no moon, but an increasing proliferation of stars, washed with the beautiful tides of Tír's galaxy. Mo's face was extremely pale, her eyes shining. Her voice was a husky whisper: "I'm getting another message, but I don't think it's coming from the True Believers. I think it's coming from the creatures themselves—from the Akkharu."

Alan stared hard at Mo, whose Torus was blazing. "Be careful, Mo. We don't know what's going on here."

Qwenqwo, Magtokk and Bétaald were all silent.

Alan was unable to suppress his anxiety. "Mo—maybe Ainé is right. Maybe we should put a stop to this right now."

"No—wait, Alan. There is a message coming through. You wanted to know if we could communicate with the Akkharu. They are about to . . . Oh!" she shrieked.

Alan clapped his hands to his head.

"You're getting this too?"

Alan heard shouts from Ainé and Magtokk, who were holding their heads exactly as he was.

It felt as if his mind were being invaded. There was something extremely disturbing about the black clots that looked as if they had been flung violently against a bone white sky. They were moving, metamorphosing, coalescing into patterns that were as threatening as they were indecipherable.

"Mo?"

She was speechless, her pale face staring back at him, shaking her head from side to side.

Alan was climbing to his feet. As he did so he saw the Kyra reach out and snap the Torus from around Mo's neck. He saw Magtokk hold out his hand to the Kyra and demand the amulet back from her reluctant fist. "I understand your concern, Kyra of the Shee. Mo is confused and terrified and indeed she has good reason for her consternation, but you cannot disconnect her from her destiny."

The Kyra held the Torus in her fist. "What do you imply, magician?"

"Her destiny is approaching."

"What do you know of this?"

"Enough to realise that she needs support and guidance. Her destiny is a great burden for one so young."

Ainé reared back, even more suspicious of Magtokk and reluctant to return the Torus to Mo.

"Did you place those frightening images in our mind?"

"No, but magic comes in many forms. It can be disturbing when we do not grasp its message."

Ainé shook her head. She looked at Alan: "Mage Lord—what does your oraculum say?"

"I think you can return the Torus to Mo, but we'll ask her not to wear it for a little while. We all need time to settle and get a better handle on what happened just then."

The Kyra handed the Torus to Mo, but she remained obdurate. "We should leave this place."

Alan nodded. "Yes—I agree."

Mo accepted her Torus, but kept it within her hand. She looked up into the broad, orang-utan face of Magtokk with its twinkling dark eyes. She felt the shuddering of his belly laugh as his huge arm, so shrouded with ringlets of hair they resembled Rasta dreadlocks, enfold her shoulders.

"You and I," he whispered, "we'll explore. When the time is right."

"And when might that be?"

"When the magic calls again."

"Is this Magtokk the Mischievous talking?"

"Of course."

Mo wasn't sure if she could face that call when it came.

The Blue Light

When Gully woke he was still arguing with Penny in his dream. He was explaining how he hadn't let her down. Then his eyes sprang open, blinking through the fog of the clinging dream. He felt for his glasses where he always left them. Finding them, he shoved them roughly onto his nose and sprung out into the freezing cold room. A wintry light was oozing in through the blinds on the window next to the sink. When he opened the blind, it didn't feel right. The light was wrong for dawn. It looked more like falling dusk. Penny's sleeping bag, right next to the shelves, was empty. It wasn't even ruffled. It was like she hadn't slept in it at all. He moved out of the big room, calling out her name in a rising panic. "Penny . . . *Penny!*"

Even as he scurried through the vestibule and into the map room he was puzzled as to how he could have slept through the day. Had she slipped something into his cuppa? His bare feet were sticking to the freezing concrete. He found the map room empty.

The memories of last night burst upon him: Penny coming back, her eyes red from bawling. Penny ignoring him, pushing away every time he tried to hold her. Penny telling him they wasn't safe no more. Penny curling up into a ball in the corner.

"Hey, Penny? Wot's wrong?"

"A Skull . . . He tried to . . ."

"Wot you sayin," gel?'

"He . . . hurt . . . me."

"Oh, no—oh, Penny!"

"Your fault." Penny had screamed at him, her eyes flowing over with tears. *"You wouldn't give me the pigeons."*

"I don't understand."

She wouldn't explain. She wasn't able to explain. But Gully could read it in her eyes. Something bad had happened, something terrible.

"They're sayin' you killed a Skull."

"I did. I killed him—I killed him, Gully!"

She had hurled the backpack onto the floor and the dagger fell out of it, clattering over the concrete. Gully had stared down at it, at the silver thing in the hilt what was glowing. Then it just came up off the floor and it landed in Penny's hand all by itself.

They had both screamed.

"Oh, Penny—Penny, gel."

It was so spooky it had frightened Gully half to death.

"The dagger—it saved me."

"Penny!" He had rushed forward, tried to hold her.

But she turned the Scalpie's dagger towards him. *"No! No!* No! *Don't you dare! Don't you dare touch me! Don't you dare!"*

Gully opened all the blinds in the room and that was when he found the note. Then he knew she had left him again. He couldn't read the note because his eyes were full of tears.

Penny was sitting against the wall in the entrance hall of the ghost Tube station. Last night she had slept, a few hours, curled up into a ball on the gantry under the map ceiling. She had not wanted to wake Gully by returning to her sleeping bag. Now she felt like curling into a ball again. She could feel the weight of the heavy dagger in the backpack between her shoulder blades and the grimy wall. She could sense it too, not just physically, but in the deeper crevices of her mind, as if it were calling her. She was breathing deeply, too deeply—hyperventilating. Already she could feel pins and needles in her fingers and painful cramps in her feet, but she couldn't help herself. The muscles around her mouth were jumping, like a purse with somebody jerking at the strings.

She had been unable to talk to Gully about what had happened in the garden of St. Paul's Cathedral. She would never be able to talk to anybody about that. It was why she had slipped two tablets into his mug of tea. She knew she couldn't talk to him and she needed time to finish the ceiling. Gully wouldn't have let her do it. He was too upset. She knew she was leaving Our Place for good and she needed to think, to collect her thoughts, so she could finish the map before she left. She had known it would be hard, heartbreaking even, and all the while uncertainties were reeling in her mind.

She needed to think about the Grimlings' nest.

Maybe she shouldn't think of it as the Grimling nest—that extraordinary place she had barely glimpsed immediately below St. Paul's Cathedral. But really, of course, it was much more than a Grimlings' nest. It was the true City Below. That juxtaposition could not be accidental. She knew that it was somehow closely related to important landmarks—important spiritual landmarks—in the City Above. But she still needed to know how far this closeness extended. It seemed logical to assume that the spiritual landmarks were like nodes that linked world to world.

If St. Paul's was a critical node in both worlds, the fulcrum of everything perhaps in both City Above and City Below, she needed to know a lot more about the labyrinth that extended below it.

She had caught a glimpse of that labyrinth when she had peered into the Grimling nest through the cleft in the rock. She recalled it now, vividly: the roaring sound of the river falling in the background and the creatures, the most alien creatures she could have possibly imagined, who were . . . constructing something within the natural caves, something huge and strange and marvellous and terrifying and wonderful.

Penny had followed an eastern course on her map of the City Above and she had figured the most likely nodes that would, almost certainly, give rise to deeper, vitally important, connections with the City Below. She had focused her mind on filling in some of the missing pieces on her map, even though her desire to leave Our Place would not be suppressed. It felt as if the drawing was infused with her own blood in blues, mauves, charcoals and black.

She thought about many things while she was hyperventilating in the ghost Tube station. She thought about the wrongness of putting the sleeping pills into Gully's tea. She knew, when she did it, that it was unforgivable, and that she would have to write a note for him, apologising and explaining. She also knew that she would have to apologise to Gully for blaming him in their argument that last night. Gully wasn't to blame for what had happened to her. It was that horrible man—the Skull.

Now Penny tried to clear her mind of that memory. She knew she had to think clearly to be able to make her way carefully back along the left hand tunnel.

Stop! Look! Listen!

There were no sounds to worry her any more; no ticking of the deathwatch beetle, no rustle of the mouse scuttling. It was as if the ghost station were holding its breath.

Anticipation rose in her, like a physical wave. She felt the shape of it and began breathing too fast again, making the pins and needles and cramps worse.

If Gully had only given her the live pigeons, she might not have gone to St. Paul's in the City Above. Here and now she was faced with returning to the Grimlings' nest and she had nothing to distract them with. All she had was the dagger. But now she recalled the Scalpie back at the little Church of the English Martyrs and how the Grimlings had buzzed all around him when he was holding the dagger. They hadn't appeared to threaten him at all. It was more like they were protecting him. Now she was here and she had the Scalpie's dagger. Would the Grimlings recognise the dagger and leave her be?

She retrieved the torch from her backpack before slipping the bag back onto her shoulders. In its light she could see the green and the creamy white tiles of the walls and the winding staircase leading down.

But she wasn't quite ready to go yet.

It was no good. She couldn't suppress it, or forget what had happened. She couldn't forgive the man who had done that thing to her: the man who had regarded her as a thing to be abused for his pleasure. She just couldn't force the memory out of her mind. The terror surged in her as if it had found its own niche in her heart and soul. As if it would never go away but just crouch there, ready to spring back at any moment. She felt the powerful hand around her throat, the blow that had broken her nose, the horror of the knife blade slicing through her clothes—and then . . . Thank heaven—the dagger! The dagger was the only thing left that she trusted now, the dagger was her only friend.

I know I killed a man. But I don't feel guilty. I don't feel guilty at all . . .

It was hard to take a breath deep enough to fill her lungs. She was weeping copiously. *I don't care! I don't care! I don't care! I'm glad. I'm glad the dagger killed him. I'm glad, I'm glad—I'm glad.*

But then a voice came into her head, a voice that was eerily consoling. It was the voice of the man she had met in the dark and rainy streets when she emerged from the City Below, and the . . . *thing* . . . was hurting people in the caravan.

<It's natural you should be angry, Penny.>

Jeremiah. Penny's fingers pressed against her lips. Jeremiah's voice was talking to her inside her head.

She didn't understand how his voice could come to her inside her head. It puzzled her that he knew her name. Had she told him her name? She didn't think she had. She was very careful who she told her name to. She couldn't rightly remember, though normally she remembered just about everything.

A new sensation flooded her mind. An uncontrolled—uncontrollable—flood. Jeremiah wasn't right about the word, anger. He should have said it was natural that she should feel rage.

<You are right to feel enraged, Penny!>

Yes, she thought, *yes, yes, yes!*

She thought back to the man who had tried to rape her. As he had torn her clothes off he had ignored her screams. He had laughed at her as if she were . . . as if she were an unfeeling, unthinking thing. Rage consumed her. It burned in her like a furnace. In her mind she reached out and she hurt him back. In her mind, she clawed at him with a tigress' nails, she bit him with a tigress' teeth. She tore his flesh apart into mincemeat. She felt herself gasping for breath, like a beast that had ripped asunder and fed and fed.

The rage clawed and snapped inside her. She felt as if she were drowning in it. What could she do? How could she stop herself drowning?

Jeremiah's voice returned, calm but insistent. <Imagine yourself become as an undying being whose heart is unconquerable, whose will is fire.>

Penny blinked repeatedly, thinking about what he was saying to her. How could rage turn one's will into fire?

The blue light became progressively brighter as she made her way back down the left-hand tunnel. She waded through the pool of stagnant water, uncaring that her teeth were chattering with cold. She didn't even fear the beast with the many faces anymore. Time moved through her as sluggishly as her thoughts. It seemed to take an age for her to arrive back in the giant cave, but finally her ears filled with the sounds of the falling torrent. There was still the opportunity for her to climb back out. The backstreets where she and Jeremiah had watched the monster divide after feeding on the travellers in the caravan were just overhead. She forced herself to pause and take her time.

There was no hurry.

She forced herself to hold her breath and allow her ears to fill with the roar of the cascade, to allow her other senses to explore.

The air felt different here. A bit stuffy, but there was a wild energy gambolling through the cavern that lifted the hair not just on her head, but even on the backs of her hands and forearms. When she looked down at her hands she saw that they glowed with the blue light. She followed the source of the light. It grew progressively stronger, leading her to the cleft in the rock and the marvellous and terrifying constructions she had glimpsed on her previous exploration: the Grimling hive, the City Below.

Penny climbed to a niche in the wall above a metal arch that braced a section of roof. She moved fractionally so her right eye could see through the crack between a strut of the shoring and the lower edge of the niche.

Stop . . . Look . . . Listen . . .

She saw bracelets and necklaces of white lights shining through the dark, forming patterns within patterns which ran away into the distance. She saw red lights ahead on either side of two reflecting multicoloured tracks. The lights had coronas and radiating rays, like stars seen through eyes blurred with raindrops. In the dead centre, at the focus of the avenues of stars, was one enormous blue flare with dagger-like vertical and horizontal spikes, making it resemble a cross.

She climbed down into the hive of the Grimlings and removed the dagger from her backpack. She was no longer afraid of them. She held the pulsing dagger upright in her two hands as waded into the icy cold running water.

At first she was startled to see tunnels everywhere, as if she had shrunk to the size of a gnat and found herself in a cheese full of holes. But then she realised they weren't just ordinary holes or tunnels; she had truly entered a labyrinth, lined by glowing crystals. The Grimlings weren't the builders here, but the guardians and gophers. Other beings—huge, slow-moving beings like slugs—were shaping things. They had jaws that moved side-to-side, which spun fibres like silkworms spinning silk. There were thousands of them, perhaps even tens of thousands, reminding her of factory assembly lines. They were all so slow moving and yet, when you looked down the labyrinth of tunnels, they were working in a frenzy.

Penny stared at the things around her in wonderment as she moved deeper among them. The Grimlings buzzed and darted around her, the noise of their flight echoing like miniature helicopters, their fanged mouths agape. Their goblin eyes were aware of her and examined her from head to toe, but were held back from attacking her by the fact she was holding the dagger in her trembling, clasped hands.

There were shafts leading down into incredible depths. She saw eerily beautiful, quasi-mathematical shapes in black, gleaming crystal, with a fine, almost musical hum of energy about them. The air glowed blue from crystals suspended in it. As constructions were completed they floated in the air to be towed away by armies of Grimlings. The calm hustle and bustle of the Grimlings comforted her somehow. The airborne crystals were so fine and weightless they diffused about her, provoking rainbows. The constructions, equally uninfluenced by gravity, were massive; they had tissue-paper-thin walls, yet seemed utterly indestructible. Some of the largest resembled the roots of gigantic trees, ramifying through myriad tunnels. If these were roots, she wondered, what structure, mightier by far than any great forest oak or ash tree, were they designed to support?

For a time she felt overwhelmed by it all and so she sat down, cross-legged, in the creative furnace of the City Below. She let the Grimlings buzz about her hair and brush closely by her flesh. She offered no resistance to their scrutiny, allowing them to touch her with their feathery palps, to nip and taste her with their scratchy side-to-side jaws.

She moved on through tunnel after tunnel, turning left or right at whim, exploring a tiny fraction of the labyrinth with its stretching lines of hawsers and Grimling hives. She peered in through waxy membranes at their young being incubated in cells like wasps and bees. She even glimpsed an enormously rotund queen, being attended to in an incubation chamber lined with crystals. There were so many different structures, so very alien and wonderful, all constructed out of the gleaming black crystal: tunnels, living quarters, intersecting planes and oblongs, soaring structures that might be monuments of the City Below. This was the city she had always known existed, whose reality was now confirmed to be so deep and extensive it took her breath away.

Only then did she see Jeremiah. He had materialised out of the air before her and was smiling at her. Penny opened her mouth to ask what he was doing here, but when she drew closer she saw, to her astonishment, that his eyes were all black.

Chaos Unbound

Kate didn't know if she was rising or falling—but she was moving. Whatever was happening to her, it involved colossal forces. There was an impression of screaming velocity. She thought perhaps she had fallen asleep for a while. More likely, she might have fallen unconscious. Frantically she tried to figure out what had led her to this.

I'm not here . . . not in the flesh. I'm present as a . . . a soul spirit.

But where was here?

I freed Nidhoggr. I freed the enormous dragon, or serpent, or whatever it really is. Once freed, it destroyed the legion of parasites that were feeding off the roots, weakening the Tree. And then . . .

And then there was a sudden rush of recovery. A feeling that flooded all of her senses—what senses she retained as a soul spirit—of soaring panic.

"Elaru—help me!"

But there was no reply.

Kate had to force her panic down to recover control of her mind. What was really happening to her? The truth was she had absolutely no idea. Her surroundings were blurred, as she moved through them at colossal speed. It was bewildering. Was she still within the roots of the Tree of Life? She had previously glimpsed the immensity of what that implied. Her soul spirit felt sick—massively out of kilter. She remembered something Alan had tried to explain to her when they were sailing down the Snowmelt River amid the thrilling but awesomely cold landscape. When they had entered the gate of Feimhin on Slievenamon, he had felt his *being* come apart. She felt something very similar. It was mentally harrowing, but without the extreme physical pain Alan had spoken of. This felt as if her soul spirit had dissolved into . . . she knew not. As if she were no longer the sum of all that made her, the organs, and sinews and tissues, and brain.

Kate felt like screaming. *How in heaven's name am I to grasp anything that might be important here?*

The impression of movement was so intense she felt giddy, hopelessly confused, by it.

Where had Elaru gone?

Surely she couldn't have abandoned her?

Elaru was somehow within her. Kate had subsumed her, but then she had released her again. She was bewildered by her own role in what was happening. This was a terrible world, a vast and utterly incomprehensible world, in which forces too powerful for an ordinary girl to comprehend fought one another for supremacy.

"Elaru—please!"

<I . . . I am here, Mistress.>

"Tell me what to do. Tell me quickly."

<Mistress—do you not realise what you have already done?>

"What?"

<You have released Nidhoggr not merely from its weakened slumber, but also from the chains of its imprisonment amid the roots of the Tree of Life.>

"What does that mean?"

<Confined, it fed on the roots, but in doing so it kept the Tree healthy. Unconfined, it is consumed with elation and triumph. Since you were the instrument of its release, it has subsumed you.>

"But I didn't do anything other than to waken it."

<Mistress—you underestimate your power. You bear the power of the Holy Trídédana. Even to make contact with a being such as Nidhoggr, such a power would evoke a response that could not be predicted.>

"What can I do? Please help me?"

<I can do nothing. The forces are too powerful for a half being such as me. It is you, beloved Mistress, who must try to restrain him.>

"How in heaven's name am I to do that?"

<So exulted is Nidhoggr by his freedom, it flees anywhere and nowhere. You could try to direct its journey.>

"Where—where must I direct it?"

The voice in her mind deepened to a mocking laugh.

"To the Land of the Dead, idiot."

"Urale! Elaru—you're still bound up with that trickster?"

<We are one, Mistress, though I am also a part of you an' he is not.>

A vulturish cackle: "A miscegenetic marriage, in my humble opinion."

"There is nothing humble about you, Urale. But I don't care what your differences are any more. I need to know what to do here and now."

"Could it be that even at this critical juncture, you have forgotten your miserable mission?"

"I have not forgotten it."

"If any must undo the folly of your recklessness it must be you yourself. Abandon this foolish enterprise immediately."

"I will never abandon the Momu."

Urale was never going to help her. He would revel in the opportunity to lead her into a trap. But did she dare to direct Nidhoggr to the Cathedral of Death? Or to where her own selfish instincts bade her—the Momu's chamber, where Granny Dew might save her?

"Elaru—help me! Tell me if the Land of the Dead is where we must go."

<Oh, Mistress! I cannot be trusted with such advice. You know how loath I am to return to the place of my own imprisonment. I would prefer to go anywhere else but to that temple of despair.>

"You must force yourself to be unselfish, Elaru."

<Oh, dearest, blessed Mistress, I want to help you, but I struggle to free myself from a stronger and darker yoke. If you would sense for yourself?>

Sense what for herself? What it felt to be subsumed by another being, one whose spiritual essence felt elemental and terrible; a soul spirit that was as dark as obsidian; a serpent-dragon that did not flap its wings to fly, but to rip and tear its way through the fabric of existence.

Kate felt a lump in her throat, as if something was caught there that was too terrifying to swallow. But she had to swallow it.

I have unleashed chaos.

The notion of uncontained destruction terrified her. Would it be a widening chaos that, once liberated, might extend beyond Dromenon?

Oh, lord preserve us!

What was it that Elaru had suggested? That she sense a way out of the terrible dilemma for herself.

Am I being asked to guide the destruction?

Surely, if ever there was a direction she would have wanted such a chaos to visit, it was the Land of the Dead. She brought the awful landscape into her mind, then focused her entire being on that dreadful memory, urging it to become the single, all-consuming focus of her oraculum until the image crystallised into being. And then it was as if a single great glowing eye were tearing its way through veils of existence, searching for the eerie streets of black ice that she now held fiercely in the focus of her oraculum.

Her spirit hands reached for her spirit mouth in dread as her vision was invaded by that graveyard of putrescent green. A moment in which she felt the same heart-sinking dread as before, and then . . .

Chaos!

The strangely etched streets and buildings crumbled before the elemental storm that was Nidhoggr. There was a vast, slithering succession of collisions, as if the great serpent-dragon were tearing through the ethereal substance of Dromenon itself. The damage of their coming was everywhere to be seen: the Land of the Dead was being rent asunder. Horrible as its malignant oppressiveness had been, its ravishing by Nidhoggr was even more horrifying still. Kate closed her eyes against it; she closed her senses, attempting to calm her disordered thoughts. But even with closed eyes she could not block out the rising cacophony of screams. When her eyes blinked open again the immensity of the Cathedral of Death was looming. Collision, gargantuan and terrifying, was imminent.

She screamed, "Please stop!"

Then, realising the hopelessness of appealing to Nidhoggr, she curled herself into a ball, focused every ounce of her energy on the oraculum and, through its window into this madly disordered world, issued the command with all of the force of her oracular power, even as the Lord of Chaos erupted through the adamantine walls of the Cathedral of Death.

"Halt!"

Nidhoggr's arrival had destroyed the entire atrium, making a gigantic rent in the Cathedral wall. Kate's vision was filled with the shimmering cascade of blue-green needles, each one of them a soul spirit of the dead. The screaming that was the sum of a billion motes of terror flooded her being. The light no longer coalesced on what had been the floor. It whirled about her, the structure of the Cathedral now caught up in the chaos.

Kate's mind was frozen with grief. That terrible sense of exhaustion was back, leaching into her spirit, her will.

Despair!

She heard the outraged shriek of Urale. "In mere moments you have destroyed the wonder of ages."

"A wonder to you—but a never-ending torment to so many souls."

"What matter mortals?"

"I am a mortal." Kate dismissed Urale. Rage at his cruelty revived her. Her mind, her thoughts, struggled back to consider why she was here. She sought his gentler twin. "Elaru—where is she? Where is the soul spirit of the Momu?"

<Look for the keepers. The pentagon.>

Kate's senses were overcome by the rising torrent of destruction. She could smell the despair—the sulphurous stink of it was invading her nostrils. But then she felt drawn to a dreadful centre of gravity within the chaos. She willed her being towards it, assuming that only the pentagon, with its kneeling keepers, could explain the ominous attraction. She glimpsed the focus of her purpose and her spirits lifted. The soul spirit of the Momu hovered in front of her, dignified as she recalled it, ethereal and still at the eye of the storm.

When Kate manifested in the ruin of the Cathedral she felt tremors of uncertainty running through it. She turned to look back at the thing that had borne her and saw something like the foothill of a mountain—a mountain over which a dreadful crackling energy sparked and ran in cascades of blue-black lightning.

Reaching out, Kate stroked the elongated face of the Momu, the tips of her fingers brushing the eyelids down over those mother-of-pearl eyes. She felt the rush of tears and knew that, back in the chamber of the Momu, her physical self was weeping. The flesh of the Momu was still transparent as smoke. The whirling, screaming fall of the crystals still passed through her soul spirit, even as the Cathedral of Death disintegrated all around them. Kate wondered if, back in her tomb of roots within the chamber, that great heart was still beating, however slowly and faintly. She prayed that there might be a mote of life still holding on there, desperately waiting for her help.

And now, as she gazed with love at the soul spirit of her friend, she realised the truth of it all. She sensed the purpose in the mad glee of the serpent-dragon. She trembled amid the moiling cyclone of chaos, absorbing the lesson that she should perhaps have grasped instinctively from the start. The Momu, the Tree, Nidhoggr—all were somehow linked together in some extraordinary cycle of existence. Kate recalled how the Momu had drawn her attention to this in their first meeting. "*Nidhoggr, the serpent—who gnawed at the roots of the world—fertilised a seed of the Tree of Life. That seed grew into the One Tree, a chimera of serpent and tree, in whose roots we converse. Sadly, the One Tree is dying, as is her beautiful city, Ulla Quemar. I, the first child of Ulla Quemar—who am almost as old as the One Tree herself—am dying with her.*"

Kate stared into the eyes of the nearest kneeling figure of one of the keepers. But surely there was a vital lesson here still, a very needful lesson? Were they consciously, or even accidentally, pointing out the lesson to her? Then she heard the voice of Granny Dew in her mind.

<The Momu must produce the egg, child.>

"What?"

<The soul spirit must become one with the flesh.>

"The flesh . . . ?" Her eyes returned to the insubstantial yet graceful form hovering in space before her.

Elaru cried out. <Mistress. You must subsume her—you must subsume the soul spirit of the Momu.>

Through the oraculum, Kate communicated her need to Nidhoggr. “The Momu pointed out your plight and the plight of the sacred Tree to me. She begged my help. I came to you through great danger, and woke you from your poisoned slumber. I made you aware of the peril that infested the roots of the Tree of Life. You had been starved to a husk of your former self. Now you have recovered your strength, and the Tree its power. It is time you completed the cycle. Help the Momu in turn. Or are the powers of being that . . . watch over worlds . . . themselves devoid of gratitude? Have you no conscience? No responding grace?”

Kate waited.

There was no response from the titanic serpent.

“Very well, then. I will enter your mind, with or without your will, and I will compel you to subsume my friend.”

Her anger mounted so that she didn’t truly understand what she was doing, other than the fact that she was turning the power of the oraculum inwards, on herself, which, in what little she understood, was now an integral part of the soul spirit of Nidhoggr himself. In a fraction of a moment she felt herself become part of the maelstrom. She was opposed by an obdurate resistance, ponderously slow, but leviathan in strength, which threatened to engulf her.

“Granny Dew . . .”

<It knows neither grace nor conscience. It knows not the spirit of friendship, like your Driftwood. The servant of Ragnarok harbours only chaos.>

"Elaru—if you wish to survive?"

<Mistress—I harbour no hope of survival. Yet you showed me kindness, which none other did. What matters it to you if you free your spirit from the worm? What matters the fate of such an undeserving world to you?>

But Kate knew it did matter. She recalled the advice of both Driftwood and Granny Dew.

<I must be clever—cunning even.>

"Elaru—please! There is so little time. Advise me now."

But it was Urale's mocking voice that answered. "She has already advised you. Abandon the worm. Flee for your life!"

"I will save the Momu. All that I have ever wanted in coming to this dreadful place was to save her and her people, the Cill."

"Foolish mortal. Why do you think the keepers are here? You have released Chaos in Dromenon. Pray that you have not released it into your own world."

"Elaru—are you too submissive to speak?"

<Mistress. Oh, how I share your anguish.>

"Words are no comfort to me here."

<The reunion of spirit and flesh you seek comes not from the great serpent, but from the Tree. Have you not seen . . . >

Elaru's voice ended with a shriek. Kate had to presume that Urale was still capable of silencing her, but it was too late, her words had suggested an idea.

The roots of the Tree of Life were now free of their parasitic infestation. Even Nidhoggr had abandoned its feeding off them. The One Tree in the Momu's chamber was an offshoot of the Tree of Life. It must also be regaining its vitality and strength back within the chamber.

What had the Momu said? Could Kate, in the midst of such violence and panic, recall her precise words? *"The One Tree is dying . . . I, the first child of Ulla Quemar . . . am dying with her."* But the One Tree was no longer dying. It must be budding—as if caught up in some extraordinary new spring. Coming alive back there in the chamber . . . The roots . . . The branches . . .

"Nidhoggr! I release you!"

Kate hardly dared to hope there would be an answer.

<You are presumptuous to think so.>

"I do not seek to influence you. I relinquish what claim I might have in your liberation. You are free to render this cathedral of pain to the chaos that is your nature."

<There is another power, one greater than yours, that wishes it otherwise.>

Kate's heart quailed. Nidhoggr could only have sensed the Tyrant.

"Then you, Nidhoggr, must decide if you will help me or not."

Kate kept her focus resolutely fixed on the translucent spirit of the Momu. She willed that spirit to her. She continued to demand the subsumation even as the hovering spirit paled amid the chaos of the disintegrating cathedral, and the dreadful landscape faded along with the kneeling keepers.

Elaru screamed, <You must depart, Mistress! You must depart the Land of the Dead without delay.>

The world around Kate was disintegrating, but she persisted. *If I could subsume the soul spirit of a minor god against his or her will, I can surely subsume the soul spirit of a dying friend.* She screamed the command, feeling it rise out of her heart and mind and explode into the chaos about her, a shockwave expanding into the disintegrating Cathedral of Death.

Refuge

Mark woke to find Nan curled up beside him facing the gable wall of the barn, fully awake. She looked forlorn with her lovely hair cropped close to her skull. The dawn sunlight was streaming in through gaps in the plank wall, dividing the air into golden shafts and streams. All around them people were stirring, children chattering, babies crying.

He moved to prop himself on one elbow so he could kiss her. "How are you feeling?"

"Alive," she whispered back.

Then she sat up, looking at him with concern, brushing the cuts and scrapes that covered his brow with her fingertips. "Where are we?"

"I think it's a barn in the grounds of an ancient manor house." Then he realised that she would have no idea what a manor house was. “A very old farm with lots of outbuildings.”

The cluster of buildings they had seen on their arrival had looked like a warren in the dark. But Mark had glimpsed the house in the headlights of their bikes as they had followed the Mamma Pig. It was a ruin, its decaying red brick inset with limestone window surrounds, mullions and leaded glass. This morning that tranquil scene had turned to bedlam. It was as if they found themselves in a medieval village caught up in the War of the Roses.

His nostrils were swamped by the odours of closeted human existence. She stretched and yawned, the T-shirt she had slept in rucked and wrinkled over her ribs. She pulled on a pullover so she could lean back against one of the huge oak uprights; a whole tree trunk at least two and a half feet square.

“What manner of place is this?”

“A refuge, from the looks of it. I know we crossed the Thames in the dark. We’re somewhere south of London.”

Mark was surprised to find so many people hiding in the building. It looked like there were 200 or more in the barn alone—and there were even more, lots more, being catered for in a ramshackle collection of other farm buildings. His tired eyes roamed over the forest of beams, arches and trusses that supported the naked roof high overhead.

Nan’s face looked so grimy he couldn’t help grinning at her. “We’d better make a start—find the others?”

She wrinkled her nose at him. “Hah!”

They stepped out through the plank doors into a world of confusion and desolation. People stared at them out of unwashed faces, still pouchy with sleep. Children ran in and out of a variety of tents and ramshackle caravans. The air was filled with the smells of coffee, barbecued sausages, beans and the paraffin and Calor Gas used for cooking their breakfasts.

“My senses . . . they still feel enhanced,” he said.

“I think we haven’t fully unwound from the battle and escape.”

“We need to check out how Sharkey is doing.”

Sharkey had been shot in the neck last night during the dogfight with the paramilitaries. They had transferred him to the Pig, where Tajh had seen to his wound before setting out. Luckily, the bullet hadn’t hit anything major. Mark had taken Sharkey’s bike so he and Nan could cover the Pig’s rear, while Bull rode point. Cal, Bull and Tajh had taken Sharkey to an emergency station within the main house as soon as they’d arrived. Mark and Nan were heading there when Nan spotted Jo Derby stepping out of a Landrover. She looked absorbed in her own thoughts, carrying a briefcase. They called to her and she hurried to join them.

“My goodness—I didn’t expect to find you here,” she said in a low voice. “But now I have, we need to talk. I assume the others are here?”

“Yeah—we’re all here. But where are you living now, Jo?”

"Moving around. Safe houses—if anywhere is safe these days."

They headed for the manor house, which loomed four storeys high. Mark saw how dilapidated it was. Loose tiles were sliding down the roof and some of the diamond panes in the windows were cracked or missing. They stepped through a strap-hinged heavy oak door into a reception hall covered with a chequered pattern of black-and-white tiles. The interior smelled musty. Heavy drapes hung around the windows and ornate plastered ceilings and faded tapestries decorated the walls. An elderly lady rushed forward to catch hold of Jo's free left hand. A small Pekinese dog yapped at her ankles as she spoke in an amiable, upper crust voice. "My dear—thank goodness you're here."

Jo stared back at her, nonplussed.

The old lady wore a floppy purple hat, a green T-shirt under a tartan dress and a damp-looking anorak. "Fay Breakespeare," she said. "I was an actress in another life. My late husband Bertie inherited the manor and farm. We're trying to organise some schooling for the unfortunate children. You must be the teacher?"

"I'm afraid not."

She turned to take Nan's hand. "Then it must be you."

"It's not Nan." Mark smiled. "But it's great that you're setting up a sort of school. I'm Mark. We're looking for a friend—a fighter who was brought in injured in the early hours. You have some kind of field hospital here?"

"Oh, dear." The hand was withdrawn. "You'll find what you're looking for in the drawing room, second on the left."

"Thank you."

But she was no longer interested in them. She was already heading for the front door.

The drawing room was cluttered with sick and injured, spread out among half a dozen narrow cots and assorted chairs. They found Sharkey sitting up in one of the cots, close by a big square window. His left shoulder and part of his neck was buried in a thickly wadded dressing. A drip, with an attached bag of saline, was running into his right hand. Tajh and Cal were squeezed into the narrow space to either side of him. Bull and Cogwheel were nearby, chatting to a man they appeared to know, whose splinted leg was dangling on the end of a hoist.

"How are you, Sharkey?"

He grinned. "Doc tells me the bullet went clean through my trapezius muscle. More painful than life threatening."

Nan smiled. "I think, perhaps, you are not an easy man to kill."

"Not while I got my little guardian here." Sharkey patted Big Ted, who was sharing the cot with him.

Jo looked around the crew. "Isn't anybody going to tell me what happened?"

Tajh explained the attack on the camp.

"You're sure it was an air force chopper?"

Sharkey lifted his eyebrows. "Tell her, Cal."

"Those other guys—the ones in the truck who were waiting to mop us up—there was regular army among them too."

Jo stared at him. "You're absolutely sure?"

"I know army when I see them."

"Then they really are working together."

"Who are?" Mark asked.

Jo shook her head. "I'm sure it won't be the whole army. I think it's going to be certain elements."

"What elements?"

"We need to have a proper talk."

The only empty room they could find was a disused kitchen with an ancient-looking Aga stove. The place was damp and freezing cold, but there was a convenient table and half a dozen chairs. Jo dumped her briefcase on the table.

Cal and Tajh sat on either side of Jo, cigarettes already alight. Mark sat opposite, with Nan hugging his left arm. Cogwheel pulled up his wheelchair at the end of the table next to Nan, while Bull filled the space on the other end. Jo looked from Mark to Cal. "You two settled your differences?"

Cal shrugged. "He takes some getting used to."

"Anybody who can take out an Ugly with a battleaxe is good with me," said Bull.

Mark glanced at Nan, who nodded back. "Nan and I, we need to know more about the organisation behind he crews. We think you know something, Jo. If so, can you give us some idea?"

Jo stared back at him, thoughtful. "I know a little, but I'm not allowed to talk about it, certainly not here and now."

"Okay." Tajh slapped the flat of her hand on the table as if in support of Jo's reticence. "So, let's hear your news."

Jo sighed. "It isn't just London any more, *all* the big towns and cities are in chaos. But look here . . ."

She pulled a flat screen out of her briefcase. She switched it on then passed it around the crew. They stared at a recorded newscast. Whole city districts were on fire. Paramilitaries were seen shooting at rioters in smoke-obscured streets.

Tajh said, "I don't recognise the setting."

"Just wait."

The scenes were clearly being filmed from a news chopper. Then, for a moment, there was a break in the smoke.

"It's not London."

"No. It's Times Square—New York."

Mark stared at the blazing street scenes, dumbfounded. "Bloody hell!"

"It would appear that New York City has its own Razzamatazzers. It's still small scale, compared to London, but that's pretty much how it started here."

Tajh shook her head. "It's insane—how could chaos be catching?"

Jo shrugged. "I wish I knew."

Mark looked at Jo. “We know there’s a horrible, implacable logic behind it and we know Grimstone is at the heart of it.”

“But Grimstone is here in London.”

“Yeah, but he has disciples everywhere.”

Jo pressed on: “The latest news is that the government here, if you can call it a government any more, has declared a national emergency. Parliament has been suspended. We’re now under martial law. They’ve set up an emergency body that will run the country until such a time as the emergency is contained. They call it the New Order.”

“And Grimstone?”

“He’s an ad-hoc member of the New Order.”

“More like ad-hoc leader,” Mark muttered.

“The paramilitaries?” Tajh asked Jo.

“They’ll become an integral part of the emergency response to control the civil unrest.”

“Along with the armed forces—the army?”

“Yes, but it’s a qualified yes.”

“And who will be in charge of emergency response?” Cal asked.

“A single senior army officer will take immediate control of the reorganisation and deployment.”

“Don’t tell me . . .” Mark was thinking back to the big meeting at Wembley Stadium and the crescents of white-robed disciples with hooded faces gathered around Grimstone on his podium.

"Yes—Field Marshall Seebox."

"Who will answer, personally, to Grimstone?"

Mark pressed Jo. "You said, in relation to the army, it was a qualified yes. What did you mean by that?"

"There's something else, something of specific interest to Mark and Nan. Can I have a few minutes with you both in private?"

They left the hall and wandered among the crowds of refugees. The morning air was bitterly cold, with a promise of snow.

Mark asked Jo: "What did you mean by qualified in relation to the army?"

"I was hinting at an answer to your earlier question—about who is regulating the crews."

"And?"

"Sections of the armed forces have broken away from Seebox's control. They're setting up a secret regional headquarters in the north."

"Where in the north?"

"I can't tell you more right now. It's all somewhat on the hoof."

The whole of society seemed somewhat on the hoof right now. Mark and Nan looked with interest at a nearby cluster of Hindus, Sikhs and Muslims talking animatedly with a clergyman in a purple shirt: a bishop.

Jo read their minds. "The various religions are getting together. It's hardly surprising, since they're facing a common threat."

"What threat?"

"A moral one from their perspective. An arena is being erected close to the Guildhall Art Gallery."

"You mean, like a Roman arena?"

She nodded.

"I don't understand," Mark said. "I can't see what an arena would have to do with Grimstone or these religions."

"You might not, but I do," said Nan.

"What is it?"

"On Tír, the Tyrant's legions celebrate with the shedding of blood through sacrifices. These sacrifices are often made in arenas where men fight men. There is a very large arena in his capital city, Ghork Mega."

Jo nodded. "The Guildhall Art Gallery—or at least parts of it—were built over what was, once upon a time, London's original Roman arena."

"It still feels bizarre and somewhat contrived," Mark said. "Unlike the Grimstone I know. So what's the big event?"

"A celebration—or maybe some kind of tribute."

"A celebration or tribute to what?"

"I don't know." Jo paused to think. "In Roman times, it might have been victory in war, or just the emperor's birthday or name day."

"But you think this might be linked to Padraig?"

"Word is that Grimstone will make an example of a false prophet—a former enemy, now vanquished."

Mark stared at Jo, shaking his head. "It all sounds a little too pat. Grimstone is up to something."

"You mean, like the trap he laid for you at the Wembley meeting?" Nan said.

Mark was recalling something Grimstone had said to him, when they had met under the tunnel at Wembley. He saw that hated face laughing. He heard his boast: *"I could deal with you now—effortlessly, but that would be too easy. It's not a fitting punishment for your disloyalty."*

"There's something I do wonder about," said Jo. "The Roman circuses were dedicated to gods. The sacrifices were made to those gods."

Mark snorted.

"What?"

Nan answered for him. "The Tyrant is Grimstone's god."

Jo closed her eyes. "Then maybe it's beginning to make some kind of sense?"

Mark recalled how Grimstone used to talk about Padraig when they had visited Clonmel. He hated Padraig's veneration of the Trídédana—the trinity of goddesses that were the Tyrant's enemy on Tír. "Grimstone is spreading the rumours. He wants me to hear about it. He's going to sacrifice Padraig. Just to draw me in."

"Why?"

"Because he intends to make a spectacle of it."

"A spectacle of what?"

"Destroying me."

A Child of the Dreamtime

<Wake up!>

Mo Grimstone refused to wake up. Yet the voice that called her, a faint whisper within her mind, was persistent. She recognised the half growly, half comforting voice of Magtokk. <You must rouse yourself! You must come with me if your deepest wish is to be granted this night.>

Her eyes reluctantly opened to confirm that it was, indeed, deepest night outside her tent, but the Torus that had been restored to its leathery thong around her neck was pulsing with light, filling the interior with a milky blue glow. How warm she felt, how comfortable, cuddled up within the furry embrace of her Shee guardian, the tigress, Usrua, whose six-inch whiskers twitched as she lay curled up into a circle around Mo's body: nine feet of big cat devouring every morsel of space beneath the seal-hide tent. Mo's eyes drifted closed again.

<No, no, no, no!> She must be dreaming.

Her mind was overcome by the exhaustion of another hard day's riding through treacherous terrain on the shoulders of her onkkh. They were still only a few days further down the slopes from the valley of the skull pyramids, but there had still not been any attacks from the Tyrant's forces. Maybe they didn't need to attack, the landscape was more than hazard enough.

No human arms and legs could have brought her and the vast Shee army this far across such daunting slopes. It wasn't just the pitch of them—it was the vicious broken nature of the rocks themselves; a morass of sharp ledges, deep horizontal fissures and looming crevasses that made the journey hazardous beyond belief. Only the giant birds, with their tenacious claws and the ability to hop and leap between ridges and ledges could have brought them this far. And only an army of giant cats that had the surefootedness of four powerful limbs with their own feline claws could have kept pace with the onkkh.

Mo envied the Gargs flying overhead. If only they could all fly like Gargs, the journey would have taken two or three days.

The whisper came again: <You must rouse yourself!>

Mo shook her head, somewhere close to sleep again. <Whoever you are, leave me be.>

<Mira!>

That woke her. The whisper was coming from somebody—some being—who knew her real name; the name given to her by her birth mother before she was lost to her adoptive parents' machinations.

She spoke aloud: "What . . ."

A leathery finger was pressed against her lips.

<We must make our way in silence.>

Magtokk! It *was* his voice. Yet, when Mo opened her eyes, she saw nothing, not even a shadow, within the gloom of the tent.

The leathery finger withdrew from her lips.

Her voice fell to a whisper: "Where are you?"

<Mind-to-mind, if we need to speak!>

Mo jerked to full attention. How could Magtokk possibly know the name given to her by her birth mother?

She spoke, within her mind: <What is it? What's happening?>

<These are perilous times. The bloom of chaos is flowering. It is time that you discovered more of who you are.>

<But people will see us. We are surrounded by aides and Shee—and there will be Gargs in the sky.>

<Look around.>

When Mo looked down, she was startled to see her sleeping self still folded within Usrua's mighty embrace.

<Oh my goodness!>

<We journey as soul spirits. No eye of Shee or Garg will see us.>

<But they are not our enemies?>

<Indeed they would protect you with their lives, but even when most securely guarded, the eyes of malice will discover a way to peek and pry. I have discovered the usefulness of invisibility.>

When Mo blinked again, or at least when she thought she blinked, she was already outside the tent staring out over the extraordinary spectacle of the mountainside camp. There was a strange low-pitched roaring sound, but now she realised that it was the flapping of tens of thousands of tents. She could hear the onkkh farting and snoring where they were tethered to iron stanchions driven deep into the rock. Beside her, she was aware of the ghostly shape of the orang-utan staring up into the navy bowl of moon and stars. Mo followed his eyes to see a shockingly familiar shape swoop down out of the starlight, its fierce black eyes and raptor's beak agape. She recalled the Temple Ship ploughing through the central currents of the Snowmelt River after their escape from Isscan . . . the dark cruciate shape of an eagle, with flashes of white fletching over the outer reaches of its enormous wings had accompanied their journey after the arrival of the dwarf mage.

<It's Qwenqwo's guardian.>

<No, it is your guardian.>

<But it protected him, it saved his runestone.>

Mo recalled how the eagle had pounced to save Qwenqwo's runestone when, enraged by what she mistook for treachery, the mother-sister of the present Kyra had hurled it far out over the water.

<The runestone was an additional, if poor, protection for you until it was restored in power at Ossierel.>

Mo looked on in silence. <Why me? What's so important that I need two such powerful guardians, and perhaps even three, if your behaviour is anything to go by.>

<You are special. Your role may prove the most important of all. And now your destiny is near.>

<What destiny?>

<We have a journey to make. It is as important to me as it is to you. The eagle will bear you, it is a True Believer named Thesau. We shall visit a special time and a special place.>

Mo shrank back in terror as the giant shape, ten times the size of any eagle on Earth, wheeled and flapped, to come in close to where they waited. She saw the yellow knob of raptor's beak and the knot of the enormous taloned feet.

<You may take cover in me.>

<Take cover?>

<Lose yourself in my embrace.>

She hardly had time to think of what he meant before, thankfully without time enough time to shriek, she found herself wrapped around Magtokk's neck. He then took a comfortable perch just between the shoulders of the giant eagle, where he clung on with all four feet. Mo felt the giant eagle soar, with no apparent effort, until the sky and the mountains below them became a blur of light and shade.

She had no memory of the journey that followed. It just seemed as if, in a moment, she had been transported from Tír to Earth to find herself in an unfamiliar landscape. Day had become sunset in a desert landscape that she did not recognise, surrounded by strangers who sat cross-legged around her. Some of the women had sleepy-headed children, who clung to their necks. They were dark-skinned and naked, their faces were sombre, their hair, silhouetted by the setting sun behind them, was ruffled and bleached. Directly in front of Mo was a pond of very still water and further back, glowing with the russet light, was a low rock face covered with stencilled etchings of hands, boat-shaped ovals, hatchings like ladders, and serpent-like curves containing rainbows.

<Where are we, Magtokk? Who are these people?>

<You will see.>

Suddenly she was within the mind of a young woman, looking though her eyes at her reflection in the pond, where she saw a young face, dusky in hue, with a nimbus of curly black hair. The face was not Mo's face, but she felt comfortable within it and within the tall, slim, girlish figure. Mo's mind filled with new knowledge. She knew that the rock face bore the clan markers and dreamtime stories. She knew that her name was Mala, a name taken from the ancestral spirit hare-wallaby, which was fleet but vulnerable, and thus kept itself out of sight during the day. She also knew that this day was her sixteenth birthday.

An old woman climbed to her feet and came towards her, the edges of her figure glimmering in the dying rays. Her skin was ruddy and glowing with ochre. Around her neck was a thong of leathery material on which hung a flattened stone disk. The disk was torus-shaped with a rough hole carved through the centre by tools of bone and granite. The surfaces of the disk were worn smooth by the flesh of countless elders who had worn the talisman from the time of its creation. Mo recognised it as the Torus she now wore around her own neck. The basket the old woman carried—on a thong attached to a broad strap across her brow—was long and cylindrical, woven from something finer than rushes. She took no notice of an emaciated dog that was yapping and whining around her legs. With fleeting touches of her ochre-stained fingers, she urged Mala to stand and then turn to face the setting sun.

Mo saw from within Mala's mind how her feet created arcs of indentation in the bright red sand.

In the basket, the old woman carried sprigs of two different kinds of flowers. One of these Mo recognised as clematis and the other was ivy. The old woman—in Mala's mind, Mo caught the respectful expression *minyma pampa*, tribal elder—chanted a hymn containing lessons of mental beauty and fidelity, making a corona of the ivy and clematis, which she placed on the young woman's head, like a crown.

The elder's face was deeply lined, her dark features contrasted sharply with her white bush of curly hair. Her breasts were flaps of leather. Her features were those Mo associated with a native Australian. Mo realised that Mala's features were also aboriginal, though less dark and unlined.

The language of the chant sounded powerful and familiar to Mo's ears. She understood the words mind-to-mind. In her actions, in her speaking, the elder was curiously unhurried. She called Mala *minyma,* which meant woman. She hesitated on the word, as if, through her posture, she infused some additional significance. Then she reached into the basket again and raised a stick with a rattling pod at the end of it and she waved it here and there. She said *tjitji,* which Mo understood to mean child, and she chanted things and waved her stick with its rattling pod.

A woman—a child . . .

She said: "*Tjoti a-nu.*"

It meant that the child went.

<What does it mean, Magtokk? Went where?>

She bade Mala to lie down in the sand and open up her legs. She examined her down there whilst chanting, turning from time to time, sometimes to the left and sometimes to the right, as if addressing the land, the red dirt, and the semicircle of perhaps thirty odd people gathered between Mo and the sunset. She talked about the dreaming, and the making of the sun and moon. She talked about the spirit of the child, which must become real and then grow in the womb. She talked of how the spirit of the land must enter the child there in the womb, in the fifth month, and only then would the woman feel the new life move within her. This was the *tjoti a-nu*. This movement was accompanied by a pause—a silence that was imbued with additional significance. "Thus," spoke the elder, "is a woman's child—a *minyma yjoti*—made alive by the spirit of the land, so the land is the spirit is the dreaming."

The old woman turned to the semi-circle and she called out: "This *minyma* is with special child."

Mo's heart almost stopped.

<It's me—I'm the child?>

<Yes.>

The old woman's words provoked a murmur among the people gathered around her. Mala looked at the semicircle of people with anxious eyes, fixing on one of the women, presumably her own mother.

"The *minyma* is with child—but she is unbroken."

This provoked an excited murmuring. In some it provoked cries of disbelief, or something else, something that made the young woman flinch. Mo stared up out of the eyes of Mala at the old woman. She didn't understand.

A woman cried: "It is a demon child!"

The elder thought about this. She seemed undecided. Mala shivered, and in soul spirit, Mo shivered with her. Both their eyes looked beyond the semicircle into the distance, beyond the small coppice of spidery trees with their leaves shivering in the rising breeze of evening. She looked at where the sun was setting behind a gigantic red mountain glimmered with light. The caves within it looked like open maws.

Mo heard Mala whisper the mountain's name: "Uluru."

Uluru was the dreamtime place of Mala's unborn child. That it was a girl, she already knew. She had sensed that girl in her from the time her blood had stopped. The notion of a child within her felt so strange and disquieting that she felt a rising panic in her breast.

Mo shared her panic.

Magtokk whispered: <Now they come!>

Mo gazed into the heavens above the red mountain, where an ocean of stars were sweeping down out of the sky. She recognised them as True Believers. They were weaving patterns amongst themselves, moving in strange but meaningful rhythms and streams. When the old woman gazed up at them, her eyes wide and staring, Mo saw the twinkling reflections of the starlight in her eyes.

The elder declared: "This child is born of no fellah. Her father is the spirit of the Dreamtime, Tjukurpa."

<Magtokk> Mo's spirit voice trembled, <what does this mean?>

<In truth, I do not know.>

The seated figures within the semicircle began to chant in deep, throaty cadences, their heads lowered.

The elder's head inclined as if she were listening to voices speaking to her inside her mind. She turned to face the sky. A fiery corona of rays radiated from the broad mountain of rock, pitching rainbows of colour down into the valley of sandy scrub and straggling trees.

She said: "Her mother name her."

Mala spoke: "I name her Mira."

In spirit, and she sensed in her physical person back in the tent, Mo wept openly and gratefully.

The elder spoke, and the gathering echoed her, as if with one voice: "This dreamtime *yjoti*—this name belong her—it is Mira."

Mo felt a tremor run through her, from the nape of her neck to the tips of her fingers and toes. Even as she understood what was happening, she felt herself withdraw from her mother, Mala. She didn't want to leave her, she wanted to know more about her. She wanted to talk to her, she wanted to embrace her and be embraced by her. Mo resisted this drawing back. She heard Magtokk speak to her quietly mind-to-mind.

<She's little more than a child herself.>

The shock of the old woman's words felt like a wound in Mo's heart. Yet she had met her birth mother for the first time. That she had been allowed to be one with her senses, even with all the fear of what Mala knew expected of her, was comforting. Mala, her birth mother, was a young woman, no more than sixteen—little different from Mo's age.

The old woman began to chant anew. She removed the thong that carried the Torus from around her neck.

"This *tjurunga* is the sacred thing. It was fashioned from a star that fell. The snake skin that holds it is blessed in the name of Wanumpi."

She began to chant anew, telling the story of Wanumpi the rainbow serpent and how it guarded the water of life. As she chanted, she threaded the leathery thong around Mala's neck. A loud, rhythmic shouting erupted among the people as, with wide eyes, they saw the Torus glow with inner light. The ultramarine flowerets within the darker green and grey crystals pulsed in time with the young woman's heartbeat.

The elder took several steps backwards with her head bowed. Mo's heart was beating so wildly she thought she might faint.

Mala rose to her feet.

She turned so that she, too, was facing the dying sun over the horizon of rock they called Uluru.

The elder spoke: "Something has happened in this time. *Tjoti a-nu*—the child has moved within her, making the songline of this place. This daughter-child will leave her mark in the land. That is her dreaming."

Mo blinked away the tears so she could see her mother, so young and afraid, bathed in the light of the pulsing Torus.

A single star came down to hover in the space between the elder and the gathering of her people, but the voice came from the Torus hanging around Mala's throat. It spoke the tribal language, the words invading every mind as clear as still water: "The child, Mira, is special. The people of Uluru must guard her. She will be hunted by her enemies. You must leave this place of the dreaming before the sun has washed the sleep from its eye. You must do everything you can to protect her."

"This must we do," the people called.

The vision, the dream journey, began to fade.

<Please, Magtokk. I don't want to leave now. I can't leave Mala now. I've hardly met her. I want to know everything about her.>

<We must. There are other journeys we need to make.>

<No! No! >

As her vision faded, Mo heard the voice of the True Believer, issuing through the Torus around Mala's throat. "You must abandon this place. You must leave no trail of your passage. Always, from this day forward, you must move and move again. The danger will never leave you. This *tjurunga* will help to protect the birth mother, Mala, and the child within, who was fathered by the dreaming."

No Place to Go

Gully emerged from the crack in the ground trembling from head to foot. It was much colder up here than underground. A light sleet was drifting down onto his head. He had twisted his left ankle on the climb out of the cavern and now he limped painfully as he made his way across the rubble-strewn land, heading for an abandoned caravan he saw opposite.

"Shit!"

He shifted some rags so he could get inside and even then there was no way of locking the door because the bleedin' lock was broken. And then he had to wipe the filthy Formica table with his snotrag and all the time he was arguing with Penny inside his head.

He had brought her a cuppa, even though she said she didn't want it. He was standing there, offering it up to her on the gantry, only she wouldn't stop scribbling even to take it out of his hand.

"Penny, gel, why won't you come down 'ere for a cuppa an' a bit of bread an' butter with me?"

"You know why."

"I don't know nuffink."

"You wouldn't understand, Gully."

He watched her left hand twirl her hair. He watched her scribbling again. Scribbling, filling in bits of paint, scribbling, panting for breath, like her bleedin' life depended on it.

"Don't it matter I been taking care of you? Gettin' in the food. Takin' chances. I made that gantry so you could scribble up there on the ceiling. But look at you now, sayin' no to a cuppa tea with me."

Her face, now she turned it round to look down at him, was red and swollen with what looked like a broken nose. She was bawling all the time as she was drawing. She blinked her tearful eyes at him. *"I have to concentrate, Gully."*

"I think you should stop it now. Just come down 'ere an' let me hold you. There ain't nuffink wrong with me just holding you. I been tellin' you that for ages. It's just natural."

"I'm leaving you, Gully."

Her words cut him. They cut deep into his heart, like a blade. *"No, you ain't. I won't let you . . . I won't let you."*

"You can't stop me."

"You won't even say why you're doin' this—why you doin' it to me? It ain't right, Penny. It ain't natural."

"Please don't be angry with me, Gully. Let me finish it while I can. It's all in my head and I have to finish it before I lose it."

"You already gone an' lost it, Penny."

"You don't understand. It's all linked, Gully. The City Above and the City Below. They're linked. They're one."

"There ain't no such thing as no City Below. You gone an' lost it, gel. Them maps is playing tricks with your 'ead."

She had stopped her scribbling to look down at him then, the lank blonde rat-tails of her hair falling unkempt to below her shoulders, her eyes such a pale grey they looked like water in a glass. He could see she was thinking hard. She was struggling to make her mind up about something—about him. *"You're wrong, Gully. It's real. It's real and it's important. Something extraordinary is about to happen."*

"Them's not even proper maps. Them's just pictures—them's not even proper pictures. *Them's just scribbles."*

"There's a pattern—I'm telling you the truth, Gully. There's a pattern so big you just don't see it at first. You don't see it because it's so enormous. I was just seeing bits of it, but now I see the wonder of it."

"Things like that, they're not real except inside your 'ead. All them things, that stuff about the dagger and the Scalpie and the Grimlings. You been imaginin' it, an' now you're tellin' yourself it's real."

"Go away, Gully."

"No, I won't, not until you come down. Come on down, now, and 'ave a cuppa an a bit of bread an' butter with me?"

Gully saw her face then, and the haunted look on it. *"Okay, Gully. I'll come down. We'll have a last cup of tea together."*

Wot she up to now?

He saw at the time that she was up to something. And now, sitting slumped on the Formica table in the derelict caravan, he saw her face again. He recalled her expression and wondered what she'd been planning inside that head of hers that would need him to sleep for a night and a day to get it done.

The sense of betrayal rose in Gully. It caused him to clench his teary eyes tight shut. Then he heard a voice speaking to him and it seemed at first to be inside his head.

"Evrytin' gonna be all right."

Gully's eyes sprang open. He was staring at a tall black woman, wrapped in a dress so colourful it blurred into rainbows. A matching blaze of colour was tied around her brow, with a big knot holding a bun of thick black curls at the back of her head.

"Who the bleedin' 'eck . . . ?"

"Henriette—a friend to poor lost boys."

She was so massive, she seemed to fill the entire caravan. There was no way Gully could make a break past her. How had she got here without his noticing? A woman her size and yet Gully hadn't heard a squeak of her entry to the caravan.

"Dry up dem tears, Dahlin'. Dis shithole wet enough already."

Gully trembled so violently that the Formica table was making a racket against the floor. He started counting one to twenty. He went through the ritual of patting his six pockets, in the right order, his right hand, P for protection, O for ordinary, C for clear . . . The fingers of his left hand brushed by K for Keys. They discovered the hard oblong shape of the mobile phone in the second down on the left, E for emergency, before the T for traps. The mobile was in E—the mobile what had been given to him by Mark.

"Go ahead, Gully. Time to ring him."

How the shit did she know his name? Gully's hands lifted to brush his cheeks, stubbly with a ginger, boyish beard. He removed his glasses and wiped them with the filthy snotrag from Pocket 2, making the smudging worse. He wiped his glasses and stood up. He sat down again and still he wiped and wiped and wiped.

"You're one of them. Like Mark an' Nan. You're jiggerin' about with the thoughts in me bleedin' 'ead."

"Penny for them, Gully?" Her whole body wobbled as she cackled a wicked sounding laugh.

"Slipped us a Mickey, she did, so's to make me sleep. Knocked me for six a whole night an' a day."

"Clever of her, wasn't it?"

"Not so clever after she gone and drawn it all out there on the bleedin' ceiling."

"So clever Gully follows her map?"

"Took a snap with the mobile."

"All de way to de ghost Tube station?"

"Once inside I didn't need no map. There was a trail of Penny's footprints showing me the way."

"Clever bwai!"

Henriette laughed, showing two rows of large even teeth. She slapped a shiny black walking stick down on the Formica table. The stick was dripping with rain. It had a sharp tip on the end of it that was hot and steaming. In Gully's vision the walking stick writhed like something half alive. She said, softly: "You jus' go ahead—call him, Gully."

In the smelly caravan, with the sleet coming down outside the window, Gully blew onto hands that were raw with cold. The mobile was slippery in his wet fingers. A hot key number, the geezer, Mark, had said. There was just the one number to press, to make the call . . .

He thought: *You did it, Penny—you left me.*

He saw that look on Penny's bruised and forlorn face, all red and blubbery with bawling. That look had followed him all the way down the tunnel and into the big cave where the waterfall was roaring. He had followed her footsteps up to the crack in the wall. He had peered in there, that place full of blue light, where Penny had gone.

He didn't care that the alien woman was watching him, listening to him. "I'm sorry, Penny, but I couldn't follow you in there. Just couldn't do it. Me bottle was gone."

He switched on the phone. Tears surged again, blinding him. He heard Mark's voice in his ear. "Is that you, Gully?"

"Yeah." He wiped the snot from his face with his sleeve.

"You sound upset. Is everything okay?"

"Penny's gone."

"She came back?"

"Yeah, but now she's gone again."

"Gone where?"

"She wanted me to catch her some live pigeons so the Grimlings would let her through."

"What?"

"The Skulls was huntin' 'er. She . . . She killed one with the dagger."

"Gully—we need to find her."

"I followed her down a Tube tunnel to this waterfall cave. There's Grimlings down there. Grimlings all over the bleedin' place, buzzing about! There's some kinda Grimling factory goin' at it like jack 'ammers."

"Grimlings?"

"Yeah."

"Where are you, Gully?"

"Dunno."

"What can you see nearby?"

He stared, blinking, at the terrifying woman opposite him, who was grinning encouragement. "I can't see nuffink with the sleet, but I can smell smoke. There's streets burnin' all around the place."

"Which streets?"

"Round about St. Paul's—I can see the bowl on the roof."

"Where do you think Penny has gone?"

"The City Below."

"What are you talking about, Gully?"

"I took a picture with the mobile."

"A picture of what?"

"Penny's map—the City Above an' the City Below. I took it before I left. So I could follow 'er on the map."

Gully could hear voices, the two of them, Mark and Nan, talking. Then Mark's voice came back on the phone. "Gully—I'm going to ask you to trust me. Will you please trust me? We'll come and get you."

Henriette was nodding, still grinning over the Formica table at him.

"I got no place else to go."

Battle Ready

"You look worried."

Alan's thoughts were interrupted by the arrival of Mo, bobbing and weaving on the back of her onkkh amid the bustle and dust cloud of the marching army.

"Hi, Mo." He shifted position to ease his aching bum. He had never thought much about the tiny bone at the bottom of his spine before, but he was all too aware of it these days, and of how it could become the seat of excruciating discomfort after another day's ride.

"You're still worried about the pyramids?" She said.

"I don't like the fact we had to leave the place without understanding the creatures that live there. We don't know if they're entirely innocent. Or even if the pyramids themselves might have been some kind of warning."

"Magtokk is equally concerned. He can't keep still for a moment. He's constantly disappearing and reappearing and then flitting from one place to another."

They were facing into powerful winds, hot and uncomfortable under a cloudless azure sky. For several moments they could hardly hear one another speak as hundreds of onkkh added their honking to the roaring of the winds. It wasn't hard to figure where they had gotten their name. The army was passing a row of conical black hills, which forced the columns to stream around them. The beasts were sensitive to any kind of change—a rise in the wind, a slight increase or decrease in the slope of the land or, as now, an unusual degree of undulation underfoot. The gritty landscape was volcanic again: the conical hills were small calderas and the ground was splattered with ancient eruptions of spongy black lava.

Alan had to wait a minute or two for his beast to settle. "To tell you the truth, Mo, I don't like mysteries."

"You sense danger?"

"We're getting closer to Ghork Mega's outer defences. The Tyrant must know we're here. We have to expect attack. It's only a question of when it happens—and what form it will take."

Alan looked up at the Garg lookouts wheeling overhead. Iyezzz had taken the bulk of them forwards, fanning out in a wide crescent to scout the land ahead. They estimated that the Tyrant's capital city was, maybe, fifty leagues to the north, and the outer defences were now much closer, but so far they had encountered no resistance.

Mo said, "I keep worrying about Mark and whether or not he made it back to Earth. I wonder what he found there."

"Me too—I keep thinking about Mark and Kate." He shook his head. "You getting any more information from the True Believers?"

Mo hesitated. She looked perplexed, her fingers toying with the Torus hanging back around her neck on its thong.

Alan had the impression she might be holding something back. He sighed, waiting for another chorus of honking to settle before speaking.

"I know that Magtokk thinks we missed a trick back there. Perhaps there was something to be discovered in the pyramids, or maybe the creatures that created them."

"The Akkharu," Mo nodded.

Alan could hardly fail to notice how Mo was changing. The shape of her face was lengthening, her eyes were turning up at the outer edges. She looked stunningly beautiful, if also wonderfully alien.

Mo interrupted his thoughts: "Now's your opportunity to ask him if we did."

He wheeled to find the bulky form of the orang-utan knuckle-trotting in their wake. Magtokk could keep up his own good pace when he wanted. Alan slowed the beast down so the magician could come alongside. He said, "You sure look worried about something."

"What could possibly worry me in these clement pastures?"

They were forced by the pressure of the army around them to continue moving. Alan glanced down at what looked like a scuttling shag-covered rug. "Something you're not telling us?"

Those dark eyes looked back up into his own. "I have been giving some thought to a mystery."

Alan rubbed at one of the many sore points in his back. "Uh-huh?"

"Ask yourself what the Tyrant will benefit if he succeeds in taking complete control of the Fáil."

Alan thought about it for several onkkh paces through the black spongy terrain. "Immortality?"

"That, maybe, and more."

"What more?"

"Who controls immortality?"

Alan shook his head. "Fate? The gods?"

"Perhaps."

There was excitement among the Gargs overhead. The crescent was closing together, hurrying towards a single focus.

Alan followed the direction of Mo's gaze before returning to their conversation. "What are you implying? He will become a god?"

"Not *a* god."

Alan inclined his head, his eyes finding the orang-utan's. "What—he will become *the* god?"

"Take it a step further. Who might thus be threatened?"

"The Trídédana?"

"Who brought you into this world?"

Alan felt a shock of understanding pass through him. Mo was studying Magtokk with widening eyes.

"This might explain something else that has puzzled me."

"What?"

"Why the Tyrant did not trouble himself to kill all four of you back in your home world before you assumed your powers."

Alan hesitated. Magtokk's question reminded him of a thought that had nagged at him since even before they had arrived in Tír. Mark and Mo—they had been adopted by the sadistic Grimstone, who would also have had plenty of opportunity to kill them. "What conclusions did you draw?"

"He killed some, perhaps all, of your parents without much difficulty. This was the brutal challenge that brought you together as friends."

"He tried to kill me—to kill Kate."

"Not hard enough."

"I don't get it."

"What if he wanted to frighten you while allowing you to live?"

"Gee—he wanted us to come here?"

"It is, at the very least, an intriguing question." Their small party was obstructing the flow of the central columns of Shee, many carrying aides on their backs, who eyed them as the cats trotted by.

Mo could remain silent no longer. "But why would the Tyrant possibly want us here? We've brought nothing but trouble for him."

"Ah, Mo, your enemy is capable of great subtlety as well as ruthlessness. No doubt you, and Alan too, have asked yourselves what purpose the Trídédana might have had in bringing you to Tír."

"The Trídédana?"

They had all accepted the word of the high architect, Ussha De Danaan, when she had explained their purpose as she lay dying on the gates of Ossierel. Her world—a fairer world, one that respected life and the beauty of nature—had been threatened by the Tyrant. De Danaan had brought the friends to Tír because they were born into a world uninfluenced by the Fáil. But now Alan wondered if he should have questioned this idea further. Had the De Danaan merely served the purposes of the Trídédana? Could it be that it was the Trídédana that actually felt threatened by the Tyrant?

Magtokk inclined his head a little to the side. Those dark eyes still held Alan's, encouraging him. "You are now part of a war that has lasted thousands of years—for mortals. But thousands of years are nothing to the divinities."

"Well, okay. You're asking me to consider if the Tyrant might also have some vested interest in our coming here?"

"I'm merely asking you to consider all possibilities."

"But why—what would he gain?"

"That is part of the mystery I have been considering."

"And your conclusion?"

"What great prize lies at the heart of it all?"

"The Fáil?"

"Have you not wondered as to the nature of this all-powerful entity—this so-called malengin of the Arinn, which controls fate?"

"The Fáil controls fate?"

"The Fáil *is* Fate."

Alan's mind reeled. He thought back to what had happened to the demigod Fangaroth at the Tower of Bones. "You're suggesting that Fate—the Fáil—is more powerful than the gods?"

"I'm asking the question: is Fate all?"

"What you're really asking is: what would happen if the Tyrant wins and he takes over ultimate control of the Fáil?"

"Might he then control Fate?"

The conversation was deeply unsettling. His eyes swept upwards to see a dense gathering of Gargs in the sky. They were growing larger, swelling in size. The scouts were returning in a single block of hundreds: the bearers of news, perhaps?

The onkkh that was carrying Alan wobbled as it encountered an unexpected crater. Alan had to hold on for dear life as the saddle heaved from one acute angle to another, before righting itself again. His eyes returned to the swooping Gargs who were alighting at the head of the column. The Kyra was calling out his name. She was standing next to a breathless-looking Iyezzz.

Alan jumped down from the onkkh and then helped Mo to do the same. They both ran clumsily because their muscles were so exhausted and aching from the uncomfortable ride. Though he was nearly as tall as his beanpole grandfather, Padraig, Mo no longer seemed tiny beside him.

The Kyra addressed him when he was still a dozen paces away. "The Garg Prince has identified a fortification up ahead."

Iyezzz's skin was a shimmering scarlet from his hurried flight. The parallel gill flaps in his throat were panting for breath. His voice was no more than a husky purr, but Alan understood the words perfectly. "It's a guarded fosse—complete with a heavily garrisoned fortress. We are not fifty leagues from the outer defences of Ghork Mega, but fifteen."

Alan conducted a rough calculation in his head: fifteen leagues—just forty miles.

STARDUST

PENNY WAS HYPERVENTILATING AGAIN, STARING ahead to where Jeremiah was sitting on a ledge feeding a gathering of small creatures. Something resembling a bat was eating from his open hand, but when she got closer she saw that the creatures were alien to her, and some as spectral as wraiths or ghosts. What she had taken for a bat was really a baby Grimling. A winged creature with eyes as red as coals and the figure of a minuscule stork alighted on his left shoulder as Jeremiah turned to look at Penny with those all-black eyes. She saw his lips moving, but the words came to her not through her ears but her mind. <They are very loyal, you know. They would die for me in their millions if I commanded it.>

Her voice shook as she spoke: "Who—or what—are you?"

<I go by many names.>

Penny didn't know what to think of his reply. "Are you going to hurt me?"

<Hurt you, Penny? Oh, my dear, do you not sense how special you are to me?>

Penny felt faint. She began to tremble. The trembling spread to her thighs and her legs, then her whole body began to shake.

"Where is this place? What's happening here?"

His voice was the same soft voice she had heard before, in the rain-drenched street when she had seen the monster come out of the caravan. <It is the place you have long been seeking.>

"The City Below?"

<Indeed.>

"It's . . . awesome. Terrifying."

<But beautiful, too—don't you think?>

"Yes. Yes—it is beautiful."

His calmness scared her. <Yours is a rare mind for a human. There is so much for you to learn, but I'm sure that you will not disappoint me. I know that you have always felt isolated from your fellow humans, surrounded by those who did not understand you. Who in this world can see, as you do, into four or even more dimensions?>

Penny wasn't sure what he meant. "Why am I important?"

<Why?> He laughed. <I could speak to you about beings that called themselves Arinn. Their minds must have been even rarer than yours.>

"Nobody cares for me other than Gully."

<Your street urchin friend—I know.>

"Nobody has ever seen me as special."

<Well then—tell me what you make of this.>

Her mind was invaded by black discordant shapes constantly changing, as if being reborn again and again and again against an ash white background. There was something disturbingly organic about the shapes, as if the clots of black were being torn from a living organism, the rent fragments being constantly and violently remodelled. The vision both frightened and excited her. Her heart rose into her throat as her lungs struggled for breath. Then, abruptly, her mind felt more at ease with the dark mystery of it.

<Tell me what you see.>

"I . . . I think they are like living fractals. They are beautiful, but there is a message in their changing beauty. I'm trying to understand the message."

"I'm certain that you'll succeed."

Her instinct was to let her mind go perfectly blank, then she willed her blank mind to be completely taken over; willed it to be consumed by the strange, metamorphosing images. She made herself focus on a single fractal, following its changing shape and pattern as it writhed and twisted in every axis within the glaring ether of white. Her concentration was unrelenting until she had grasped the wholeness of its existence in three-dimensional space. And then she did the same to another, close by, and then another.

She watched the shapes blend and change, and blend and change again. She saw how the sum of the metamorphoses of the individual fractals become one with the entire swarm. Then she understood. The triumph of revelation shuddered through her, exalting her mind, her spirit.

She clapped her hands. “They’re blueprints.”

<Indeed they are.>

“Blueprints for what?”

Jeremiah stopped speaking mind-to-mind and spoke gently into her ear. “Something that will fascinate you. Come—the makers are waiting for you.”

He was referring to the huge slug-beings. Their bodies undulated with waves of movement, their relatively large but simple heads had sets of exquisitely sharp teeth, which were assembling what looked like fibrils made out of a very fine blue-black wire. When she looked closer, she could see that their side-mounted jaws were actually spinning the fibrils, joining columns of crystals together.

“They are called Akkharu.”

“What are they?”

“The Akkharu are creative beings. They mine the most precious secret in this world, or any other. They have no name for it, such is their reverence for it, but you might regard it as stardust.”

Penny stared, her eyes wide. She wondered if she had heard the words correctly. *Stardust?*

Some of them were weaving bubbles, in which other creatures seemed to be cocooning themselves.

Others were weaving whole strings of *gigantic* bubbles which, when they coalesced together, became tunnels, which were then further refined and strengthened by ribs and barbs of the same crystalline substance—the stardust.

By now she was assimilating the black, changing images, reconstructing their instructions within her mind and interpreting the three dimensional geometry that was emerging from them. She saw the instructions become reality, the crystalline structures—the dreams of the makers—appeared and changed in three-dimensional space, and then shadows emerged from them that extended into . . . other dimensions!

"Do you like what you see, Penny?"

"The Akkharu—they're architects," she marvelled. "They construct with their minds because the crystals follow their thoughts. I think . . . Oh, there's only one word for it. They're magicians."

"Magi."

"A whole race of magical beings."

"Only a mind as beautiful as yours would perceive it."

"I feel the need to capture it—to draw it."

"It is enough to paint it in your mind, to savour its elegance with your senses. Your mind sees what is, not what your human nature would make of it. The language of the Akkharu is related to what your people would call creativity. You understand it effortlessly, naturally and instinctively."

"I still don't fully understand it."

"That's because you try to understand it in words. It cannot be understood in words—it is enough that you can admire its manifold dimensions."

"What does the name of these magi mean—Akkharu?"

"In your language, the closest concept might be the same as a dreamcatcher, but it might also be taken to mean dreamstealers or dreamweavers."

To Penny the notion of a dreamstealer was frightening. It reminded her of ravenous monsters from the more unpleasant fairy tales. She preferred the idea of dreamweavers. How wonderful to weave architecture out of one's dreams! She felt a wave of delight sweep through her.

"Oh, now they're singing."

"What you hear is their hymn of creation. The dreams enter, become common to the weave, and through the weave the stardust is woven into the fabric of *being*."

Penny was aware of a growing sense of wonder. She watched some smaller creatures, perhaps baby Akkharu, spin shapes with walls that were thinner than gossamer. They took joy in invoking starry or radial symmetries; objects of great beauty and charm that floated in air, like children playing with soap bubbles.

"They are wonderful. Yet still I don't understand—why are they here? What is it that they are constructing?"

"You know it as the City Below."

"But what is its purpose?"

"Soon you will understand."

In that instant he turned into the figure of her father, but the image of her father retained the all-black eyes. She stared at him, dumbstruck. The trembling had never gone away and now it was more violent than ever. Her throat tightened, making it hard to speak. Her left thigh was jumping as if she had climbed a very tall building.

"Who—what are you, really?"

His voice had changed, too. His voice was the voice of her father. "You might regard me as your adoptive parent—a mentor." He brushed a finger over her broken nose.

"Oh!"

"Surely you remember, Penny. The summer house, the one place you could be alone, the one place you called your own. You could escape from Mother and me, wind the big lever and follow the sun."

One special day, above all, she recalled. A sunny day, with the golden light flooding in through the dust on the panes. Penny felt the pain ease as her nose healed.

"I remember."

Penny had never been able to talk about her life to anybody before, but the growing feeling of intimacy with Jeremiah was soothing and the growing halo of lights so calming, she felt she could talk to this figure that had borrowed the face of her father. Indeed, she felt that she must talk. As she was speaking to him, now, she saw the memories so clearly within her mind it was as if she had returned to inhabit them.

"There is no meaning here," she saw her younger self strike her breast. "There is no welcome anywhere for me." She saw herself drop her head into both her hands.

"In your mind, in your heart, you have known loneliness and alienation. But soon you will discover tranquillity. You will discover your destiny."

The trembling worsened. It felt as if her entire being had been caught up in an irresolvable conflict for all of eternity.

"I don't believe you. I think you are going to hurt me."

"No."

"There was a man. He . . . He . . ."

"I saw what happened. I helped you to escape him. I promise you that nobody will ever hurt you again."

"What will happen to me?"

"You will become my avatar in your world. You will do and see extraordinary things. You will be adored as a goddess."

Penny felt faint.

His hand reached out to steady her, resting on her left shoulder. In that light contact she sensed the immense power in him. Awe overwhelmed her.

"What must I do?"

"Can you remember what you asked yourself that special day, when you were alone in the summer house?"

"I . . . I wondered why we existed. If there is no meaning to it all, no purpose, as Father insisted, why spend all those years and years at school? Why struggle to find a job, struggle to support a family, and then die? It isn't worth it."

She had thought a lot about that. She had wanted life to mean something, to be worth the bother of living.

Penny was aware that a lot of people her age talked about fate, about what they thought they were on the Earth to do, but she didn't believe a word of it. Sometimes, like when she was reading about people who had fought to achieve something—like great explorers, or composers—she would come across passages where they talked about the place their life was headed. They really believed they had been born to do a certain thing—they wouldn't be chopping and changing their mind in a day, or a week, or a year.

"Do you remember arriving at your decision?"

"Yes." It was the great moment, the ultimate decision in her life. "It was when they were sending me to university. I knew they wouldn't like me there and that there would be no summer house to escape to. So I decided that I would run away—to London."

"Do you remember why you ran to London?"

"To discover my destiny."

"Now you realise that you have always been coming here to discover your City Below. You know that you were right in the decision you made all by yourself, on that fateful day in the summer house. There really is a City Below. It's your city, Penny. It's the place you have been coming to, all your life."

"It feels different to how I imagined it would be." She sensed the earthiness, the strangeness and the magic . . . that was what she had hoped for. That was what she had prayed she would find when she was drawn towards that blue light. The calling that had made her leave home and come to London was her desire to discover a kind of truth. A truth that would tell her what life was all about, what mattered to her and what would give meaning to it all.

"But why are you here?"

"That isn't the question you really want to ask me—is it?"

The question invaded her mind and it spiralled endlessly within it. The question was: *Why am I here?*

"There's something happening right here in London. I sense it. I sense that something really big is about to happen."

"What you sense is the coming war."

"War?"

"Your world—this world—has involved itself in a very ancient war taking place on another world. It has taken sides against me. In doing so it made an enemy of me."

"I don't understand."

"It wasn't a very prudent thing to do—not for a world that has become ultimately dependent on machines."

Penny felt herself tense up. She felt her lips tremble again. "What will you do?"

"I have done it already. It was begun long, long ago, when the Akkharu manufactured a weapon of magic—a sword."

"A sword of magic?"

Penny thought about that for several seconds. "What do you want of me?"

"Of you, of this city, of your imagination? Nothing. I have brought you here to bequeath it to you, Penny. I will make you queen of your City Below."

"But you will hurt people."

"I don't have your concerns for humans."

"Why—why do you hate us?"

"Like you, Penny, I have dreams. Certain people from your world are attempting to end my dreams."

"What will you do?"

"It is already begun. You have seen one of my servants at work—the people in the caravan."

"The monstrous creature—Shedur? You never told me what its name really means."

"Hunger. It is a destroyer of worlds."

"I don't understand."

"You saw how it reproduced."

"Reproduced?" Penny was reluctant to visit that terrifying scene, even in her mind. The creature of smoke with all the heads ate people up. Then she had seen how it had broken up so each head was surrounded by its own little cloud of smoke.

"But how could that monster possibly serve you?"

"You saw it give rise to sixty-four beings, each the fruits of its original hunger. And each of those began the cycle again." He paused, allowed her to look directly into his all-black eyes. "There is a beautiful, if cruel, mathematics to it, Penny, as you will already have calculated in your extraordinary mind."

"The sixty-four will give rise to four thousand and ninety-six."

"When the cycle will begin again . . . and repeat itself again and again."

"The people, the army, will stop it."

"Do you really think that their guns, their machines of war, will overcome the power of magic?"

"That's what you—through the Akkharu—are creating here. You are creating a weapon of magic."

"You do not disappoint me." He—it, perhaps—smiled. It was a frightening smile.

"How can you do these cruel things?"

"Do you imagine that humans are not cruel?"

"I thought . . . I thought you were offering me something wonderful."

"Oh, but it will be wonderful. You will discover truths that even your most learned would have died for."

Penny didn't want to be part of some plan that hurt people. She found it hard to think. She didn't know how to deal with what was happening. She felt a clutch of panic invade her stomach. Tears welled up into her eyes.

"Are you concerned about your City Above—the city you have been venerating in your art?"

"Yes."

"I will save your city—if you will serve me."

The tears were streaming down her cheeks.

"I don't want them to hurt Gully."

"Your street urchin friend?"

"I know they're hunting for me—the Skulls. He'll be much easier to find. Our Place won't be safe for him any more. I don't want anybody to hurt Gully."

He turned those terrible all-black eyes on hers. "And if I promise to save your friend?"

She hesitated. She could barely whisper the words: "I . . . I will do what you want me to do."

"That can't be an easy thing for you to promise."

"No."

She felt so faint she might have died. She might have preferred it if she had died.

He put his arm around her shoulders. He was still wearing Father's body. Neither of them spoke. Then the landscape disappeared. They were hovering as if weightless under a black sky over a white empty space. She saw him extend large diaphanous wings. The wings should have shocked her, but she accepted them without question.

"We're flying!"

There was a part of her that exulted in the fact that she was flying through veils of light and dark, oblivious of what was to become of her or where she was heading.

The Birthing

Kate attempted to open her eyes, but her lids were sealed shut. A jolt of alarm shot through her. She struggled to scream, but her lungs felt solid, as if laden with concrete. *Help me . . . Help me . . . I can't breathe.* A well of nausea rose from her stomach. She needed to retch, but her stomach, her gullet, even her mouth were full . . . *Not full . . . My mouth, my throat . . . they're blocked.*

Memories of where she was . . .

Oh, lord! I'm back in the Momu's chamber. I'm trapped within the roots of the One Tree.

The need to scream rose in her again.

Those things . . . the creatures . . . they had fed her and kept her oxygenated. She could still feel them crawling through her open mouth. A stream of tiny living creatures, packing her mouth, lungs.

She was attempted to gasp for breath, but she couldn't even do that. She could neither move, nor retch nor breathe. All she could do was try to suppress her rising panic. She had to think, to remember what had happened. The dying Momu . . . The journey the Land of the Dead, the terrifying cathedral of lost souls, the serpent-dragon Nidhoggr.

<Granny Dew!>

She screamed her need with every fibre of her being.

<The oraculum, child!>

<The oraculum?>

<Let it happen—what must be.>

The power in her exploded. Her body twisted and turned, writhing in a furnace of green flame. She tore herself out of the blazing fragments of dirt and roots, vomiting the writhing a stream of living bodies out of her stomach and gullet and mouth. It took several wretched minutes just to clear her vital organs and tubes. All the while she huddled in the dirt on hands and knees, her fingers clawing the hot ashes of her own conflagration from her face. Her mouth and nostrils streamed as the final creatures were ejected in fits of retches and coughs and sneezes. Her clothes had been ripped to shreds. Staggering to her feet she felt as thin as a scarecrow, but inside her, in every tissue and organ, every living cell, the Second Power was rampant. When she gazed at her hands and turned them over, they were marbled with livid green. Her flesh glowed and pulsed with the power of the oraculum.

But there was something still to do.

She tore away all that was left of the singed rags that still clothed her and, still gasping, she looked around, flaring her oraculum to illuminate the fire-blackened chamber. The grey, flat outline of the birthing pool and the decayed remnants of what had once been the fleshy branches and roots of the Tree were still. A tremble, registered through her bare feet, warned her that the walls and streets and caverns of Ulla Quemar were collapsing. The city was being reclaimed by the ocean that had once succoured it.

I must act . . . Do it—now!

She put as much power as she could command into her voice: "Elaru! Are you still here? We have little time."

No reply, but why should she be surprised. Was not Elaru the alter ego of the spirit of duplicity, Urale?

"If you abandon me now, I will feed you, the scheming pair of you, to the hunger of Nidhoggr. You will be permanently subsumed to chaos." Kate felt the power of the oraculum flare again, but this time it exploded throughout the chamber, invading roots, trunk, branches. She called out again.

"Granny Dew!"

<In your spirit, child!>

Kate remembered: she had subsumed the soul spirit of the dying Momu. She looked at the chamber, where the green pulse of life was surging back into the One Tree. Where was the body? With a cry of panic she scoured the reviving roots with her oraculum. A whirlwind of green swept over the ground, blowing fragments of burnt wood, ash and scorched dirt away.

There!

Kate stood before a pit in the dirt, where the giant figure lay withered, still half enmeshed in the burnt and shrivelled roots. She looked so wan, so unmoving, she could have been dead already. But Kate would have known, she would have sensed the death of the Momu within her soul spirit.

<Ach! The Momu must produce the daughter-child.>

"I . . . I don't understand."

<The birthing pool.>

"But how do I make that happen?"

<You do not.>

Kate moaned with frustration. "For goodness sake—what am I to do?"

She threw herself onto the body within the pit of dirt and ash and hugged it to her breast. She attempted to drag the Momu towards the pool, but even in her emaciated state, the Momu was too heavy for Kate to move without help. She sat in the cinders and dirt and wept.

"Help me—Elaru! Granny Dew! Somebody!"

A dishevelled and emaciated body squeezed through the broken doors and into the chamber. Kate's eyes glanced across the grey murk of the soot-filled air, unable to make out who it was that was wading across the birthing pool, followed by a rising wash of sea water—the ocean that was now flooding the streets and hidden chambers of Ulla Quemar.

"Greeneyes!"

Kate wasn't sure if she really had heard the voice. It was little more than a moan creeping into her terrified mind. But it was a familiar voice, soft and musical.

"Shaami? Shaami—is it you?"

As he came closer, the face and the eyes looked like Shaami's, but there was little resemblance to the childish face Kate remembered. This figure was taller, the features thin and wasted. And yet the voice . . .

"Shaami! You've survived."

He had waded to her side, but looked too exhausted to clamber out of the pool. He looked around, a mixture of grief and wonder filling his turquoise eyes.

"Is anyone else left?"

"Some warriors, they are hard to kill. When they went berserk and sacrificed all, I hid and waited. I waited for so long I had given up hope."

Kate reached out to help the dripping figure to climb out of the water. "Oh, come here. Let me hug you."

"You are afire, beloved Greeneyes. The light of your bravery is illuminating the entire chamber."

Kate was blinking away tears, thinking furiously. "If the Momu must produce a daughter, then you . . . It must also need you, Shaami?"

"Yes, I must be the seed."

His body felt as light as a ghost as Kate threw her arms around him, one naked emaciated body embracing another. He sighed. "Is she . . . Is the Momu . . . ?"

"No—her spirit survives in me." Kate released Shaami from her embrace, then took hold of his skinny shoulders. "Do you have any strength left? Can you help me to get the Momu into the pool?"

"I will try."

As they attempted to slide and manoeuvre the long, wasted body over the ash-strewn ground, the reclaiming ocean came to their aid. It flowed around the body of the Momu, lifting it so it became almost as weightless as her dying spirit. As the Momu floated into the pool, the crystal about her breast began to glow, faintly at first, but in slowly rising pulses. *The crystal!* Kate switched the focus of her oraculum onto the crystal as she and Shaami waded out into the middle, where the water was also beginning to pulse in time with the crystal.

"Shaami—help me to bring her head against my breast."

Kate felt the body of the Momu come to rest against her own, her upper back against Kate's belly and legs, and her brow just below Kate's chin. Cradling the elongated head within the embrace of her arms, her hands cupped the Momu's chin, Kate bent forward to kiss the brow. Then she turned the oraculum inwards, searching for the soul spirit of the Momu within her own being. She found it, sensing little more than a whisper of life. Kate kept a firm hold of that wisp of hope at the focus of her being, then turned the force of her oraculum onto the Momu's crystal again, pouring green fire into its pulsing matrix.

She whispered, her lips close to the brow, her mind in touch with the mind of the Momu. "The Tree of Life is cured. Here in the chamber, the One Tree is recovering. Now you must find what little strength is left to do what is necessary."

She heard Shaami's cry.

A turquoise light diffused into the water around the figure of the Momu.

Kate felt a shiver run though the flesh of the Momu as it withered and dissolved, but it wasn't the release of death. In that same moment Kate felt her own soul spirit swell and grow, even as the face she cupped started to shrink. She watched it become tiny, vulnerable within the fold of her cupping fingers. The entire pool glowed with a shimmering mother-of-pearl opalescence.

Kate felt her own being pervaded by the thrill of change. All around her the water of the birthing pool became alive with darting movement and an apparently rapacious feeding. A swarm of tiny beings darted everywhere like tadpoles, mouths clicking in a feeding frenzy on the crustaceans and other tiny creatures that had formerly been food for Kate. Tiny limbs whirred with movement, their bodies covered with the glittering reflections of what looked like shells.

"What are they, Shaami?"

"Milawi."

The darting, hunting movements were all around and over Kate's skin. She recalled the discussion around the pool in the City of the Ancients. The Gargs had called the Cill the people of the shore. If ever she needed reminding, the Cill were not human. They were an amphibian race that were one not only one with the shore, but also with the tide. Kate heard the faintest of keening sounds. It might have been the beginnings of the song of the Cill, but this was more primitive, a sound made through gills between creatures bearing shiny carapaces, with the big eyes of octopuses and tiny feeding tentacles. Then she heard a different cry—a deeper, strangely musical one. She could not fail to recognise a baby's cry.

"Oh, blessed mother!"

Kate was cradling the New Momu, a strange and willowy baby, in her arms. Already it was as big and as heavy as a human child of two years. In the background Kate heard a growling acknowledgement emerge from Granny Dew.

Kate said: "Did she know, the Momu, before . . . ?"

<She gave herself so that her people might survive, but that sacrifice would have failed had you not the courage to confront the Tyrant for her sake. You have confounded his plans in Dromenon. Yet even your combined courage will have availed you naught if you fail her now. The new Momu needs your help to make all that courage and sacrifice worthwhile.>

The new Momu!

Kate felt her body rise as the pool deepened with the incoming tide. She threw her arms around the baby, still curled up in its foetal embrace with its eyes tight shut, the Momu's crystal dangling around the baby's throat.

"Shaami, you might survive the ocean, but I won't—and I doubt that she would at this stage. We have to get out of here."

The head and shoulders of Shaami surfaced beside Kate. The delicate fan-like fronds were opened wide over the dome of his head, gills that enabled him to breathe under water, now sheening with rainbow reflections like a freshly opened shell. His turquoise eyes were shining with panic. "I fear there is no way out. The chambers that would normally allow entrance or exit are all flooded. The water seals have lost their purpose."

Kate heard an almighty crack, followed by a resounding, echoing thunder. She turned to discover a squat triangular shadow lift a heavy staff in a grimy fist. Granny Dew struck the stony wall of the cavern with her staff again, pausing a moment as if harking to the thunderous echoes for signs that only her ears were attuned to. She struck the wall a third time. There was a much louder, thunderous crack and the wall of the cavern split open, the rocks cleaving into a fissure wide enough to allow entry. But entry to what?

<Pah!>

The all-black eyes in that heavily lined face glowered back at Kate and Shaami and the newborn Momu. A wider glance around the Momu's chamber warned

Kate that the roots of the One Tree were writhing and moving, the trunk and the boughs filling and swelling, the fleshy leaves sprouting into new life. She glimpsed the presence of others: a new danger breaking through into the chamber from the ruined city.

<Quickly, child! It is time to flee!>

"But where can we go?"

<The ways of beginnings.>

"What?"

<The ancient ways, where the ancestors came to hide from the Great Witch, long, long ago.>

Kate felt a powerful body crash into her own. An arm, hard as iron and carapaced with a thick iridescent shell, lifted her off her feet. Her breath was squeezed from her lungs. Turning to look behind her she saw the ugly, elongated skull of a Cill warrior, its eyes glaring with madness. It thrashed out with its webbed feet and one free arm, hauling her through the water of the pool into which the roots of the One Tree were already invading, quickly, thickly, as if intent on filling the entire chamber before it was filled by the arriving ocean.

"Shaami! The baby!"

"Greeneyes!"

Thrashing within the iron grip of the warrior, Kate was forced to hold her breath as she was borne through the widening fissure, already several feet under water. As her terror rose, her face submerged within the moving torrent, she heard a musical exclamation, mind-to-mind. It didn't sound like Shaami's voice. The mind she sensed was inchoate, a confusion of curiosity and terror and dawning awareness. Kate had been expecting the growth to be more gradual, more like a human baby only recently emerged from its mother's womb, its mind empty of anything other than the need for nourishment, love, sleep. But this baby was already different and much more aware of the world—a fury of growing sentience.

Kate's face broke the surface of the water and she gasped for breath, aware that they were being swept along through a system of winding tunnels. Still gripped by the powerful arm of the warrior, they were carried along by the churning rush of water. But she had not been harmed, if anything the warrior's arm was holding her head above the racing current. Was it possible that the warrior had recovered his senses with the birth of the new Momu? That he was in fact protecting the baby and the nurturing arms that held it—Kate herself?

She realised that her terror of drowning was not shared by the swell of life within her arms—a presence, however naïve, that appeared to be growing stronger by the moment. Kate squirmed within the powerful grip of the carapaced arm, loosening her arms sufficiently so she could turn the baby around to face her. The eyes in that beautiful elongated oval of face were crinkling open.

"Oh, baby Momu—I'm here!"

The response of the new Momu was not in words but in pure musical tones of delight. Kate watched as those beautiful mother-of-pearl disks irised slowly wider, then slowly closed.

It was the Cill greeting: a way of saying so many more things in a single gesture than could be expressed in words alone.

Return to London

The Mamma Pig trundled out of the Tudor farm at noon, its metalwork decorated with the abstract blue and grey of paramilitary camouflage and emblazoned with the Tyrant's triple infinity on either flank. The heavy wheels cut deeply into the mud as Cogwheel directed it between tall sandstone gateposts and into a maze of winding lanes. The cab was so high they could peer over the hawthorn hedges and into fields dusted with snow, which still fell and blustered around them thick and hard, like a swarm of gnats. Luckily, visibility was still okay up to about a hundred yards ahead. Sharkey had had to be left behind, nursing the wound to his neck, so Mark and Nan had taken charge of the Minimi machine guns within the body of the Pig, though Mark intended to rely more on the Fir Bolg battleaxe when it came to close quarter fighting. Cal and Bull operated as scouts, riding BMW R1200s up front and behind. They were disguised as Skulls and armed with the MP5s, which were stored for action in leather holsters slung from the front of their saddles.

"You're all lunatics." Tajh had said at the meeting last night, but she had still shaved Cal's head before decorating the bare skin with a mock triple infinity tattoo. Her face had been drawn, and she had been so nervous her fingers were shaking.

"Good job you're not shaving me throat," Cal had said.

She snorted then, pulling his head roughly to where she wanted it. "It's not a plan. It's a bloody suicide mission."

Mark could understand the strength of Tajh's feelings. The plan was so full of holes it didn't bear close scrutiny. They just didn't know what they were heading into. They had little or no intelligence other than the fact that Grimstone was holding a major celebration that afternoon at an arena near central London—and the likelihood was that Padraig would figure in it. They were all charged up from drinking coffee and Mark had a migraine-like headache from the combination of all that caffeine and too little sleep. However they worked on it, the mission was subject to contingency. Tajh was absolutely right; it carried enormous risk. So much risk that Mark hadn't felt like talking about it with Nan when they had been alone. He had just hung about in a pensive silence keeping an eye on the worsening weather. To start with there had been sleet and then, an hour or two before the dawn, snow.

Made no difference, sleet or snow. And there was nothing like standing out in the cold morning air to clear your head.

He had helped Cal and Bull set up the heavy Minimi at the rear of the Pig, together with half a dozen spare belts of ammunition. From time to time Cal's eyes met his with the suggestion of a mocking smile. Mark stood on the step and had a glance at his face in the Pig's side mirror. His short-cropped hair was standing to attention. Damn—he had more hair on his chin. It was the face of a stranger. Even his eyes looked different: the gaze of a man who had already seen too much to ever accept things at face value again.

The triangle in his brow was quiescent, a brooding absence of light. It had moulded itself so closely to his skin that its black gloss could have been a birthmark if it hadn't been for the sparks of strange life within it; the moving and metamorphosing arabesques that pulsated with his heartbeat.

Back to London, then. Back to those streets where he had witnessed the strange green glow and the swarming, hungry spectres.

"The timing has to be perfect," was Cal's brooding comment to Mark as they prepared to set out. He passed the red-highlighted route map through the cab window to the disgruntled Tajh.

The Mamma Pig had to slip into central London—if *slip* was an appropriate word for a vehicle as big and heavy as a tank—to arrive at the arena at about 2:30 p.m. *Perfect timing, my arse!* Mark had thought. By the time the convoy of Pig and two bikes nosed into the outer reaches of the south-eastern suburbs, they would have just half an hour to spare.

But, by the time they got there, they could see that any chance of a quiet entry had gone up in smoke. Whole blocks were burning in a new, monster Razz. The mayhem continued through the ravaged streets as they rumbled closer to the inner city, with Razzers setting up roadblocks to loot vehicles. Cogwheel had to veer and swerve and use the giant guillotine blades on the front of the Mamma Pig to smash through blazing barriers and mob-organised obstructions, until they were within half a mile or so of their initial target: the looming bottleneck of London Bridge.

Up ahead, apartment blocks on either side of Great Dover Street were ablaze and a maniacal gathering was taking place at the junction with Borough High Street. Cogwheel idled next to a public house, painted green and cream, under a street sign with forks going left to Southwark and right to London Bridge. The snow was not letting up. If anything it was thickening and beginning to settle even in the warmer city streets. Smoke issued from the gaping door of the pub and flames were licking out through the broken windows. Trees blazed on the broad pavement in front of a red-brick church with a big sign running along its side, LUNCHTIME RECITAL. A magnificent white steeple, complete with a clock face, soared out of the smoke and flames just before a crush of vehicles that obstructed passage through the junction up ahead.

Over the radio Cal asked if they wanted him and Bull to clear a way. Tajh shouted into the radio com, "Don't even think about it!"

Cogwheel whistled. "It's unbelievable—the numbers of Razzers. You don't want to be stopped on a bike in the middle of those bastards."

The traffic lights up ahead were still functioning, though nobody was taking any notice. The jam of vehicles—mainly armoured cabs and trucks—wasn't held up by the lights, but by a blazing barricade, and the drivers were suffering the Razzers' attentions. As they watched, one of the cabs burst into flames.

Cal's voice on the intercom: "Molotov cocktails!"

Cogwheel called out over his shoulder, "Okay, folks. That right hand lane is beckoning. Hold on tight."

Mark peered ahead over both Tajh and Cogwheel's shoulders. No vehicles were coming through from the other direction. Revving the heavy engines in low gear, Cogwheel crashed the Mamma Pig through the central road barriers and bumped and rocked their way out onto the opposite lane, accelerating along the wrong side of the road towards the barricade. The two bikes fell into single file behind the Pig, hanging onto its tail. The world around them became a maelstrom of broken metal, screaming lunatics and petrol-stoked inferno.

Then, somehow or other, the Pig was through and the broad outline of London Bridge filled the oncoming view.

"We're being followed," Nan shouted from the back.

Mark joined her in looking out of the rear porthole and saw a black van thirty yards behind them, rapidly catching up. "Shit! We've got to deal with them here. We can't afford to draw attention to ourselves nearer to the arena."

They were about a third of the way across the bridge when Mark flung open the rear flaps on the Pig and used the heavy Minimi on the swivel stand, firing it at the van. A stream of fire ripped the cab of the van apart, rupturing the tyres and causing it to veer to the right. The van flipped over onto its side and its momentum caused it to slide, in a shower of sparks, over the broad pavement. It ripped through the parapet of the bridge and down into the river. Through the gaping hole, Mark caught a glimpse of the distant tracery of Tower Bridge.

They crossed the bridge to continue along the dual carriageway of King William Street, where they encountered a paramilitary roadblock with large blocks of concrete and an armoured vehicle obstructing the left hand turn at the top. They were forced into bearing right onto a curving track through towering ruins. Cogwheel thundered left and then right in low gear through defunct traffic lights.

"Bloody hell!" Tajh exclaimed. "I don't believe it!"

Mark came forward to look over her shoulder. A whole district, at least half a mile square, had been levelled to the ground.

Tajh said, "You think there's a pattern?"

Mark grimaced. "Who knows?"

"Shit!" Cogwheel was staring out into the cleared space, which was thickening with Razzers. "There must be thousands of them."

"Tens of thousands, more like."

"What are they doing?"

Tajh stared. She threw open the forward flap and then they heard them. "They're chanting." The noise was thunderous, deafening.

<Mark—do you sense what I am sensing here?> Mark heard Nan's whisper, mind-to-mind.

<Nan, we're sensing it calling—we're sensing the Sword!>

It felt powerful, overwhelmingly so. The Sword was calling, seducing the Razzamatazzers. Just like it had drawn in the feeding spectres that Henriette had shown him.

"Heading left," Mark heard Cogwheel's cry.

It felt like dusk as they entered a smoke-obscured side street. There were no scurrying hordes of Razzers and no armoured cabs or trucks. They made another turn to find themselves in a curving street. There was a street sign bent into a right angle that read MONUMENT in one direction and LONDON BRIDGE in the other, but there was no telling where it had originally pointed. They passed a gang of Skulls running from the arcaded entrance to a shopping mall underneath a seven- or eight-storey hotel. Scaffolding screened the entire front of the building. There was a series of explosions, followed by shattering glass, then the lick of flames in the windows high above them.

The Pig paused, shaking them with its throbbing, as Cogwheel considered a temporary road sign that warned against any right turn entrance onto the upper reaches of King William Street. He ignored it, forcing his way out into traffic again.

They were back on track, but the Pig was forced to screech to a halt close to the burned-out Bank Tube station. Mark's phone sounded. He put his hand on Cogwheel's shoulder, and called out:

"Stop."

A bespectacled ragamuffin figure emerged from the ruin, running headlong through the half inch of snow. A tall, matronly figure leaning on an ebony walking stick watched him run from the doorway into the ruin.

"Hey—shit!"

Tajh threw open the cab door on the passenger side. Mark called out past her. "C'mon, Gully. Jump in!"

They hauled him in by the seat of his jeans, manhandling him past the cab and over the seats into the back.

"No sign of Penny?"

"Nah! She's gone!"

Nan took charge of Gully. "You look half starved. Do you want something to drink—some coffee or water?"

Gully shook his head. His eyes were puffy as if he'd been crying. "I . . . I got the picture. Wot Penny calls the City Below. Here on the mobile."

"Well done, Gully." Mark accepted the phone as Nan put her arm around Gully's sodden shoulders.

The Pig was moving on up into Princes Street, following the jam of other vehicles heading towards two towering cranes. Cogwheel down-geared, edging through a narrow gap of another roadblock.

"Tajh—can you get the image off the phone and onto a monitor?"

"I'll see what I can do."

Cogwheel had somehow got them to Gresham Street, passing the battered signs for the Mayor and City of London Court—somewhat redundant since there was nothing here but ruins.

"You see it now—a definite pattern?" Cogwheel accepted a lit cigarette from Tajh, who was squinting at a tablet screen.

"What is it, Cogwheel?"

"One block demolished after another. And those big cranes up ahead."

"What about them?"

"Somebody's levelling the place, but it ain't random. They're making a single big clearing—round about where the Razzers are gathering."

"But what could be the point?"

"You're the brains. You tell me."

They were held up in a queue of vehicles several-hundred yards long, leading towards the arena. The pavements on either side of the road were thronged with paramilitaries and Skulls making their way towards a series of turnstiles. The celebration was clearly limited to Grimstone's bother boys. Mark and Cal watched a minibus approach two large steel-and-wire gates to a car park. The gates were manned by armed paramilitaries. There was a delay as the minibus driver showed tickets and identification to the guard. An armoured car to one side had a cannon trained onto the entrance. The level of security indicated a frame of mind close to paranoia. Mark had no idea if the armour on the pig could take cannon fire, but given the level of security he'd already seen, he assumed the paramilitaries would also have RPGs. He caught Tajh's furious glance back at him. She didn't need to say what she was thinking, they could only hope that their forged documents would pass muster. He continued to watch as, satisfied, one of the guards clapped the bonnet of the minibus with the flat of his hand and the gates opened to allow it through, then they closed again and the guards began checking the next vehicle in line. Mark figured they had at least half an hour to go, given the queue between them and the gate.

He moved back into the body of the Pig, studying the tablet screen that had just been passed back to him by Tajh.

"Hey, Gully, come show me what you mean."

Gully came forward with Nan, her comforting arm still cradling him. He looked as if he might burst into tears at any moment.

"We've put the picture you took onto this screen. I can see it's some kind of mural with pictures and a very complicated map."

"I ain't altogether sure I can follow every bit of it—but I followed Penny's trail down to the ghost Tube station."

"Do you think she might have been heading for this arena?"

Gully shook his head. "Nah! I followed 'er footprints down there, underground." He pointed to part of the map close to the extraordinary superimposed vignette of St. Paul's Cathedral. "She went through the crack in the waterfall cave. In there, where the place was crawlin' with Grimlings."

"Shit!"

Mark returned his attention to the image on the tablet screen. The artwork—the extraordinary proliferation of overlapping images—was astonishing in its complexity and dexterity. Certain images were easy to recognise: churches, monuments like St. Paul's, Piccadilly, Cleopatra's Needle, Trafalgar Square. They were drawn with a curious distortion of perspective, as if

Penny had been able to see, and portray, something beyond photographic accuracy.

"You're going to have to help us with this, Gully."

"Penny—she can see things you and me can't. She was goin' on about someplace she called the City Below."

"What's that supposed to mean?"

"You ask me it's bonkers. Like there's this City Above an' there was this other place she called the City Below."

Mark rubbed at his brow, looking hard at the extraordinary pictorial labyrinth.

"Nan, can you figure it out?"

They stared at the images together.

Nan pressed Gully, "Are you saying there are two cities—the city we can all see and a second city underneath it, a city that most people don't see?"

"Somefink like that. Yeah."

Cogwheel spoke from his seat in the cab. "Have you guys ever heard of a palimpsest."

"What's that?"

"It's where you find one image superimposed on another—or even more than one above the other."

Mark stared at the picture again, thinking about what Cogwheel had said. The picture took up an entire ceiling. It was dense with information and images curling and crawling around the fixed points of monumental buildings, yet the whole thing was eerily beautiful and strangely alive. But it was also, clearly, a recording of Penny's vision; a vision that was incredibly imaginative and intelligent. The idea of a palimpsest made some sense. If you could imagine the old, central city as some kind of complex living whole, and beneath it a much stranger, more alien presence: the City Below. You could see, through the pictures, that the City Below was invading and overwhelming the City Above. Wheeling trails of golden stars—like force lines—interlaced, interconnected various elements of the composition. It was the most mysterious, most extraordinary picture he had ever seen.

"Gully," Mark gestured to him, "let's see if we can make out where we are right now on Penny's map. Can you make out where we are?"

Gully stared at the map. He pointed to an area with a trembling finger, the nail of which was black with dirt. Mark and Nan looked at the spot, close to the centre of the picture. The image that greeted them might have been a cleft in the fabric of a world; multitudes of the strangest, most monstrous creatures were issuing out from it and into the City Above in a continuous stream, like a swarm of wasps.

Gully prodded the screen with his finger. "I think that's where Penny was headin'. She told me there was a Grimling's nest close to Saint Paul's. She told me she had found the way to the City Below."

Mark looked at Nan in the gloom. The Mamma Pig lurched forwards again, inching closer to the gate into the arena—which, if Mark read Penny's map accurately, was directly over the cleft in the fabric of Penny's world.

The Labyrinth

<Wake up, Mira!>

Mo Grimstone came instantly awake. The voice of Magtokk was in her head as before, but this time he had addressed her by her true name, the name given to her by her birth mother.

The hackles on her neck pricked as she sat upright. But, seeing the sleeping form of the guardian Shee, Usrua, by her side, she remembered to keep the conversation mind-to mind.

<I . . . I was expecting you to come, after what happened with my mother, Mala. There's so much I need to ask you. I've barely had a wink of sleep. I toss and turn all night long, going over what we saw, what the old woman said—and the warning of the True Believer.>

<You did not speak of our journey to Alan?>

<No.>

<May I ask why not?>

<He has so much on his mind with the impending war. I didn't want to burden him with any additional worry.>

<Perhaps it was wise.>

<Oh, Magtokk—I know Mala is in great danger.>

<Mala is dead, Mo—or should I call you Mira now?>

<Mo, please—Mira is strange to me as yet. But Mala dead? I only saw her a few days ago. She had only just realised she was pregnant.>

<We visited the past, Mo.>

<I don't know if I can bear not meeting her again.>

<The past is always near for True Believers. Perhaps you will meet her again.>

<I hope so. But I don't know how I'll bear it knowing my mother is going to die just to protect me. That's why I cannot sleep.>

<A heavy responsibility has been placed on such youthful shoulders.>

Mo's head fell. There was another questions that pressed upon her mind: who was her biological father? The worry gnawed at her, like an indigestible stone in the pit of her stomach.

<Where are we going this time?>

<We must return to the Valley of the Pyramids.>

<What for? What so special about that place, Magtokk?>

<You will see.>

<Am I to be carried by Thesau—the eagle?>

<This time Thesau will not be necessary.>

<I don't understand anything of what is happening.>

<Then it is time you did. You must discover how to use the talisman that was entrusted to you before ever you arrived on Tír.>

Mo's hands went to her throat. With her eyes closed she brought the talisman to her lips. The three-headed figurine, shaped by nature from black bog oak, had been given to her by Padraig back in Clonmel, so long ago. She couldn't help shivering. She thought: *Padraig! Just how much did you know even back then? Did you have any inkling of what was to come when you gave it to me during that beautiful summer?*

When she opened her eyes again, they had arrived as soul spirits into the night-shrouded Valley of the Pyramids. Their journey had been effortless, and the landscape no longer appeared so ravaged and spoiled. It looked dreamlike and eerily enchanting when compared Mo's earlier fleeting inspection with Alan and the others.

<Why has it changed?>

<It wasn't possible to explore the true nature of this hallowed place when you were last here. You alone may witness this.>

Mo was already jittery with expectation at the thought of another dream journey in the company of the magician.

<Behold> he said.

She saw something glowing on the floor of the stony valley a short distance away. Then the strange wasp-goblins fluttered out of their stone-capped holes in the ground, their wings sheening in what she assumed to be starlight. Their faces, with the bulging multifaceted eyes, were pallid as ghosts and in the air above the vast proliferation of pyramids something strange was happening: arrays of glistening black filaments, gossamer fine and vast, streamed out of the skull pyramids, spiralling and rising through the moonlit air, reaching out into the starry firmament. They were independent of gravity, like some of the feathery fronds that soared into the oceans out of coral reefs.

<What am I seeing, Magtokk?>

<The weave of the Akkharu. Nets designed to monitor the cosmos.>

Mo tried to imagine something like the antennae of insects—such as butterflies and moths—but so vast that they could reach out and measure the night sky, like radio telescopes back on Earth.

She found that, when in soul spirit, she could move through the landscape traversing great distances at will. The thrill of that was exciting as well as frightening. Beside her, Magtokk gazed up into the streaming net, in awe at its ambition and purpose. Meanwhile, Mo's attention was distracted by a flurry of movement on the valley floor, where the vast numbers of lids they had noticed previously were now thrown wide open to the night air, spread over the entire floor of the valley, so spaced and regular that they looked somewhat like the open pores of a giant's skin. And from every pore the whirling weave erupted, so the observing net extended over the entire sky. There must have been millions upon millions of individual filaments. Approaching one of the vents, she saw dozens or more of the wasp-like creatures fanning the opening with their wings, as if ventilating the tunnels beneath.

Magtokk's voice startled her from her musing. <The eye of the weave is woven from crystals of stardust.>

Mo looked up with him into the sky. <They are magical.>

<Look for their shadows on the ground.>

It took several moments of study before Mo saw the flickering matrix he was referring to. <I see what you mean. They're not casting shadows at all. They're casting light.>

<Stardust is light's shadow.>

To Mo that sounded like a riddle. But what did it mean?

<You have a great deal to learn in so short a time. It is high time we explored the labyrinth below.>

<We're actually going down there?>

Even in soul spirit form, she sensed the heavy rug of Magtokk's arm wrap itself around her shoulder. He was already guiding her into one of the larger holes in the ground.

<I don't know if I can go there. I'm petrified.>

<Trust me. We face no danger here. If at any moment you demand it, I shall return you to your tent in the blink of an eye.>

Mo wasn't sure she entirely trusted the magician. If only the sceptical Turkeya could have accompanied her on the exploration.

<We're about to enter the labyrinth.>

<I can't see a thing.>

For all of Magtokk's encouragement, and in spite of the fact she was, at least in spirit, cradled within his arm, Mo's anxieties did not settle as they drifted down through a pit in the valley floor. There was the unpleasant sensation that they were being sucked down past the frantic buzzing of the wasp-like creatures' wings and into what felt like a dark and dangerous interior.

<Do you recall your first day at school?>

<I was utterly terrified.>

<You were but a child, now you are a mature woman. Consider yourself a scholar opening the first page of a book containing ancient and sacred knowledge.>

Mo found herself wondering what lesson she was intended to learn. The act of bringing her here suggested that there was some important message. It seemed hard to credit that this secret world lay beneath the desolate Valley of the Pyramids. As if some intelligence had read her mind, her vision opened. She glimpsed what appeared to be underground farms where worker beings cultivated a wide variety of fungi, of every size and colour and shape, in endless but apparently highly organised consortia. She focused on a single mushroom garden, gloriously coloured, buzzing with colonies of insect-like beings that tended and fed on the mushrooms, and which, themselves, fed great flocks of fatty winged creatures resembling white-haired bats. Meanwhile, the bat droppings provided fertiliser for the mushrooms. She thought: *am I witnessing an ecosystem at work?*

Now she looked more closely, many of the creatures had eyes that were reduced to balls of skin, reflecting the evolution of creatures that lived in the dark; they were blind. She glimpsed more lowly creatures that chewed on root fibres to make bedding and clothes for their young, which, from what she glimpsed, were as ugly as kangaroo embryos in their nakedness. She knew, without needing to be told, that they cannibalised their dead. It removed the need for burial, or cremation, while recycling proteins and essential minerals.

She held onto the thought: *without needing to be told . . .*

She spoke to Magtokk aloud: "Nothing here is quite as it appears. I feel I could be within the mind of a magician."

<You are within the matrix of a mind, but a common mind rather than that of any individual magician.>

It was no accident that Magtokk had become her tutor. Though he had claimed it was fated when first they met, fate could mean many things on Tír.

Already, the more mundane sights had melted away as she moved further through the labyrinth. She still had no idea where she was, or why she was there. In spite of her reservations, Mo clasped the spirit arm of the orang-utan, sensing that she was being guided through dimensions of place and experience stranger than she cared to imagine. <I'm beginning to see something new. It's like peering through smoke into a kaleidoscope of colours.>

<There is rather more to witness here than your ordinary human senses could assimilate. Accustom your senses to a more universal perspective.>

<I'm not sure how to do that.>

She felt the big hairy arm hug her closer to him. <Explore through the Torus as well as the bog oak talisman.>

Mo tried to calm her overexcited mind. She did her best to expand her consciousness so as to allow her to examine her surroundings through the two very different amulets.

<Help . . . I don't know how.>

She had expected the rough walls of a narrow burrow, or cave of sorts, but instead she found herself drifting through an immense hall of . . . mirrors? But then, no, not really mirrors . . . She had no idea, she only knew that she was flooded with powerful impressions she neither recognised nor understood. Her spirit being was drifting through veil after veil of twinkling images, like a series of frosted panes of glass that extended to the horizon of her senses in all directions.

<Oh, Magtokk—I feel bewitched.>

<The Tyrant stole the Akkharu's dream song and used it for a baser purpose. We True Believers rescued what little that remained—this single free colony, abandoned in the Wastelands, like lost children searching in never-ending despair for their former paradise.>

Mo was aware of a sense of wonder, of exaltation, so beautiful that tears moistened her eyes. <I can see stars.>

<You are seeing through the eye of the weave.>

Mo clapped her hands in delight. <Magtokk, I must know, is this a dream or am I truly seeing it?>

<It is no dream.>

<I'm floating through the Milky Way.>

<It is difficult not to be overwhelmed.>

<I want to be overwhelmed.>

<Alas we don't have time to explore even a fraction of the wonder of the Akkharu's vision.>

She said: <Why am I really here?>

Magtokk's arm was around her again, gripping her shoulders so tightly she could hardly breathe. <We have little time. We must enter the cynosure.>

Even as he spoke, Mo found her vision blinded with light.

<Here the weave converges. Close your eyes for a moment. Close every one of your senses. The talismans

will compensate. You will be less likely to be overwhelmed by it.>

When, after several minutes of acclimatisation, Mo felt able to look around through narrowed lids, she saw that she had entered an enormous chamber filled with dazzling while light. The lambency came from the floor, which was up-curved, as if the face of a minor sun were pressing into the rounded emptiness beneath her feet. Out of the resultant meniscus, a vast weave of crystalline filaments emerged to whirl and flow through every morsel of space, illuminating every crook and crevice with their shadow light.

As her eyes, and senses, became more accustomed to the ambient brilliance, Mo saw that the chamber was no cave but a vast stellate composition, its ceiling a profusion of intricate cones, like the spiny carapace of a sea urchin. And as she became even more accustomed—and observant—she saw that the weave followed the architectural conduits, rising and passing through the apical cones to the connecting labyrinth above.

<It's so beautiful—so glorious.>

<Indeed.>

Mo considered for several moments. <I think I can understand that these structures, the eye of the weave, might be some kind of astronomical instrument—an instrument of heavenly observation woven from stardust. But what's the point of it?>

<To observe the workings of the stars.>

<What are they looking for?>

<The first ripple of the change.>

<No more riddles.>

<I will speak plainly. The cycle of being is everywhere. Are we not born, live, reproduce, then die? Water falls as rain, enters the rivers, flows to the sea, evaporates to the skies and then falls as rain again. Everywhere you look, you discover such cycles. Even in the heavens suns are born, die, and are reborn. Those great cycles can be observed, the mathematics of the great changes observed and measured.>

<The Akkharu—they created this?>

<They could not have done so without direction.>

<Then it's the True Believers who are observing the change. They're directing the Akkharu through the eye of the weave, aren't they?>

<Yes.>

<Why are the True Believers looking into the stars?>

<Because they anticipate an extraordinary new cycle: the end of this universe and the birth of another. The time when—if—the Tyrant takes full control of the Fáil, will coincide with the moment of change in the great cycle.>

Mo was shocked into silence for several moments, gazing up into the night sky. <What about me? You also said I would discover my purpose here.>

<Your destiny, Mira, daughter of Mala, is to confound his plan.>

Mo considered this. She turned round in a slow circle, gazing around the giant stellate chamber of light, her senses numbed with astonishment. Then she realised that the chamber was filled with movement. Starry points of condensed light swept and swirled all around her, following the tracery of the weave.

<Magtokk—they're everywhere.>

<Please don't be frightened by them. Let the True Believers come to you, let them be one with you.>

She shivered, unable to suppress it, as the starry constellations whirled and flowed around and through her spirit. <Why? Why do they want this?>

She had forgotten the shaggy arm around her shoulders, but now it squeezed her tight to remind her. <Calm your fearful heart. Remember what you have witnessed. We can come back here to the labyrinth at any moment of your choosing.>

Fear of what was expected of her impaled Mo's heart like the coldest, sharpest splinter of ice.

<Take me out of here. Right now, Magtokk.>

<Of course.>

She felt herself flow, just like the stars, along the course of a gossamer thread of black, strung out like a silk, but constructed out of the finest crystals. They traced its course upwards through the swirling weave and through one of the spines of the sea urchin, to arrive at the bleak surface above. There they abandoned the thread as it emerged from a pyramid, there to become part of the weave that splayed against the sky.

River of No Return

The landscape rumbled with latent volcanic energy. Alan lay awake, listening to the splitting and cracking of the rocks that passed for the dawn chorus outside the tanned leather walls of his tent. How invitingly easy it had seemed when Iyezzz had flown down to warn the company that a mere fifteen leagues was all that separated them from the outer defences of Ghork Mega. A rising tide of excitement had carried them through most of that distance in a single day of hurry, through a landscape that had remained arid and windblown, but devoid of military threat. Admittedly the going had become tougher on the second day, and markedly so as they neared the fosse that brought them out into a wide gorge, the ground gritty with slag. The smell of brimstone was very strong here, just a couple of leagues distant from the defensive wall and fortress up ahead.

He had been a member of the advance party that had crept forward during the evening to scout out the defences. He had looked across a steeply-pitched gorge, perhaps half a mile wide, to the most fearsome bulwark that he had ever seen: a grim curtain wall of pitch-black rock rose a thousand or more feet high, capped by giant dagger-shaped spikes. At the heart of it was a fortress built out of the same rock, its black turrets bristling with hundreds of cannon trained down on any enemy foolish enough to come within range.

Even the approach to the defences had been gruelling: a six-mile trek over uneven ground pitted with sharp edges and chasms. How could they possibly overcome it? There had been much discussion among the advance party about potential weaknesses in the slopes to either side of the fortress, but from what he saw, the apron walls merged seamlessly with the sheer mountain slopes to either side of it. It seemed that even with an army of a hundred thousand Shee the task was going to be formidable.

He had woken in his tent while it was still dark, his mind preoccupied with the looming conflict, his thoughts going over and over in his head. To add to his worries, he remembered something from a conversation he'd had with Magtokk two days earlier. *"Your enemy is capable of great subtlety as well as ruthlessness."*

What if the Tyrant was corralling them into a trap?

As he lay awake, the light of dawn crept over his tent and he heard a low-pitched humming noise nearby, as if a fly were trapped in a bottle. He heard shouts—the warning roars of Shee. Then a series of cries . . .

Qwenqwo's head poked into his tent. "We're under attack."

"What sort of attack?"

"A swarm of biting vermin."

Alan left his tent in the company of the dwarf mage, gripping the Spear of Lug in his right hand. Not that the Spear would be much use here, but his instincts bade him keep hold of it. He looked into the pallid sky. Huge clouds of insects wheeled and twisted in the air above him. They were three or four times the size of any wasp he had ever seen and their numbers were so colossal that what sounded like the roar of the wind was actually the beating of their wings. They soon blotted out the rising sun, pitching the camp into twilight.

"Aides!" He heard the roar of the Kyra.

Alan accepted the fine veil shoved into his hands by one of the aides and threw it over his face and head, already bleeding and blistered from stings. Qwenqwo was trying to light a pipe for the benefit of its smoke, cursing and swearing under a similar veil.

"Bloody hell, there must be trillions of these things. Where are they coming from?"

Qwenqwo shook his head. "It's no accident of nature in this barren place, and too closely timed with our attack on the fortress."

Was it some kind of a distraction? If so it was the most annoying distraction Alan could imagine—enough of those stings and the bugs would put half their army out of action. He hurried ahead to the northernmost periphery of their camp, trying to make out what was happening with preparations to march on the fortress, but the air was so full of bugs he could see nothing of the landscape ahead.

"Damn! It's worse than a blizzard."

He went searching for the Kyra in the thickening swarm, discovering her not by sight, but through localising her commands through his oraculum. She was calling out to the Shee and aides, instructing them to light fires and brandish torches. It was a good idea, so Alan grabbed a flaming torch from one of the aides and waved it over his head. It had little effect beyond a few feet of his flailing arm. He spoke to the Kyra, shouting over the noise. "The enemy is up to something. I worry that we're facing a sneak attack."

"If so, we are ready for them." The Kyra metamorphosed within moments into the form of a giant snow tigress. All around them Alan saw other Shee do the same. Presumably the thick pelts were more resistant to biting and stinging than the less hairy skin, but it could only protect them to a limited degree. He saw the great cats clawing at the air and snapping all around them.

Qwenqwo said, "What of the Gargs? Can they get above them?"

"I don't think they'd be able to fly in this. We're going to have to sort things out for ourselves."

The aides were passing out more blazing torches, but it didn't help very much from what Alan could see. He probed the valley with his oraculum, turning it in the direction of the towering fortress. He sensed change there, some movement, but one he couldn't make out clearly. It felt more like a gathering thunderstorm, a force of violence invading the landscape.

The Kyra, in cat form, growled mind to mind. <I fear that you are right. This is a ploy. We cannot allow ourselves to be distracted. To delay might be our undoing. I intend to give the order to attack.>

<You have a strategy?>

<Their strength is the great tower at the centre of the fortress, where most of their cannon are located. We shall approach the vale below in a triple-headed pincer formation. The central pincer will be a feint. Our real assault will involve a lightning-fast move to their left flank. Here we shall scale the iron-black slopes, if necessary, warrior will lock with warrior to construct a ramp of ascent. Shee will clamber over Shee until we reach the summit and then we will burst centrally to take the fortress from within.>

<Okay, go for it! I'd come with you on an onkkh, but I fear the swarm would drive the animal mad. I'll follow you on foot, instead. Signal me when you are about to begin the attack, maybe when you make your central feint, and I'll join in with the power of my oraculum. But

we'll need to be closely coordinated, I don't want us to end up attacking one another.>

The Shee began their attack formation with six miles between their current position and the fortress. Alan was joined by Qwenqwo and an armed guard of one hundred Shee as he forced his own way northwards. He pressed onwards with his oraculum blazing through the long twisted blade of the Spear of Lug, cutting paths through the wheeling, thrumming swarm. His progress was very slow. He peered through the thick veil of insect bodies, his boots slipping and sliding over the inches-deep mass of writhing forms on the ground. All the while the airborne masses continued to envelop and sting them in impenetrable numbers.

The Shee army had closed its eyes for better protection. They would be led by the oraculum of Bree alone. Mind-to-mind Alan heard the Kyra order an increase in pace. He turned to look back. He could make out a glow some few hundred yards in the distance that was the vanguard—aides coming up the rear with a huge wall of blazing torches.

What a terrible risk the Kyra was taking, to go in blind under the noses of the enemy. They already knew the Tyrant had hundreds of cannon and other weaponry on the fortress wall. The Shee would draw that fire not knowing what they might face to either side of it. It demanded such bravery that he felt a lump in his throat.

I've got to find a way to help them.

He felt a hand grasp his shoulder. Turning he found himself confronted by an exhausted-looking Mo, accompanied by her guardian Shee, Usrua. Mo ignored the swarm of biting insects to take hold of his hand.

"What is it, Mo?"

"Magtokk took me to see my birth mother, Mala."

"He did what?"

"It was a dream journey, like when Qwenqwo took us back into the past at Ossierel. Tell him, Usrua."

Alan turned to look at the experienced Shee warrior. "Last night—and three nights earlier—I slept with Mo in her tent. I wake at the drop of a feather. On the first night I woke to find Mo calling out in her sleep. She spoke a name, Mala, which she now explains is the name of her birth mother."

"Usrua—Mo! I don't have time right now to talk about dreams."

Usrua shook her head. "I would not disturb you with a dream. But last night she became restless again in sleep. She cried out, more than once. Then when I sat by her I saw a star appear out of the Torus she wears."

"A star?"

"It hovered over her all the time that she was restless, as if protecting her. I believe it was the magician, Magtokk, adopting the form of a True Believer."

Even in the confusion of the insect attack, and with the Kyra and her army already heading out for the fortress, Usrua's words troubled Alan.

"Mo—what the hell is going on?"

"Magtokk took me on a second dream journey." She was apprehensive, her fingers toying with the Torus, as if seeking comfort there. "We returned to the Valley of the Pyramids. We explored the labyrinth underground."

"There's a labyrinth under the valley?"

"I was shown my purpose in being brought to Tír. I saw extraordinary things, Alan. You and I—we have to talk."

"Mo!" Alan hugged her exhausted body to him.

"It's really important."

"We'll talk. I promise you, at the first opportunity. But right now the Shee are about to attack the fortress." He turned to Usrua. "Take Mo back to her tent and seal it off from the swarm. Guard her well, every waking and sleeping moment, until we can get together again."

There was a look on Mo's face, a sense of urgency that tugged at him, but he really didn't have the time right now to talk. The Shee nodded and withdrew, with the fretful Mo looking back at him even as she was led away.

Alan felt Qwenqwo's hand on his shoulder. "Man! I don't need some additional worry about Mo when I'm already out of my mind with worry for the Shee."

"You must focus your mind on what needs to be done."

"You really believe that the bugs are a distraction?"

"I do."

Alan pressed on through the battering thuds of solid little bodies, with their stings and biting mouths.

Qwenqwo was hurrying along beside him. Alan tore the bugs out of his hair, where they were stabbing at his scalp.

He heard a command mind-to-mind. The Shee were moving forwards in three great pincers and gathering speed. Ainé's plan was so risky. He calculated just how long it would take them to cover six miles in their cat forms: perhaps ten to twelve minutes. That was how long he had to find a way to help them. He thought hard about that while still moving forward in their wake.

The Shee's battle horns were sounding out through the thrumming and buzzing. Up ahead, Alan heard alien sounds: the groans and squeals of heavy machinery. He could smell sulphur more strongly now.

Qwenqwo said, "I don't like the sound of that."

Alan didn't like the smell either. He heard the thundering of hundreds of thousands of paws beating determinedly against the stony ground.

"Qwenqwo, what can I do?"

"Use your oraculum."

"But how do I use it against the swarm?"

"Make one storm to destroy another. Remember how you controlled the elements back at the ice-bound lake."

Alan took a deep breath. He tore the veil from his head and looked up through the obscured heavens above them. He lifted up the Spear of Lug, directed its spiral blade into the sky and drew on the power of the land. The triangle in his brow flared a blood red, the fire of his power rising in a crackling sleeve of lightning to become one with the blade. The Ogham letters of magic on the spear, carved by his grandfather Padraig, burst into flame and the expanding sleeve of red lightning rose, tearing through the wheeling blizzard of flying bugs, igniting everything in its path as it burst into ground-shaking thunder. Storm clouds swelled to fill the sky from horizon to horizon, their black bellies crackling and spitting with lightning.

Staring up into the funnel of clear sky created by the rising torrent of power and lightning, he began to twist the spear in his hands, creating a vortex. There would be damage to the camp and tents uprooted and torn, but it couldn't be helped. He spun the heavy spear round and round, causing the vortex a mile or more above the ground to wheel and gather force. The gale of wind caused him to narrow his eyes as it whipped at his hair. Suddenly the focus of the swirling clouds, wracked with blood-red forks of lightning, exploded. A cyclone tore across the sky, rippling across the valley and sucking the air up into its vortex. The vast swarm of bugs were sucked up into its gaping spout, whirling higher and higher before spinning away into the distance. Qwenqwo tore the veil from his face and shouted, "Look up ahead—the fortress!"

Alan stared into the distance at a sight that made no sense. Something lurid and glowing was creeping out from beneath the black cliff wall that supported the tall angular outline of the fortress. Something glowing, fiery and red . . .

"Shit! What is it?"

"A lake of fire."

Alan used his oraculum to look at it more closely: through the forbidding vista of black rock and moiling vapours crept a broad snaking river; a seething, crackling furnace of magma hissing and spitting flames. Gases ignited from the tormented rock at its banks while with white hot wavelets moved across the molten flow—a river of no return crossed the path of the charging army.

"That's what we've been hearing and smelling, Qwenqwo. They must have dammed back the magma from an underground volcano and now they've opened the gates. They're flooding the valley."

"Mage Lord—the Shee!"

Ainé's army was thundering at full speed towards the flowing river of magma, already at least a hundred yards wide.

Alan's oraculum was flaring. He sent the vision to the Kyra, mind-to-mind, but there was no response.

"Something's blocking me. It may be the fact the Kyra has entered blood rage. I can't stop them."

"We have to stop them. They'll die—every one of them."

Alan felt a wave of panic tear through him. What could he do? He saw the moving front of the three sharp prongs of Shee, the vanguard of the columns tearing up the ground and ripping bravely through the cindery desert. They were only a couple of miles from the lip of the steeply pitched valley, seeing nothing of what flowed beneath the lip, unaware of the peril that awaited them.

A powerful explosion flared with thunder and red lightning was breaking through the blood rage that consumed the Kyra. There was a voice inside her head, the same two words, repeated over and over.

<A trap! A trap! A trap! A trap . . . > The swarm that had occluded her vision was gone, but the morning was shrouded in shadow from spreading thunderclouds that stretched from horizon to horizon, their underbellies a crackling web of blood-red light.

The pounding heartbeat of blood rage had not entirely cleared from her breast and head. Her blue eyes, wide with the glare of battle, moved their focus from the sky above to the fast approaching bend in the cinder-strewn approach. A great heat beat on her face and the pungent stench of sulphur filled her nostrils, and in her ears was that same voice in her head.

<A trap! A trap! A trap! A trap . . . >

A warning from Alan!

The Kyra wheeled in that instant and issued the order to slow all three columns. But it was too late. Rows of huge cannon discharged from the fortress and enormous steel-tipped missiles made of whole tree trunks tore lines of death through the charging Shee. Trebuchets hurled a hundred huge balls of flaming lava to tear through the approaching Shee army.

The Kyra's claws were extended into the cindery ground, eliciting a shower of sulphurous smelling dust. Three such dust clouds filled the air behind and to either side of her. She was at the lip of a river of raging lava and broiling brimstone two hundred yards wide.

Alan looked up into the storm-wracked sky. He recalled the deaths of his parents. He took his anger and the grief that remained red raw, and infused it into his actions. His need for revenge caused the oraculum to flare brightly. The runes blazed in the spiral blade of the Spear of Lug, the surge of power building. No clouds could contain the force of his lightning. The red flare turned the entire bowl of sky red even as he lowered the Spear of Lug. His entire body and directing arm became an exploding furnace of power.

In the heightened vision the oraculum gave him, Alan saw the shield wall illuminated by arcs of fire and fragments of burning rock hundreds of feet high. He struck out against the base of the gigantic fortress, carved out of the solid mountainside.

There were cries of terror all around him as the colossal force of the strike caused an earthquake that rippled back through the landscape, even through the miles of distance that separated them.

Through the eye of the oraculum he saw how the entire mountainside was collapsing in a cataclysmic deluge of rock and debris; a tide that overwhelmed the river of lava, paving it over immediately in front of where the fortress had stood.

<Now> he spoke mind-to-mind to the Kyra, <continue your charge.>

He watched the ongoing battle as the Shee charge intensified, his arm now limp by his side, though the lightning still crackled and blazed in decreasing circles around him. He saw how the landscape heaved and rippled with the living torrent of great cats that moved over it. A tidal wave of fury struck what was left of the curtain wall, racing over the fallen rock and deluging over what was left of walls and towers. The defenders crawled over the bodies of their dead, hurling themselves off the remains of the walls and fleeing from the widening fan of slaughter that was spreading outwards on either side of the destroyed fortress.

Lovesong

Kate's feet had been taken from under her by the swell of ocean pouring through the cavern. The roar of the current filled her ears. So violent was the upsurge that it was tearing rocks out of the walls and hurling them headlong into the waves. A huge boulder was carried through the stream in Kate's direction, missing her by just a few feet. Her vision blurred and her mouth and nostrils filled with brine. <I'm drowning. Save me, Granny Dew—or all will be lost even now.>

A claw, hard as a grappling hook, grabbed her by the hair, and she felt herself lifted and hauled through the onrushing torrent. The warrior was still looking after her. She felt the power in his armoured arm and saw the webbed fingers of his free hand pedalling through the ocean. The water had completely filled up the chamber of the Momu and was now pouring through the tunnels discovered by Granny Dew.

There were intervals of a second or two when she managed to snatch a breath before she found herself beneath the turbulent water again.

She was not alone. The water around her seethed with the same darting movement and rapacious feeding she had seen in the birthing pool. The Milawi! Their same frenzy of movement and excited hunting was accompanying her. Even in the bewildering nightmare of seething water Kate heard other sound: a hint of something lovely, a fairytale tinkling.

The advancing swell carried her into a huge cavern, vastly bigger than the chamber of the Momu, and the expansion was so broad and rapid that the depth of the water fell instantly. Kate felt her feet touch the bottom and for a few seconds she and the guard were able to stand, however buffeted by the rising tide. In the distance, through the green light of her own oraculum, she could make out the triangular figure of Granny Dew demanding a continuing channel through the rocks with thunderous raps of her staff of power. Kate heard her muttering words in the language of beginning, weaving a continuous, ongoing spell. Kate was exhausted by the effort of keeping her face out of the water. She had hardly recovered from her ordeal within the roots of the One Tree and now her face and her fingers, all felt numb with the freezing cold. Blinking to try to clear her vision, she used the light of her oraculum to look around. The cavern was even vaster than what she had thought from her initial impression, and so spacious both horizontally and vertically that the light of her oraculum petered out without reaching the ceiling or the distant walls. The floor immediately in front of her was littered with rocks, both large and small. Then she jerked as the surface level of the water rose again to her chest and she was unbalanced by a new swell of incoming flood, held upright by the warrior alone. His ungainly head was swivelling from side to side and his iron-cold eyes stared at the surrounding walls. His nostrils moved as he sniffed the air. Some of Kate's hair was caught up in his lobster-like claw, with its curved, overlapping blades.

Then Kate felt a sudden release.

Shaami was by her side, his hands reaching out for hers. Numbed as her skin had become she could still feel the strangeness of the absence of nails on the webbed fingers shaped for swimming. The flesh of his hands now became even softer and more gentle, a gesture of friendship. The incoming deluge was continuing, the roar of the pressure coming from deep below the surface, But Shaami was looking around the cavern with the same interest as the warrior. Kate followed his eyes to the nearby walls, which were unnaturally smooth. In the pallid light of her oraculum she thought there might even be carvings within them, and natural shapes—a suggestion of stars and prickly things, of fronds moving with the current.

"Shaami, what is this place?"

"I think it may have been the first refuge of the Ancestors."

Kate heard the awe in Shaami's voice. "What do you mean? A hiding place?"

"Where they first fled the ravages of the Great Witch. Our home before the construction of Ulla Quemar."

"What a discovery!"

"See—the histories—they are written on the walls."

His eyes were better adapted to the dark than hers. Kate could make out very little other than the size of the chamber and the suggestions of patterns.

"What a pity it will all be lost to the ocean."

"No, Greeneyes! You do not understand."

Shaami's eyes were open wide, glowing with wonder. "What does it matter to us if the ocean fills the chamber? We inhabit both tide and shore. We shall return here to cherish this place."

She had forgotten that, for Shaami, home was as much the sea as the land, yet it could hardly be accidental that they had found their way into this place. Kate realised that Granny Dew must have cleaved her path through the rock with the express purpose of arriving here.

Even as she reflected on this, the enormous chamber continued to fill with seawater. Kate feared that the eruption from the deep would begin again. It might not matter to the Cill, who could breathe underwater, but it might drown Kate herself. She heard a thunderous crack. The rock beneath her shook so violently she was thrown down onto her knees, her mouth barely above water. Then sunlight flooded the gigantic cavern, pouring in like a new incoming tide around a distant corner, and with it arrived a new stream of warmer water. Water that surged in to meet the colder stream of deeper ocean, the union accompanied by an altogether recognisable and welcome sound—the wash of tide over a beach.

Shaami's head disappeared under the surface, as if he was overwhelmed at the arrival of daylight.

Kate could now make out the walls and contents of the cavern much more clearly. High above her she could see huge stalactites of many different sizes and colours. All around her she saw the rippling streams of surface- and deep-water rush together in wavelets and foam. The level of water stabilised around Kate's lower chest, but the floor of the complex cavern had different levels. In some of the more peripheral areas, the floor was a foot or more out of the water. But there were glimpses of a more coherent structure. In places, particularly on the higher plateaus of rock, she saw broken-off sections of what might once have been the walls of buildings. Bit by bit her exhausted mind put things together. Some remnants of walls had the organic shapes of starfish or sea urchins, other fragments had the shiny surfaces of sea shells, such as periwinkles, clams or nautili. Buildings, like those she had so admired in Ulla Quemar, that took their inspiration from the organic shapes and creatures of the sea-shore . . .

Kate squealed.

Beneath the surface she felt many gentle nibbles against her skin. And when she ducked her head below the surface, in the dappled shadows she saw the shapes and colours of eyes.

A thrill of something wonderful and impossible was racing through her, causing her pulse to rise to giddy heights.

On a sudden impulse she dived under the rippling surface and swam among them. The Milawi were everywhere, darting to and fro. Her oraculum pulsed brightly, in tune with her astonishment. In its light she made out tentacles and circular mouths ringed with tiny, finely-barbed teeth. She could see hearts—three separate hearts beating within a single, semi-translucent chest wall, then there was a spreading circulation of blue blood within the same small body. In the moment or two that she beheld it, she glimpsed how bright that blood became. It was the iridescent blue of a clear Italian sky when leaving the three hearts, and the deep blue of the sky over the Comeragh Mountains at midnight when it returned. On the heads of others, of many more than she could possibly have hoped for, she saw the wide radial fans of the gills, and luminous turquoise eyes of the Cill. They were looking back at her, irising their slow expansions and contractions of friendship, while shoaling around her. Kate realised that she was the entire focus of their attention. They darted to and fro around her with a jet-like locomotion by squeezing water through the ring of their tentacles. They brushed against her, touching her skin with those tentacles and nibbling at her with sharp-toothed mouths.

<Granny Dew!>

<They grow quickly in the presence of the Second Power. In mere minutes they mature to what would have taken months in the wilds of the ocean.>

Kate's heart was bursting with excitement.

Of course, she had known all along that the Cill weren't mammals. She hadn't expected them to bring babies into the world, like humans. Now she knew that, like a great many marine creatures, the Cill's egg were fertilised in the wilds of the oceans. The Milawi were their hatchlings; feeding embryos! She was so mesmerised by the realisation that she had almost forgotten her need to breathe. She surfaced, whooping. Shaami put his arm around her, supporting her until she had recovered her breath and until her pounding heart had settled closer to normal. He pressed her forwards, helping her towards the light. They were surrounded by half-a-dozen warriors whose presence wasn't threatening, as she now realised. They were there to take care of her and him—to protect the miracle of what was about to happen.

It was a happy shrieking sound, the sing-song of children's voices, that woke her. Kate sat up, rubbing the sleep from her eyes, to look out onto a landscape full of sea and sky and sunshine. She was sitting in the shade of a pine tree, resting in a nest of feathery soft needles. The shrieking voices drew her attention down to the meeting of tide and blindingly white sand, where a large rounded hump was making its ponderous way out into the shallows. Kate's eyes followed the dimples of its tread on the sand, running from where the gigantic turtle had laid its eggs to the shoreline, where a melée of naked bodies were climbing excitedly over its slow-moving hummock. The melodious sing-song chatter of what could only be Cill children melded gracefully with the sweep of the waves over the shore and the breath of wind in the branches over her head.

Kate felt so refreshed she might have been asleep for a year and a day. And she was no longer naked. She lifted the hem of her ankle-length diaphanous silk dress, which matched the green of her eyes. Underneath the silk she discovered the softest, lightest white cotton undergarments. Her mind was a confusion of happiness and disappointment. Disappointment because she had slept through the evolution of Milawi to what, for want of a better term, were now infants, or at least the Cill equivalents.

"Shaami—it's paradise."

"A paradise, beloved Greeneyes, where we can languish in the tide and turn our faces to the sun for the first time in many thousands of years!"

Kate enjoyed walking through the soft warm sand to the water's edge, following the dimpled trail made by the turtle, to gaze out over the lagoon with its scattered islands of palm. The unmistakable shape of a sunstealer caught her eye, making a suspiciously rapid movement through the surf in her direction. She pretended to be surprised as a cluster of six or seven children broke the surface, their excited faces erupting from the water, those beautiful turquoise eyes staring up at her.

"Momu! Momu!"

Shaami smiled. "They call you Momu in their song of welcome. It is the greatest honour my people could bestow on you."

"How lovely!"

She saw gill rays retract over the domes of their heads, reduced to tattoos of stubbly lines, as they clambered out of the water. All around her, more and more of the children were emerging from the lagoon. One of the last to break the surface was a figure much taller than the others. The young Momu emerged with a slow and gentle grace under the watchful protection of the warriors. She clasped the pulsating crystal in her cupped hands, light spilling out between her long and delicate webbed fingers. Those gorgeous mother-of-pearl eyes irised slowly open and then closed. The children surrounded Kate and the new Momu, hugging them.

"Who will teach them the arts they once knew?"

"All that was known will be recovered from the crystal."

Kate recalled the terrifying circumstances in which she had first met Shaami. His delicate body had trembled with terror in the clutches of the Great Witch, Olc, in her Tower of Bones. Kate had saved him from being sacrificed to the furnace of the rising titan, Fangorath. Now Shaami had become the elder of his people.

She closed her eyes and heard an unexpected whisper, mind-to-mind. <Oh, Mistress. That I should live to hear the love-song of the Cill.>

"Elaru?"

<I am present in soul spirit only. Your goddess, Mab, permitted me this wonder. I had the honour of helping her daughters clothe you as you slept.>

Kate struggled to take it all in.

"What will become of you now? Will you have to go back to partnering that monster, Urale?"

<I fear my time has come. I begged the goddess to allow me this opportunity to ask forgiveness for the part I played in deceiving and tormenting you—and to thank you for your charity.>

"I forgive you, Elaru."

<May the fates preserve and protect you, Mistress.>

As the presence of the succubus faded, Kate was silent for several moments, gazing into the distance, her thoughts confused. She had spoken aloud, but Shaami could not have heard her mental answers from Elaru. He must be wondering what to make of her.

"Have you decided on a name for your new home?"

"Ulla Moimari—the City of Beach and Tide," he said.

"It's a lovely name." Kate hugged him for several long seconds, and then she hugged the young Momu.

"Then you are leaving us already?"

"I have called the dragon Driftwood. I must go with him without delay. The Great Witch is gone, but the danger is not over. I must return to join my friends, Alan and Mo."

They sang to her then, amid the beauty of the coral bay, and it sounded like fairy music. It was as if she were listening to the weave of nature; the delight of the flight of a butterfly, the soar of swallows when they came to signal that summer had arrived, the leap of salmon in the choppy rivers that led to their homes, the fecund, glorious warmth of summer. It was so lovely it broke her heart not to stay, to lie in the warm briny swell of Ulla Moimari and stare into the sky at the passing clouds and simply glory in the wonder of it all.

"Oh, Shaami!"

Shaami wept, as did all the children. Kate nodded, unable to speak, her eyes filling up with tears.

The Black Rose

Looking around, Mark and Nan attempted to figure out what was really going on. The so-called arena was more makeshift than they had anticipated. An entire congested oblong of the old city stretching westwards from Moorgate had been cleared, seemingly deliberately, to allow for this singular celebration. Ruthless razzamatazzing, followed by wholesale demolition, had eliminated venerable buildings, blocks and streets. An army of diggers were still scattered around the periphery, under the shadows of the two enormous cranes that had guided the Resistance there. Giant bonfires were still burning throughout the derelict wilderness to the east, and through the rising smoke they could make out the surviving shadowy outlines of the monoliths of the financial district.

Mark said: "My God—it's incredible."

They were only just coming to realise the size of the cleared space, which covered at least a square mile, over which sprawled groups of ramshackle caravans, stalls and tents teeming with Razzers.

Nan murmured. "There's a whole army of Skulls and paramilitaries gathering around the arena."

Mark shook his head, focused on an oblong of heavy vehicles immediately opposite the car park. His apprehension grew.

"I think we should take a closer look."

Nan looked across to where a gathering of generator trucks screened off the central oval, where the thunderous activity of hammering and drilling pointed to continuing construction. She squeezed his arm. "This does not make sense. Something is very wrong!"

"Just about everything here feels wrong."

Cal's voice came through the plug in Mark's left ear. "I hope you're happy, now you're here."

"Happy isn't the word for it."

"Shit, man! No chance we're going to get out of here alive."

"Let's just see about that."

"All for the sake of one old man, who might, or might not, be here."

"Padraig is here."

"You sure of that?"

"Yeah—I'm sure." Mark wished he was half as confident as he pretended to be. Nan was tugging at his arm. "Look around, through your oraculum."

Mark closed his eyes and looked through his oraculum into the surrounding landscape. The cleared area with its vans and tents and the oval where they were still cobbling together a makeshift amphitheatre, was etched with the same sickly phosphorescent green light he recalled from his earlier walk with Henriette.

He opened his eyes, gritting his teeth.

Snow was gusting again. They had gained entry at the gates with surprising ease, their false tickets arousing no suspicion. Cal assumed it was the trouble they had taken with their appearance, and the camouflage decoration of the Pig, but Mark wasn't so sure. He had left the Fir Bolg battleaxe in Cogwheel's cab, with instructions for Cogwheel to release it if it showed evidence of his calling it. And now, barely twenty feet from where they had parted from the crew, a mockery of the Union Jack flapped over an unrecognisable stubble of a monument. It felt ten degrees colder here; a fierce cold that felt alien for an English winter. Mark looked down at his hands. The hairs on his fingers were frozen erect.

"You sense it?" Nan asked.

"Yes."

"Grimstone knows we're here."

"I think you're right."

"Then it is a trap."

He sighed. "Yeah."

He recalled the feeling that had overwhelmed him when he last saw Grimstone, and recalled Nan's words, *"A furnace, like a black sun, burns inside him."*

"I'm afraid, Mark."

He hugged her fiercely and kissed her frozen lips.

"It's too late to change our minds. I know Padraig is a prisoner here. I sense it. If there's the slightest chance of rescuing him, we have to take it."

Brave words, but had Grimstone used his concern for Padraig to bring him and Nan here to their deaths? Mark's left hand had risen to touch the oraculum, burning now, reacting against the suffocating sense of evil that surrounded him.

Something was happening. Crowds were beginning to mill around them. They tried to force their way through a crush of Skulls arriving through a pedestrian access from the main car park, but the crowds were so dense they were carried along with them. A swell of panic brought a lump to Mark's throat. The weight of vicious enthusiasm pressed in on them. There was a sudden deafening roar of military music—a band practising. Mark fought to stay close to Nan. The crush took them into the oval arena with its concentric tiers of rough-hewn wood.

The oppressive sense of malice was much stronger closer to the arena. Mark was struggling to think clearly. Then they were clattering up a wooden staircase and entering the arena through a tunnel leading part way up the seating. The oval was already filling up. Mark gauged that the theatre as a whole was about eighty yards in diameter. There was seating for 30,000 or more, sloping down into a central pit covered with sawdust under a spreading layer of snow. Even as he glanced around, the atmosphere became expectant.

<Padraig—I'm coming. I'm near!>

Mark cast the thought through the force in his brow. No answer. Yet his instincts said otherwise. He was certain that Padraig was there and that he was really close.

Two young warriors swaggered into the pit. They were armed with short Roman-style swords and circular metal shields. Their heads were covered in steel helmets, with face-guards and flaps over the back of their necks, and their right arms, from shoulder to gauntleted hand, were covered in overlapping strips of leather, making the armour resemble the segmented carapace of a lobster. Their upper torsos were bare, oblivious to the cold. Their left legs, from knee to sandal, were also armoured with steel and tethered by leather straps, but otherwise, they wore no more than a loincloth under a broad leather belt. Two men dressed in togas and sandals stood back towards the periphery. One held a huge wooden mallet; the other stood by a brazier in which an iron bar glowed red.

The gladiators stood to attention and waited in the swirling snow.

There was a wild cheering and a thunderous stamping of feet on the hollow plank floor of the tiers as a group of figures entered at a measured pace from an opening in the eastern wing.

One of them took his place on a raised platform protruding over the rim of the pit. He resembled a Roman emperor presiding over the Coliseum. The man must have been forty yards from where they sat, but even from this distance Mark wilted under power that radiated from him. He smiled in their direction, a full-lipped cruel smile, as if he were fixing his eyes on Mark amongst the screaming adulation of the crowd. Then he took his seat on the rostrum.

Grimstone had arrived.

At his signal the men within the circle began fierce hand-to-hand combat. Mark had hoped it would turn out to be ceremonial, but it took barely a few minutes of thrusting and parrying before one of the combatants took a wound to his right shoulder. Blood ran down in a thick stream over his sword arm and onto the snow-carpeted sawdust. The fighting did not halt. The victor struck home a second wound, deep into his adversary's chest. Mark stared at the young man who had gone down onto one knee, his sword fallen and his shield-arm trembling. His opponent struck him with the boss of his shield so that he fell, then placed his foot against his back between the man's shoulder blades. The victor raised his sword aloft, looking in the direction of Grimstone. There was a rolling of drums and a blare of trumpets, during which Mark could see the cold expression on Grimstone's face, then recoiled in horror at the earth-directed thumb. The victor plunged his sword into the back of the neck of his defeated opponent and twisted it, with a grisly snap. The crowd roared, hungry for more blood.

Nan whispered, "It is rumoured to be the manner in which the Tyrant chooses his Legionary soldiers on Tír."

As the body was dragged unceremoniously out of the pit, Mark searched the entrances for any sign of Padraig, but he detected nothing. While he was searching, another pair of gladiators entered the pit and stood facing one another, awaiting the signal to fight. In only a few minutes the horror of ritualised murder was reenacted before their eyes. There was another roll of drums and a baleful trumpeting, and a third combat began. The two winners, already bloodied from the earlier combat, were now facing one another. The pattern had a horrible inevitability about it: the ruthlessness of the killing, the celebratory trumpets, the howling of the mob. There was no prospect of mercy for the loser. Only one of the fighters, all presumably their bravest and hardiest men, would emerge victorious.

Mark stared incredulously as the final victor knelt before the figure on the platform and raised his bloodied weapon into the air.

Grimstone stood. In his two hands was the Sword of Feimhin. The blade was glowing with power. The gathering was on its feet, chanting a hymn-like dirge in an eerily harmonised baritone that was frighteningly familiar. He remembered it from the ritualised combat between the Storm Wolves and the Shee back on Tír: the battle hymn of the Death Legion. Shock froze Mark rigid.

"Look through your oraculum," Nan whispered.

Mark closed his eyes, and opened the senses of the stone in his brow. The landscape had turned into a nightmare world of wraiths and goblins with shining eyes, razor-like teeth and gauzy smoke for hair. It was the hidden London he had witnessed in the company of Henriette. He heard her chuckling voice, *"All drawn to de Sword."*

Mark heard another throaty roar from the crowd. He saw every face turned towards Grimstone, who was raising the Sword of Feimhin with its long black blade aloft to kiss the sigil of the triple infinity in the hilt.

He spoke, his voice calm and deep. Mark could see no microphones and no loudspeakers, yet that quiet voice penetrated the large gathering through the blustering snow. How did his voice carry that far in such a large arena? With a sudden conviction borne from his experiences in Tír, Mark realised that Grimstone's voice was not exterior, but interior. He was addressing them through the power of an oraculum—which had to be the Sword. Every head in the arena was turned towards him, every mind laid bare to his words.

<My brave and fearless Legion! I applaud your sacrifice of blood in veneration of the Master. We have

witnessed the moment in the existence of the pure warrior when the divine and inexorable purpose of his life will be revealed. What else gives meaning to the meaning of destiny? What does a warrior have to contribute other than the willingness and the heartfelt joy of offering his life for the cause?>

Nan was right. Grimstone was no longer human. He had to be a Legun. And he wasn't alone on the platform, he had been joined by two additional presences—a small, slight man, with a vaguely Asian face and a neat white beard, and a girl, tall and slender, with a wild mop of tawny hair. Both faces were a little blurry, as if out of focus.

Mark heard Nan's exclamation of shock. The girl was Penny—and the man . . .

"Oh, Mark!"

"Yeah . . ."

The small man had to be the Tyrant of the Wastelands. How calm and undemonstrative he appeared. *The Tyrant*—Mark thought—*he has come to London!*

Bewildered by shock, his mind racing with the realisation of the new danger facing the crew, Mark also thought to ask himself why the Tyrant would see this pathetic, brutal circus as important. Even as he thought about it, he sensed how, with the new arrivals, a numinous explosion of power now filled the arena.

There was a movement in one of the narrow tunnels that led into the pit. A captive was being carried into the arena by a cluster of white-garbed acolytes; a lean, emaciated figure, battered and bloody. He was clearly unconscious and tethered by the wrists and ankles to a crude X-shaped wooden stretcher.

Padraig!

He felt Nan take his hand in hers.

"Is it definitely him?"

"Yes."

They saw the acolytes sprinkle the unconscious body with petrol. They stood by with what looked like flame-throwers.

Mark spoke into the intercom to Tajh. "They're about to sacrifice Padraig. We need the Mamma Pig—now!"

A power of darkness was invading his mind. He felt a stiffening paralysis in his muscles and a dulling of thought. Turning, he saw that Grimstone had lifted the Sword of Feimhin aloft again. He was directing it into the encroaching darkness of the late afternoon sky. Grimstone's face glowed with a greenish light, as if it were reflecting moonlight. Their oracula pulsing, Mark and Nan forced a passage through the crowds, heading down into the pit. An ocean of unshaven faces turned to glare at them. The Skulls and paramilitaries tried to block them with their bodies. Mark was filled with horror at the massed stupidity of so many bald and tattooed heads, the mindless obstruction of their physical presence.

Grimstone's words continued to insinuate themselves into his mind.

<Those who deny these self-evident truths profane our purpose. They weaken the purity of your destiny. Today—on this ominous and fateful day—all will glory in the flowering of that destiny, the opportunity at last of being one in heart and spirit with the Master.>

The multitude was on its feet, their eyes rapacious with hunger, every mouth agape.

Mark felt his mind reel under the persuasiveness coming from that figure on the platform. His oraculum was blazing, but even with its help it took all of his will and strength to resist the suggestibility of the Sword. Where were Cal and the Mamma Pig? Had his radio signal been received? That horrible roll of drums sounded out again, the strident trumpeting insinuating itself deep into every mind. The power of the Legun gathered force from the idolatry of the multitude under its power. The malignant spell was utterly overwhelming. Mark sensed it coursing through his own heart and spirit.

A false sun of white-green fire came into being in the swirl of snow in the air above them. It grew rapidly until it was a circle, covering the centre of the arena. Every eye was staring up at it, unblinking. The Skulls were chanting in an orgasmic slow motion, a sound that was eerily in harmony with the light. As Mark and Nan neared it, the circle extended four tangents that moved out, twisting and spiralling as they grew and evolved.

Grimstone lifted the sword aloft for a third time and the alien light invaded the entire sky, flared with green and blue and carmine brilliance. It burned beyond their eyes into their brains, overwhelming all thoughts and desires other than that coruscating emblem of malignancy. <Take strength from this virile symbol. Glory in the power of the Master.>

The power of the sigil descended over the arena, overwhelming the force of Mark's oraculum.

<The triple infinity is your purpose—the glorious light that must be consummated by the purifying flame of sacrifice. The torment of our enemies is the ichor of its need.>

With horror, Mark saw the white-robed acolytes light their flame-throwers. There was a shimmering in the air above the pit, a twisting and turning, as if a dreadful force of hunger were rising.

Where the hell was Cal?

Mark smashed his fist into the sickening grins of the faces immediately below him, those who barred his progress. A Skull with the glaring eyes of mania tried to grab hold of his jacket. Mark slammed his knee into the groin.

Grimstone was looking in his direction. There was a lubricious smile on his lips, as though he savoured Mark's dismay. The magma reeling overhead was centred upon the body of Padraig. It weighed upon Mark's spirit like a malignant ocean. Grimstone still held the Sword of Feimhin as high as he could reach. The drums were rolling.

<The strength of union embraces us. Already the power of the Master takes force from our common purpose on this glorious day.>

Mark screamed for Vengeance. He hurled his call with all of his might, through the blazing oraculum in his brow. Within moments there was a screeching through the air as the battleaxe found its way to his upraised palm. Already he was carving his way through the obstruction of Skulls, moving forward in a fury of motion.

"No!" He heard Nan's roar shake the arena like a sudden great squall of wind. The flame-throwers were extinguished as the men holding them were thrown bodily against the sides of the pit.

Grimstone's face was impassive, the sword still aloft, a monolith against the tempest gathering in the sky overhead. Mark followed Grimstone's eyes to the sky, which was nascent with foreboding. Mark smashed his way down through the remaining rows of Skulls, toppling down through several of the lower tiers into the pit where he regained his feet in the bloodied sawdust and snow.

A wash of sweat erupted over his skin. As he turned towards Padraig he heard the flame-throwers coming back into action. His lungs searing from the effort of breathing, he stood before the petrol-soaked figure of the elderly druid, defying any man to approach.

There was a thunderous crash high above him, to one side of Grimstone's rostrum. The guillotine blade of the Mamma Pig appeared like a glittering new gate between the tangled wreckage of tiers. The cab windows had disintegrated. Mark saw Cal and Bull come running down the tiered steps. Then Bull's heavy machine gun crackled into the reeling and panicking mob.

Mark infused all the power of his oraculum into the battleaxe, from his left arm to its twin curved blades ensheathed in blue-black lightning. With all of his power he hurled the battleaxe, its twin blades casting lightning at the figure of Grimstone on the platform above him.

He saw the Sword of Feimhin drop to confront the whirling blades. His eyes were blinded, his ears deafened, by the massive detonation of force as the battleaxe struck the blade of the Sword. He saw the battleaxe disintegrate into sparks and splinters of glowing dust.

He thought: *Cal was right. We're dead.*

Then Mark saw a bespectacled, ragged figure tearing down the aisle between the tiers of screaming Skulls. He stared disbelievingly as Gully ran into the arena and confronted the figures on the platform.

"Penny!" he cried.

Mark saw how the slim girl on the rostrum lifted her head. He heard her answering cry, "Run, Gully. Run from the City Below!"

Time roaring past him, fractured, so he was uncertain of the passing moments. Bull still wheeled the spent machine gun around himself. Cal, his face a mass of tiny bleeding points with splinters of glass glittering in his brow and cheeks, cut Padraig free. With the torches extinguished, the daylight was fading into twilight and was further darkened by the black clouds obscuring the sky from horizon to horizon. He glimpsed Bull throw Padraig's emaciated body over his shoulder. Cal gripped Mark's shoulder, half-pushing, half-dragging him back up to where the pig's steel nose poked through the stands. Nan followed close on their heels.

"Why aren't we dead?" he shouted to Nan.

"The girl—Penny."

"I don't understand . . ."

"Don't ask me how, but I know she saved us, I saw it in her mind, but I think it might have been more as a result of her trying to save Gully."

Mark was struggling to regain control of his limbs. He still couldn't credit the fact that they were still alive. "Where is Gully?"

"He's fine—he's here with us."

Mark shook his head. He had clearly lost several minutes of memory.

There had been a moment, as Cal was hauling him back from the platform, when Grimstone and Mark had come within yards of each other. Grimstone was oblivious to the spitting machine guns, making no effort at all to take cover. His flesh was numinous, etched in a nimbus of green light. Then, in that moment of contact, Mark had witnessed his look of triumph.

Triumph!

"You were right, Nan. Grimstone is a Legun."

"Even if he is a Legun, do you imagine him capable of what you have seen? Is he capable of destroying your battleaxe, powered by the goddess? Why is he now ignoring you and me? Why is he clearly unafraid of us?"

"What are you saying?"

Nan was speaking urgently into his ear. "Did you not see—up there, on the platform? The third figure—"

"Yeah—I saw him."

"You know who . . . ?"

Mark nodded. The Tyrant was here in London. But now, through his continuing bewilderment, he also recalled that the Tyrant was standing close to Penny, resting a hand upon her shoulder.

Mark felt his entire body begin to shiver, but then he realised that it was the ground underneath the Mamma Pig that was vibrating. The whole arena was shaking as if an earthquake had struck.

Nan shouted to Cogwheel, who was brushing a rain of glass off the driver's seat, "We must get out of here—now!"

The arena was disintegrating. The wooden tiers were pitching and tumbling, crushing and rending the bodies of the audience. A monstrous eruption shook the ground in the centre of the excavated wilderness to the east. The thunder of it went on and on, increasing from moment to moment. The ground fissured over a vast area, extending eastwards to the monolithic outlines of the financial district. Mark saw one of the buildings implode, as if from some dreadful internal calamity; the windows disintegrated and the skeletal steel shook from side to side before collapsing in an avalanche of concrete, steel and glass.

Something enormous, dark and glittering with incandescent power, was forming at the heart of the disturbance. It grew rapidly, like the birth of a sun, ripping and tearing itself into being from the tormented air. A series of thunderous explosions numbed the senses, provoking a storm of energy rapidly expanding like a maddened ocean: a tsunami of blood red, sulphurous yellows, incandescent greens; a seething maelstrom of monstrous birth, growing outwards and upwards into the frenzied sky.

The Pig lurched and shuddered as Cogwheel gunned the engine. With a huge jerk they slewed backwards in an arc, then accelerated forwards, smashing through one obstacle after another. Cogwheel was whistling between his teeth, performing a five- or six-point turn amid the carnage. Then he accelerated madly, ripping through the tail ends of tiers adjacent to the aisles. Mark glimpsed Bull pulling open a crate of ammunition, then staggering, almost falling, before he managed to secure the heavy machine gun to its pin at the rear porthole, where he began to open up. Nan had taken Gully under her wing. Tajh was ministering to the unconscious Padraig. Cal was up front, in the seat next to Cogwheel, using the lighter Minimi on anything that moved. Front and back, Mark saw the spent shells pattering out of their discharging guns. Cogwheel smashed his way out of the car park, cleaving through barriers and vehicles driven by panicking drivers, their machine guns firing and firing, the cabin of the Mamma Pig a choking fog of cordite . . .

They were through the gates, smashed asunder by the guillotine blades. There was the sound of following vehicles: bikes and four-wheel drives, struggling to escape the exploding hell of the arena. Then they were thundering through burning streets. Cogwheel turned to look back at Mark from the cab, his pupils big in his glittering eyes. He battered through a series of road junctions, heading, as far as Mark could determine, anywhere he could.

Night was falling. Or, at least, it looked like the darkest night, devouring what was left of the day. They were driving through the grassy slopes of a park, the wheels of the Mamma Pig gouging deep ruts in the snow.

"Oh, Jesus—man!" Cogwheel's voice came from the cab. "Hey, everybody . . ." He braked, slowing the vehicle down to a halt.

Bull slid the door in the side open and jumped out, helping Nan and Gully to follow him. Mark climbed stiffly down to join them, leaving Tajh by the side of the deeply comatose Padraig. Cal then jumped out of the cab and Cogwheel hung out through the window, intent on missing nothing.

"What the bloody hell is going on?"

Even from what must have been ten miles away, the sight of what they were witnessing awed them to silence. A black rose a mile high was forming over what had been the financial district. Where the skyscrapers had stood, ring after ring of concentric petals were coalescing, their surfaces and edges glittering darkly, as if constantly changing, infused with nascent power. Torrents of indigo, carmine red, virulent green and sulphurous yellow—frightful rivers of energy—were deluging out of the constantly metamorphosing petals and seething through the streets of the city like the flow of an erupting volcano.

They stared, spellbound, at the stricken city, the shock of what they were witnessing reflected in their eyes and faces.

"What in God's name . . . ?"

Nan was barely able to whisper, "The Tyrant has declared war on Earth."

Mark was too devastated to reply. He felt Nan's hand enter his own, her fingers crabbed and cold.

Waves of blue-black lightning deluged from the giant petals of the rose as a storm battened and thickened at its core. Mark thought he heard something through his oraculum, a rumbling voice monstrously deep, speaking words as ancient as the universe. He sensed, even before he saw it, the blade of an enormous sword several more miles high, rising out of the heart of the rose; a vision of immense gravity and power, with the spectral brightness of a star. It, too, was constantly metamorphosing, turning slowly in the gigantic curled tunnels of power that were erupting between the petals of the rose. Streaming, dazzling tides of energy, finally took up the shape of a vertical infinity, bisected by a horizontal infinity, bisected again by a third infinity at right angles to the second: a triple infinity three miles high. It rotated and glittered, shimmering, its elements reforming from moment to moment, shockwave after shockwave emanating from it in every dimension.

Dramatis Personae

Human Characters on Earth

Alan Duval—One of the four friends. Bears the Oraculum of the First Power, the Power of the Land, in his brow

Bethal Grimstone—Adoptive mother of Mark and Maureen Grimstone. Wife of R. Silas Grimstone

Bull—Member of the "Crew"

Caleb Dunne (Cal)—Leader of the rebel Crew

Cogwheel—Member of the Crew

Father Noel Touhey—Retired Catholic priest in London

Fergal Shaunessy—Paternal uncle and guardian of Kate Shaunessy

Field Marshall Marcus Seebox—Ally of Grimstone

Gully Doughty—Shares the London squat, Our Place, with Penny Postlethewaite

Jo Derby—Sociologist

Kate Shaunessy—One of the four friends. Bears the Oraculum of the Second Power, Life and Healing, in her brow

Mala—Maureen's (Mo's) biological mother

Mark Grimstone—One of the four friends. Bears the Oraculum of the Third Power, the Power of Death, in his brow

Maureen (Mo) Grimstone—One of the four friends. Bequeathed the Torus of the True Believers by her Aboriginal mother

Nantosueta (Nan)—Mark's girlfriend and co-sharer of the Oraculum of the Third Power. Queen of Monisle on Tír

Padraig O'Brien—Alan Duval's maternal grandfather

Penny Postlethwaite—Shares the London squat, "Our Place," with Gully Doughty

R. Silas Grimstone—Brutal adoptive father of Mark and Maureen (Mo)

Sharkey—Member of the "Crew"

Tajh Madine—Member of the "Crew"

Non-Human beings on Earth

Henriette Boleyn—Father Touhey's Belizean housekeeper

Jeremiah—Darkly spiritual being with a secret agenda and identity

Humans on Tír

Ebrit—Prince of the City of Carfon

Milish—Councilwoman and Ambassador for the High Council-in-Exile

Non-Human Beings on Tír

Ainé—Hereditary leader, or Kyra, of the Shee
Bétaald—Spiritual leader of the Shee
Elaru—Spirit being, linked to Urale
Granny Dew—Earth mother
Iyezzz—Garg Prince
Kehloke—Wife of Siam
Kemtuk Lapeep—Original shaman of the Olhyiu
Layheas—An aide
Magtokk—Wizard of legend, said to have great wisdom and powers of prediction
Mahteman—Garg high shaman
Momu, the—Leader of the Cill
Nidhoggr—Dragon of chaos coiled around the roots of the Tree of Life
Qwenqwo Cuatzel—Dwarf mage and sole survivor of the Fir Bolg
Qwenuncqweqwatenzian-Phaetentiatzen—Garg word for the Dragon God
Shah-nur-Kian—Garg queen and mother of Iyezzz
Shikarr—Great serpent and queen of the Snowmelt River
Siam—Chief of the Olhyiu
Siri—A succubus
Snakoil Kawkaw—Olhyiu traitor and spy
Soup Scully Oops—Preceptress and spy for the Tyrant

Thesau—a True Believer in the form of an eagle who can ferry people through Dromenon and across time and space
Topgal—Siam's brother-in-law
Turkeya—Son of Siam and new shaman of the Olhyiu
Urale—a minor god in *The Sword of Feimhin*
Usrua—the Shee who protects Mo on the journey to Ghork Mega
Ussha De Danaan—Last High Architect of Ossierel
Valéra—Shee-in-novitiate
Yoolf, the—Demon twins
Zelnesakkk—Garg king and Iyezzz's father

RACES, CREATURES & GROUPS

aides, the—Assistants to the Shee, skilled in herb-lore and healing battle wounds, and weaponry
Akkharu—Creators of the City Below
Cill, the—Amphibian race who inhabit Ulla Quemar
Fir Bolg, the—Dwarf warrior race of ancient times, extinct but for Qwenqwo Cuatzel
Garg, the—Winged warrior race, also known as the Eyrie people
Grimling—A flying goblin
Keepers of Night and Day, the—beings who witness the ends of races and worlds
Leathers, skull squads—Thugs under Grimstone's control
Olhyiu, the—Warrior fisher people of bear origin

onkkh—Enormous flightless birds carrying high-walled baskets of food and shelter for the invading army
Paramilitaries—Mercenaries under Grimstone's control
Shee, the—Race of female warriors who can metamorphose into great cats
Scalpie—Sacred warrior and servant of the Tyrant

Acknowledgements

I should begin with my deeply felt thanks to Jo Fletcher, of Quercus Books, who has been a model of patience with me in the genesis of this book. A similar accolade is due to my editors, David V Barrett, who was as tough on me as I deserved, and to Nicola Budd, who was perceptive and sensitive in the polishing. It is a special pleasure, as always, to acknowledge the sterling efforts on my behalf of my agent, Leslie Gardner. I would also acknowledge the role of Brendan Murphy, whose belief and practical support was important in getting the project off the ground. I should also, belatedly I now think, thank my wonderful but sadly late mother, May, for the songs she sang to me and the endurance and inspiration she thus inspired within me, in the magical landscape of the foothills of Slievenamon. Finally I am indebted, as always, to my long-suffering wife Barbara for her patience, timely criticism and indefatigable support.

About the Type

Text set in Utopia Regular at 10/14.25pt.

Utopia is a multifunctional typeface designed by Robert Slimbach in 1989. It is solidly based on types of the eighteenth-century, with the addition of contemporary type innovations.

Typeset by Scribe Inc., Philadelphia, Pennsylvania